First and always I have to thank Rabia Gale and Miquela Faure for being more than just amazing beta-readers, but a cheer squad and counselors too. Thank you also to Tehani Wessely, for your support and enthusiasm. It means more than you could know.

I would also like to thank the crew at Giant Bomb for their Persona 4 endurance run. The best cure for a difficult year.

And finally, but most importantly, my husband. Thank you for your understanding and never-ending support. None of this would have happened without you.

Also by Jo Anderton

Debris (a Veiled Worlds novel)
Suited (a Veiled Worlds novel)

The Bone Chime Song and Other Stories

Guardian

Book Three of the Veiled Worlds Trilogy

Jo Anderton

First published in Australia in 2014
by FableCroft Publishing

http://fablecroft.com.au

This book © 2014 Jo Anderton

Cover art by Dion Hamill
Cover design by Amanda Rainey
Design and layout by Tehani Wessely
Typeset in Sabon MT Pro and Ambrosia

FableCroft
Publishing

National Library of Australia Cataloguing-in-Publication entry

Author: Anderton, Jo, author.
Title: Guardian / Jo Anderton.
ISBN: 9780992284442 (paperback)
ISBN: 9780992284459 (ebook)
Series: Anderton, Jo. Veiled worlds trilogy ; bk. 3.
Subjects: Technology–Fiction.
Quests (Expeditions)–Fiction.
Cities and towns–Fiction.
Science fiction.
Dewey Number: A823.4

The Keeper makes his report

The Keeper sits in the chair his programmers made, and tries to ignore his brothers beating down the door. All the screens in the abandoned comms room are dark, the hubs dull, and everything is coated in a thick layer of dust. He presses the palms of his hands against his ears, long fingers criss-crossing his bald scalp, and squeezes his black eyes shut. It doesn't help, of course, because his body isn't real. But he can't help trying. It's the way he was designed.

"I've come," he gasps and rocks forward, "to make my report."

He's travelled long dark paths and entire continents to reach this station, but his brothers follow no matter where he goes. Maybe this will at least distract them, from Tanyana and Kichlan resting in the mountain above Movoc-under-Keeper. So far away.

"The disintegration is not my fault. You have to believe me. It didn't even start with Tan, not really. My brothers and their schemes are much, much older."

If he tries really hard, scrunches up his unreal eyes and bends all his fragmented mind on it, the Keeper can block out the sound of his brothers. That doesn't mean they're not there, hunting him. He just can't hear them anymore.

He remembers his programmers instead.

It's almost like they're alive again, and in the room with him. The light of shining crystal hubs scatters the dim blanket of dust and the entire underground station buzzes with energy. Half a dozen different programmers emerge from the shadows, some grown up, some still children, but all fully aware of the people they used to be and in regular contact with the world they left behind. Not like it is now.

"Actually," the Keeper breathes, and straightens. He feels stronger, bolstered by his memories of a time when he was whole. "It's *your* fault."

Everyone turns to him in shock.

"Yes," he says, more confident by the moment. "Yes, it was all your doing. You created them! Then you set them loose. You should be fixing this, not me. Not Tan."

One of the programmers—wearing the body of a ten-year-old girl, but so very much older—approaches him. She carries a notepad of shimmering crystal covered in code written in globules of debris. "What do you mean, Guardian?" she asks. "I'm reading all sorts of strange errors on the feed, and have received multiple queries from across the veil. Can you explain?"

"Call me *Keeper*," he replies. *Keeper* is the name the people of the light world first gave him, and it is the name he has chosen for himself. "And that's why I'm here. To report."

She nods. "Then we are recording you."

"It wasn't Tanyana's fault they picked on her," the Keeper says. "She just took the wrong job. Caught the attention of the wrong people. They would have chosen any powerful pion-binder. She was such a good architect before the accident that gave her all those nasty scars. She made pretty buildings. I saw some of them, like the big blue art gallery. I liked that one. Lots of doors to close, you know, wherever she and her nine point critical circle went."

"Doors?" the programmer frowns. "Ah, you mean a weakening in the veil."

"You should call them doors!" he snaps at her. "On this world I'm the Keeper, and they're doors. Got it?"

The girl doesn't argue, but he can see her making notes. She's using debris to do it, so he can *feel* her. Reporting back to the programmers on the other side of the veil. Telling them all about their broken little Guardian program and his delusions.

He squeezes his hands into fists, and concentrates. No time for that now. His brothers are coming.

"I know you can't see them," he continues, trying to sound reasonable and fully functioning. "But most people on this world can see *pions*: semi-sentient particles glowing deep inside of all things, that can be persuaded to manipulate the very fabric of the world. Tanyana and her circle used them to deconstruct raw materials and remake them into grand buildings and giant statues."

"And all that pion manipulation creates a lot of debris," one of the programmers chimes in. "We know all about that. You're right, we can't see pions, but your programmers can see debris. It looks like, well, like sludge. Dark and wet and wiggly. That's probably why the people here think debris is a waste product. All they know is that it appears after the binding of pions, and too much of it entropies their carefully created systems."

The Keeper nods. "After her accident Tanyana lost the ability to see and command pions, but gained the ability to see debris. So they made her into a debris collector."

A small shudder runs through the programmers. "Horrible procedure."

"Yes." The Keeper looks down at his fingers, nervously fiddling in his lap. He's never told Tanyana that he saw her being suited. All the machines and the blood and Tan strapped to that table, unable to fight back. He knows how horrible it was. "Because debris cannot be touched by human hands, she had a *suit* drilled into her bones— six glowing metallic bands around her wrists, ankles, neck and waist." His brothers created that suit, and put Tan through the torture of its installation just to test it. "The suit looks like silver, but it's not. It's made of debris. Just like me."

He looks up and waits for the incredulous reaction. No one should be able to do anything like that, because no one on this side of the veil has the skill to work with debris. That's why it took him so long to understand what was happening. That's why he didn't fight back, until it was too late. Until Tan. Because only his programmers should be able to recode debris. His brothers, and the things they did, were impossible.

But the programmers in this ancient comms room don't react. They are just memories, after all. Hallucinations summoned by his lonely, shattering mind. They keep plugging away at their ethereal keys and scribbling their pointless notes.

"Over time she learned to control the liquid metal that oozed from those bands," he continues, voice little above a whisper. He used to give regular reports, and the programmers on both worlds hung on his every word. Now, he just wants to tell someone. Anyone. Even if they aren't real. "Mould them into any shape she needed, from spoons to pincers to swords. But the life of a debris collector is a low one. Tan hated it at first. I think that's how he tricked her. Devich, I mean. Because she'd been so rich and everyone had looked up to her, and then she was at the bottom of society, spending her life picking up trash. Devich made her feel like she still belonged with the elite of Movoc-under-Keeper, even though it was a lie. I didn't like him from the beginning, but she couldn't hear me properly at the time, so how could I warn her?" The Keeper shakes his head. For countless years he's watched from the shadows, unable to interact with the people he'd been created to protect. He'd known Devich was lying. He'd seen him ingratiate himself with Tan, then report back to the veche on every single thing she did. If only he could have warned her not to let Devich get so close, then the little bastard couldn't have betrayed her, and hurt her.

And she wouldn't be pregnant now either. But that bit wasn't any of his business. Made him blush black just to think about. Poor Tan. Poor little baby, somewhere inside of her like a glitch in her code.

"But, after a while, she started to realise that being a debris collector wasn't all bad. She made friends with the rest of the team, especially Kichlan and his brother Lad." He pauses, and sighs gently. "Lad."

Lad should have been a programmer, like the little memory-girl listening to him with a faintly bemused expression. But the programmers are different now. Broken. What did Tan call it? *Half*. Tan found the term in an old book written by the Unbound, and it was supposed to mean Half in the real world, and Half in the Keeper's. That wasn't exactly right, but it was pretty close. Because Lad really had been only half a man. He had lost the programmer part of him, and it made him childlike and strange.

The Keeper's programmers started failing not long before Novski's critical circle revolution changed pion-binding from something only a few people did really well, to the foundation for a civilisation of sprawling, automated cities. For a long time the Keeper hadn't understood what was happening to his programmers, why they were arriving broken, without memories of their true selves, and unable to program anything. But he is pretty sure he knows now.

His brothers.

"Who is Lad?" the programmer asks.

The Keeper can't answer straight away. "I think Tan blames herself," he whispers, eventually. "But maybe it's my fault too. We all should have looked after Lad better. Instead Tan got involved with Fedor and the Unbound in their struggle against the veche. They believed that the Unbound—that's another name for people who don't see pions and can't bind them—shouldn't be forced to become debris collectors. They believed in me, even though everyone else nowadays just thinks I am a myth." It was nice to have people believe in him again, even if they got some of the details wrong. He wasn't actually a god, for one. "They convinced Tan to help them attack the veche, and she brought Kichlan, Lad and even members of her old critical circle along. They broke into a secure storage facility and they were going to release some of the debris the veche had been hoarding. You know, to help me. But it all went badly. So badly." He sinks his head back into his hands, black tears streaming hot against his cheeks. He doesn't want to remember this part. "And Lad died."

"Why are you crying?" The little girl programmer crouches beside him. "Programs can't cry."

"Tan held him in her arms when he died," the Keeper sobs and gulps the words. The girl is right. Programs shouldn't cry. But he does. "I saw it all happen, and I couldn't do anything to help. His blood splashed all over Tanyana's suit, and that greedy silver drunk it all up. The debris in her suit absorbed the programmer paradigm still buried somewhere inside him. When he was alive, Lad didn't know what he was. But dead, he was able to access her code. When my brothers tried to take back control of the suit they had created, Lad *reprogrammed* it and freed Tanyana from their shackles. Thanks to him, she was able to escape, and rescue Kichlan." And destroy Movoc-under-Keeper, but he doesn't mention that part. "It was amazing. It reminded me of you."

The girl recoils. "Your *brothers*?"

"This is what I'm trying to report. My brothers are behind everything. None of what happened to Tanyana was an accident! They planned it all! She didn't *fall* eight hundred feet from the palm of *Grandeur* and hit her head. She was pushed! They bound her to an experimental collecting suit, and created monsters for her to fight. They kidnapped Kichlan and tried to undo the pion bonds that hold his body together, just to see what she would do." The Keeper staggers to his feet. "Everything they did to Tanyana, it was all part of their plan to kill me. They keep cutting off little bits of me, and reprogramming them. It hurts. It makes me feel so small."

"But why?" the little girl says, sounding worried. "I thought you called them your...*brothers*." She says the word like it makes her feel sick.

"Because they want to bring down the veil between worlds," the Keeper answers.

"But that will destroy them!" one of the other programmers stammers. "This world, the light world, and the dark world on the other side. The worlds are so different that they destroy each other when they come into contact, and the only thing that stops that happening is the veil in between."

And it's the Keeper's job to keep it that way.

He's just a program, really, created on the dark world to keep the veil strong. Sometimes, he looks like a black and white sketch of a man. Most of the time, he's just code. And in this world, the light world, that code is debris.

He tries his best. Anywhere a pion is manipulated it weakens the veil—opens a door—and he will appear to keep it strong, and save everyone. All the time. Over and over again.

Until his brothers arrived, and started messing with everything.

"That's why they're trying to kill me. If I'm gone, there's nothing protecting the veil. No one to close the doors." He walks slowly through the room. Runs white fingers through the insubstantial bodies of the programmers from his memory, but no one takes his hand. No one ever treated him like a person, before Tanyana.

"But maintaining the veil is too big a job for just one Keeper. I know you think I'm not good enough. I know you've been upgrading me. Because I'm a tool to you. Not a friend."

"You are just a program," the girl says. "Programs don't need friends."

But he does.

"You altered me, over and over, and the bits you didn't like you threw away, into the veil between worlds. But they didn't die there. They told me, the veil is not what you all think it is. The veil is lush, the veil is rich. It's where my brothers were born, from my discarded off-cuts. All because you don't believe in me."

The Keeper releases a pent-up breath, and lets his memories fade. The comms room is dark and dusty again, all so long dead. There is nothing but the silence of ages, and the banging of his brothers knocking down the door. He places a pale hand against its cold metal. An ancient construction of silex and steel, sealed by a complex pattern of locks built of both pions bonds and debris programming.

"Tanyana calls you the puppet men," he says to his brothers just on the other side of the door. "Because those human masks you wear don't quite fit. Underneath, you are something closer to me. Code, given life. Poor little lost programs, hurting. I know why you want to tear down the veil. You don't belong in either world, so you will make a home in the ruin of both. Can I blame you? Can I blame the programmers who made us?"

The Keeper shakes his head, and steps back. "Does it even matter whose fault it is, anymore?" He waits, breathing heavily. They will break through, he's certain. They've been hunting him for so long. Is there really any point in fighting?

Keeper?

The voice is like a whisper, at the edges of his hearing, and yet it comes from somewhere within.

We need your help.

He is still connected to all the debris his brothers have taken from him, from the furious monsters to the bloodthirsty collecting suits. He thinks they did this on purpose, to hurt him. But then, they never factored in Tanyana, did they?

I'm not giving up, but I can't do this on my own.

A slow smile spreads across his pale face, the inside of his mouth darker than the shadows in the room. No one ever factors in Tanyana, do they? That suit they forced on her has become his lifeline. It allowed her to hear him, then speak to him, and even see him. Hold his hand. After eons of loneliness, it brought him a friend.

Help me fight them!

Something worth fighting for.

1.

no one had lived in the Keeper Mountain for a very long time, but the hints of their lives that remained were tantalisingly familiar. Glass-tiled murals on the arching ceilings sparkled in the light from my suit, depicting images of the mountain, the Tear River, and the very beginnings of Movoc-under-Keeper itself. Small white buildings. The first sketches of a bridge. Little figures of people and animals. Strings of different coloured pions tied it all together, so simple compared to the complex knots and intricate patterns I was used to—and had once created. This was Movoc-under-Keeper before the critical circle revolution. The people who made these murals could not have imagined the massive towers of steel, glass and stone the city had become, or the factories full of binders working in unison that powered it.

That was the Movoc-under-Keeper I had lived in all my life. And it was the city I had just destroyed.

"Another one," Kichlan said.

I glanced back at him. There was still ash smeared on his face and great shadows beneath his deep brown eyes. He clutched his ruined left arm beneath his tattered jacket, hiding the stump of suit silver I had fused onto his elbow. Guilt dropped into my stomach with a sickly lurch. I'd saved his life when I gave him that stump, but it didn't make me feel any better.

"Another what?" I asked, keeping my voice soft. It wasn't necessary. Apart from the Keeper, who led us, we were alone within these ancient mountain corridors. But this was a place for hushed voices.

"Keeper." He didn't point, just nodded to a spot on the ceiling. I followed his gaze.

He was right. Images of the Keeper were everywhere within the mountain, from the massive statue in the room where we had sheltered, to the mosaics, and the carvings on every cornice.

"It is called the *Keeper* Mountain," I replied, but the truth was I found it unsettling. Not because of his presence—even in modern Movoc-under-Keeper he could still be found decorating veche buildings and public artworks—but because these images were accurate. Really accurate. They could only have been made by someone who had seen him.

We must hurry, the Keeper whispered in my ear.

I nodded. "Come on," I said, and wished Kichlan would let me take his hand.

The Keeper from my childhood storybooks was a figure of myth, an archetype—the hero who had saved his people from the darkness of the Other. Sometimes he was drawn as a knight, sometimes a powerful pion-binder, sometimes even as an innocent child. My suit had showed me that the Keeper was not a myth, and he didn't look like that at all.

He looked like the drawings and the carvings in this ancient, quiet place.

"Tan, stop," Kichlan gasped. "Look at this."

"I don't think we have ti—" I turned, and stammered into silence.

So many of the corridors within the mountain were in ruins, weighed down by age and neglect. We wouldn't have even got this far without the strength of my suit. I'd shaped my hands into great spades and dug where the Keeper had told me to dig, then sharpened them into saws and cut through solid rock to create an opening when the accessible pathways ran out. We'd come across many dead ends, and doorways hidden behind slabs of fallen ceiling, the ghostly shapes of glass figures still twinkling, broken in my light. But nothing like this.

"I think it's been sealed," Kichlan said.

I stood close beside him, and he took a shuffling step sideways so we weren't touching. "Sealed?" I asked, as I forced away the hurt. Lad's death had changed so much between us. Could we ever go back to the way things were?

Kichlan found it, the Keeper said. He sounded like he was right beside me. *I couldn't feel it. It's dead. Nothing working. You cannot turn the power on.*

"We have to try," I replied.

Then hurry. They are coming.

The puppet men. I clenched my hands into fists, and sharpened the suit that slid out of my wrists into blades. The puppet men were why we were doing this in the first place.

The door Kichlan had found was as tall as the ceiling, wider than the two of us standing not-too-close together, and seemed to be made of the mountain rock itself. It was covered in carvings of the Keeper. Faces of actual marble, eyes of onyx. So many of them, all over the door. Behind the figures, a landscape I did not recognise, made from protruding shards of crystal and glass. And at their white, floating feet, a strange array of coffins.

It made me shiver. I traced the edges of the door with the tips of my blades. It did, indeed, look like it had been sealed. No random collapsed rock blocked it. Instead, there was something wedged around the frame, like mortar, but hard and shining black. My suit barely made a dent in it.

It will not work, the Keeper said. *Even if you get inside. You should run, instead. I—I don't want them to hurt you again.*

But there was nowhere to go where the puppet men could not find us.

I shoved the tips of my blades through a gap between Keepers, where the rock still retained faint traces of colourful paint. "It's too late for that," I said, braced my feet, and pushed. Nothing was as strong as the silver of my suit, and my blades tore upwards, shattering stone, raining marble and glass down around us in a rush of stale air.

Lights flickered on as we stepped cautiously inside. They were faint and unsteady, shining like moonlight behind bars from grills in the walls.

"What is this place?" Kichlan hissed, close behind my shoulder.

The air inside was heavy with the strangest aroma. Coppery, like blood; burning, like a lightning storm. A thick layer of black dust covered the floor and congealed into stalactites on the ceiling. It tugged at the bottom of my shoes as I approached a clear, glass coffin in the centre of the room.

I swallowed hard, tugged the sleeve of my patchwork coat down over my hand and wiped dust away from its surface. Underneath it was, thankfully, empty. "Is this," I asked, my voice unsteady, "how I will cross the veil?"

I told you, the Keeper said. *It will not work.*

"Look at the lights—the power is on." I gestured to the wall, as Kichlan crept around me and investigated the rest of the room. "I can do this."

Not enough.

"Cross the veil?" Kichlan asked, glancing my way, even as he ducked beneath a great tangle of cables and tubes that coiled snake-like from the ceiling to hook into the coffin. My stomach lurched at the sight of them. So similar to the puppet men's laboratory, the place I had destroyed when I rescued him, and had set off a chain reaction that brought Movoc-under-Keeper down with it.

"Yes," I said. "It's the only way to stop the puppet men. I'm certain of it."

Kichlan paused at a wide bench sticking out from the wall, and ran his hand across its surface. More lights sprung up, hundreds of little designs and symbols within the rock itself. They were so familiar—the same symbols floated, rising and falling, in the bright and spinning bands of my suit. I knew what some of them meant, but only two or three, and yet I'd seen whole books written in them. The language of the ancient Unbound.

If only I could read them. Maybe they were instructions? Maybe one of them said 'press this button to cross the veil'?

The symbols cast bright patterns across Kichlan's face. His hair was a mess, dirty blond curls falling across his forehead, making him look so much like his brother it hurt.

I crouched beside the coffin. The Unbound rebels, led by Fedor, had built something similar for Lad when he died. They said it was tradition, the reasons lost over time, but now I thought I understood.

"The programmers on the other side of the veil made the puppet men," I said. I ran fingernails around the edge of the glass until I found a lid. "So the programmers can help me defeat them. I need to go over there, to the dark world, find these people and make them help us before it's too late." All it took was a little pushing to open it. Cold air rushed up at me, icy fingers numbing my face.

Don't. Please.

Kichlan wrapped his jacket tighter, and I shivered. The chill leaked into the room in drifts of pale mist. "Will that work?" Kichlan asked.

Doesn't work. No power. Hubs all quiet. Too late.

"It has to work!" I snapped at both of them. "Or do you have another suggestion?"

"I thought the worlds were opposites?" Kichlan asked, not daunted. "Won't you just dissolve into dust? Like the sewer wall. Like—" he paused, and swallowed hard "—like Aleksey."

"Halves cross the veil," I said, between gritted teeth. "If they do it, so can I."

*Minds extracted. Reworked into code. Uploaded on a trail of light, through me. Seeded into an unformed body. Final. Like life, or death. Not just walking back and forth like—like—*The Keeper dissolved into senseless laughter and sobbing.

"What about this then?" I slammed my fists against the coffin. It seemed to set something off, as gears shifted above us, sending cracks through the ceiling and rattling the loops of cable. Several of the lights in the walls flickered red, and the symbols began changing, frantically.

"All right, all right!" Kichlan edged away from the wall. "Calm down. I was just asking."

Just for talking. Hello, how is the Guardian today? Does he need another friend? Is he lonely and sad, so sad? Thank you for saving us all, Guardian. You get to be lonely, for your reward.

"What?" I pushed myself away from the coffin and stood. "Fine, just for talking." The Keeper was getting worse. I was used to him being broken, I was accustomed to his riddles and his clinging presence, desperate for friendship, desperate to be heard. But this was bad, even for him. "Let me talk to them then."

Doesn't work. Can't talk to them. All gone all gone.

I could hear him breathing, beside me, behind me. All around. Panting. "Keeper, I—"

Shut up, Tanyana. Stop telling me. Just listen to me, Tanyana. Listen to me!

I crept close to Kichlan. "Something's wrong," I hissed. "The Keeper. He's—"

I said listen to me!

I could feel his breath against my face, his hands against the sides of my head. He was shaking. He was hot—how could the Keeper be hot? I released the bonds of my suit and let it slide over me, a second skin of hard yet malleable silver, covering me head to toe.

Even now, after all these moons, it was not a pleasant sensation. Especially now. I'd fought the suit for control of my own body, and nearly lost. Every time it covered me, every time I drew a blade, part of me was waiting for it to try again. The suit was so much of me now, from the bands, to the heavy lines of silver across my abdomen, and the newest scars, the deeper scars, the ones right through my heart. It made me strong, even as it hollowed me out. I had no idea where the suit ended, and I began. Not any more.

I placed a hand on my stomach. What had it done to the unborn baby resting, quiet, within me? Devich's child. Nothing, surely, could survive what I had put the poor thing through.

The suit slid over my eyes, and the world changed. No more mountain, no more ancient Unbound room. Nothing but darkness, and doors. And the Keeper.

He was right in front of me, so close he was almost on top of me, gripping my face with his hands. Panic pulsed through him, in the surging beat of debris visible through his pale veins, and his gaping, black mouth. I tried to draw back, but the Keeper held me tightly. "They're coming!" he cried. "Coming for me. Coming for you. Can't you feel them? Too blind, Tanyana. So much suit and Half in you, but still so blind!" He tipped back his head and howled with laughter and tears.

I swallowed hard, tried to force myself to keep calm, but the Keeper's madness was contagious. "Keeper, what's happening? Calm down. Just explain to me—"

"My *brothers* are happening!" he actually spat the word, with the kind of venom I'd never heard from him. "You destroyed their machines and took control of their suit, but did you think that was enough? They're coming! Mountain rock doesn't mean anything to them, we follow our own dark paths. Run, Tanyana, while you can."

"But—" I tried to turn my head towards the coffin, hidden now behind doors, but the Keeper gripped me even harder.

"Waste of time!" he screamed into my face. "*Listen* to me! The feeds are all dead, the programmers are Halves, and I am all alone! This will not work."

I gripped the Keeper's wrists with my silver hands and pulled him away from my face. Around us, the doors all rattled, rotten wood hollow against rusted hinges. Laughter like malevolent ghosts echoed through the mountain.

"Did you hear that?" Kichlan's voice was muffled on the other side of the suit, so I withdrew it from my face.

I glanced around the shadowed corners of the room. Nothing. "Maybe we imagined—"

Three puppet men materialised out of the darkness right in front of us. They smiled their too-wide smiles, fake skin stretching, their eyes the colour of mould flickered between rage and bland amusement. Pristine white coats, darkness in their mouths, and the only sign that something was amiss—that I had destroyed their laboratory and ruined their plans or, at least, delayed them—was a stinking muck stuck to their shoes. River-mud and writhing tendrils of debris.

"Other curse you!" Kichlan staggered back from them, shocked.

As one they turned toward him, and said, "The Other cannot curse anyone anymore."

Too late. The Keeper slipped from my hands.

"What are you doing here, Miss Vladha?" one of the puppet men asked. "The connections here are lost. The programmers abandoned him. Our brother, your Keeper, sad and all alone."

"Stay back!" I hissed at them, and fashioned fresh blades. I edged closer to Kichlan, putting myself between him and the creatures that had hurt him so much. I wouldn't let that happen again.

Dimly, I could hear the Keeper's hiccupping sobs. They sounded so empty, so hollow.

"Listen to him." The voices were coming from all around us now. "He has failed."

More puppet men materialised out of the walls, three—no, five, no, so many of them. "He cannot maintain the veil, as he was created to do, so he undoes himself. You might call it grief, Miss Vladha, though we do not feel such things. His programming fights for an answer. It finds none. And so it goes, twisting over and over until it tears him apart."

They were barring the only exit. I glanced at the floor. How thick was the rock? Could I break through it fast enough to get Kichlan away from them?

"It is time," the puppet men continued. One voice, many voices, all tangled together. "We have come for our brother. We will save him from such an unfair fate."

Tanyana? I could feel the Keeper's fear through the debris we shared. *Please, don't let them—*

"Get away from him!" I snapped. I'd done it once, I could do it again, escape from the puppet men with both Kichlan and the Keeper in my grip. Even here, deep in the mountain rock. The suit made me strong.

"You had your turn, Miss Vladha, and you did so well. The destruction you wrought to save that man—" they all nodded to Kichlan, who shuddered behind me "—has done more damage than we could have hoped. The pion systems in Movoc-under-Keeper lie in desperate, misfiring ruins. See how it weakens the Keeper, even now? It spreads him so thinly he can barely hold himself together. It's time for us to save him. And that is all thanks to you."

"No. I didn't..." I felt like I was going to be sick but stood firm. "I didn't—I couldn't—I won't let you!"

"We have been given life by the veil itself. We are of both worlds. We are debris and pions. We are everything and nothing. You cannot stop us, Miss Vladha."

I lifted my bladed hands, guided the suit back over my face. "Try me."

The world of darkness and doors was in chaos. Doors rattling, rust creaking out like disease from beneath the puppet men's feet. The Keeper huddled beside me, crouching, covering his face. "Come on," I cried. "We have to—"

"Tan!" Kichlan shouted, then something slammed into me. I was thrown to the side, the suit absorbing most of the damage, only to be hit again, and again. The silver dropped from my face so I could see—great spears of rock springing from the walls themselves. More came. They tore the ancient cabling, they shattered the programmers' coffin, and hope fell out of me like air from my lungs. But suit was still strong.

"You can't kill me that way!" I shouted, found my feet, spun and sliced at the next shard speeding my way. "You made this weapon!" Anger and frustration raced through me. "You know I'm stronger than this."

"Are you?" voices whispered from the rippling darkness.

Hurts, the Keeper whispered. Where was he? If only I could grab him, and get us out of here. If only I could command pions again, just like the puppet men were doing. I could calm the mountain, I could repair the coffin. I could... No. I couldn't do any of that. I had to focus.

Tendrils of pulsing, animated debris licked out at me. The mountain shook. Great cracks at my feet—I leapt out of the way, straight into a wall that hadn't been there seconds before. Steel hands clutched at me, pinning me, just for a moment, just for as long as it took hundreds of tiny saws to breach from the silver of my suit and cut them all away.

I fell back. Debris wrapped around my ankle, my wrist and—and all my silver trembled. Somewhere, a whispering, at the very edge of my hearing, words I couldn't understand. And very slowly, out of my control, my blades began to retract.

"Get out of my suit!" I pushed myself to my feet, tore the debris away. The puppet men were trying to reprogram me, the way Lad had done, using the debris to infiltrate and regain control over their weapon.

"How strong are you again?" The puppet men chuckled. "Tell us, Miss Vladha."

The floor fell away. I sent a grappling hook into the ceiling, pulled myself up. Rock slammed into me, sending me flying. I crashed into a wall, rolled awkwardly, stumbled to my knees. Something hitched in my side. The suit absorbed so much of the blows, but the suit was a part of me too. How long could I take this?

"How strong?"

I looked up. Three solid puppet men held Kichlan, while a mess of mist and disembodied faces writhed gleefully behind them. He hung limp and unconscious in their fake-skin hands, blood running from a fresh blow to the side of his head. The breath caught in my throat. The puppet men were dangling debris in front of his face. Not just any debris, the pale, scarred stuff that had nearly killed him. The kind that wiggled inside of you, undoing you, one pion bond at a time.

"Kichlan?" I called to him, but he didn't move.

The puppet men all smiled, as one, and dropped the debris. It slithered inside his chest.

"No!" I lunged forward, scrambling at the debris, at Kichlan. The puppet men, laughing, shoved him into my arms. I gripped him tight, and together we fell through the gaping holes in the shattered floor.

Laughter still around us, as I crashed down, down, through corridors, rooms. Crushing ancient glass murals. So much rubble, it felt like the mountain was coming down on top of us. Down. Down.

Until, suddenly, there was no floor, just a roar rising up from below.

We smacked hard into rushing water, and were swept along. The source of the Tear River, from deep within the mountain itself. Even with my silver-strength it stunned me, and for a moment I couldn't quite feel anything, didn't quite realise what had happened. Kichlan was torn from my grasp. Then all was riverbank and water flow, and the only light was the faltering glow from my suit, and Kichlan was a limp shadow, lost and carried away.

"Kichlan!" I tried to call to him. Water in my mouth for my trouble.

I fought to right myself, but the weight of the suit dragged me down. Into darkness, deeper and darker than I thought the Tear could go. She smashed me against rocks, she forced my face into gravel and her murky, unseen bed. I tired to swim, but her pressure was intense. And while the suit saved me from her crushing hands and tearing teeth, it added so much weight.

My lungs burned. I'd promised Lad that I would look after his brother. And now...now Kichlan was gone. Had I killed them both?

The dark paths. The Keeper sounded so distant, so faint, voice thin and wavering. *Take the dark paths.*

I ignored him, I had to find Kichlan, but eventually my suit chose for me, spreading over my head, easing the pressure in my chest.

There was no river in the Keeper's dark world, only doors. All around me, they shuddered and splintered, Movoc-under-Keeper in thick wood and ruining steel. Once before, I had walked between them. The Keeper had held my hand and led me along the calm between each door.

"What dark paths?" I whispered. There was no calm. Doors in the torn earth beneath me, doors in the sky above me.

"We make our own paths." The puppet men had followed. A stairway of entirely different doors arched up from that mass of breaking wood. Smooth metal with gleaming dials instead of handles, lights captured in glass instead of hinges, hissing steam and all of them, being steadily eaten away. A mass of rust, flecking copper like shedding skin.

They brought the Keeper with them—well, what was left of him. Half his face had peeled away, revealing only darkness like his eyes. Hands too, and up to his forearms, strip by strip, piece by piece, the Keeper was losing form.

"They're winning," he gasped, and his half-a-mouth flapped like cloth in the breeze.

"Oh, Keeper," I whispered. "I'm so sorry."

"You should not be," the puppet men said. They moved as one great mass, so many faces all the same, bleeding into each other. No longer even pretending to be human. "He has been alone for so long. A cruel fate, for a guardian."

The Keeper's single eye moved as he turned his head, looked around him, behind him.

"But no longer. Now, now he has brothers."

Countless hands reached out of the mass, and tore at the last remaining strips of the Keeper's skin. And then he was nothing but darkness—living, beating debris—and then, he was gone. Absorbed into the puppet men.

Leaving the veil unguarded.

With a terrible, rusty creak the handle of the door closest to me turned, unlocked, and opened.

"No!" I lurched forward and gripped it. In the past, I had struggled simply to touch these doors. Not any more. Even without the Keeper's help, I was debris enough.

"We programmed the suit inside you in our image." The puppet men closed around me. They pressed, shifting, rustling and warm. Strangely warm. "You are just like us, and just like the Keeper. We could even call you sister, if you liked."

"Sister?" I choked over the word.

Emptiness leaked in through the open door. It wrapped like tendrils around my arms, my shoulders, and my body. I gritted my teeth. I had watched the emptiness from that other, opposite world dissolve everything it touched: from steel to stone to suit metal and flesh. It was only a matter of time before that happened to me.

"You would not be alone, not with us."

I clutched the door harder, even as the metal on my arms wavered into particles like sand and dissolved from my skin. I could close this door. But around me the handles of the city and the sky turned. Not even the Keeper could close them all and he had been created for the task, designed for it. I was nothing but an architect, turned against my will into a weapon, used to help facilitate the end of two worlds.

"Isn't that what you want? A circle, a team? A lover, a brother? We can be all of these." Laughter. "We will be everything, soon. We will be all that remains."

My circle had long ago tattered. My collecting team was now disbanded. Lad was dead. Kichlan—

Was there anything left to fight for in this world?

I placed a hand on the silver unwinding from my belly. "Well," I whispered to the baby within me. "There *is* you."

"Join us, Tanyana." The dark mass of puppet men closed in.

Other curse them to the deepest hells, Other chew on their fake-flesh and spit out those mould-coloured eyes, I was *not* going to become a part of the puppet men!

"No." I shook my head. "No, I will not give up. No matter what you do, no matter who you take from me, I will find a way to fight you!"

I turned my back on the puppet men. Before me, nothingness stretched out with its impossible arch of stars. I smelled smoke, caught a sound like the faint crashing of distant waves. Strange, because surely nothingness could not have a smell?

The Keeper had told me it was impossible. I could not cross the veil, and even if I tried, the other world—the dark world—would undo me. But the Keeper was gone, and I couldn't think of anything else to do. And nothingness was better than the puppet men.

So I stepped forward, into that world, and slammed the door closed behind me.

2.

A face hovered above me.

It leaned close and frowned with deep worry lines. Brown eyes, unruly blond curls, stubble. I knew that face.

And it was impossible.

It spoke, lips moving slowly. I heard nothing but waves crashing somewhere in the distance.

"Lad?" I tried to whisper in reply.

But I didn't have a throat. And he disappeared.

3.

He crawled out of water that clung to him like hands, heavy and cold. All alone he climbed sharp stone, clutching rosemary bushes for purchase. The scent of crushed leaves tore sobs from his burning throat. It mingled with a layer of ash, disturbed by his scrambling, and the unmistakable smell of death.

Lying on his back in the rubble, he dug at his chest, pushed clothes aside, scrambling fingers searching, searching. But he found nothing. Thankfully, impossibly, nothing. He was still alive. The river that had almost drowned him must have also saved him. It washed everything away.

He forced himself to his feet, staggered, collapsed against the broken roof of a fallen tombstone. The sharp edges of shattered tiles cut into his hand.

But he managed to walk. Just one foot in front of the other. Then again. And again. Down the ruins of the cemetery path. He did not look for broken names, did not want to think which recently buried bodies had been flung up to reek of decay in the sun. Just keep moving.

Away from the river.

All alone.

4.

I opened heavy eyes. I was floating, surrounded by a humming light of many bright colours, always shifting, from sharp blue to a deep-salt sea green.

This was not what I had imagined nothingness would be like.

I blinked with difficulty. Gradually, the light dimmed, and I could see. The world seemed strangely wavy. It consisted of a tiled wall, square lamps, and a large dark slide scrawled with pale writing.

With a jolt I realised I was looking through glass. I turned my head. I was in a tube, supported in a thick liquid. Small, clear solids—like glass, or crystal—floated beside me, gently knocking against my face, my arms, my legs. Whatever this liquid was, it didn't appear to be drowning me. I could breathe in it, despite the airless feeling in my chest. I was alive and suspended in a tube.

None of it made sense.

"She's awake." A distorted voice came from above me.

Who was that? The puppet men? Had they caught me? Brought me back to the laboratory, trapped me in this bizarre prison while they waited for me to wake up to begin the next experiment?

I tried to struggle, but I could hardly move. Just like the suiting table! I wasn't going to let them—

"Don't move!" The voice was tinged with fuzzy, metallic panic. "The silex structures haven't properly formed yet. Quick, knock her out before she does herself any more damage."

Something whirred above me, the unmistakable spinning of gears.

I would not let them do this! But my arms would not respond, and I couldn't feel much at all from the neck down. Dull pain etched strange lines through me, following the path of the suited scars that held so much of me together.

"No!" A real voice, not above me but from somewhere on the other side of the curved glass. "No more drugs. Let me talk to her."

"Now is not—"

"Fuck off Marcus. I'm not going to interview her. I'll just calm her down."

A pause, and the whirring quietened.

"Think she'll listen to you?"

"Yes." A figure rippled into view. I couldn't make out any real details, except for a white coat, what looked like a pale mask that covered mouth and nose, and something dark over the eyes. "I'm certain."

I knew that voice; it called to me like a ghostly memory.

"Lad?" The word came out weak, semi-formed, and muted. When I spoke, I realised my mouth was full of the strange liquid. It had no taste at all, but the feeling of it filling my throat made me want to gag.

Lad pressed both hands against the glass, and leaned forward. I wished I could see his face. I needed to. Like a fluttering in my belly, a craving. Lad, here. Alive. Where we both should have been dead, taken by nothingness and cast like dust to the winds. But he was here.

"How do you know my name?" he asked, voice low.

I tried to move again. Slow, this time, not in panic or fear, I lifted my arms and reached for him. Palm to palm, either side of the curving glass.

Until I saw my wrists.

The suit was gone, and in its place I was nothing but light. The glow that filled my tube, the strange shifting of colours, they came from me.

I tried to cry out, but made no sound. Other's eternal darkness—my throat! If the suit on my wrists was gone then what about my throat? My waist? What had happened to the silver scars in my abdomen? The plug in my heart, the suit in my lungs?

What was going on? Where was I? What had happened to me?

Was I even alive?

"I thought you were going to calm her down?" The distorted voice. "She's redlining! We need to bring her under again."

"No!" Lad tore the masks from his face and pressed his nose against the tube. His brown eyes pierced me through the glass, through the liquid, through all my panic and fear. "Please, I don't know who you are or how you're even here, but please calm down. You made it this far. We don't want to lose you now."

He didn't know. Somehow, that was what calmed me. Why didn't he know who I was?

"She's stabilising," the voice said. "It's working, keep talking."

Slow kicks in my tube and I managed to propel myself closer to the glass. Lad watched me from the other side, eyes wide and concerned but fiercely thoughtful. So much like him, yet different entirely.

"Don't move too much—"

"What is this?" I whispered, and silenced him. My light-made throat could only manage the smallest of sounds. "Where is my suit?" The very act of talking was exhausting, and painful.

"Suit?" Lad whispered back. "I—" he glanced up, away from me "—I'm sorry, but I don't understand."

I tried to shake my head, but quickly discovered that was not such a great idea. My hands shook, where they pressed against the glass. I was strangely grateful for the fluid holding me up, because I certainly did not have the strength to do so.

"This, then?" I peered at the light, held down the tides of fear washing through me. "What is this?"

Lad glanced up, somewhere above and behind me. I wondered if he was seeking permission. "That is a Pionic Flare," he replied, and I almost did not hear him. "Powerful, but held in check by your program and the silex we are binding to you." He leaned forward. "Who programmed you? I have never seen coding like—"

"Aladio, be quiet." Not the distorted voice from above but another, outside the tube. Sharp and angry. "Enough!" I caught the hazy outline of another figure, somewhere toward the back of the room, but could make out no details.

Aladio? I had never heard Kichlan call him that.

Lad drew back, visibly hesitant.

"No." I pressed my hand harder to the glass. "Stay." The light brightened, and beamed from my wrists. That was suit light, I realised, unbound from its symbols and silver.

"What the—?" The distorted voice. "I don't believe this. You need to take a look at these figures, Sir!"

The indistinct figure disappeared.

Lad leaned forward again. "Who are you?" he whispered. "What are you?"

"Don't you remember me?"

The look in his eyes as he backed away was enough to break my heart. Maybe I deserved it. I had, after all, killed him. I had convinced him to fight the puppet men, to follow me to the laboratory basement. And he had flung himself in front of Aleksey's blades for me, taken their brunt, all to protect me. I no longer deserved his trust. The fear in his brown eyes, the panic and confusion...yes, I had certainly earned them.

So I turned myself away, with my slow-paddling movement. And noticed another tube, only half as tall as mine. The top was capped with metal and cables, ringed with flickering lights, and what could have been dials or numbers that moved.

Something shifted inside the tube. Small and slow, turning, glowing.

I watched, in morbid fascination.

A face—tiny and barely made, only the very beginnings of a person, the merest of sketches. The curl of semi-fists pressed close to a chest. The soft curve of a delicate spine.

It almost looked like a child. But it was mostly light, hardly flesh at all. What skin it had was so thin it was transparent, and colours shifted inside it. They rippled like sunrise on a pond.

A knot of fear tightened low in my stomach.

I had always wondered what the suit was doing to the child growing inside me. Just how much silver it had become.

I glanced down. No suit scars across my naked abdomen, only strips of light, as though it was shining up at me through a grate. Light and—stitches.

*Stitche*s?

"You cut into me?" I wanted to cry but I could only whisper. I tried to bang on the glass but I could only tap. I pressed my whole body against the tube and shone so brightly I had to close my eyes. "How dare you!" I finally managed to scream.

And my throat tore with it.

"The silex bonds have ruptured!" A terrible wail like an injured cat shattered the room, echoing through my tube and deep into my very bones. I opened my eyes to great red lights flashing in time to the noise, drenching everything in blood.

I had never truly made the kind of decision Sofia, Mizra and Uzdal had wanted me to make. I had never known what I wanted to do about my unplanned pregnancy. Terminate it, or risk giving birth to a debris collector—doomed to scrape out a poor life at the bottom of society—or a Half—broken and living in constant danger. But that had always been my decision to make. And it should not have been taken from me, not like this, no matter what the child would have been. No matter what.

"We have a freeforming Flare!"

More voices, all at once, some from a distorted distance and some in the room with me.

"Lock down the sector."

"Institute secondary control mechanisms."

"Up the silex count, we need to reform those bonds."

Were any of them Lad? I didn't care. I tried to bang against the tube but the liquid was thickening. And I couldn't make any sound anymore, only open my mouth and try to scream. To call to it. The semi-flesh, semi-light unborn creature they had taken from my body.

"Redlines all over the grid."

"Knock her out, now. I want so many drugs in that soup she doesn't wake up for a week."

Darkness pooled down with the tinny voices and the whirring at the top of my tube. A soft darkness that was dissolving my panic, my fear. Everything.

"I'm sorry," I thought I heard Lad say. But I had heard his ghost so many times before, I couldn't be sure if he was real.

Darkness was far easier, much more what I had expected a world of nothingness to be. So I let it take me.

5.

movoc-under-Keeper's wall was gone. It had stood strong for centuries, unbent by storm or quake or the force of an invading army. Tan, however, had destroyed it in one night.

Figured.

Kichlan climbed the ruins of the wall to escape the cemetery, and headed back into the city. It was difficult with one arm. At least the metal stump where his elbow had been didn't hurt, no matter how hard he knocked it. But it wasn't a hand, and it couldn't grip.

His city had moved on from chaos into a heavy melancholy. The fires had been doused; in their place smoking timber and scarred stone remained. The streets were torn, some made impassable by fissures in the cement, others risen up into jagged peaks spouting pipes and the ragged ends of steel frames. So few buildings remained. Most were shells. How could anyone survive this?

Yet they had. The citizens of Movoc-under-Keeper dug through the ruins of their city, shocked, numb, every movement slow, every word hushed. It felt like a great silence had fallen over the city, broken only by bodiless weeping coming from somewhere in the distance.

Hunched over, elbow hidden beneath his coat, Kichlan walked steadily down the broken streets. He wasn't really sure where he was going, or what he was hoping to do. He just knew he had to keep moving. Because if he stopped, if he just sat at the side of the road like he so desperately wanted to, then everything would come crashing down on him, and he might never get back up again. He was exhausted beyond anything he had ever known. Yet he walked, threading a slow path among the pion-binders dragging bodies and body parts out of the rubble.

Where were the bodies being taken, now that the cemetery beyond the wall had given back her dead? Perhaps the Tear River could have them, drag them down into darkness and nothingness. Like it had done Tan.

Tan.

He ran the back of his sleeve over his face. He'd always thought she needed looking after. Liked to pretend strength, to push her way forward and bear the brunt. But he would never forget her standing small and near frozen on his doorstep, that precious book in her hands. Or the defiance in her eyes, the challenge, when she had first shown him her scars.

Other damn her. Prideful and stubborn and oh so blind.

And gone. With his brother. Because he had failed them both.

He couldn't think about that. *Just keep moving.*

He grasped his silver elbow as he walked. His shoulder hurt; it was so much heavier than a normal arm. What had Tan been thinking, when she forced it on him?

He walked until his legs could hardly move. A constant mess of tiny debris grains brushed against his feet like sludge, but he ignored them. His debris collecting days were well and truly over. A ragged looking street vendor pressed poorly roasted sweet potato into his hand, but Kichlan couldn't find the will to eat it. Just to walk. Deeper and deeper into the city, past leaking effluent channels, collapsed factories, smouldering apartment blocks. Over broken glass, inches thick in places. The city grew hazy, his head spun, and everything smelled like sewage, and death.

Until a shadow passed over him, and Kichlan looked up. He blinked. Where was he? How long had he been walking? Somewhere, he'd dropped the sweet potato, but he was still clinging to its wrapper.

Two Strikers flew low above, passing overhead with the deep rushing of displaced air, leaving heat and debris in their wake. Strikers were the ultimate soldiers, held aloft by invisible pions, their mutilated faces hidden in sleek hoods of white leather. All around him, recovery work stopped. Stones were dropped, bodies placed gently back against the earth.

Kichlan paused, glanced around. Something didn't feel right. It was unusual to see Strikers deployed above the city, yes, but given the circumstances Kichlan wasn't all that surprised. The veche had imposed martial law even before Tan had destroyed Movoc-under-Keeper, thanks to skirmishes on the Hon Ji border and Fedor's Unbound insurgency. He'd seen the Mob, Shielders and Strikers marching through the city streets. So why were all these people so shocked?

Kichlan frowned. Now that he was getting a better look at them, they didn't look like normal pion-binders. They were wrapped in rags and digging through rubble, just like everyone else he'd seen. But they were...too big. All solid-looking figures, faces obscured and turned up to watch as the Strikers turned in a wide arc across the sky.

An overwhelming desire to run swelled with the quickening beat of Kichlan's heart. He didn't know what was going on, but he was certain he really didn't want to be in the middle of it.

The sound of fast, heavy feet echoed from the streets around him.

Kichlan ran. A staggering, broken-stride of a run, hardly any faster than walking.

Shouts. The feet marched faster. Strikers swooped down again and this time hovered.

"Stop!" Mob ran toward him like a tidal wave, so many, so large. "By order of the veche!" He had no way of fighting them. His suit was not as strong as Tan's had been.

He turned, met the Mob face on. But they weren't after him, and surged around him like thick, dark water. Black armour riddled with the silver hints of pion-powered weapons, golden eyes glowing behind wide, thick helmets. One, the large bear head on his black armoured breast ringed with nine circles, paused to scowl down at him. Which was an achievement in itself. Not many people were taller than Kichlan.

"Get out of here!" he snapped, shoving Kichlan aside.

Breathing hard, Kichlan staggered and struggled to right himself. His body was shaking uncontrollably. The suit metal cap on his elbow rolled, squirming, questing out with small lumps, like it was alive. Damn you Tan, he thought, and clenched his teeth. The movement he could not control started somewhere near his shoulder in the twitching of muscles, and ended with the unruly suit. It felt like an invasion of his body. *What have you left me to deal with?*

The large figures he'd seen digging through rubble, the ones he'd just assumed were normal pion-binders like everyone else, pulled off their robes as the Mob ran towards them. And Kichlan couldn't stop a gasp. They were Mob too, some Varsnian—from various local and regional veches, if the coloured bars on their heavy armour were anything to go by—but some were distinctly Hon Ji. Their bright blue armour shone in the crisp sunlight, dimmed only by the black dragon twisting across their breastplates. They all drew weapons, hidden in their rag disguises.

Hon Ji Mob in the city? Running battles in ruined streets? He had to get away, and he had to do it now, before he was caught in the rush of pion weapons he couldn't even see.

But he couldn't stop the shaking. And he had only stumbled a weak step forward when suddenly, everything flashed white. Then cries around him, behind him. He spun, desperately rubbing his eyes.

The Mob were fighting each other, and spilling back towards him, weapons like humming, vibrating swords that flickered and buzzed as they clashed; projectiles fired; flares burned; blood sprayed; chaos and violence around him in a terrible ring. He scrambled back, lost his footing and fell hard.

A great shadow loomed over him. Varsnian Mob, a bloodied blade lifted and ready, held out an armoured hand. "Hurry, let me help you."

Kichlan stared up at the roaming golden eyes and did not understand what was going on.

"Quickly, before—"

Two more bursts, so bright they hurt, then explosions rocked the street. The Mob cursed, dropped to a knee, swung to deflect the blade of one of his fellows and followed through with a blow to the man's gut. It took two vicious hacks to cut through the black armour, and then the man fell to pieces on the street.

Kichlan turned, stomach heaving.

"Get out of the way!" The Mob bent, hooked arms around Kichlan's chest and swung him around with strength born from the massive pion manipulations going on inside his body.

An instant later the Strikers fell, crashing to earth right where Kichlan had been. He stared at them, their bodies broken and burned. Charred leather, terrible smoking gashes blasted through masks.

What could possibly—

Natasha emerged from the battling Mob. Natasha as he had never seen her. Dressed in a strange arrangement of pieces of Mob armour, with a Striker's hood, over her debris collector's dark, boned uniform. She smiled when she saw him. Blood plastered her hair to one side of her face, and the other was darkened with soot. The silver handles of countless small knives protruded from her armour, and she held a small clay-looking disk in her hand.

She paused beside him, took in his exhaustion and silver-healed injury with one sweeping glance.

"Other's fiery hells, Kichlan," she said. "What happened to you?"

6.

I had been dreaming about Kichlan. And in my dreams, he was alive.

My eyes opened slowly. Lad stood on the other side of the tube. He watched me.

I wanted to tell him I had dreamed of his brother. He would like that. Did he dream about Kichlan too?

But the darkness still held me. So I could only meet Lad's eyes, just for that moment, before mine closed again.

But in the darkness, I dreamed of Kichlan. In my dreams, he was alive.

And that was better than nothing.

7.

"Please just sit in the wheelchair, Tanyana," Aladio said, red in the face, exasperated but obviously trying to hide it. He gestured again to the hideous chair with its lime green cushions and large metal wheels, as though that would possibly help his argument. "It's for your own good."

I narrowed my eyes at him. He was not the Lad I knew. Not the man who had sacrificed himself to save me from Aleksey's vicious twin blades, and not the ghost who had reprogrammed my suit and liberated me from the control of the puppet men. It hurt every time I saw him, looking so much the same. So I had to keep reminding myself, in the face of my memories and my guilt—this was not Lad. This was *Aladio*.

"I can walk," I said, throat grinding, sore and always thirsty. It hurt to speak, but there was no way I would keep silent. "I will walk."

He shoved the chair. "You're being obstinate just for the sake of it now!"

I gritted my teeth. "And you can stop treating me like a child whenever you like."

Apparently I'd been out of the tube for two days. It was impossible to tell, because I'd been kept in this room since then and it had no windows. I wasn't certain windows would help, either. Did a world of nothingness even have a sun?

Lad—no, *Aladio*—was the only person I'd seen. He didn't come to keep me company, he didn't come to talk, and sometimes he couldn't even look me in the eye. Instead, he came to test the integrity of my silex bonds. He couldn't even bring himself to touch me, and when he had no choice— when the silex splintered and he had to patch it with tubes full of viscous liquid—he wore thick, white gloves.

I glanced down at the strange band of crystal around my wrist, and the light inside it brightened. This *silex* was delicate stuff. It looked like ice-shavings. Thick around my wrists, ankles, waist and neck—in fact, anywhere the suit had been drilled into my bones. A fine layer coated most of my body, like a dusting of sugar or the crust of a shallow pond. It itched against my skin and made disturbing creaking noises when I moved.

Aladio took a deep breath, and when he faced me he was calm again, his expression false and all too patient. "And that's very good, Tanyana. Very good. You are healing very well."

I hated that look on his face and that too-sweet tone of voice. It was all so wrong.

"But you know you need to be careful. If you're too rough on your silex bonds the Flare inside you will eat you all up, and it would destroy all of us at the same time. So be a good girl and sit in the wheelchair, or you'll have to go back in the tube. Do you want that, Tanyana? Do you want to go back in the tube?"

It made me sick. But my neck hurt, and my piecemeal body felt so fragile—divided by light and held together with little more than glass. So I gave in. I sat in the wheelchair and let Aladio fuss over me.

"I don't understand," I said, quietly, as he wheeled me around to face the door. "What is a *Flare*? What have you done to me? Where is everybody else?"

He tapped symbols glowing on a glass panel riveted into the wall beside the door. Something like a pion lock, I'd decided, but it required a code. I'd studied those symbols for bells. Not only because that door was the only way to escape, but because they reminded me too strongly of the symbols that had bobbed and glowed on the bands of my suit. The same symbols the ancient Unbound had used to write books with, the ones we'd found glowing inside the Keeper's Mountain.

That had to mean I'd come to the right place. There were programmers here, people who could—I hoped— help me defeat the puppet men.

I swallowed against crystal and a faintly warm, burning sensation. "Where are you taking me?"

Aladio hesitated. "To someone who can save you," he answered. "I hope."

My dim, hazy reflection wavered in the door's smooth steel as it slid open. My eyes were red, irritated and always vaguely itchy. The skin around the edge of my mouth and nose was dry and cracked. They'd shaved my head, and it emphasised the pale ridges of my old scars, now running beside protruding patterns in silex. I was grateful there were no real mirrors here, and I could not see myself in detail.

He wheeled me out into corridors of white tiles and blue paint. There was something loose in the left wheel and it rattled, incessant, grating. The floor was a kind of strange, spongy polymer that squeaked beneath us and was coloured to look like stone. I tried to memorise the way he was taking me, the number of silver doors we passed, the corners we took, left or right. But it all looked the same, and I lost track.

Finally, we stopped at a set of large silver doors. More tapping, and they slid open. I noticed a larger symbol shining in red above the panel on the wall, and I recognised it instantly—*debris*.

"Wait." I clutched at the top of the wheels but could barely grip them, let alone slow myself down. "What is this place?" Memories of my suiting, of the puppet men with their needles sent shivers of panic rattling through my crystal.

"Calm down or I will have to strap you to the arm rests!"

We entered a long, narrow and dimly lit room. It was cold. The clothes they had given me were thin cotton shirt and pants, and slipper-like shoes I did not bother to wear. I had not needed anything warmer until now.

Lidless coffins of solid crystal lined the walls. So similar to the one we'd found in the mountain room, but some of these held bodies. A woman, young, dressed in a white robe. The skin of her neck and hands was so pale it was almost blue. She appeared to breathe, but long breaths ever so slow. They steamed out from beneath a silex mask, condensing in the cold air. The end of her coffin was capped with a silver cone. A prism spun at the very tip. About the size of a clenched fist, it scattered light across the room. Tiny mirrors dotted the ceiling and the walls. They caught this light, reflected it, and sent it to a giant shard of crystal floating in the centre of the room.

Aladio parked me in front of the giant shard. Almost as tall as the ceiling, with a sharply tapered top and bottom, it rotated slowly. Light rippled inside it, the same light that rippled inside of me.

"What is that?" I whispered, and leaned forward to touch gentle fingertips to its smooth, warm surface.

Aladio paused. He glanced over his shoulder. He bent to fiddle with the left wheel.

I turned my hand, wrist close to the giant crystal, and watched the way our rainbow of lights entangled. "Lad, please."

He shuddered. "Don't call me that," he whispered, his voice hoarse. "My name is Aladio."

"*Lad*," I said again, insistent, and shoved my wrist at him. "Explain this to me. Why am I here, and not dead? Why am I glowing the way that crystal thing is glowing? What have you done with my baby? *What is going on?*"

"Just—just calm yourself. Don't do anything that might weaken your silex bonds. Just—sit, quietly—and fuck, woman, don't call me that. No one calls me that anymore." Lad stood, placed a hand on the crystal. "Not for a long time."

I tried to do what he said. Deep breaths. I rested my hands in my lap. "There," I said. "I'm calm. Now it's your turn. Explain this to me."

He shook his head. "Not my job. Just had to bring you here. Because you seem to like me. Because, when

I'm around, your silex holds. Don't know why. It doesn't make sense." Finally, he met my gaze. "Nothing about you makes sense."

"Other's darkness, don't I know it."

"*Other*? Why do you keep saying that?"

I shrugged, and winced at a cracking somewhere in my shoulder. "It's a curse. You know, something you say to add…emphasis to a situation." I'd never heard Lad swear, although he'd seemed to enjoy it when other people did.

Aladio bent to inspect my neck and upper back. "A curse, truly?" His gloved fingers, as they pressed the skin around my silex, were gentle. And warm. "How odd."

"La—Aladio, please. Why have you brought me in here?"

"This room has a direct connection to the veil," said a voice behind me. "This is where we upload programmers to monitor the Guardian program. And this is how we will send you home."

I twisted in my chair. A small group of men and women entered the room, all wearing crisp white robes. Most were tapping at bright symbols on the clear class panels they carried—like pion slides, just larger—one was empty handed, and smiled at me. An older man, head shaved like mine, his face lined with age rather than scarring. There was silex embedded in his temples. Only small crystal shards, about the size and shape of a fingerprint, each shining with a different coloured light.

Aladio turned me around to face him. The man crouched, and held out a hand. "I'm sorry for the belated welcome, Tanyana," he said. "I am the Specialist, head programmer of Fulcrum. I apologise for your treatment, but we needed to stabilise the Pionic Flare within you before we could do anything else."

"Head programmer?" I took a deep breath. I had to concentrate. No more panic, no more weakness. I was here for a reason. "Good. You're just the person I want to see." I took his hand. He touched me gingerly.

"Am I?" He lifted his eyebrows and sat back a little, dusting off the silex I had left on his palm.

I started to nod, felt something crack and ease at the back of my neck, and stopped. "Yes. I need your help." The door behind him opened, and more people came through, this time pushing something on wheels. I ignored them, and held the Specialist's gaze. "You see, back on my world, the doors are opening, and the puppet men—creatures that you created!—have undone the Keeper so there's no one to close them. If we don't stop them, then both of our worlds will be destroyed."

The Specialist looked at me like I was speaking another language. He glanced up at Aladio before patting my knee, gently. "I'm sorry," he said. "I don't understand you. I wish I did. You can't know just how much I wish I could help you, and talk to you, learn about your world and find out just how you managed to cross over into ours. This has never happened, not in all our history, and it shouldn't even be possible—" He paused, and sighed, shaking his head. "But we just don't have time. Tanyana, we're going to send you home. Now."

He stood, and gestured to Aladio. I found myself wheeled deeper into the room.

"Wait!" I cried after him. "Home? But I need your help!"

This time we stopped at a single glass coffin in the centre of the room. Thin, transparent wires trailed their way from a large prism at its top, pulsing with light and leading directly to the giant glowing crystal. Was this what the coffin in the mountain would have looked like, long ago? So bright instead of dark, pulsing rather than quiet, almost a living thing rather than a dusty tool.

"Now, don't struggle," Aladio said. Before I even knew what was happening he lifted me from my chair and laid me in the cold, hard bed. This close, I realised there were flecks of gold threading through the crystal so tight around me. I recognised that too—I'd seen rubble of the same material in the ruins of the underground Unbound street.

"What—" it was hard to talk. "What are you doing?"

The Specialist leaned into view. "This is for your own good. Aladio, calm her down."

Aladio crouched beside me. "Really, it's for the best," he said.

Cold seeped up from the coffin and wound itself through me. I had to focus so hard just to move my arm and clutch at Aladio's sleeve.

"Lad," I gasped. "Lad, don't let them. Lad, please."

He pulled back, expression hard. "I told you not to call me that."

"You have to listen to me!" The light within me surged with my effort, and it was warm. It dissolved the clutching cold and held the numbness at bay. I wrapped both hands around the edges of the coffin and slowly, ever so slowly, pulled myself upright. "I came all this way, I risked so much, so you would help me! My world, your world, both our worlds are under threat. There are these...these things... I call them the puppet men. I don't think they have a real name. They are trying to bring down the veil."

I managed to sit up. The Specialist stood between my coffin and the giant crystal, surrounded by large, floating screens covered in bright symbols. His fingers danced across them, the silex in his skull flickered to the same rhythm as his hands. All around me was so much light. It gathered in the crystal, it shone in hard, steady beams from the mirrors in the walls, filling the room with a complicated pattern, a labyrinthine mesh of colour. The other programmers stood at regular intervals around us, each with their own group of smaller, floating screens.

The Specialist frowned at me. "Bring down the veil? No one in their right mind would want to do that."

"But they do!" I tried to push myself out of the coffin, but my strength only extended so far. My arms wobbled, I fell back against the side, and winced as something cracked around my waist. "The puppet men do! They're not people, they're—" what did they call themselves again? "—code! Programs. Parts of the Keeper himself. The leftovers, the upgrades that didn't make it." I tried to remember everything the puppet men had spouted, right before I destroyed Movoc-under-Keeper. "You programmers didn't want them, so you cast them into the veil. They grew there. Now they want to bring down the veil to create a world of their own, and that's just what they will do, unless you can tell me how to defeat them."

"What's a Keeper?" one of the programmers called.

Beside me, Aladio shuddered, and for a moment, just a moment, he looked lost.

"The Keeper is the Guardian program," I answered. And I met Lad's—*Aladio's*—eyes as I did so. "That's what we call him, on my side of the veil. We don't have programs there, or code. We always thought he was a god." I reached for Lad's face. "And he had messengers. We called them Halves."

He jerked away, and I slipped back against the coffin.

"Tanyana," the Specialist said. "You need to stop fighting this. Please, lie back in the chamber."

"But—"

"Listen to me. We can't help you, because those things you said, they are impossible. The veil can't create anything, it doesn't foster or feed. Nothing can live inside it. Or spring from it, fully formed."

"But they are real—"

"Secure her, please."

Aladio placed a white-gloved hand against my chest and pressed me slowly back into the coffin. He didn't look at me, just stared at nothing, jaw square, eyes hard. The cold took hold again, and the lights inside me dimmed.

"Hook her up. And the child."

Fear dropped into my heart. "What—" I forced out the words, one slurring syllable at a time. "Are—you—do—with—"

"Tanyana, hush." The Specialist appeared above me. Two of his screens had come with him and floated at the edge of my sight. I couldn't move my head, had no hope of sitting up again and seeing what they were doing to my child. All I could see was his fingers moving, and the symbols flickering, some shining brightly then dimming as others took their place. Such an arcane dance. So much like the way they had bobbed, crested and sunk on the bands of my suit.

"I think—" Aladio said, beside me, his voice breaking. "I think you should tell her what you're doing to her. And to the child. I think she has a right to know." For a moment his face was above me, and his eyes met mine. They were hurting. How that made me ache. "Isn't it the least we can do?"

The Specialist paused, then nodded. He looked over his shoulder and said, "Keep it going," then he stepped back from his panels and knelt beside me again. I wondered why they didn't fall.

"I don't know how you came here," he said. "I don't know how you're even alive. You seem to know something of our worlds and the veil between us, so you know you should be dead. Hell, more than dead. Your world is utterly incompatible with ours, so you should have been undone on a fundamental, subatomic way. But you weren't. You came to our world on the back of a powerful Pionic Flare, just dropped out of it like it was birthing you. I wish we could find out why—"

"Pi—Pi—" I struggled to speak. Pionic Flare? As in, *pions*? What was he talking about?

"I wish we could study you, get to know you. Translate your code, and work out who could have programmed you. But we can't. Because, Tanyana, you have a Flare inside of you, one just as powerful—if not more powerful—than the one that brought you here. The silex has managed to contain it for now, as has your own programming, but that won't work for long. If we don't send you back, you will die. And you will take Fulcrum, and me, and Aladio, and all the people who work here, with you."

"Sir, communication beam has been established," one of the programmers called. "We're sending signals to the Guardian program and await response."

The Specialist nodded. "Prepare for extraction." He smiled at me. "This won't be too hard on you. Unlike the programmers we send into the veil, you're already code as well as flesh. We won't need to translate the electronic pulses in your brain into light, purify them into manageable code, and send them on a beam back through an open

Flare. All we have to do is link you to the Guardian and let it carry you across. Easy."

Lights flickered through the crystal around me, following the fine tracks of gold. Strange, sharp little feelings, like pinpricks on my skin, surged through me in response. So, this was what it took to make a Half.

"I'm sorry you have been caught up in this, and I'm sorry you have to suffer for it. We never wanted that. Your world was not to blame."

Your world was not to blame? The Keeper had said that too. "Don't—understand," I gasped. "Pions—my world. What—Flare?" My throat felt strange, all liquid and empty again. I couldn't see it, but I could just make out my wrists. The crystal coffin and the crystal in my flesh were merging, the thin gold wires worming their way inside of me. Just like the suit again.

The Specialist sighed. "A long time ago our ancestors—programmers and Specialists just like us—made a bad mistake. They thought they could control the very fabric of space and time. Instead, they tore it. There are many different realities—your world and our world are just two of them. They all exist in parallel, one beside the other, so close and yet so far. Normally, we're not aware of them, because they are so very different to us that we can't see, can't touch, can't measure them. Opposites, incompatible. But the ancient programmers forced our realities too close together. So close, in fact, that they began to bleed into one another, destroying each other. The only thing that saves us is the veil."

He paused to reach up, drag one of his panels down, rearrange symbols, then pushed it back to hover beside its fellow.

"The veil is a side effect of the experiment that first weakened the line between our realities," he continued. "It seems to be some kind of wave function semi-reality, we think, visible on our spectrum as light. It can host programs like the Guardian program, or the programmers whose brain functions have been translated into code themselves. But it can't give life to mathematical concepts, Tanyana. It's not a place, or a thing."

I would have shaken my head if I could have. "Know—veil—Keeper. My world—doors." The puppet men had told me, smirking, vicious, that the veil was not what the programmers thought it was. But I didn't have the strength to warn them.

"Don't try to talk," Aladio admonished me. "You'll only hurt yourself."

The Specialist raised his eyebrows. "Doors? How strange."

"Sir?" one of the programmers called.

The Specialist raised a hand, "A moment." He smiled down at me, probably trying to be reassuring. "We are all very lucky to have the veil. Remember I told you that our realities have been forced so closely together that they bleed into each other? They still do. And we are opposites, and cannot co-exist. We should be destroying each other, we should have been destroyed a long time ago. Only the veil saved us. It acts as a filter, and changes the particles as they move through it. So they rush into our world, burst through with sound and heat and light and, if left unchecked, would unmake, remake, warp and ultimately tear our world apart. That, Tanyana, is what a Pionic Flare is. It is a burst of particles that change the nature of our reality. That is what you have inside of you. It might not sound like we're lucky, but we are. Because we can capture these Flares in silex, as we have done for you, and as you have seen floating in this very room. Through silex we are able to use Flares to power everything around you."

"Sir?" The programmer tried again. "Sir, I really think—"

"I said wait!" The Specialist sat back on his heels. "So you see why it is so important to send you home, and do it now. You have a force within you capable of altering the fabric of reality. We could trap you in a silex Shard like the one in this room and draw on you to power this station, but

I hate to think what that could do to your body, and your mind. I will not do that to you. Not if I have a choice. So, please, Tanyana, don't fight this. Let me send you home."

But I wasn't listening, not to him, not really. Instead, I listened to myself. The rush and flow of particles within me. Of *pions*. Particles that had the power to remake the world? I knew what that was. Not exactly the same as the pions of my world—ours did not arrive in a burst of heat, although they certainly did shine, and the pions I knew responded so eagerly and did not need to be captured in crystal. But still...

After all these moons, cut off from the lights of my childhood, from the world I had loved, suddenly I was filled with pions again, filled fit to burst. A Pionic Flare.

Was this Flare inside me really the mindless destructive force the Specialist thought it was? Or would it listen to me? Could it be cajoled, like the pions I knew?

"Sir!" the programmer called again, panic in his voice. "Something's wrong."

The Specialist frowned, and looked away. "Wrong?"

"We're not getting anything back from the Guardian program. Actually, we're not getting anything at all. Not even static!"

"Excuse me." The Specialist stood, grabbed his panels, and hurried away with them.

"Won't—work," I gasped. "Guardian—dead. Puppet men—absorbed. Saw—it."

Aladio leaned forward so I could see him. "Didn't you understand? The Guardian isn't a person. It's a program—numbers and symbols translated into light. It can't die. It was never alive."

"You were—too. Half. But you—still—died."

Aladio's eyes took on a distant look. "H—Half?" he whispered. "That word, it calls to me. Why does it call to me?" He focused on me. "You do too. I don't understand. I feel like I know you, but that's impossible. I find myself thinking about you, worrying about you, knowing things. Like your name. I knew it before you could even speak. Why?"

"Lad—"

"And why do you call me that? That's what my mother used to call me, before she died. No one's called me that for more than fifty years."

"Interference," the Specialist was saying, somewhere in the background. "There's too much traffic on her Flare! It's not us. What *is that*?"

"I—know—you." I had to work so hard, just to speak, even haltingly, even whispering. It wasn't just the weakness in my throat anymore, there was something else, like buzzing, like voices, so many voices, all in my head. "You crossed. To my world. You were—my friend."

The mesh of light above and around me started surging to a desperate beat I could feel even deeper than my veins. The rush and the flow, the movement between worlds, all trapped inside me. *Can you hear me?* I whispered, silent, to the innermost parts of myself. *Are you there, lonely, waiting for me to call to you? Little pions, little particles, little friends?*

"Crossed the veil, you mean?" Lad leaned forward. "Yes, I did. For twenty-five years I lay in this room, frozen in my chamber, while my mind was beamed into the veil to monitor the Guardian. I don't remember any of it. At least, I shouldn't. But then, there is you."

The room shook. Beams of light wavered. The crystal coffin seemed to contract around me like a living hand.

"Sir!" the programmer was shouting now. "I'm losing connection. Our beam is being rejected. Code unravelling."

"Rejected?" the Specialist shouted. "That's impossible!"

Another shake. Something crashed behind me, glass on the floor. Several beams snapped off. The gold wiring retracted from my silex, slithering free of me like countless tiny snakes.

Aladio finally seemed to notice what was happening around him. He stared around us, expression horrified. "Tan?" he whispered. "What are you doing?"

I could move my hands again. With a grunt, I pulled my wrists free of the clutching cold and wiggling wires, gripped the sides of the coffin and levered myself upright.

The room was drenched in red. Warning lights flashed from every single one of the coffins that lined the walls. The great crystal at the centre was burning too, crimson like glowing blood churning, spilling, crashing against its smooth facets.

The Specialist turned to me, horrified. "Get back in there! Let us do our job!"

Aladio jumped up, hurried to one of his fellow programmers, grabbed an inactive panel and dragged it back with him. He pressed fingers against its dark surface and symbols flashed into life across it.

"Tanyana, you need to stop doing whatever you're doing in that Flare. You're destroying our code and weakening our connection. We can't upload you when you do that!"

"I don't want you to upload me." I looked around for my child. It was set up, still in its tube, in a coffin similar to mine. Its half-face was tranquil, its single flesh hand loosely curled. It even yawned with a tiny, pink mouth. A little spot of calm. Its coffin, and that alone, did not flash with warning red. "I came here to get help, and I'm not going back until I do."

Whispers surged through me, around me. I lifted one arm, drew my hand close to my face. Something was leaking out of the cracked silex where the little golden wires had drilled into my wrist. It was light, yes, the ever-shining of the rainbow inside of me. But there was something else too. A disturbance in the air, like heat rising. "Can you hear me?" I breathed on it, and for an instant—so quick I couldn't tell if it was real—a tiny shimmering form of countless bright lights danced, then vanished.

"Sir!" another programmer cried. I turned to watch them smacking palms against unresponsive screens, all scrawled with red lines like some terrible toddler's drawing. "Access denied! Programmer feeds coming back at us! Something's pushing our beams back. Disconnect from the veil in five, four, three …"

"No," the Specialist abandoned his panels and ran to

an occupied coffin. "They're waking up—"

A screaming-cat wail cut across him. Thick tendrils of mist rose from the floor a few feet away from me. The programmers grabbed their screens and all scrambled back.

The great circle appeared on the floor, broke in two, and retracted like an opening door. Cold rushed out, the rumble of gears grinding deep below us sent fresh shudders through the room. A jagged pillar of crystal rose slowly, terribly.

"What is that?" I choked over the mist to Aladio, who remained crouched beside me.

"Our graveyard," he whispered. "Oh Tan, you've got to stop this."

"I refuse to—" I stuttered to silence. Bright lights wavered inside the pillar, their beauty and movement broken only by the dark shapes of bodies.

These people were most definitely not sleeping. The deeper they were in the crystal, the less of them remained. They did not decay, as such, as bodies buried in soil decay. Rather, they had faded. From solid skin and muscle and bone to thin shadows of shape, more reflection than real.

"These are what remain of the programmers who cross the veil. Some who've spent their life in service. Some who couldn't handle the extraction, and died before they even had a chance to try. This is where we all end up, where our code is analysed for variations that could be used to upgrade the Guardian. This is where I should be."

"But you woke up."

"I should not have, Tan."

I stared at the bodies of dead Halves and remembered the Keeper's fear that he would fail. These programmers who gave up their lives to help him, they were his creators. He had always wanted to do them proud.

Then a familiar face called me from the crystal. The most recent of the bodies, still whole, still recognisable, close to the surface. The Hon Ji Half.

And she twitched.

"All the Other's hells!" I gasped.

And all around her the parts of once-were Halves were moving, spasming, jerking against the crystal that held them so tightly. A bone here, a shadow there, arms and what was left of a head.

"That's it!" the Specialist shouted. "We're aborting! Lock down all beams in and out of this sector, don't let this spread to the rest of Fulcrum. I want her drugged, keep that Flare down to a matchstick flicker until I'm certain she's contained."

Three programmers grabbed me, one plunged a needle into my upper arm.

"No!" I struggled to fight them off, and only managed to crack silex. "What about the puppet men? What about the Keeper? You have to help me! That's why I came!"

Then I couldn't feel my arms, or face, not any part of me. And darkness seeped in at the edges if my vision, a darkness I knew too well.

"Sir, you have to see this." The voices were distorted and sounded so far away. I couldn't quite understand them, couldn't quite hold on to the words. "It's the child, Sir. Its connection is...fine. Strong, clear. No interference, no pushback. It's perfect."

Child? No! But I couldn't do anything, couldn't even feel the pulse within me. I had the strangest sensation of being lifted and floating, gently, out of the room.

"You're joking, even in the middle of all of this?"

Someone was holding me, carrying me.

"Get everything back to normal and then I want tests done. Find out what's so special about this child. And what the fuck just happened back there."

Lad. I wanted to turn my face into his chest. I wanted to hold his hand, feel his warm skin, the way we always had, the way that had always comforted him—and me. But I couldn't do anything. As they took me from the room, and turned their attention to my child, all I knew was floating. Then darkness. And dreams.

8.

He still couldn't believe it. Tan had said something about Natasha being a spy; she had chased the woman down, bound and beat her when she'd tried to escape. But still, he couldn't believe it. Natasha's lethal grace, her plundered armour and the power of her weapons. The army of Mob, Shielders and Strikers at her command—some Hon Ji, some rebellious Varsnians.

"*You?*" he asked, again.

"Will you stop saying that?" She flashed him a furious look. "And don't use that tone!"

"I'm sorry." He should be sorry, and careful. Natasha was dangerous. *Natasha.*

"You remind me of Tanyana."

"I'll bet." He could imagine the look of surprise on her face when she'd found out, and the image made him smile. Even now.

Natasha paused, clenched a fist in the air and the mass of armoured bodies around her halted. Two Varsnian Shielders waited at the rubble of a nearby corner, the crimson of their uniforms like a splash of blood against the city's broken stone, the dark glass visors on their helmets lowered to obscure their eyes. The pion-bound barrier around them was only visible in the crushed shards of gravel suspended in its curve. A moment of tension, between golden roving eyes and shaded gaze, then at some signal Kichlan couldn't see Natasha's Mob seemed to decide these Shielders were on their side. One of the

Mob whispered to her, she nodded, and unclenched her fist. They continued to march.

Kichlan kept his eyes downcast, and focused on the ruined, unsteady street as he passed the Shielders. How many soldiers did Natasha command, and just what was she planning to do with them?

"Where is Tanyana?" Natasha whispered, barely audible beneath the marching of heavily reinforced feet. "She left me to go and save you, right before the city destroyed itself. Obviously she was successful. But where is she now?"

Kichlan shrugged deeper into his jacket, clutched his amputated elbow to his chest. "She is gone," he whispered, even quieter. "The river took her."

Somehow, Natasha heard. She reared back. "She, what, drowned? That's impossible."

Kichlan shrugged. He didn't know, he hadn't seen. All he remembered was the puppet men, the twisted crawling of debris inside him, then falling, crashing, and dragging himself out of the water. He pressed his remaining hand to his chest, the memory of that feeling of being undone making him breathless. Somehow, the Tear River had saved him. Even as it had taken Tan away, it had ripped away the debris trying to kill him. Impossible? Natasha didn't know the meaning of impossible. Everything Tan and the puppet men had said, that was impossible. This damned arm and the fact that he was even alive, impossible. But he did not bother to argue. "It doesn't matter, not any more."

Natasha shook her head, drew one of her small clay disks from a pocket hidden in her armour and began rolling it between her fingers. The closest few Mob hung back, a little, at the sight of it. Strange, to see such large men so nervous around her. She muttered something incomprehensible, the stuttering and biting curse of another language, then, "She should have stayed with me instead of running off to save you. I told her what we were trying to do, even offered her a place in that future. What a difference she could have made."

"Well, thanks for your concern." Kichlan knew he should be hurt, or angry. But he didn't seem to feel anything, anymore. "But I told you, it doesn't matter. None of us will be here for much longer."

"Oh?" Natasha gestured to her Mob, even as she spoke. Silently, the company disbanded, and smaller groups dispersed down alleyways, until he was left with Natasha and only two Mob. "Really?"

Why didn't she sound surprised? Or fearful? "The Keeper is dying, dead already, maybe, and the doors are opening. Soon, this world will be swallowed in nothingness, torn apart and scattered like dust to the stars." Now, why had he said that? Didn't sound like him. Sounded like Tan, when she recounted the Keeper's words.

Natasha did not so much as pause, but drew him along in the wake of her steady march. "It's taking a while, wouldn't you say?"

"What?"

She stamped down on a smooth portion of unbroken cement, before vaulting onto the jagged bones of a fallen apartment block. "This world still seems pretty solid. How long does it take nothingness to get here, anyway?"

Kichlan could not hope to follow her strong, lithe movements, so walked the long way around the rubble. He frowned at her. She had pocketed her disk, and looked far too smug.

"I remember that sewer, Kichlan. Tanyana said it was open only a crack, the door that nearly destroyed us in an instant. If the doors are opening, like you say, and there is no Keeper to maintain them, then why are we still here? How long is it going to take?"

He could not answer. Natasha was right. He had been so sure the world would end. He had been waiting for that nothingness, like he was holding his breath.

"So maybe you'll just have to learn to live with it," she said. "Tanyana is gone, Lad is gone, but the world isn't ending." They halted at what was left of a shop on the Eastear bank. "You might think nothingness would be easier, but thinking won't make it so. The world is still here, Kichlan. Why don't you fight with us to make it better?"

The banks of the Tear had fractured in the explosion, the river carrying most of the rubble away. Instead of wide, well-paved streets lined with shops and upmarket housing, the Eastear and Westear were little more than rough cliffs. Their foundations, guts of steel frame, cement and brickwork, were exposed, obscenely open beneath the cold blue sky. The river rushed between them, foaming white in anger, steadily tearing more and more of the city away.

"I don't understand," he said, watching Natasha crawl nimbly through the rubble.

"I know, and that's a pity. Tanyana did." She scanned the ground, lifted a rock and peered at it closely, before shaking her head and tossing it aside. "Took some explaining though. I never understood that. You and her, you should have been on my side from the beginning." She glanced over her shoulder. "Your national veche is run by a group of warmongering old families, wasting the resources of this once-great nation to consolidate their power. What has happened to you and her, and even Lad, you're all proof of that!"

Kichlan swallowed hard. "Don't bring Lad into this—"

"But it's true." Natasha abandoned her search to jam hands on hips and glare down at him. "While Lad was alive, you lived in constant fear that the veche would take him away. Not everyone treats their Halves like that!" A quick glance at the sky, and she resumed searching. "I was born in the colonies on the disputed border, my father Varsnian Mob, my mother a Hon Ji civilian. I've lived on both sides, I've seen the difference between the veche and the Emperor. I chose my side, Kichlan." She paused at some invisible signal, gestured to her Mob and pointed at the ground. "And I'm not alone. So many of your local and regional veche are sick of having their authority eroded, and have turned against the old families. With the help of the Emperor, we have been sowing the seeds of revolution for years. With the city in disarray and the military loyal to the national veche already stretched, now is the perfect time for those seeds to sprout!"

The Mob clamoured after her. They twitched their steel-clawed fingers and whispered, as they began manipulating pions. From the time it took them, and the tension in their arms and hunching backs, Kichlan gathered the pions were not being all that co-operative. Hardly a surprise, given the debris released from the puppet men's underground laboratory, and all the doors Tanyana had seen.

"Hurry up," Natasha hissed, and tipped back her head to scan the sky.

Kichlan followed her gaze. The sky was hard blue, the sun distant-seeming and weak, empty but for the Keeper Mountain. Countless tiny figures flew close to the mountain, white armour glinting in the rays of the sun. It wouldn't take long for them to swoop, if Natasha and her Mob were discovered. It had to be risky, surely, to march Mob through the streets, fight the Varsnian forces, and now dig through rubble so exposed.

Kichlan jumped as the ground beneath them began to shift. It was rough, and noisy, and sent dust up into the air, but the Mob were digging deep into the foundations of the building. Far deeper than they could have gone digging by hand.

They pulled something that looked like part of a machine out of the ground. Long at the front, bulging in the middle, riddled with handles and chains hanging loose from the dark cloth it was wrapped in. It was huge, easily longer than his arm—his whole arm—and thick as a man's torso. Only a Mob, reinforced and strengthened with pions, could surely carry such a thing.

Grinning, Natasha leapt out of the ruined building. "Another block to the south, three doors back from the Tear," she said. "We need to move fast. Less than a quarter bell, I'll risk being out here. The longer this takes, the more chance we have of being seen. You too, Kichlan," she gripped his coat and dragged him along behind her.

"What—what is that?" Kichlan gasped as he staggered to keep up.

Natasha paused beside the Mob long enough to tear the cloth at the thick end of the device. She drew it back to expose a dragon's head, wrought in iron. It had no bottom jaw, and its half-maw opened too widely, too roundly. Tiny, sharp teeth glittered in the sunlight. Deeply inset eyes stared darkly up at him, and Kichlan shuddered.

"The veche aren't the only ones developing secret weaponry," Natasha said.

9.

When I woke, I was being carried. My head felt oddly disconnected, my body numb and heavy. I tried to look around but my neck wouldn't work. All I could see was the ceiling, broken only by doors and the odd red, glowing symbol.

"You're awake," Aladio said, somewhere close to my ear. I didn't need to look at him to know his expression was hard again, his jaw too square, that pent-up, forceful look in his eyes. "You should have stayed asleep, Tanyana. It would have been better that way."

"Don't talk to her," said someone on my other side.

"Let's just do this, and get back to the Specialist," said another, near my feet. "Biggest moment since the Guardian came online, no way I'm going to miss it."

So, I was being carried by Lad and more than one programmer.

"Wh—" I tried to speak. Nothing, not even the rattling of the silex in my throat. "What—" I tried again, drawing on everything I could. The Flare inside me brightened, a rush of particles whispered deeper than my bones. "What are you doing?" My voice was barely audible.

I caught glimpses of Aladio in the edges of my vision. "You're too much of a risk," he said, after a long hesitation. "We need to protect the balance between two worlds. That's what programmers have always done. Even...even if it means locking you in silex for eternity."

Fear sent sharp pulses of light out through my silex to cast hard patterns on the ceiling. "No—" I gasped. "Don't—"

"Shut up, both of you," said the programmer carrying my feet. "Or we're going to miss them reprogram the child!"

"Child—?" But all I could do was whisper, I couldn't even move.

Finally, the programmers halted. They lowered me to the ground gently, but I landed with an odd-sounding clunk. Something loosened around me, and I could feel my fingers, even move my head. Only then did I realise why I felt so heavy and numb: I was wrapped in a thick layer of hard silex, arms pinned to my sides, legs together, back straight.

They propped me up against a pillar in the centre of a great, hexagonal room. More threads of piercing gold snaked out of the pillar and floor to drill into me. A whirring sound echoed up from a spider web of lines in the polished, chrome floor.

"Hurry." The three programmers left, leaving only Aladio beside me. "We need to get this done."

Dozens of small, circular doors opened in the walls, the floor, the ceiling, and the gaping ends of pipes extended into the room.

"Don't be afraid," Aladio said, but his voice was unsteady. "It won't hurt, you won't feel a thing. It's just like sleeping."

"What—" I coughed, tried again. "What are they going to do to my child?"

He shook his head. "Don't worry about that now."

"What about the puppet men? The doors? My world? I came to you for help, Lad! Don't let them do this!"

"Aladio!" came a crackling voice from somewhere far above us. "Get out of there. There's traffic building on her Flare. We have to shut her down, now."

"I'm sorry," Aladio whispered, and leaned close. "I can't help you. I'm not who you think I am. So please, just take the peace we give you. Forget those nightmares, forget your child, and just sleep."

"I can't." I called to the particles travelling through me, to the pions in my Flare. My light built. *Set me free*, I whispered to them, *if you really are pions then please, rework this stuff into water and let me go!* But for all my light and all my pleading all I managed to do was move my fingers, just a little bit more.

"You have no choice." Aladio met my eyes with a look of such sadness, mingling with a kind of relief that hurt so much to see. He pulled the white gloves from his hands and gently, shaking ever so slightly, he touched my cheek.

And the Flare inside me surged. The whispers and rushing at the edges of my hearing became shouting, screaming, and a roar.

Great cracks ran the length of my silex prison, from neck to wrist, waist to ankles, enough to allow me to draw a deep, full breath. Lad's hand was warm against my face, and that warmth followed the cracks, filling me.

The warmth brought memories. Lad, sitting in front of the fire he and his brother had make, spooning kasha into his mouth; Lad, leaning on the ferry, laughing as I tried to coax him down; rosemary on his mother's grave; the firm set of his mouth, his first resolute 'No!'; Aleksey's blades, plunging into his back. His voice, inside my mind, loosening the control of the puppet men so I could save his brother.

But above all of them, his hand in mine. Solid, warm. Comforting, giving strength.

The light died, as suddenly as it had sprung up. Tinny voices shouted from outside the room. The programmers.

"—out of there, now, she needs isolation—"

"—Flare just dumped a shitload of data, but I can't trace it—"

"—can you hear us, Aladio? Respond!—"

Aladio? I knew, with utter certainty, that the man in front of me was not Aladio, not any more. I felt strangely thin, different, like a part of me was gone. The parts of Lad I had carried inside of me, since his death.

Lad staggered back. He stared at me, face pale, the hand that had touched me pressed to his lips.

"Aladio!"

He jerked at the name.

"That Flare needs to be neutralised, now. Get out of there so we can begin construction."

Lad backed out of the room. I held his gaze all the way.

I started to struggle when the door closed behind him. I scratched at the silex across my lap, thrashed shoulders, kicked legs. I barely moved at all, for all the effort, but the cracks were widening.

The whirring sound strengthened, and the room began to vibrate. The floor descended until I was propped up on a small, stationary ledge. If only I could unbalance myself, I could have fallen and broken the crystal, but the wires held me in place. I glanced up; the ceiling was moving too, rising to a sharp point.

Would it really be so terrible, to sleep? No Keeper, no child, no Lad to worry about.

And after all, when I dreamed, I dreamed of Kichlan.

Then fluid rushed in through the dozens of pipes in the walls, and the great empty space—that hexagon with a pointed top and bottom—began to fill with liquid.

"Lad!" I shouted. "Don't let them hurt my baby. Promise me, I need you to promise! Keep him safe!"

Nothing. I squeezed my eyes shut.

Until the rushing stopped.

I opened my eyes to sudden quiet. The room felt unnaturally still. I peered to the floor as best I could. Not even a quarter full of that thick, living-crystal liquid. Hardly complete.

My breathing sounded terribly loud.

The whirring started up, and the silex began to drain away. The room shuddered, then flattened out again: the ceiling descended, the floor rose. And silence beat hard down on me when it had finished, until the door opened again, and Lad stepped into the room.

His white coat was splattered with blood, his black pants so drenched they shone in the room's stark light. He carried a strange metallic object out in front of him, something between a hammer and a wrench. It was bent, and coated in blood. His eyes were haunted. He rubbed a hand across his cheek, left a bloody print. And slowly, ever so slowly, he approached me. Gradually, he raised the wrench.

"Lad?" I whispered.

He stood above me, both hands around the weapon now, and lifted it high above his head.

"I died for you," he croaked. His voice was raw.

I closed my eyes again. "Yes, you did." And I realised this death was better than eternal sleep, and so much more fitting. Because Lad had died for me, and that was unforgivable. "And I am so sorry."

I turned my head away.

Lad brought the weapon down on the silex that encased my body. Again and again he bashed the wrench against it, until chunks of mineral scattered across the floor, until the entire structure loosened, cracked open, and fell from me.

I sank back against the pole, my legs too weak to hold me. The Flare leaked from my neck and abdomen, dull, and without enthusiasm.

Lad threw his weapon away and sank to the floor beside me. He clutched at my pants, crawled closer, and rested his head in my lap. The light from within me brightened his golden hair, and highlighted the crimson blood caught in its curls.

"I died for you," he whispered against my legs. I ran gentle hands over his forehead, through his hair, not knowing what to believe, what to think. "And I remember it now. Other damn you, I remember it."

10.

Lad scrambled through drawers, stuffing tubes of the silex liquid into a large dark bag. I sat against a screen as the repairing crystal he had worked into the cracks at my neck and waist wove deep and uncomfortable bonds. He had also attached a heavy glass chamber called a *silex bath* to a deep crack around my ankle. It fitted awkwardly, so I had to bend my foot at a strange angle, and was full of the busy, pinching, tingling crystal. I gritted my teeth against the sensation, and focused on breathing steadily: in, out, hold, in, out, hold.

I tried not to look at the bodies of the programmers Lad had killed.

"Tell me what they're going to do to my child," I said, when my bonds settled down enough to allow me to speak.

Lad shook his head. "We have to get out of here, Tan. Just concentrate on that."

"I need to know."

He paused, head down. "We've lost connection with the Guardian. But, of course, you already knew that. Because the Keeper—the Keeper is dead." He drew a deep, shuddering breath. "Oh fuck, this is hard. I know the Guardian is a program, nothing but code and light. But I also know he's the Keeper, and I remember the way he used to whisper to me. No one believed me." He lifted his head, met my eyes. "Until you."

I held his gaze in silence.

After a moment, he returned to his packing. "Whatever the reason, we've lost the Guardian program. He—it— was our connection to the veil, and now we have none. All our programmer feeds are being rejected. We can't monitor the fluctuation of particle flow, which allowed us to predict and contain Flares before they freeformed. And no one's strengthening the veil. That was the Guardian's main protocol. Every particle that passes through the veil tears a little piece of it, carries it into our world as Flares, and your world as pions. The Guardian program infiltrates and reroutes the veil's fluid, wave-like structure to patch these holes. That's the whole reason the programmers are here and suddenly, we can't do that anymore. Nothing's getting through—nothing, that is, except your child."

Dimly, I remembered the Specialist, in the middle of the chaos when his attempt to send me home had gone so wrong.

"Tanyana," Lad said. "Your child's signal is crisp, and clear. No interference, no loss of data integrity. While we were floundering in the darkness, it was shining and strong. The particle flow within it is steady. Its body, rather than rejecting the silex as yours does, seems to have incorporated it. Your child is code already, and light, and silex, and veil. It—it's the most perfect Guardian we could have hoped for. More complete than an uploaded human mind, better designed than a program. It's almost like... that's why it was born."

"Lad," I whispered. "No."

"All we have to do is bind it to our network, and its signal will do the rest. It would become a hardwired, integral part of Fulcrum itself. It would be our shining, beating heart, and yet so much more. It would connect all the programmers of this world to the veil, it would carry the lives of Halves, and protect countless millions from death by undoing."

"But Lad—"

He turned away. "Your child could save two worlds."

"I knew the Keeper," I tried, desperate. "And you knew him too. He was a sad, tortured creature, driven mad by loneliness and the impossible task you people gave him." I struggled to swallow against the crystal building in my throat. "Don't let them turn my baby into that, Lad."

"We have to run, Tan. Now. It won't be long before they find out what I've done. Then they will banish me, and seal you away. Got to hurry." Lad slammed the drawers closed, pulled a metallic cord to close the bag, and tightened buckles to secure it.

"What about food?" I asked. I could feel the silex tightening in my waist; it pulled on the base of my lungs, wound itself through my muscles and stomach. If I was not silver then I was crystal, and I had almost forgotten what it meant to be flesh. Simple, human flesh. "And water."

Lad shook his head. "The most important thing you need is silex. Without it, the uncontrolled energy from your Pionic Flare will alter your subatomic structure, and you'll die anyway."

A pleasant thought. "What about you?"

His expression was curious, troubled, like he didn't know what to make of my concern. "You looked after me, didn't you? You and…and…"

He couldn't say it. "Kichlan," I whispered for him. "Your brother. And yes, we looked after you. We loved you very much."

A great shudder ran through him. "Where is he?"

I lowered my gaze, I couldn't answer him. But that seemed to be enough for this new Lad to understand. "He was not my brother, not really." He bent, undid the silex bath around my ankle, and tossed it aside. Apparently, his bag was full enough. "I don't have siblings. My parents died decades ago, long before I was taken from the world below to work as a programmer." He wiped what was left of the thickened, clingy liquid from my foot. "I should not grieve for him, because he was not really mine."

"He was," I said, though Lad gave no sign that he heard. "Just as real as I am."

"You might have looked after me," Lad straightened and slung the bag over his shoulder, unhindered by its awkward bulk or unburdened by its obvious weight, "but I looked after you too. I remember that. So that's what I'm going to do." He held out a hand. "Get up. We're getting out of here while we still can."

I took his hand and he hauled me to my feet. I felt weak with the silex burrowing its deep work inside me. But I could stand, I *would* stand, on my own two feet. "Not without my child." I tried to look as determined as I felt.

Lad shook his head. "We have one opportunity—"

"No." I pulled my hand from his grasp and crossed my arms, then realised how petty and childish that gesture must look so let them hang loosely at my sides. "No. I failed you, Lad. I failed Kichlan too. The fact that this child has survived my twisted, changing body is a sign in itself. I will not fail it too. Fail *him*. Do you understand? I will not leave without him, and condemn him to an unlife as a program and a tool. As the Keeper."

Lad sighed and ran a hand over his face, spreading the drying blood across his cheek. He glanced at his palm, paled and shuddered again, before scrubbing it against his shirt. "Bro used to say you were stubborn and full of pride. That it would be the death of you, and that he was cursed with such foolhardy people in his life."

I couldn't help but grin. "Kichlan would say that, yes."

He lifted eyebrows. "I could force you," he whispered so quietly he was only breathing the words. "Pick you up and carry you out of here, whether you liked it or not."

I scowled, strengthened my stance. "Yes, you probably could. But I wouldn't make it easy for you."

"Tan." That haunted expression returned and for a moment, Lad sagged beneath the weight on his back. "Bro said, Bro said…" He shook his head, as I stepped forward, hand raised. "No, don't." He straightened again. "No, I'm fine."

Fine was hardly what I would call it. But I stilled all the same.

"We will do it your way," he rasped the words, voice rough. "Isn't that what we always did?"

Bag across his shoulders, he strode out of the room. I hesitated for a moment, transfixed by the bloody shoe print he left behind, and wondered if that was some kind of subtle accusation. Had Lad just blamed me for his death? Well, I deserved it, didn't I?

I hurried to follow.

"How are we going to do this?" I asked. Only a few quick steps to catch up with him and I was already winded.

"I have absolutely no idea." He paused at a wide lobby. Three chrome doors, large and round, on one wall, several normal sliding doors with red symbols glowing above them on another. He placed the bag down against one of the round chrome ones, and peered at me, thoughtfully. "The Specialists will not give up your child, no matter how politely we ask."

I frowned at him. "Of course not."

"So we will need to take it by force."

I nodded. I missed the strength of my suit, however strange it was to feel that way.

"Surprise wouldn't hurt, either." He nodded to one of the normal doors. I recognised some of the symbols above it, but could only properly translate the one for debris. "Your child is in that direction." He explained the route to me. "Think you can find your way there and act like a dangerous, crazy person for about five minutes before they capture you again?"

I stared at him. It still stunned me to hear Lad speak this way.

"Well?" But when he smiled, his face was gentle, and hinted at the frightened child-like man I had loved so strongly. "Can you?"

I straightened and ran a hand across my shaved skull. After a moment's thought I bent, placed my palm on Lad's blood-soaked pants, and added prints to my shirt, my neck, and across the top of my head. His eyes widened. I nodded to him. "Crazy? Yes, I think I can do that."

"Then go. Quickly. Try to get your child back."

"What will you—"

"I will help."

We split up. Lad hurried through another door, and I followed his directions. I felt oddly strong, even without my suit, thanks to the blood on my hands and the fact that I was finally doing something more than sitting and waiting. My task might be impossible, but it was better than none at all.

I counted doors, my left and right turns, through all the colourless corridors, until I came to a room I recognised. I'd been held here, floating. My tube loomed tall, empty, its curved glass impeccably clean. But my child was nowhere to be seen. Dismayed, I stared at his smaller tube. Not empty, still full of silex liquid, but no small half-body, no unfortunate unborn.

"All of them?"

Voices from deeper in the room, from the higher level behind the cylinders. I ducked and hid behind the silver base of my empty tube. It wasn't actually connected to the ground. It floated a few inches from the floor, above a thick chunk of gold-flecked crystal.

"Yeah, and all at once."

Two programmers, directly above me. I peered up through holes in a metal mesh floor, to their dark shoes and white coats.

"That can't be right."

"None of the other systems have been affected. Only the security streams. Seems odd, don't you think?"

The programmers descended stairs I hadn't realised were there. "And still no word about the woman? Shouldn't they be done securing her by now?"

"Nothing. The Specialist has sent others to investigate."

We didn't have much time. I waited for the programmers to leave and hurried up the stairs. I followed flickering lights and the muted sound of voices, around more dark screens, keyboards, crystals reflecting hurried, frantic flashes of light, and more empty tubes. Many more.

Finally, I found my baby again. In the centre of the Other's most horrible hell.

He seemed to have grown, somehow, even without my body to support him. He looked more complete now. He had toes, he had fingers, and a soft smile on his sleeping half-face. I could see the faint fluttering of his tiny heart. It beat in time with the fluctuations of colour in his Flare, wavering light out into the room.

No longer encased in a tube, he was suspended instead by a mesh of golden wire. It burrowed inside of him, his skin as well as silex, pulled his little semi-formed arms up at an unnatural angle, spread-eagled his legs, forced his head back and his chin up.

The sight of him hit me like a physical blow. Rage and fear rolled up in its wake, so powerful they nearly swept me off my feet. He was my son, a part of me, and even though we no longer shared the same body that connection would never fade. I knew, with absolute certainty, that I would do whatever it took to protect him.

"No!" I roared, and rushed forward. "Stop it!"

The light from his Pionic Flare shone across the room. My own silex caught it, reflected it back, even as I climbed a small platform and reached for my son, impossibly high above me.

"Shit!" The programmers were behind me, protected from the Flare by a cage of silex and glass. "What is she doing here?"

"Sir, we have redlines on the grid again! She's interfering."

I gripped the mesh, shook it. But it was far stronger than it looked, and all I got for my efforts was a strange tingling across my skin, and the whisper of half-imagined voices. The disjointed laughter of the puppet men, very far away. And a faint child's cry, lonely, stretching on and on, tearing at my heart.

"Sir, more problems. Screens failing, level seven through to sixty four! And rising, coming this way."

"First the security, now screens?"

"Is she doing this? Her traffic interfering with Fulcrum's internal signals?"

Behind me, a door opened. "No," the Specialist said, so calm and clear above his programmers' panic. "I don't believe so. She's not even connected." I spun to face him. "No, this is a different kind of sabotage." He had been wearing thick, dark spectacles, and a tight white mask but he pulled these from his face, and narrowed his eyes at me. "How did you escape, Tanyana? What have you done to my programmers?"

I shuddered, tried to focus. Lad had asked me to act like a madwoman, and give him time to do whatever he was doing. It did not take much to achieve.

"Give him back to me," I growled the words. Didn't need to force it, the sound rose from anger, and deep helplessness.

"Just tell me—"

"No!" My Flare surged, bright and sporadic, spluttering like unhealthy candle flame. Above me, my son moved. I felt it through the wire, and glanced up. He was straining against the web, peering down at me, even though his unmade eyes were still welded shut.

"It's Tanyana!" More programmers ran into the room. "She murdered them, escaped and—" They halted at the sight of me, suddenly silent, expressions pale and shocked. And I grinned. Unhinged. Not an act.

"Yes, we can see that." The Specialist scowled at them.

"Sir!" One of the newly arrived programmers pushed forward. "Aladio was not with them."

"What?" he snapped.

"He was not among the dead!"

A thoughtful look—too thoughtful for my liking—spread across the Specialist's face.

I released the web, stalked forward. "I killed him, just like the others!" I screeched, too loud, too painful in my throat. "And I'll kill you too!"

"Did you?" The Specialist did not believe me. He turned back to his programmers, not at all afraid of me.

"Sabotage. Aladio has betrayed us. Lock down everything below eighty, don't give him access to any of the deeper hubs. Divert as many beams as possible to the Crossing room, and this one. We need to maintain the stability of this connection, no matter what."

Programmers scattered at his command.

"And summon the Legate."

Then all the lights snapped off.

Everyone froze. The only light that remained was the unstable flicker of my Flare, and my son's steady glow.

"That motherfucker," someone growled, one of the programmers still hidden behind their cage. "He's switched off life support."

"That's impossible." The Specialist strode back toward them. "There's no way he made it down to the bottom level that quickly."

I pressed back against the web.

"Don't let it faze you. Continue."

"But sir..." The other programmers did not sound as certain. "We will run out of breathable air!"

Another crystal glittered in the darkness, carried on Lad's upraised palm. He walked into the room so calmly that I wondered, for a moment, if he had gone as mad as I was supposed to behave.

The programmers did not notice him, not at first. "Sir, the error is isolated. This floor, ten above, ten below. The rest of the building is functioning normally."

"Send a distress signal to the Legate, quickly. And replicate it throughout the building. Maybe the lower floors can funnel us up some—"

"I wouldn't try to do that, if I were you," Lad said, and silenced them all, instantly. "It won't work."

The Specialist turned. "Aladio? What are you doing?"

Lad shook his head. "That is not my name, sir. I am Lad. I heard the voice of the Keeper. I am Tan's friend. And I am helping her."

If this surprised the Specialist he did not show it. "Now, listen—"

But Lad cut him off again, this time by holding out the crystal in one hand, and lifting something large, heavy and silver above his head in the other. "This is the primary life support hub for this sector," he said. "I have removed it, shattered the bonding silex and diverted the control beams. If you were to replace it now, I'd say it would take you three, maybe four hours to reconnect and get it working. I'm not sure how much air we have left, however. So I would stop arguing, if I were you." He bounced the crystal in his palm, once, twice, and around us the programmers drew a collective, shocked breath. "If you don't, I will smash it. And tell me, do we have any spares?"

"You bastard," one of the programmers hissed.

"That's right." Lad's expression was hidden in the darkness. "We don't, not this far up. I believe they have some on level fourteen. But I think you'll find their screens aren't working, and they don't even know you need help."

Terrible silence. All I could hear was my own laboured breathing.

"So that's enough arguing." Lad gestured to the web behind me with the large, metal bar in his hand. "Now, take him down."

"Alad—"

"Do it!" Lad tossed the hub of crystal, higher this time, and fumbled his catch. I think that was what convinced the Specialist. Not the threat of what Lad meant do, rather the accident waiting to happen.

"You are dooming us all, Aladio," the Specialist said, as his programmers handed him a dark panel from behind the silex cage. Symbols sprung to life on its surface. "Both worlds need this child, and you know why."

I held Lad's gaze. He did not waver. For a moment, I doubted what I was forcing him to do. Wasn't this just the way he described it? Lad, following me again, unquestioning, even to his death?

But he held no such doubts. "Faster, sir," he said. "Every word is eating up oxygen, precious molecules you might just need to breathe."

The light above me faded, slowly. Then the web shook. Wires slid cleanly out of the baby's silex, and his skin, and he fell. Gently, like a snowflake caught in my sunlight. I held out my arms and he drifted down into them, so soft he barely seemed real. Which he wasn't, entirely.

I pressed him to my chest. He tucked up his bent legs, and seemed to fit perfectly in my arms. He smelled like the air before a storm, like moisture and energy. His slow breathing trilled quietly. A tiny hard reached out, and wrapped lightly around my thumb.

"Hurry," Lad snapped me back to reality.

I scowled at the Specialist as I hurried from the platform. He followed my gaze, expression heavy and judgemental. "You won't live long without our help," he told me. "Your Pionic Flare will destroy you, and your child, and Aladio. And who knows how much of my world."

Lad tossed the metal bar to the floor, grabbed my arm, and together we ran. Back through the room with the tubes—Lad paused to collect the tube that had held my son, and as large and heavy as it was he managed to tuck it under one arm—out into the corridor, around corners, beneath red symbols, and back to the lobby with the three chrome doors. The programmers followed. They were not, I realised, trying to stop us. After all, I could not move that quickly, and my slowness held Lad back. Rather, they wanted the precious crystal in his hand.

We halted at the chrome doors. Lad placed the tube on the ground, swung the full bag over his shoulder, and tapped a small panel on the wall beside one of the doors. Something behind it whirred and grew gradually louder, as though approaching from a great distance.

"Where are you going, Aladio?" The Specialist had also followed. He and his programmers hung back, crowding the doorways. "You know she will die if you take her down to that world. The child too."

Lad shook his head. "Take this," he whispered to me. I cradled my son in one arm as he placed the crystal hub in my palm. He picked up the tube, and backed into the chrome door. I followed, holding the crystal out in front of me.

"I look after Tan," he said, and my stomach clenched. "From anyone, from anything. Even from you."

I hated myself for this. But my child was safe now. He had to be.

The whirring rose to a grinding-metal crescendo behind us, and the chrome door opened. Lad stepped through it. I followed.

"We will call the Legate," the Specialist said, his voice nearly lost behind the echoing, grinding noises. "Not even your programmer status will protect you."

"I'd worry about myself, if I were you. Can't call anyone without air, without heat." Lad leaned forward, whispered in my ear, "Get ready to throw it."

He dropped the bag and the tube to type frantically at a bright keyboard on a curved wall.

"Don't do this—"

"Now!"

I tossed the crystal hub back through the circular door. As the programmers and the Specialist leapt for it—a single mass of white coats and black, pressed pants and a communal, panicked expression—the door closed. And we were moving.

I spun. We were inside a small room. The walls were curved, the ceiling too, and the floor a raised platform. It was a large ball-shape, big enough to hold maybe a dozen more people. I couldn't work out how we were moving, but I felt it in a dipping, sick feeling in my stomach, the pressure in my ears, and the way the entire room seemed to jolt. Like an enormous, and truly bizarre landau.

"Hurry." Lad tipped the tube up, tapped more buttons. The crystal on the bottom lit up, while the metallic top slid free. "Put him back in here."

I baulked. "What?" I had to hold him. After everything we had just done, how could I put him back inside that tube? Only here, in my arms, could I be sure he would be safe. "No, I—"

"He can't survive without the silex!" Lad cut across me. "He is far too young to survive outside the womb."

"You're the people who—"

"We don't have time to argue, Tan. You did this because you wanted him to live, didn't you? Don't kill him with your stupid pride."

I swallowed, hard. My neck rattled. "Are you sure?"

He nodded, expression sad. "Yes. I'm sorry, but this is the only way we can keep him alive."

I nodded, and crouched down in front of the tube.

"The silex will provide his developing body with the things it needs to live. Oxygen and minerals. It will also filter out carbon dioxide and—"

I was staring at him, and Lad must have realised that I had no idea what he was saying.

He smiled, crouched beside me. "Never mind. Let's just say it will give him energy to develop, the kind of energy your body would have provided. But it will also help isolate his Flare."

That I could understand. I kissed my son's soft cheek. His skin was so thin I could see blood pumping inside him, and light washing along with it. That reminded me of the Keeper. "Please live," I breathed against the side of his head, into his not-quite ears.

I eased him back into the tube, and held my breath as silex closed over his head. Lad replaced the lid. He pressed a few more keys, and it sealed with a hiss.

"Will he be all right?" I pressed my hands against the side of the tube, but it wasn't the same. I couldn't feel his breathing warmth. "Doesn't the tube need to be connected to a Pionic Flare?"

Lad nodded, tapped knuckles against the glowing crystal at the base of the tube. "Isolated silex hub—it's basically a piece of a Shard with some of the Flare still inside it. There's enough juice in this thing to keep that tube working for decades. At least."

Juice? I decided it was best not to ask.

"You, on the other hand, need some attention."

Lad sat me on one of the pale, leather-like seats that ringed the edge of the circular room. He drew more of the patching gel from his bag, used it to fill cracks in my neck. I leaned against the wall and watched as he tossed away two empty tubes.

"How long will all that keep me alive?" I asked, and pointed to his bag.

Lad sat back on his heels, clasped his hands beneath his chin, and studied me. "Depends on what you do," he said. "Run around like this, crack the silex, and a couple of weeks, maybe. If I'm careful."

"Weeks—?"

"Two sixnight and one," he explained.

Was that all? I stared up at the curve in the ceiling. There was a small glass window at the very top. Lights flashed past, faster and faster.

"Behave, keep as still and as calm as possible, and I might be able to stretch it out for a month. A moon."

"So, I'm dead. Sooner or later." I glanced down at my son. Then who would look after him?

Lad sighed. He stood, walked to the far side of the room. A small compartment slid out of the wall there, with taps, a sink, and crockery. He filled two glasses with water, drained one, refilled it, and gave me the other.

I touched it to my lips. The water tasted strange. Like it had been stored in a warm poly container for a very long time.

"We are not without options on Crust."

I lifted eyebrows at him. "Crust?"

He grinned, the expression genuine. "Here, let me show you."

A keyboard rose in the centre of the room, beside the tube and its sleeping cargo. Lad's fingers flew across keys. The window at the top of the sphere widened until the entire top half of the room was transparent. I stood and scrambled away as the wall was replaced by curved, clear poly.

"Don't worry," Lad said, and approached me. He wrapped an arm around my shoulders and turned me back towards the wall. "It's strong."

We were speeding through a tunnel. Lights flashed past us; everything moved so fast I couldn't make out any details.

"We are leaving Fulcrum behind."

The lights rushed past, faster and faster. Lad tightened his arm and gladly, I leaned into his strength. "Thank you," I whispered. "Thank you for looking after me."

A final burst of light. I blinked, squinted.

"Don't close your eyes," Lad said.

And then we were free.

We shot out from the tunnel into a terrible, dark and twisted sky. I stared around us, shocked. No stars, only clouds and their storm-like whirling, their solid rain-sheets, and their darkness. Reaching, clawing into each other. Darkness.

And hanging in all that torn, chaotic night, countless, giant silex Shards like deadly, shining wounds.

I leaned against the clear poly surface. Far below, much further than even *Grandeur*'s eight hundred feet, a city spread out beneath us. At least, it had once been a city. Empty steel frames reached up at us, the skeletal remains of towering buildings pierced the clouds. Smaller dwellings, made indistinct by distance and haze, surrounded them, but I could see hints of colourless cement and shattered windows. Weak, scattered lights wound vague trails through the darkness. The remnants of streetlamps, I thought, judging from their patterns.

Shards loomed out of some of the shattered buildings like they had fallen there. The floating ones were enormous, their bottom spikes nearly touching the tops of the city buildings, their peaks impossible to see. Flares pulsed inside them. In the distance, they looked like stars. Flickering, arching in a delicate pattern, beads in a dark dress.

"Tan." Lad turned me, gently, to look back the way we had come. "That is Fulcrum."

I didn't know what to think of it. It looked like a building, but was not connected to the earth. Several bright spots—like the tunnel exit—dotted the base. The rest of it was solid, smooth and grey. A windowless apartment block. It sheered up into the sky, mostly hidden by cloud, far larger than I could begin to imagine.

"That's the programmer's building?" Dizziness rocked me. Only Lad held me upright. "We weren't even connected to the ground?" Days of unspent vertigo gathered in sickness low in my stomach.

"Yes," Lad said. "That's Fulcrum. It is our palace, and our prison. It keeps the programmers safe from the denizens of Crust. Keeps our work safe, the world safe. But it also keeps us working, until we die."

"Are we falling?" I gasped out the words.

"Flying," he said. "We are all born on Crust, the surface of the world below. In the remnants of ancient, once-great cities. Show promise, show intelligence, and if you are lucky, the Legate will choose you. The life of a programmer is one of hard work and sacrifice. But it is a life. On Crust, there is only death."

I shuddered, glanced up at him. "Then why are we—"

"Because there is also freedom. And I told you, there are options on Crust. In Fulcrum, everyone has their role. Mine was to cross the veil, and die there. Your child's was to replace the Keeper, and save us all. You have changed those paths, Tan. But freedom does not come without a cost. We will find both, on Crust."

Countless Shards hung bright in the torn sky. I had come so close to joining them. Maybe Lad was right, maybe I had turned all our paths around, when I had brought his other Half with me through the veil, and restored him. But was it really the right thing to do?

I glanced back at my son. It was. Absolutely.

"The programmers will follow us, won't they?" I asked.

Lad nodded. "It will take them a while to restore life support and screen-com. But as soon as they do, they will alert every floor of the Fulcrum, send out every available pod. And contact the Legate. So yes, Tan. They will follow. They will chase us."

"Is there any point—"

"There are many places to hide on Crust." Lad held me tighter. "I said they would chase us. I did not say they would catch us."

As I watched, the city reached up to us from Crust, its dark, tall buildings like the claws of some giant hand.

"We just have to keep you alive, Tan. That's all we can do."

11.

Three days of Striker bombardment and Kichlan had never felt so cold in all his life. That was saying a lot. He'd grown up in Movoc-under-Keeper, and as the saying went, his veins were brittle with frost. But there was nothing like Striker-cold. Just as it sapped the moisture from the air, it drained the confidence from a man's spirit. If it was not for the treacherous Shielders and their pion-binding skill—and Natasha, of course, with her frightful weapons—Kichlan thought that despair alone would have defeated them days ago. But there was something in her eyes that kept her Mob on their feet and her Shielders working, while they waited. Belief, passion…madness?

"I didn't realise revolution involved so much sitting around and dying, slowly, of the cold," he muttered, through chapped and bleeding lips. "I thought there might be fighting. You know, battle. Moving around. Keeping warm."

It was Natasha who called this a revolution, not him. She filled the tedious, freezing silences with details. She knew every one of the local and regional veche who, tired of the overbearing national veche, had banded together and eventually reached out to Varsnia's most powerful neighbour to help them revolt. The Hon Ji emperor had ever so kindly agreed to aid their cause, sending spies like Natasha, and weapons like the ones she'd dug up. It'd been years in the making. Weapons smuggled in and hidden, veche members paid off or assassinated. The soldiers under Natasha's command were all defectors, loyal to local members rather than the national military body. Tan's battle with the puppet men and the subsequent ruin of Movoc-under-Keeper had not been part of the plan—but Natasha was quite willing to use the chaos it had created to her advantage.

It was all for his own good. Natasha had tried to impress that upon him, over and over. The people of Varsnia were suppressed by their national veche, couldn't he see that? Just look at what the puppet men did to Tan! Think of the way he and his brother had been treated! The local and regional were different, and so was the Hon Ji. They weren't warmongers, stirring up tensions by developing weapons like Tanyana's enhanced suit. They cared more about the common people—even debris collectors, the lowest of the low. Natasha guaranteed it.

Kichlan, however, remained sceptical. He couldn't tell whether she believed her own rhetoric, but he'd worked for the veche, before he lost his pion sight and became a debris collector. He knew what they were like. All he saw was a desperate power struggle between levels of government, and a neighbouring imperial power more than happy to weaken Varsnia however it could. No wonder Tan hadn't agreed to join in. Compared to the puppet men and the Keeper and doors, all of this felt like a terrible waste of time. And life.

And he was stuck in the middle of it.

"You complain too much," Natasha snapped at him. "You full-blooded Varsnians aren't even supposed to feel the cold."

The skin around her lips had dried and cracked so the bottom half of her face looked like the bed of a desiccated creek. Had to be painful. She was constantly dabbing it with an already-bloodstained cloth.

He had no idea how the Mob were coping, or the Shielders, with the cold. The Mob hid behind their heavy helmets, the Shielders behind their dark glass, and they were all too stoic to complain.

"There's cold," he snapped right back. "And then there's this. This is something entirely different."

Natasha refused to answer.

He grunted, looked away. Complaining was all he could do to fill the cold, dry silence. He hated the silence, the sitting, the stillness. Because there was nothing else to do but remember. And ache.

Natasha and her Mob had dug up three more weapons before the Strikers had started chasing them. Five of her soldiers had been killed, hit straight on with ice that shattered their bodies. Back through city streets, they'd regrouped, and retreated, Strikers in the sky, enemy Mob all around. Kichlan had no idea how many of her men had died, and how many weapons were lost, by the time they halted in what had once been a University. Half of the building had sunk below ground, creating a deep labyrinth of dark tunnels.

And here, they had been trapped. Strikers and Mob above them, packed earth below.

"Natasha!" A call came from the barricades. "We have company."

A fleeting look of triumph flashed across her face, then Natasha scrambled forward.

"Curse you," Kichlan muttered under his breath, and followed.

Navigating the semi-collapsed room was a pain in the Other's hairy behind. The whole structure slopped upward. Windows were now hand and toeholds, doorways niches to nest in, and walls defences to hide behind. And all if it was frozen. Kichlan had been given a hat and several layers of coats, all too big for him, but was forced to wrap cloth around his hand so the skin of his palm did not tear.

"What is it?" Natasha leaned between two of the Mob behind the front row Shielders. Kichlan positioned himself at what he hoped was a relatively safe spot, hugging the edge of a doorway.

The Mob gestured. Kichlan squinted to look past the hazy barriers. He couldn't see the complex pion-bindings the Shielders had stretched across the doorway to hold back the Strikers' attacks. All he could see was the way it caught the ice into a hard, cracking wall, and the faint threads of steam generated by its heat. A liquid drop of debris slid, every so often, from its surface to pool at the floor. Kichlan ignored it. What was the point in collecting anything now?

A single man approached, navigating his slow and careful way down the icy, sloping corridor. He carried a small pion-powered lamp and held out a veche insignia in the other hand.

"I am here to negotiate," he called, nearly slipped, and dropped the light to steady himself. He scrambled to collect it. "I will speak to Natasha Illoksy."

"Why should we trust anything you have to say?" Natasha called back.

"I speak with the authority of the local and regional veche, miss. None of us want this fighting to continue."

A wide smile spread across Natasha's face, despite the broken skin around her lips. "Let him in," she told her Shielders.

"What?" the Mob beside her sounded just as shocked as Kichlan felt. "What are you doing? How do we know he can be trusted?"

"I am unarmed," the man called.

"Meaningless," another of the Mob growled. "A well trained assassin would need nothing but pions to kill."

But Natasha shook her head. "Haven't you all learned to trust me yet?" She tapped her Shielders, lightly, twice on the shoulders. Their barrier faded with a crashing of ice, and the veche representative stepped through.

The Mob all drew weapons, silver and loudly humming in the close room. Natasha held up a hand—disk poised between her fingers—and they hesitated.

The veche man was small, thin, and very pale. He was wrapped in many layers of woollen clothing, but even so, his lips were almost blue.

"You took your time," Natasha said.

"The national veche is flexing their muscles, Miss Illoksy. They wanted to freeze you out. It took a lot to convince them a ceasefire was a better use of resources, and in the interest of the nation in this time of crisis."

"I see." Natasha lowered her arm. "Are you ready? Have you got them all?"

"We have been in position for days, miss. All your Mob are accounted for."

"Let's put an end to this fighting then."

The veche man nodded. He closed his eyes, lifted his hands, began twitching his gloved fingers and whispering beneath his breath. He was manipulating pions.

The Mob stepped forward. Again, Natasha and her disks held them back.

"Be still!" she hissed at them.

"But he is—"

More Mob crowded the doorway behind Kichlan.

"Something is happening—"

"We're in the middle of a circle! National veche bastards have—"

"Enough!" Natasha shouted, and silenced them all, instantly. Kichlan could not help but shudder at the thought of what Natasha could do, just how strong she must be, that so many Mob would so quickly obey her. "I thought you were commanded to obey me? Where has my army of Mob gone, and who are these snivelling brat-children around me?"

Kichlan stepped around the doorframe. "I don't know about them," he said. "But this snivelling debris collector would like to know what is going on."

Around him, Mob muttered agreement.

Natasha sighed. "Don't fret, Kichlan dear. You aren't involved in this circle. Unless, of course, you think you can lift one of those." She pointed to the rows of the large, dragonhead Hon Ji weapons lining the room. "You see, they are only one half of the weapon." She turned away from the newly arrived pion-binder, straining and sweating where a moment ago he had been pale and frozen. "Do you really think we'd hide hundreds of new weapons in the middle of Movoc-under-Keeper if just anyone could pick up and use them?"

"We're ready, miss," the pion-binder gasped behind her.

Natasha nodded. She looked up at her Mob, her face expressionless. "This might feel a little strange, for a moment. Don't let it rattle you. We are about to make you all more powerful than you could ever have imagined."

The binder brought his hands together.

As one, the Mob gasped. A strange sound, in such a tight space, from so many large and pion-strengthened soldiers. To Kichlan's eyes, blind to pions, nothing seemed to be happening. Yet the Mob stood rigid, shuddering. And the local veche man—a traitor, obviously allied to Natasha and the Hon Ji—fought to hold his hands together, cupped and grasping the apparently thin air.

"What's happening?" Kichlan whispered through the heavy silence.

Blood dripped from open cracks along Natasha's chin as she grinned, but she did not seem to care. She drew a short, silver blade, dusted ice from its handle and tossed it, hand to hand, rubbing warmth back into its gleaming metal. "He is the centre of a great and complex circle." She nodded to the Mob around her. "They are working inside my men, altering the pion-bindings in their physical reinforcements, so they can wield weapons the likes of which this nation has never seen."

"What kind of weapons—"

"Ah." Natasha pressed a finger against her abused lips. "You shall see, very soon, Kichlan. You shall see."

The pion-binder let out a great cry. Around them all, the Mob echoed it. As the centre's knees gave way and he fell back, the large, black armoured men were also stumbling, clutching the frozen walls for balance, and struggling to breathe.

"How will this help, exactly?" Kichlan muttered.

"Shh." Natasha bent down to the veche traitor. She wrapped an arm around his shoulders, eased him into a sitting position. "Is it done?" She whispered.

He nodded. "They are ready." His voice was so soft, Kichlan could hardly hear him. It almost seemed that his lips did not move.

"You did well." Natasha placed the tip of her blade against his neck.

With a contented smile, the traitor closed his eyes. "Take them down," he gasped. "And set Varsnia free."

"I will." Natasha drew her blade across his throat.

He died quickly. The pumping of blood and a single shudder, before Natasha laid him down against the frozen stone.

Kichlan stared at her, shocked. "What—*Why?*"

Natasha wiped her blade, spun it between fingers, and sheathed it. "The old families do not know how deep this conspiracy goes." She turned to him, her eyes hard. With the blood on her chin and her blue-tipped face, she looked like the Other, not Natasha. A twisted creature of nightmare. "Perhaps, when they find their emissary dead, they will not realise what he was. And the longer they thrash about in ignorance, not realising that most of their local and regional branches are against them, the more chance we have to overthrow them." She looked down to the body. The pooling blood had slowed in the cold. "He understood his fate, accepted his role, and did it well." She turned back to her Mob. "Now, let us do him proud."

Kichlan spun. The Mob were no longer weakened and staggering. They stood, massed in straight and regimented lines, at the doorway and further back into the rooms. But they still did not look any different to him.

"Take up your weapons," Natasha said.

A single Mob broke away from the group. He collected one of the huge dragonheads from against the wall.

"Remove the cloth."

Kichlan flinched back from the sight of the weapon fully revealed. It was freakish. The half-maw curled slightly, ending in a round dragon-nose. The eyes were deeply sunken, and surrounded by engraved swirls like creases in black-iron skin. Two fiercely clawed feet jutted out from the bottom of the head, and a long, straight tail, riddled with hollow spikes and broken scales, extended directly opposite the jaw. It looked wrong. A demented version of a child's drawing, half-made, and not quite understood.

"Mount it," Natasha said, with reverence, her eyes bright. "Teeth to your shoulder, claws to your chest."

It was awkward, at first. The Mob turned it around several times, and even rearranged the fittings of his armour, until he got it right. The dragon's teeth pressed against his shoulder and curled over to his upper back. The claws scratched at his breastplate. The tail stuck out long in front of him, and Kichlan realised the final spike on its end was broken. Instead of a smooth point, it had been shattered, so it had many sharp edges fanned out into a rough star shape.

"And hold on."

As soon as the Mob placed his hand—ungloved, Natasha insisted—on the dragon's deep eye, the weapon came alive. It bit down hard on the Mob's neck. Even as he screamed those clawed feet tore chunks of his armour away to embed themselves in his chest.

Natasha cried, "Be silent, be still! Do not resist it!"

Kichlan watched in horror as somehow, the Mob calmed himself down. He ceased screaming, resorted to a painful-sounding panting.

"Good," Natasha said, voice soft, soothing, and approached the Mob. "Do not try to fight a Hon Ji dragon."

With his free hand the Mob tore the heavy helmet from his head. Kichlan winced. Those eyes—solid gold with irises roaming—were bad enough when hidden behind the helmet's obscuring slit. Set into the bare skin of his hairless face, they were terrible to behold, too large, bulging, and wild. Maybe that was why the Mob never removed their helmets, even in a frozen underground graveyard like this. Not merely professional pride. Perhaps they too were aware of the horror of their own faces.

"What has been done to me?" The Mob hissed. His teeth were capped with something metal looking and black.

"Don't you feel it?" Natasha asked. "You are strong. Stronger, even, than you can know!"

Frowning, the Mob ran his spare hand awkwardly along the tail and muzzle of his dragon. One hand remained clamped to the eye. "I—" he stuttered, unsure. "I do not know—"

"Lady Natasha?" One of the Shielders, still perched at the opening to the room, glanced over his shoulder. "Movement in the hallway. Shall we rebuild the shield?"

Natasha dabbed at her skin. "No," she said. "No. Let me show you the power of these weapons." She waved her hand in a dismissive gesture. "Out of the way!"

Fresh ice cracked its way across the doorway as the crimson-coated Shielders rose and retreated. Footsteps and voices echoed, closer.

Natasha did not seem concerned. "One weapon," she said. "And one soldier to wield it." She pointed to the dragon-clamped Mob, and directed him to the doorway. "And we will triumph."

Unsteady, still unsure, the Mob advanced. He braced himself, legs strong, and pointed the tail of his dragon to the hallway beyond.

"Strikers!" the Shielders cried, and Kichlan ducked, instinctively, as great shards of ice crashed into the room.

Natasha flung herself to the side, "Fire!"

"There is no trigger!" The Mob cried, as ice clutched at his arms, his feet, as spears of it broke against his armour. "How do I—"

"Your pions," Natasha said, as she rolled to her feet and pressed her back against a far wall. "Your body is the trigger. You are one with the dragon, Mob. Roar your fury!"

Kichlan, of course, could not see what he did. But all the Mob around him gasped, and the dragon weapon began to glow. It started deep inside, filtered out through the scales like sunshine through lattice, and built at the tip of the broken tail. At first, a warm light. But as it strengthened it lost its colour, became cold, sharp, and reminded Kichlan of Tan's suit, when she was angry.

For a moment, the thought threw him. That light was just so familiar. He shook his half-arm free of the layers of clothing that hid it. The silver she had given him was smooth, as ever, but now it seemed to glow. Just a reflection of the dragon's breath. Nothing more.

"The pion bonds that give you heightened strength, reflexes, and senses have been altered," Natasha said to her Mob. "We have rearranged them into circles, and circles around circles, all of it intricate and deep within the nature of reality itself. Each of you is now the centre of an infinite number of circles, made from your own bodies, powered by your own unnatural strengths."

The gathered light at the tip of the dragon's tail released. It surged forward, into the hallway. For a moment, everything was light, and Kichlan covered his eyes with his single, remaining hand as the dragon-mounted Mob roared, a rage-filled sound that disintegrated, slowly, into an exhausted and pain-riddled scream.

When the light died down, and Kichlan had blinked its residue away, the ice was gone. The Mob had fallen to his knees. He no longer held the dragonhead, and it slipped, inanimate, from his shoulder. Blood ran from puncture wounds on his neck, down his back, his chest, the marks the only evidence that the dragon had ever been so alive.

His fellow soldiers helped him to his feet. He was too weak to stand on his own.

"One shot, and you will need time to recover," Natasha said. "You are an infinite circle, but no circle greater than nine is stable. No matter how much research we have done, we have been forced to admit that Novski was right about that, all along. And yet, it is that very instability that fuels the dragon."

"What good is your weapon," one of the Mob growled, "if it leaves us so weakened and exposed?"

The Shielders approached the opening. "All Striker activity has ceased," one said. And there was awe in his voice. Awe, and fear. "Their attacks—the ice—is dissolving. Some of the hallway integrity too."

"We could not replicate Tanyana's suit, no matter how we tried," Natasha said, and held Kichlan's gaze as she spoke. "But we understood one thing, perhaps better than she did. The silver was not her real strength, no matter how she used it. Rather, the destabilizing properties of the debris it was crafted from. So while we have not had the same success with debris-manipulation as the national veche, we did what we could, to replicate its effect."

She approached her exhausted Mob. It was all he could do to lift his head and look at her.

"The altered pion bonds within you, when activated by the dragon's head, create an infinite and extremely unstable pion-binding circle. The dragon draws it out of you—saving your life at the same time—and channels that instability into a weapon. One that will undo any bond it comes into contact with. The Striker's attack. The Strikers themselves. Any Mob, waiting to advance, and Shielders, providing protection. Even the building. So you see, only one shot, and you have saved us. You are exhausted, yes, but that really doesn't matter. Because there is no one left to fight."

In the unsettled silence, something groaned. The earth, shifting above them, the damaged walls, weakening.

"And now we should get out of here, before the building comes down on us." Natasha pointed at the body of the pion-binder who had set this all in motion. "Bring him. Leave him close to the entrance, so he can be found. Hurry."

The Mob took up their dragonhead weapons and hurried from the underground labyrinth. One Shielder led the way, the second waited for Natasha and Kichlan, before following. Kichlan tried not to see the cracks, steadily growing in the walls about them. Steam hugged the corners, all that remained of ice undone so quickly, and obscured what was left of the dead soldiers.

"Do you see?" Natasha hissed, as they ran. Behind them, walls were falling, the ground caving in, the entire structure giving way to the strength of Natasha's weapon. It reminded him of an underground sewer, and an opening door. His missing hand tingled, as though with the memory of his brother's strong grip. "The national veche will fall before my dragon-headed army."

But Kichlan shook his head. "What do you think your infinite circles are doing to the Keepers doors?" he replied.

Natasha glanced over her shoulder. "The doors aren't about to suck the world into nothingness, I thought we had already established that." She kept her voice tight and low. "First, we need to overthrow the veche. When we have liberated this nation from the old families, and halted its aggressive colonial expansion, then we can worry about doors."

"Reinforcements, ground level," the Shielder behind them said. "Strikers, shielded. They will attack as soon as we breach cover."

Natasha called a halt, and this time mounted up two of the Mob. "Defend them," she told her Shielders. "Just long enough to allow them to fire."

She and Kichlan hung back, as the two Shielders and two Mob crept above ground to take on the forces of the national veche.

"You're playing into their hands!" Kichlan gripped Natasha's shoulder. She shook him free, easily. "Opening more doors, weakening the veil!"

Natasha drew back. "Veil? What are you talking about now?"

Explosions rocked the already unstable underground. Kichlan tried to grab the wall as the earth shook, but his heavy left elbow unbalanced him, and he fell. Too-bright, too-cold light flooded down the corridor. His silver elbow ached.

When he could see again Natasha was standing over him, holding out a hand. He did not take it; rather he clutched the wall and dragged himself upright.

"Come on," Natasha said. "That will have cleared the way. We should get out of here."

He followed her out of the building. Smoke and steam mingled in the cold morning sun. A smell like boiling meat, charred wood and burning hair, rose up with the fog to choke him.

The Mob formed rows as he and Natasha emerged. She left him at the entrance. Behind him, the ruined University sunk deeper into the earth, sending up billowing dust to add to the already heavy sky. Hands clasped behind her back, Natasha stood before her soldiers, bloody face split in a triumphant grin

"Now the revolution really begins," Natasha said. "You remember your recon points, I assume?"

As one, her Mob nodded, saluted. Kichlan could feel something in the air, something more than steam heavy with the dead. A dangerous readiness.

"Then, it is time. Return, regroup, and carry out the cleansing mission allotted to you. Maintain contact on a secure pion flow, surprise is the second strongest weapon we have. You are now the first."

A cheer. Not, Kichlan thought, as strong as Natasha would have liked. Still a little unsure, still concerned about the weapons powered by their own bodies that drained them so fully. But these men were soldiers, regardless.

"Do not be afraid," Natasha said. "No one can stand against you now."

Tan could have. Kichlan sighed. Tan's suit was debris, not pion-made. So these weapons that destroyed pion-bindings could not have harmed her.

Then the Mob were breaking up again, splitting and disappearing along the ruinous streets. Natasha approached him. "You and Tanyana helped us, when you destroyed the city centre." She placed her hands on her hips and surveyed the damaged buildings. Kichlan realised she did not feel the loss of the city the way he did. She did not mourn for the Tear River or the bluestone bridge. She was not really Varsnian, after all, and Movoc-under-Keeper had only ever been a place to conquer, a revolution to wage. Never a home.

No matter how cold, how pion-driven, how veche-run and dangerous, to him the city had always been home.

"You didn't even leave us any veche chambers to attack." She reached up to smack his shoulder, companion-like.

Kichlan shuddered at her touch.

Three Mob, and one of the Shielders, remained with her. They waited like loyal dogs at her back.

"The veche have massed troops with the refugees outside the wall. We take the city first and cleanse it—one street at a time, if they force us to. Then we liberate the refugees. Once Movoc-under-Keeper shakes free of its shackles, the rest of the country will follow. You will be free, Kichlan." She held out an arm as she spoke, tried to draw him into walking. "And if only Lad was still with us, he would be free too. No one to hide from, no need to pretend to be what he is not."

But Kichlan held his ground. He was tired of it all. Tired of carrying the weight of the doors, tired of following Natasha around. Tired of the loss, the hurt. He missed Lad, oh how he missed him. Tan too. Tan—he couldn't even think about her.

So he did what he could to cross his arms, and said, "I'm not an idiot, Natasha."

She paused. "What—?"

"And neither is the veche. Local, regional or national. None of us are foolish enough to believe the Hon Ji are here to liberate us out of the kindness of their own hearts."

"Kichlan?" Natasha frowned, waved her military escort out of hearing. "What are you saying? Don't you trust me? Don't you believe me?"

He lifted his eyebrows, shocked. "Of course not. Why would I do that?"

"Fine." Her eyes hardened. "Of course the campaign to liberate Varsnia is in the Emperor's interest. Why would he invest so many resources if it were not? Breaking the hold of the national veche, and establishing a relationship with the regional and local authorities that will replace it: that is the Emperor's goal. The national veche is aggressive and expansionist—Tanyana and her debris weapon should be proof enough for you! That means that conflict between Varsnia and Hon Ji is inevitable, so we are merely protecting ourselves."

"But what about those?" He gestured to the dragonheads and the Mob. "You're developing weapons of your own."

"Only to defend ourselves."

Kichlan closed his eyes. This was pointless. "You're wrong about Tanyana," he whispered. "The veche was not using her, the puppet men were. And they don't care about the Hon Ji, or borders, or colonies." He opened his eyes again. "Sooner or later, none of that will matter to anyone." It was, after all, only a matter of time before the puppet men brought down the veil, and washed them all away in emptiness. He was not going to spend the rest of his brief, sorry days fighting for someone else's revolution.

Kichlan turned on his heel, and started to walk away.

Natasha lunged, grabbing his arm, "What are you doing?"

He tried to shake her off, but she was strong. "I'm leaving you to your revolution. I want no part of it. You have no right to decide the fate of the people of this city. And neither do I."

"You will leave when I say you can leave!" She would not let him go. Instead, she pulled on his arm, spun and tripped him up with ease. He fell heavily on his hard silver elbow, and she knelt beside him. "This is your fight, Kichlan." She did not seem to be able to decide between imploring him and commanding him. "Even if you don't realise it! Tanyana should have been here, but it's you, now. You're all that's left."

Was he really? What about his debris collecting team? What about Fedor and his Unbound—those people who could see debris, but had escaped being fitted with a suit and forced to collect it? What had happened to them when Tan destroyed the city?

"No." He jammed the butt of his silver elbow against the ground and levered himself up. "I'm going. You won't stop me."

Natasha released him, drew back. She muttered something to herself, a rapid-fire of spiteful sounding words Kichlan could not understand, then drew one of her blades. "I'm in charge now, Kichlan," she said. "And you will obey me." Blade out, she lunged forward.

Kichlan's suit was not like Tan's, but years of living with his strong, unstable brother had taught him to make the most of his limited strength. When Natasha attacked, he lifted his remaining arm, knocked her knife aside, and slid his suit into a blade of his own.

"Don't assume you can command me," he said. He still wasn't used to the changes Tan had made to him. He staggered a little, the lack of his arm keeping him off balance. "I'm not one of your Mob."

Natasha curled her lip. She tossed her blade aside, and drew the silver in her right wrist out into a club. "You're not the only one with a suit here, either."

Again, she leapt at him, and she was fast. He lifted his blade to parry her club, but she ducked, twisted, and he just couldn't follow. Her silver crunched hard into his left side, beneath the arm that wasn't there. He dropped to his knees, and stuck his blade into the shattered cobblestones to keep from falling on his face.

"Damn you," he gasped.

"You're not as fast as Tanyana," Natasha said, as she stalked around him. "Or as strong." She paused, and crouched in front of him. "That bitch gave me the hardest thrashing I've had since training, and you know the worst part?" Natasha drew one of her clay disks from her armour. "She wasn't even trying."

Natasha pressed the disk against Kichlan's blade. Its lightning surged into the silver of his suit, and through him, all of him, every last deeply-sewn wire, every shaving of silver, his skin, muscles, bones. His suit spasmed and retracted, completely out of his control. Kichlan fell, as his body jerked; his bones were on fire, his head filled with a rushing like the waters of the Tear trying to crush the life out of him.

Natasha sighed, a wistful sound. "She really should have joined us. What a soldier she could have made."

Kichlan couldn't move, let alone answer.

Natasha stood, walked away. "Pick him up," she said to the Mob he couldn't see. "And take him with us."

He refused to let them do that! But his suit did not respond, and his body was just as bad, and the only thing that didn't burn with Natasha's lightning was the silver cap on his elbow. The little part of Tan's suit she had forced on to him. Not connected to the rest of the metal in his body and, apparently, unaffected.

The Mob rolled him over. One wrapped arms as strong as steel around his legs, another grabbed his torso. Kichlan squeezed his eyes shut and focused on his elbow. It was still a part of him. No matter how poorly Tan had connected it to his arm, how mangled the nervous connections, it belonged to him how. A part of her, ever with him.

He remembered what it was like when he was first suited, all those years ago. After he had injured himself, taken away his own pion-binding ability so he could remain with his brother instead. Getting used to a suit was like learning to walk all over again. It took concentration, and hard work, constant training of the mind to recognise the silver and learn how to make it move. He'd done it once. He'd thought of himself as skilled, really, until Tan came along. He could do it again.

The Mob picked him up, but he barely felt it. There was nothing in the world but the alien silver on his arm, and the need to make it move.

"Careful," Natasha said somewhere, dimly. "Support his head, I don't want him hurt."

Something rippled. Kichlan felt it in twitching along his shoulders, to his upper back and even the top of his thighs. Tan's messy nerve connections, struggling into life. Another ripple, this one stronger, sent Kichlan's jaw clenching. Silver slipped free of his elbow. Long and loose at first, almost liquid, it took every inch of his focus to get it to move. But it was! And hardening, sharpening, responding to him like a real suit should.

The Mob paused. "Lady Natasha," one said. "There's something—"

Kichlan whipped out with the suit from his elbow. It sliced across the arms of the Mob, scoring deep. They dropped him with a curse, and he would have fallen hard, but the whip coiled beneath him like a spring then lowered him, softly, to the ground.

"Other's hell!" Natasha cried. "How did you—?"

The strangest feeling was rolling through Kichlan, starting at his newly awakened silver. A heady sense like victory, a need, an urge, so deep it make him shiver, and yet, almost impossible to define. He breathed deeply, and it filled his lungs. It loosened his lightning-struck body, one muscle at a time, and made his suit tingle and sting like it was new.

Coughing, shaking, Kichlan pushed himself to his feet. He lifted his left arm, drew the whip back and again, fashioned a blade. It was so responsive, this suit. Fast and sure, it seemed to know what he wanted to do even before he did. He found himself grinning, as he faced the two Mob.

"Go on," he said, his voice rough. "Go on, just try that again. I want you to!" And he really did. He wanted to plunge that blade into their pion-strengthened bodies, he wanted to see just how hard they would fight to stay alive. Let them try, let them—

—this wasn't right. This wasn't him. This need for blood, the urge for battle. Why was he—

Kichlan clutched his head. What was going on?

"Kichlan?" Natasha stepped forward, softly. "Just calm down, please."

But she was lying to him. He would read it clearly on her face, like it was mapped out for him, translated. And he could feel the dangerous, clay disk in her hand, as she made to throw it. So he lashed out again, blade back to whip faster than an instant, caught it in mid air between the finest, most delicate pincers. He was so gentle it did not detonate, and all it took was a little flick to send to flying back to its master, and her Mob.

Natasha flung herself away from the lightning explosion at the last moment. Kichlan spread a wide shield for himself. But her Mob were caught and when the light and the dust cleared, all three were lying prone.

Natasha stared at him in horror. "How did you do that?" she gasped. "Have—have you been able to do that the whole time?"

Enough of this. He'd had enough of fighting, hadn't he? Kichlan gritted his teeth, and drew his suit back in. He pointed his elbow at her, and Natasha flinched. "I'm going," he said. "Don't try to stop me."

"You could be one of us!" Natasha cried, as he shuddered and lurched away. "Just like Tanyana should have been. You would be a great weapon!"

He ignored her. His new suit throbbed inside him, across all its jagged network, and even pinched the edges of his old internal wires. Strange words whispered, at the edges of his hearing. Strange shadows, like ghosts, haunted his vision.

He ignored it all, and just kept walking.

Somewhere, beneath the chaos, in the centre of the storm, his old debris collecting team had been hiding. Innocent, dragged into battle by Tan and the puppet men. If he could do one thing before the world died, it would be to find them. To make sure they were all okay.

Natasha and her battles could just go to all the Other's hells. That was what he would do.

12.

I jerked awake, scratching at my elbow and screaming, "I am not your weapon!"

Lad hunched down in front of me. He ran his hand over my sweat-slicked hair. "Shhh," he whispered. "Not so loud."

Shuddering, I tore the makeshift blankets from my arms and stared at my left hand. It felt so wrong. In the dim, passing lights from the other side of boarded-up windows, it looked unreal. Flesh and silex, skin and light. Cold, bright light. Not silver, not fluid and mobile.

What was going on?

"Just a dream." Lad took both my hands and tucked them back beneath the blankets. "A bad dream. Don't disturb the silex any more than you already have. Take a breath, that's my girl, and calm down. That's one hell of a Flare going on inside you. Just try to relax, see if you can settle it down."

I leaned back, beneath Lad's gentle hands.

"Good, good. That's the way."

I had been so angry. But here, in the semi-dark and the stench of smoke and beneath Lad's constant, heavy worry, I couldn't quite remember why.

Except, it had to do with Kichlan, didn't it? Because when I dreamed—

"Tan?" Lad brushed tears from my cheeks; what I could make out of his expression was shocked. Perhaps he did not think me capable of crying. "Oh no, Tan. Please. Here." And he wrapped arms around me, and held me, as I cried for his brother. For Kichlan.

13.

I watched through a crack in the boarded-up windows as Lad killed a *useless piece of shit junkie* and stole the man's weapon. When I'd asked him if it was really such a good idea to attack an armed man like that, he'd only answered, "Crust is a rough teacher, and I remember her lessons well."

The *junkie* did not look healthy. He shuffled along the poorly lit street below the abandoned building we were hiding in with a strangely hitching gait, as though his legs didn't quite work. His hands snatched at invisible things in front of his face.

"He spent too much time wired to a Flare," Lad said, when I asked what was wrong with the man. "I hear it's nice for a little while. The world...changes. You change. All the darkness and the hunger of Crust are gone, replaced with anything you can imagine. And many things you can't. But spend too long playing with reality, and you lose it. Even when you disconnect, like this guy, you don't know where you are. Or what's real." He drew me gently away from the windows. "What did I say about keeping out of sight?"

But when he headed downstairs and out to the street, I returned to the windows and watched, cradling the silex bath against my chest as it repaired a crack down my left arm. I wasn't entirely clear on what Crust's lessons were, but Lad was right about one thing. He had nothing to fear from the junkie, weapon or none.

The man did not even see Lad coming, too busy swiping at invisible flies. Lad strode right up to him and punched him. The junkie dropped to the dark road like a doll, unsteady legs akimbo, arms flailing wide. Lad crouched, wrapped his large, strong hands around the man's face and smacked the back of his head against the ground. Three sharp, hard movements, and it was done. Then he searched through the junkie's clothing, found a few things apparently worth stealing, and left him there, on the pavement, bleeding wide trails of thick blood into the filthy gutter.

I stared down at the man's body in horror. I had seen Lad—*my* Lad—in his violent moods, but they were nothing like this. This was the coldly calculating act of a killer, not the desperate misunderstanding of a stressed and child-like mind.

And that was all my fault. I was all too keenly aware of what I'd done to Lad, on both worlds. Everything I'd taken away from him. And it hurt so much I didn't even know how to talk to him anymore, how to look at him, to trust or know him. All I knew was guilt.

The junkie's eyes were still open. They stared back up at me, sightless.

"I told you," Lad said, as he reappeared, "to stay away from the windows."

I returned to my bedding. The building Lad had chosen to hide us in had once been an apartment block, but that was a very long time ago. Time had destroyed most of it, eating through steel, cement and silex like a disease. I was certain it was unstable, and probably dangerous to be hiding in, but I supposed that made it the best place. Who would risk their lives to look here?

There was silex everywhere in the building, but it was different from the crystal in my skin, or the stuff that made up my son's body and powered his tube. A dull, grain-like smattering of mineral embedded with wire and threaded through the walls and floor—linking lights in the ceiling, heating units, and devices with functions I did not understand and had asked Lad to explain to me. Steam presses for clothes, screens like the ones the programmers used that had once provided entertainment, and other devices that enabled communication over great distances. Of course, only the bones now remained. I could see the heating units because most of the floors had long-since disintegrated. Their thick metallic loops reminded me of pion factories. Of the lights, only small silex hubs dangling from the ceiling remained, in some cases still semi-encased in glass. But mostly, all that remained were sockets, where any device could be activated by creating a connection of crystal and light.

"What happened?" I had asked him, as Lad led us through the decaying rooms to one that looked the most stable, and less likely to collapse on us in our sleep. "To the people who lived here?"

"Flares happened."

We could not climb to the building's roof—the upper stories were little more than steel frames and ghostly, glittering silex—so Lad risked the street, for just a moment, to show me a nearby Shard. It grew out of the very earth, the lower end of its angled, reflective surfaces hidden below the street. It reared high into the sky, dwarfing the buildings around it, and scattered light across their dark and empty edifices.

"A Pionic Flare, right in the centre of a neighbourhood like this one, causes significant loss of life and property damage. Unchecked, it could undo the subatomic structures of the entire city. As you can see, it has been contained, but everything it touched—buildings, people, pets—was destabilized. Some were euthanised, a quicker death than slow disintegration. The buildings were condemned, and the area cordoned off."

I glanced around. We had seen few people in our rush from the pod, where it had landed in another condemned area, much like this one.

"Of course, that was hundreds of years ago." Lad did not allow us to stay out on the street for long. He feared the Legate and its satellites. "Such regulation is no longer enforced. It's all the Legate can do to keep this world together. Even so, only junkies and homeless and criminal gangs would dare a place like this."

I leaned against the broken remains of a tiled wall and watched as Lad sorted through the items he had stolen from the junkie. He had made our bedding in what was once a bathroom, on a hard floor, between a ceramic tub and exposed steel pipes.

"The strongest place in a building, and the last to fall. So if this place starts to go, we might have time to run."

I'd expected the small room with tiled floors and walls to be cold. But nothing in this world, it seemed, was cold. Not any more. Even the constant heavy clouds and the bouts of hard, needle-like rain brought nothing but steam and humidity. Flares released a considerable amount of heat with all their potent energy.

Lad placed the weapon on the floor. Small, metal, and dangerous-looking, even though I didn't know how it worked. He caught me staring at it. "This is a gun," he said, lifted it, tossed it lightly in one hand. "There's nothing like it on your—on our—on that—world."

He tried so hard not to think about the world where he had died. Could he feel the blades through his back, as clearly as I could still see them?

"This is a gun," he said again, his voice rough, constricted. "It shoots bullets. Here." Something inside the weapon clicked, and the middle rolled free. Six more pieces of metal fell into his hand—small, pill-like, and edged with silex. "These hit you, at great speed, and get inside your body. Then—" he made a small explosion motion with his empty hand "—the silex inside them shatters." He studied the bullets, clicked his tongue disapprovingly, and returned them to their case inside the gun. "These are cheap, their silex is weak and not even threaded. The guns the Legate uses, for example, will release an isolated Flare inside your body. No one comes back from that. A good shot and this could still kill you: head, chest, any major artery. But more likely to leave little bits of brass and silex inside you, to fester." He snapped the gun shut again, and pocketed it. "But better than nothing."

"That's horrible!" I gasped. It still hurt, to compare this Lad to the man who had held my hand so tightly, and demanded nothing more complex than a good story. His haunted eyes made him look so ancient, so distant and different from me. His beard was growing unchecked, his hair always was unruly, and his white programmer's jacket was filthy now. Kichlan would not have let him get into this state. "Why would we want—"

"Don't be naïve, Tan. This is Crust. Everyone down here is armed." He shuffled on his knees around the ancient bathtub. Behind there, between loose floorboards and what he hoped was a sturdier lattice of pipes, Lad had hidden his bag. "And anyway, we only have enough silex to keep you alive for another week."

I'd tried my hardest to keep still, to remain calm. But we had been forced to run from the pod when it landed in a semi-abandoned slum, to climb into buildings and hide, as lights lit the sky below the distant Fulcrum and the denizens of Crust emerged to investigate. Add that to my nightmares—occurring nightly, now—and the bright Flare they summoned, and Lad had already been forced to use more of the silex than he would have liked. Soon, too soon, we would run very low.

My son, in his tube, leaned into a corner close to where I slept. Lad had wanted to hide him somewhere else in the ruin, just to be safe. I understood his reasons, but I'd still refused. When I slept, my son slept with me. When I woke, I knew he was there. So we resorted to throwing a blanket over him, to smother his steady Flare.

"Only one week." I nodded. "Yes, I know that."

"So now I'm going to try to get some more."

I frowned at him as he shuffled over to sit in front of me. "From where? And why will you need a gun?"

Lad sighed, and gestured to the windows. "That corpse out there, that junkie, he had been wired to a Flare."

"Like you said." I nodded. "To forget Crust. To change your reality." Almost sounded like a good idea.

"Thing is, it's not that easy to do. Can't just walk up to any old Shard and connect. You need implants, you need the right hacking equipment, and they all require silex. That means there must be a gang around here—not too far away, I don't think he could have walked far in that condition—with access. So I'm going to get some."

He stood. I hurried to follow.

"You'll use the gun to force them to give you some?" I asked.

He laughed, a tough, humourless sound. "Oh fuck no. That would be suicide." He shrugged. "I have some credits to my name, if the Legate hasn't wiped my funds, of course. If not, I have skill. I am a programmer, after all. I can create the kind of crystal connections those thugs can only dream of. Strike the right deal with them, and I'll keep you alive for a lot longer than a week."

"Lad." I clutched his arm. "This—I think this sounds dangerous." Actually, I'd only understood half of what he had said. "Please, don't put yourself—"

"Shhh." He unwrapped my fingers where they bunched his shirt. "I help you, Tan. Bro said—" He shook his head. "I mean, this is my decision. This is what I meant, when I said there were options, here on Crust. I didn't say they would be good ones, or safe ones. But I grew up on Crust, and I know the way things work here." He glanced down at my hand, clamped in its silex bath. "I just didn't think I would need to go to the gangs so soon."

Guilt dipped low inside me, and set off fresh flickerings of light through my mineral skin. It did that so often now. I'd already killed one half of Lad; if I let the other die here, for me—

He untangled me easily. "So just sit still, and rest. That's the most important thing you can do."

I watched him leave. But I was not good at sitting here, calmly, while he went out into the dangerous world to try and save me. Even as an architect I had never taken orders well, and had only ever been comfortable as a circle centre. The point where all the lights converged.

Could I really just sit here, nursing my injuries, while Lad risked his life for me? Again.

What choice did I have?

I paced, slow and steadily, careful with the silex in my skin and the weight of the bath.

Time was strange on Crust, just as it was on board Fulcrum. Sunless, bell-less, it passed only with the sound of my feet against hollow floors and the flickering of lights outside. I peered through the slatted window. The Flares from countless floating Shards reflected against the low, heavy cloud, and gave the ruined city a constant, twilight glow. Every so often something bright sped along the street past the building. Lad had told me they were pods, like the one that had carried us down to Crust, the carriages of this world. Only the Legate and its programmers, however, had access to them now. So I was to hide, each time one flew by.

With Lad gone, however, I did nothing of the kind. I pressed my nose to putrid wood and stared intently at the first flash of oncoming light. The pods moved too fast to see properly: a streak of silver and a blaze of light. They weren't regular enough to provide a decent way to estimate time. But in the heavy silence of eternal twilight, they were all I had. Three passed, before I began to worry that Lad had not returned. I slept a little, between the second and third. I wasn't hungry, not even thirsty either, but that meant nothing. I wasn't sure how much I needed food, any more.

How long had he been away? And what did that mean? I deserved to be abandoned, and wouldn't fault him for it. But had I sent him his death again? Fear and guilt and hopelessness played through me, and I didn't handle any of them well. So I paced, and worried, and stared outside, and longed for the strength of my silver.

I was watching the trail left by the third pod—the fade of light left behind in steam and low-cloud haze—when I saw two, as Lad would have put it, *pieces of shit junkies*. They waited in shadows across the road for the pod to leave, then hurried to the dead body still lying in the street. They were both thin, like the man Lad had killed, the skin tight on their faces. I held my breath as they searched his pockets, and found nothing.

"Fuck it." One of them kicked the dead man. "Not even a jack on him." He was almost bald; what hair there was left on his head was wispy and grey, though his face didn't look that old. His clothes were filthy and riddled with holes. He wasn't wearing any shoes.

His fellow nodded, stood, and scanned the street, his expression far too thoughtful. "He didn't overdose though, did he?" This junkie looked healthier. He still had hair, for one thing, dark and speckled with grey. He even wore shoes, mismatched, but surely better than none. "Ever seen an overdose with a head like that?"

I leaned back from the window as the junkie stared up at the building.

"You're saying someone beat the shit out of him, and took his stuff?"

"What else do you think happened? He, what, beat his own brains out on the street then threw his wires in the gutter?"

A pause. "He coulda done it the other way, threw his junk first—"

"No one breaks open the back of their own head on the floor!"

I leaned forward again, peered down. The junkies were pacing the street, kicking at doors, looking through windows. I held my breath as they knocked against the old, wire-frame door beneath me, and it gave way.

Voices echoed up from the floors below. "So, maybe they are still close by, you reckon?"

"I swear, you say one more word and I'm going to blow your fucking brains out!"

"But that's why you're looking around, right? Think they've still got his wires and jacks?"

"I'm not kidding. One more word, I introduce a bullet to your brain. I'll buy them fucking dinner."

I stared around the room. I might be able to hide in the bathtub, if I hunched down tight enough. But they would see the bedding; all they had to do was glance inside the room as they walked past. Then surely, they would come hunting. And my son was in here, propped up against the wall, a thin blanket the only thing between him and these two violent men.

But I didn't have my suit, and I didn't have pions. So I tore a long, thin pipe from the wall, tucked my left hand—encased in silex bath—into the folds of my loose shirt and held the twisted, rusting weapon out in front of me. I stood, facing the doorway, bare feet braced against the floorboards, stance as strong as I could make it. And watched as the junkies emerged from the stairs.

There was something strange about them, something I hadn't noticed while they were out on the street. They seemed to…waver. Like waves of heat rising from their skin, encasing them. But when the floating dust of ages passed through the oddly shifting air around their bodies, it changed. Some suddenly shone like tiny, trapped stars before falling to wink out on the ancient floorboards. Others snapped into deep darkness that buzzed around like flies. Some even grew large, long, and dropped, slithering, alive, to the junkies' shoulders.

I shook, a little, but held my ground. The Flares these men had connected themselves to were Pionic, I knew that. They were bursts of energy capable of rewriting reality. So maybe I was seeing the residue effects? But if that was true, then what was it doing to their insides? No wonder the man Lad had killed had looked so unhealthy. This was what happened if you wired yourself to a Shard? No matter how hard Crust and her teachings were, could this be worth it?

I swallowed against the silex in my throat. Wasn't the same thing inside me? Killing me?

"We ain't gonna find anything here," the bald and unhealthy looking one said. There was a certain weakness to his knees, a wobble in his gait that made stair climbing difficult. He clutched the railing, hauled himself up, and didn't even bother to brush newly formed wiggling wormlike creatures from his shoulders. One sprouted legs and skittered away, inside his clothes. He didn't seem to notice. "Reckon we go back and—"

The sarcastic and healthier one turned on him. He drew a gun from the back of his pants with a single, smooth movement and pointed it at his fellow's face. "What did I tell you?" he hissed, and used the tip of the gun to wipe away the creatures on the first junkie's shoulders. "Fuck man, at least clean yourself up!"

The stupid one flinched back from the gun in his face, and as he did so, he saw me. Our eyes met for the long moment it seemed to take for him to realise I was there, then a look like wonder, and hunger, crossed his face. "There's a woman," he said. "And she's glowing."

The sarcastic junkie paused. "What?"

"There."

Then the gun was pointed at me. I remembered what Lad had said about silex exploding, about festering splinters of brass and crystal, or direct blows to the head and chest. But still, I lifted my makeshift weapon higher, and the Flare within me brightened, casting its fluctuating weave between us.

"Get out of here," I said.

The gun shook slightly.

"She's wired." When he laughed, I realised the unhealthy junkie barely had any teeth left at all. "Can't see the cables, but she got to be. Look at her glow!" He tried to move toward me, but his partner held him back.

"No," he said, his voice tight, low. Far too thoughtful for my liking. "No, she's got no wires at all." He approached me, slowly, gun still lifted. "I've never seen anything like it."

The junkies entered the bathroom, and I stepped back, unwillingly. They split up, circled me. Strange things were happening to the floor at their feet. Wood splintering one moment, mending the next. Water oozing out of dry boards. Copper wires flecked with silex rose like charmed snakes. I backed toward the corner with the tube, determined to keep my body between them and my son.

There was no way I would let them find him.

"Where's your connection, little thing?" the man with the gun asked. "Did you kill that man out there and take his junk? You using that to glow so hard?"

I didn't answer, just waved my pipe in front of them.

"That silex?" The stupid one muttered. I glanced toward him. He was closer than I had realised, and I nearly tripped to keep distance between us. "In her neck, and arm, glowing like that. Is that silex?"

"You know, I think it is. And not just any silex, there's a Flare in there."

The way they spoke, it was like they had forgotten I was here, even as they pushed me into the corner and trained that gun on my head.

"Fuck, there is. She's not connected, she don't need to be! She's a Shard, all on her own."

The sarcastic one laughed. My feet knocked the tube and it rattled against the wall, the sound thankfully muffled by the blanket it was wrapped in. "Is that what you are, little thing? You a Shard? What if we wanna wire you? Would you lie there, just lie there, and take it? Or do we have to tear that silex out of you first?"

"Never wired a girl before."

"No!" I swung my pipe at them. The stupid one skipped back, and his partner laughed. "Get out of here!"

In one quick motion, the sarcastic junkie pocketed his gun, stepped forward, and grabbed my pipe. He yanked it from my hand, and threw it aside.

The tension in my clutching grip sent tiny cracks up through the silex in my arm. Light spilled out in fitful bursts, colouring their hungry faces.

"Amazing," the idiot gasped. Before I could even try to move away he had wrapped arms around my waist and pressed the side of his face against my neck. "That's strong, isn't it?"

His companion nodded. He grabbed my right arm, yanked my shirtsleeve back and peered at the newly formed cracks. "Surely it is."

They did not look afraid of the death, the undoing, leaking into this world from beneath my skin. I saw, in their ravenous eyes, none of the fear and horror I had seen in programmers'.

"Don't you know what that means?" I gasped. The junkie's grip was tight, I could barely breathe against his arms. "This Flare will unmake you, if you stay here. If we don't repair the silex, it will kill us all!"

Sarcastic twisted his lips in a dry smile. "Think we're scared of a little changing?" He grabbed a handful of the strange creatures from his shoulders and held them right in front of my face. Leeches, I thought, just like leeches. Except in the waves of heat from his skin they were changing, ever changing. From living things, to dust again, one to a tiny perfect flower that crawled away on fat white hands.

"Already happening." The stupid junkie's breath, so close to my face, was rancid.

I struggled against their hold, I tried to kick. All I got for my trouble was cracking along my waist and in my ankle.

"Hush." Sarcastic wiped his hand on his pants then gripped my chin. His touch made my skin itch.

"What will you do to me?" I whispered.

"Don't tell me, that with all that light inside you, you've never been wired?" He pouted a fake expression of regret. "Now that's exciting. To be first."

A harsh chuckle close behind my ear. "Yeah, exciting."

"Let me show you." Sarcastic released me, and pulled back his own sleeve, revealing a filthy arm covered in scars. Some old and white, others fresh and still red and tight. "You looking?" He dug at a ridge of newer scars around the underside of his wrist until the skin peeled back to reveal a small nib of silex. He pinched the silex and drew it out. A long stream of wires followed.

He took my cracked wrist again. I tried to recoil, but his fellow held me tightly. The wires were inside him. And even though these did not kick like insect legs, they were just too close—oh too close—to the suit that had been inside of me.

"This is my jack," the junkie said, grinning widely. Most of his teeth were missing, and the wavering aura around him made the darkness inside his mouth squirm like it was alive. "Use it to hack into Shards. Shards a lot like you."

He pressed his silex nib hard against the cracks in my wrist. For a moment we were nothing but crystal, grinding. Then the nib softened, and liquid bubbled up from within me, and they bled into each other, wrapped around his wires, and we were joined, the junkie and I. He tipped his head back and took a deep, shuddering breath. "Now, we're wired."

My Flare flickered. Its light danced along his wires then followed the scars in his arm, shining beneath his skin. Particles rushed within me, filling my head with their pressure. I felt thin, strung out by their movement, like they were wiping me clean inside, hollowing me out. Like I was nothing but a shell. A conduit.

Behind me, the other junkie leaned forward, bending me over. "What's it like?" he asked, in awe-hushed tones.

"Pure." A gasp, a shudder, eyes closed, ever smiling. "Fucking pure."

He started to change. His teeth grew back. His scars healed. His eyes lost their haunted, unreal look. Then the room followed. The floor became grass, the walls trees, the air so crisp and cool and clean.

"See that?" the junkie asked. His wires were gone too, and he was holding my hand instead. I felt a rush like affection as he smiled at me, like we were close, like we understood each other. I followed his gaze, and looked up. The sky was a hard, brilliant blue. I knew it. It was mine. Movoc-under-Keeper on a Widesky day.

"Trees are mine," he whispered. "Saw 'em on a screen, once. They were green. Ground too. But that blue. That blue is yours."

I wanted to touch it. To lift my hands and plunge them so deeply into that open sky, and stay there, floating, forever. Filled with this lightness, this affection.

Are you sure about that? something whispered, behind me, and its voice was the rush of pions. *Is that really why you came?*

I tore my hand free and spun. For an instant I thought I saw Kichlan, only as solid as a shadow, but his expression so disappointed it wrenched at my heart. Then the room snapped back to hard, solid reality. The sky was a rotting ceiling, the grass floorboards, the trees walls.

The junkie held his limp wires in his hand, the nib flashing a sharp and warning red. Silex liquid dripped from my wrist like blood, my Flare spluttered weakly.

"Fucking bitch!" The junkie knocked me to the side. "Couldn't you bloody hold her still?"

The world reeled as I fell into the corner, slipped on the tube's blanket and scrambled desperately to keep it covered. What had just happened? Had I imagined it all?

"I saw it!" his fellow didn't even seem to notice he was being shouted at. "Wasn't even wired but I was there too. Purest Shard you've ever found. Fucking wonderful!"

That calmed the sarcastic junkie down. He crouched, grinning again, and in the aura around him I saw blue sky. He smelled of cut grass, and when he smiled, all his teeth were there, white and clean.

Longing, and fear, both fluttered low in my stomach. "Was it real?" I whispered.

"Of course. Real as the Flare makes it. Changes you. Changes the world around you. Into something beautiful." He crawled closer. I pressed my back against the tube. "At first. So much more than this shit. You change and change until you can't tell, anymore, because you're not real, and the world ain't real. But doesn't matter, by then. Worth it, don't you think? A little light, a little peace, a little green, before you die?"

I almost did. If not for the tube pressed against my back, and the look on that unreal—impossible—Kichlan's face, I would have agreed with him. But that was not why I was here.

So when the second junkie crouched beside him, and dragged more wires out of his arm, and they both leaned

in with the world around them shifting I said, "No!" and
kicked out. They grabbed my ankles, dragged me down to
the floor, away from the tube. The blanket wrapped itself
around my arm and slipped down with me, revealing my
son, small, half-made, glowing as he spun.

The junkies stared at him like they had just stumbled
upon gold.

"What is it?" Stupid asked.

Sarcastic glanced down at me, then back to the baby,
a terrible smile spreading across his lips. "It's a fucking
jackpot, what it is."

"But I thought we were going to wire *her*?"

"Oh, we are. But we're going to sell this one." He
stepped over me, ran his hand down the smooth glass tube.

"No!" I punched up at him with the heavy silex bath
on my hand. It caught the back of one knee, knocked him
against the wall, then snapped open and spilled silex across
the floor in a crystal-studded puddle.

I wouldn't let this happen. I rolled to my stomach and
scrambled along the floor as the second man lurched to his
feet. I reached for my pipe; he stomped at my back, grazing
badly down my left side. More silex shattered beneath his
boot and pressure pinched at my lungs.

Work with me, I whispered, inside, to the particles I
had heard only moments before. *I know you can. You're
pions. Your brothers and your sisters were my friends, on
the other side of the veil. So work with me. We can build
wonders together.*

Light surged through me and again, my head with filled
with sound. My vision blurred, all I could see was light,
colours, dancing from the fissures in my second skin. Tiny
little specs like suns. I gave up on the pipe, and opened my
hands to them. My mind. Myself.

"Yes." I could breathe again. I pushed myself to my feet,
grinned, though I could barely feel my face. "You want to
change reality? I'll show you how to fucking change reality!"

And I showed the pions what I needed them to do, the
way I always had. Form rock and steel from the dust in

the very air and pin the junkies down. Repair the silex throughout my body, add strength to my muscles and bones. I was Tanyana Vladha, and I might not have a circle of nine but I had my pions back and I—

Thunder shook the building. It rattled every last crystal inch of me.

"Shit!" one of the junkies cried. "What are you doing?"

I blinked. They weren't pinned helpless to the floor. I wasn't healing. Instead—

Something like lightning ricocheted through the room. It cracked across the walls, it set the thin remnants of the carpet alight. Somewhere, something crashed to the ground, and the building shuddered.

"Stop it!" Suddenly, the sarcastic junkie was right in front of me. He hit me, hard across the face. I fell, again. Lightning above me. Thunder through me. But that wasn't what I'd asked! The rush filled my ears and the excitement of countless, powerful pions pressed hard inside my every vein, but they weren't helping me.

"Too much strength?" I whispered to myself, to the memory of the Specialist, trying to explain the bursts of energy tearing into his world. "Too many pions, all at once?" But I'd felt them. I thought they wanted to help remake the world with me. Instead of this.

"Now that's much better." Sarcastic peered down at me as behind him, his fellow used my blanket to put out the small, smouldering fire. "No point wasting it all at once, is there."

I didn't know what to do. There were pions inside me, beaming out into this world. I could feel them. They longed to create, they pleaded for guidance. I was certain of it. So many of them, they were a clamour. And yet, when I'd tried to use them all I'd got was light, and cracks, and pain. Thunder. Lightning. A pointless, directionless burst of energy.

It hadn't touched the junkies at all. In fact, they were more worried about *me*.

I chuckled, softly to myself.

Pointless.

"Reckon she can walk?" the stupid one asked, somewhere that sounded so far away. "Or do we have to carry her too?"

I stared down at a hole in the floor beside me, and tried to ignore the sounds of tapping on my son's tube. More silex and wires beneath the rotten wood. I was sick of the sight of them.

"Carry her," Sarcastic answered. "Don't want her to break."

Silex and wires connected everything here—even connected the junkie and me—and all of it powered by a Flare. By the uncontrollable, mindless, destructive rush of too many pions all at once. Just like what was happening inside of me.

"Okay, but I want her," Stupid muttered. "Didn't even get my turn yet."

I shifted, slightly. Inside of me? I reached beneath the rotten floorboards and wound my fingers around the frayed wiring. Everything in this world was powered by Flares, and that's exactly what I was. So, what would happen—

Silex liquid slid down my fingers. It found the wires, encased them. Hardened.

And the entire building flooded with light.

"What the fuck?" Both junkies froze.

I stared around the room. The lights, those broken knots of silex, wire and glass, blazed brilliantly. Something rattled in the distance, a sound that deepened, that grew, and rolled up from the bottom of the building in a wave. Then water shot from the pipes in the wall and the shattered faucets above the bath. Thickly dark stuff, tepid and laden with sludge.

As water gushed over me, and the junkies retreated from it, cursing and brushing ooze from their clothing, I stood. Carefully, lifting the wires with me.

I felt the building's pulse like it was another part of me. It was silex, all of it. The crystal connected everything, it formed the foundations just as much, if not more, than cement and steel alone. And I powered it all. With a thought, I dimmed the lights. Another, I tightened creaking valves far below ground and held the water back. It was all so fragile, all weakened by time and disuse. An eggshell cracking.

"I am not weak anymore," I said.

Above me, wires snapped. Old, frayed, they could not contain the strength of my Flare. Shocks buzzed across the ceiling in their wake, following the track of water seeping in from the floors above. The junkies like insects on my skin. I knew every silex hub close to them, every heating unit, every dangerously eroded or crossed wire.

They should have run. They should never have come here; they should not have threatened my son.

"It might not be suit-metal," I said, and squeezed the wires harder, "and I might not be able to bind your pions. But I will not simply lie here and let you harm us." I sent a surge of energy through the silex. Lights began exploding. I flooded heat through the ceramic units beneath the rotten floorboards. They shattered with the pressure, and flames surged into the room. That, finally, convinced the junkies.

Hands above their heads they ran from the bathroom, out into the hallway and toward the stairwell. But the building had slumbered long, and had not wakened happy. Even as I pulled back from her wiring and released her into sleep, she shook like a lumbering monster. And the high stories gave way. Steel beams crashed down, through layer and layer of rooms, dragging splintered wood and cement behind them. I pressed myself against the side of the tub as they crashed down on top of the junkies, tearing out the hallway floor and shattering most of the stairwell, to finally settle in a mountain of rubble at the ground floor.

Fine cement dust rose like smoke, as the building settled back down around me.

Lad had been right about the bathroom. It survived the collapse quite well.

I hardly dared to breathe. Without me to power them, the broken heating units died, and soon, the flames receded. The smoke burned my nose and the back of my throat, sending me into coughing fits that added fresh cracks down my neck and around my chest.

It might have survived that, but it probably wasn't a good idea to stay here.

I dug Lad's bag from its hiding place, grabbed the silex bath from the floor, and slung the lot over my shoulder. I tied several more blankets around my son's tube. One to wrap it up, to obscure its contents from view. With two more, I created makeshift straps, so I could hold it against my chest and tie it there. So laden, I could hardly move. But it was the best I could think of.

Most of the stairs were gone. The rubble, at least, provided a kind of a pathway down. I struggled, slipped, almost overbalanced several times, but made it outside the building. And almost as though it knew, as though it had waited for me to leave, the apartment block finally gave way as I stepped out from beneath its shadow.

It fell slowly, with a strange kind of grace. What was left of the upper stories—the steel bones and timber framing—folded inward, and carried the rest down. Like a flower closing, I thought for a moment. It was strange to mourn a building so, but I had been a part of her. If only for an instant, I had felt the strength she once had. The flow of light through her silex, of heat beneath her floors, and water along her pipes, the power she had once used to sustain generations of uncounted lives.

"Foolishness," I muttered, but still smiled at myself, and ran a hand over the smooth curve of my son's tube.

Silence and the heat of the constant twilight settled over me. I glanced up and down the street. Nothing but broken-teeth ruins tearing up from the cement. In the distance, fires burned.

No sign of more junkies. Or Lad.

"Now what?" I asked my son. Of course, he couldn't answer, but that didn't stop me asking. We were in this together, after all.

At first, we waited. Because Lad was coming back. He had to be.

Then lights appeared in the distant sky. I watched them for a little while, the way their swerved and danced. And hummed. They sung a deep tune that grew louder, and they grew larger and...closer.

I swallowed fear, looked down to my hand. The silex that had bubbled out of my cracks to bond to the building's wiring had solidified in trails across my palm. And even though I still leaked a constant flicker of light, the Flare within me did not seem as urgent. It felt eased. Like it had needed that release, that directed pulse of energy.

So, I was not helpless in this world. Still dying, slowly, one ripple of light at a time. But still, this wasn't my world. And those lights were coming closer. And I thought of satellites, and the Legate, and the programmers, always searching.

Lad has promised his brother—he would look after me. And no matter what world, no matter what kind of Lad, he would never break a promise. I knew that deeply, even without the parts of him that I had carried. So Lad was coming back.

But we couldn't wait for him. Not any more.

I strapped my son to my chest again and shuffled, awkwardly, as quickly as I could manage, beneath the shelter of nearby ruins. Just in time. Spotlights swept over the building I had destroyed. The ground vibrated with a deep rumble I could feel in my chest. I hurried, head down, close to the wall, draped in shadow.

The rush of a passing pod added its wail to the sudden cacophony. He'd been gone so long. Too long. Where was my Lad? What had happened to him?

I struggled on. I'd learned to live without him once before. It hurt that time, and it hurt this time. But I could do it again. If I had to.

14.

For countless, silent bells, Kichlan slogged north through the city.

Movoc-under-Keeper had been built around the Tear River, and all roads led to her banks. But now, with the river running amok, the ground caved in, so many buildings falling, and Natasha's heavily armed Mob roaming the streets, the city was nearly impossible to navigate. It didn't help that he didn't really know where he was.

He had almost given up looking when he finally found a street sign. Somehow, it had survived, still drilled into a street corner—all that remained of a once-large building. He had to touch it to believe it was real. Old copper letters left to bleed into green. Flakes of pale enamel paint. Rust stains on the weathered wall.

13th Effluent, Section 15

He sagged and rested his head against the stone. Still so far to go. Two whole sections. He'd been walking all day, he'd hardly slept, and there was still so far to go. Who knew what else he would find in his way to slow him down—

His left arm shuddered.

Kichlan straightened, and withdrew it from the folds of his coat. Not that there was anyone here to hide it from, but it was habit now.

The silver was moving. It rippled, it bulged, then faded back down into his arm.

He hadn't told it to do anything. Since leaving Natasha it had been quiet again, calm. "What are you—?"

"*No!*" someone screamed, right beside his ear.

Kichlan spun and stared back along the ravaged street, heart beating frantically against his chest. Mob? Strikers? Natasha, about to try and take him again? He'd been lucky to escape her last time, he knew that. He really didn't want to try again.

"*I am not weak anymore.*" The voice was right behind him, so close he should have been able to feel her breath—her breath?

"Other curse you." Kichlan swallowed, hard, and looked down at his silver stub. He could have sworn that voice was Tan. Damn, but it sounded just like her.

Feelings he could not place rolled up inside him. Fear, a desperate fear, something that clutched his entire body in a sweat-slick and muscle spasm. What was this? Some residual memory, carried on the silver she had forced into him? Was he feeling what she had felt when the river took her? Or something earlier? Maybe this was what it had felt like to fight Aleksey, or to risk everything to rescue him from the veche. If she was going to die, if she was going to leave him, couldn't she have just done it cleanly? Did she really need to dredge all this—

Then hope swelled up within him. And heat, like a rising sun, like the power he used to feel, when he could bind pions and do it oh so well. The feeling was so intense it flattened his fear and silenced his questions—what memory was this?—and he was smiling, grinning like a fool.

Until all the world went black.

For a stunned moment, Kichlan blinked, convinced there was something wrong with his eyes. Then he realised his arm—his left arm—was whole again. Silver, and glowing strongly, a shifting multicolour light he would have thought was beautiful if it hadn't been so impossible. He flexed his hand, it responded. And it felt strong.

When he looked up again, the darkness was crowded with doors.

Great and ancient, wood cracked, handles rusted, hinges rotting away. And he knew what they were—he'd heard Tan describe them so many times—but he didn't understand how he could see them. This new arm appeared to be made of suit metal, yes, but the rest of him was not encased in silver. Not the way she had done it, head to toe, in order to access this world and speak to the Keeper. Even though Tan had given him a part of her suit, it was only the very edge of him, the stub of his mutilated elbow and some of the nerve connections she had overridden. His suit, the one that still spun slow and dull at five remaining points on his body, was nothing like hers, and should not be able to bring him here.

"Did you do this?" he asked his own left arm. His voice echoed, travelled far. Nothing answered.

He stepped forward. The doors were everywhere. Crowding around him, threatening, looming. He trod on them; more floated above him. Of the darkness, only tiny cracks remained. But they were closed. All of them. They did not even rattle. Tan had said they rattled, like something on the other side was trying to get in.

He clasped his hands together, wove silver and flesh fingers, and squeezed just to be sure they were real.

"Tan?" he called, uncertain. He had seen her dragged down into the Tear River, and had not seen her emerge. What else could she be, but drowned? But this, what did this mean? Could she be here, somewhere, waiting for him in the gaps between reality, in the Keeper's world of darkness and doors? Could she do that? Was it even possible? He just didn't know. "Tan? Are you here?"

Nothing. Not even another half-imagined cry.

"Impossible," he whispered to himself. "Damn me for hoping."

"Impossible," said a toneless, unemotional voice behind him. "We are tiring of the impossible."

Kichlan spun. A single veche man—a puppet man—stood behind him, surrounded by a mist thick with shadowy, half-seen figures. It watched him without expression, and wore its skin poorly. The face did not fit around the bones of its skull: the seams along the edges of its mouth had torn into a too-wide, manic grin; its nose was nothing but a misshapen black globule; rough stitches were visible along the hairline. Its eyes were empty.

Kichlan stumbled back. In the darkness of those eyes he saw the insect-head, the horror the veche men had strapped him to, the debris they had attacked him with. Snakes in his skin, tearing, pulling him apart. His arm, gone, and Tan's terrified face above him.

He lifted his silver arm. "Get back!" he cried, and at the same moment smoothed his fist into a sharpened blade. "I won't let you take me this time."

The puppet man tipped his head. "We know you," it said, and followed him. It didn't even bother to walk, but floated, feet inches above the doors. The mist rolled behind. "You are our interrupted experiment. You should not be here. You should have been terminated." It paused, and shook its head, the movement violently jarring and too fast.

Then an arm reached out of the mist, just below the puppet man's feet. It dug and clawed at the doors, before gripping those floating, pale trouser legs and pulling half of its body free. White skin, black eyes, skull a criss-cross of dark veins, and expression set in fear, in horror. "Run!" it cried. "Kichlan, run! Don't let them take you again!"

The puppet man looked down, shook its leg, but could not dislodge those pale, grasping hands. "Integration is not running as smoothly as we would have thought," it said, and glanced at the doors. "Communication flow has ceased. All programmers have been blocked. Veil has not weakened as planned. We suspect manual interference." Then it trained that half face back on Kichlan. "Do you know what's happening behind the veil? Can you tell us, what has she done?"

"I—" Kichlan backed away until he ran into a door. "I don't understand a single thing you've said."

"Our programming was flawless." The puppet man began kicking at the body attached to him, and Kichlan winced every time one of those too-polished shoes hit the pale head. "This is impossible."

He had to get away. Kichlan focused, again, on his silver hand. He tried to pull it back into the cap, but it was fighting him. One finger down, two. Pain in his shoulder, knots down his back. He gritted his teeth, and—

<emergency repair required>

—ignored the lies inside his own head.

"Like you." The puppet man paused. "You should not exist in this place. Tell us, what has she done, to bring you here?"

The thing attached to the puppet man's leg looked up. "Please run," it said. Its hands were wet and dark with its own black blood, and it was losing its grip. "Don't let them kill you too."

"I don't understand."

"Tanyana would not want you to fall into their hands again." Such a small voice. Weak, strained, and childlike. "Not after everything we went through, just to keep you alive."

We? A chilling thought occurred to him, a surreal and impossible thought. But Kichlan remembered the statues in the underground Unbound street, and the murals in the mountain, the images Tan had said looked so much like the Keeper. White, crystalline stone and large black eyes. Who else could it be? "Are—are you the Keeper?"

"Continued interference shall not be tolerated," the puppet man snapped. It lifted its foot a final time, and kicked the Keeper down. Once it had finished with the Keeper, the puppet man looked back up at Kichlan. "Reprogrammed," it said. "Yes, you have been reprogrammed. You will return with us for evaluation."

It lifted a hand and pointed at Kichlan. The silver within him seized up, all his control torn away, and he took a step forward.

"No!" he tried to cry, but his mouth wouldn't move. Silently, he screamed, "We won't!"

Sizzling, burning, followed every nerve connection through him. He managed to twitch his fingers, flesh and bone, then silver—

<protocols demand a return to the hub for correction and analysis. I suggest we stop resisting>

"No!" he shouted, this time, out loud.

The puppet man recoiled.

"This is my body and you're my suit and *you will do as I say!*"

Nonsensical whispers filled his head, random numbers and letters. There was something earnest about them, something in that quiet voice—not his own—that was begging, pleading with him. Trying to make him understand.

"We have to get out of here," he whispered in kind. "That's the most important thing. Just concentrate on that. For now."

The voice receded.

"Coding error detected!" the puppet man cried, its voice sharp, unnatural. "Protocols corrupted. Suit shall be extracted and returned to the primary hub for reintegration. You—" it snapped its fingers, as though to a dog "—retrieve."

The doors beneath its feet began to roll. The wooden doors slid down, while strange metal and glass alternatives rose to take their place. Then a creature—that was the only word Kichlan could think of to describe it—appeared. It walked along a path of newly risen metal doors.

Part of it was silver, like Tan's suit. Long and twisted limbs gave it a loping stride, hips too high, back bent so it almost walked on all fours. Neck elongated, back of the head capped in silver.

"Bring him to us," the puppet man said as the rippling doors carried it down, out of sight.

"We have to get out of here," Kichlan said to his own suit. "Quickly. Do whatever you need to do, just get us back to the real world." He crouched, as the creature reared above him. It had a mostly human face, though the lower jaw was twisted so its mouth hung open, and its teeth were wrapped with metal.

And it was familiar. Kichlan knew it. Damn it, he recognised those eyes. That look. "Devich?"

A blink, a frown, lips shuddered, jaw movement. Was it trying to speak?

Kichlan's left hand smoothed, retracted, without a fight. The doors began to dissolve, like water washing away paint. As easily as it had taken him, the darkness and the doors let him go, and he was back at the street corner, leaning against the wall with its old, rusted sign.

Kichlan drew a deep and shuddering breath.

Then behind him, something growled.

15.

The tube was heavy. It pulled at the muscles in my back, and the makeshift straps dug into my shoulders and rubbed at my waist. It sloshed. That motion, perhaps, was the worst part of it. If I wasn't careful my gait started up a movement of silex liquid, a roll inside the tube that knocked my son's small, delicate body repeatedly against the side of the glass. So all I could manage was a tedious shuffle, feet scuffing against the ground.

The ruins stretched into eternity. I couldn't imagine how big the cities of Crust must once have been, to have bones this large. Silence stretched on with the road, never ending, never breaking, smothering me.

I had never felt so alone.

"Wonderful idea, Tanyana," I muttered.

I was glowing again. I wasn't sure how far I had walked before the moon-soft light waving through my silex began to regain its strength. I still had no way of telling the time. But one short rest, and three fully-grown blisters later, it was shining a rainbow into the darkness.

"Step through the door, that'll help. I mean sure, it got you away from the puppet men." I stopped, and slowly bent forward—twisting at the back, bending ungainly at the knees—to rest the base of the tube on the ground. Then I shrugged myself out of the straps, dropped the bag, and sagged to the floor beside them. "But only so you could wander aimlessly across a dying world. Brilliant."

With a sigh, I leaned back, and stared up through the holes in the roof of the ruined house that sheltered us. Shards shone against the torn clouds, and my Flare strengthened in response.

"Lad," I whispered. "Where are you?" Every breath hurt, not just from the weight of my child and the newly formed cracks in my silex, but with fear. Lad had said he was coming back. He had to be. But now, he wouldn't find me waiting.

Something skittered across the roof.

I blinked, and held my breath.

Nothing. I released the breath, began to relax and— there it was again. A shape, dark against the light of distant Shards. It paused half way across a gap in the roof and twisted. Then two lights blinked on. Silex-hazy, one blue, one red. I stared at them, they blinked, rhythmically, and I couldn't help but think of eyes.

I struggled to my feet. The red light blared brighter, and then disappeared as the creature scuttled away, hard feet clinking over tiles and iron and wood, above my head then down a nearby wall.

A shudder wound its way up my spine.

I moved as quickly as I could, heart beating rapidly and hard against my ribs while the Flare pulsed in time. I slung the bag over my shoulder. The tube was difficult to collect. I knelt, began tying the straps around my waist when those two lights—eyes, curse it, they were eyes—reappeared in the corner of the room.

I stood, wrapped arms around the tube, and dragged it with me as I backed away.

"Not yours," I hissed. "You can't have him."

The eyes approached. Slowly bobbing, low to the ground, hesitant.

I couldn't see it, not properly, with its eyes so bright and the world around them so dimly monotone. Only the faint outlines of a shape resolved itself. Six legs, maybe more, segmented and arching like a spider. The eyes were lopsided, the red angling away from the body mass, the blue high and centred. It didn't attack, didn't start waving a gun around and demanding to use me.

"Stop," I whispered, when I could back away no further. Could it hear me? Could it understand? "Get away. I will hurt you, if I have to." I scanned the nearby walls and floor for loose wiring. The only weapon I had.

Then three wide beams of light swept into the building, travelling over cracks in the floor, revealing holes in the walls and finally settling on the spider-creature.

And it was all I could do not to scream.

The creature's legs were metal, black like iron, mottled with rust and clumps of ugly orange fungus. They arched and bobbed on hinges, they rolled and lifted around gears. A body balanced at their centre. Half metal, wires and bulging silex that bled, constantly, a thick and pus-like ooze. The red eye sprung from that side, held out on a metal arm with a rotating hinge.

The other half of that body was human. Or, it had been once. And even worse than that, it had once been a child. At least, a child's head, shoulders and upper torso, fused to the metal and the silex and carried around on those metallic spider legs. A blank face, small mouth hanging open. One eye had been replaced with a hub of blue-glowing silex and countless wires that crawled out over forehead, cheeks and chin before embedding in its skin. The other eye was gone. Just gone. This poor child was so obviously dead, long dead, skin sagging and dry, flesh hollowed out and bones too apparent, too sharp.

The red eye swivelled between me and the beams of light, while the blue silex hub brightened, flickering in an odd pattern. It reminded me of something, but I couldn't place it.

Then three sharp cracks, so loud I pressed hands to my ears, and three tight explosions. Two of the spider creature's legs tore apart; it staggered, almost falling before righting itself, balancing on its remaining four.

"Got it!" A cry from outside the building.

A frightful scream rose from the creature, made all the worse for that dead, open mouth. It scuttled to the wall and climbed at terrible speed, up into the ruined floors above me.

"Not enough to stop it!" another voice shouted.

Three people ran into the building. They carried bright silex hubs in one hand—the source of those beams of light—and guns in the other. When those lights, and the guns, trained on me, they skidded to a halt.

"You—?"

"It's got to be."

"I don't believe it. We actually found her."

I drew myself up. "You can't have him," I said. "And you can't have me. I killed the last two of you that tried to wire me, so get out of here, now. You—you useless piece of shit junkies!"

Stunned silence, and slowly, the lights lowered. I blinked, trying to clear my vision. Two men, one woman, all dressed in dark clothes, faces hidden behind masks. For a moment, we stared at each other.

Then the woman lowered her gun as well, and peeled back her mask. "Junkies?" she snapped. "Listen, we're not—"

The spider-creature dropped from the ceiling. It crashed between us, sharp legs biting deep into cement, red eye swivelling to focus on the woman even as she leapt to the side.

"Replace your mask!" One of her companions shouted. "Quickly, before the Drone sees you!"

She fumbled, dropped her gun, swore as she leapt for it only to send it spinning across the floor.

"Meta, watch out!"

Two more shots rang out, but the spider swerved, skirting them with an agility I would not have believed if I hadn't seen it myself. It ran at the woman—Meta—smashing more cement.

"Too late, it's locked on." She grabbed her gun, rolled to her back and fired, wildly.

Explosions against the ground, close to my feet. One in the wall just behind me, another in the ceiling.

"I'm out!" Meta screamed, finger clicking against a gun that would not fire. "Hit it! *Hit it*!"

But the spider swerved as it ran, eye spinning, the entirety of its dead body-mass pivoting to face me.

"Mother fucker." The two men had split up, dimmed their lights, and crept around the outside of the room, guns trained on the creature. "She's the one the Drone is after."

"That's even worse!" Meta cried. "Fucking shoot it, will you?"

Two more shots, but the Drone was moving again, speeding across the floor toward me, eye bright and hub flickering. One bullet caught it just below the shoulder, splattering blood and rot and tiny pieces of bone. It didn't stop. Another hit metal, but did not penetrate, rather it exploded in a blinding flash of light on the surface of the Drone. Didn't even slow it down.

Then the Drone was in front of me, its terrible face in mine, mouth gaping, eye flashing red and clicking. And I couldn't run, because I was the only thing between it and my son. So as it jabbed a sharp and curious leg at me, as two more bullets took it in the back but made no difference to its long-dead body, I did the only thing I could think of.

I plunged my hand inside the Drone, where skin and metal met in a mess of silex and cables. The Flare inside me surged. My silex wrapped itself around the protruding wires, and connected us.

Like an abandoned building, like a desperate junkie, I flooded it with the strength of my Pionic Flare.

The Drone screamed again, and tried to scramble away. But I grabbed its wires and held on, so all it managed was to drag me with it. I fought to stay on my feet as it reared up, red eye twirling, blue hub pulsing madly.

"It's signalling the Legate." Meta was standing again. She replaced her mask, and caught something small and black that one of her companions threw at her. She opened her gun, the way I had seen Lad open his, and used it to replace the bullets she had spent. "We need to get out of here, fast. More will come."

"The Legate?" I whispered. I thought of satellites and pods and lights in the sky, and braced my feet as strongly against the floor as I could manage. "No. I can't let it do that."

"Damn right we can't," Meta hissed. She pointed her gun at the Drone again.

I couldn't control it, not the same way I had controlled the building's silex systems. But I could still feel inside of it, and it was crowded. Two presences batted against my Flare, as I overrode the weaker energy systems of unthreaded silex. One rattled numbers and random letters at me, a language I couldn't understand. And the other... the other wept. Such a small voice, so lonely and scared.

"It's the child," I gasped.

The Drone was weakening. It sunk to the ground, one leg kicking, the rest going limp. Slowly, I began to understand. My Flare was just too strong. Its internals were old, recycled from dead children and ancient machinery. It simply couldn't contain me. I felt every shattering hub, each wire that snapped, the tiny flames taking root in dry bones. The Drone was telling me things, through our connection. Its primary AI couldn't keep up with the damage I was doing, couldn't repair in time. Secondary processing going offline. Backups engaged. Signal loss. Protocols wiped.

"Whatever you're doing there, just keep it up." Meta approached the Drone, slowly and crouched low. She placed the end of her gun right against the red eye—camera, the Drone told me—and pulled the trigger.

I felt it, as the camera shattered, and flinched back, lifting an involuntary hand to cover my eyes. Silex and shards of metal and glass spilled across the floor, and inside the Drone the child screamed. The second presence faltered, its rambling drowning in a single, high-pitched tone.

"Don't," I gasped. "You're hurting him."

Meta and the two men encircled me. All three removed their masks, and for the first time I could see Meta properly. Her hair was cut very short, so it hugged her head like a tight, curly cap, and was pure white. She didn't seem old enough for hair like that, though her dark eyes were world-weary and suspicious. She had complicated patterns of scar tissue at her temples, with a few lines running down to the peaks of her eyebrows.

"The Drone is a thing," one of the men said. "A very dangerous thing. But not a he." His skin was dark, whites of his eyes stark in his face. His cheeks were heavily scarred by countless, tiny marks, all slightly paler.

"It was once a he," I said. "And still, some of him remains." The boy, I was certain. Kept alive by the silex inside him, even as his body decayed.

It was terrible, unnatural. Something the puppet men might do. The thought filled me with horror. The puppet men were programs, created in this world, twisted when they were rejected and discarded into the veil. But what was this Legate?

"It's summoning more Drones," Meta said. She waved the tip of her gun toward the flickering blue hub. "See that?"

I realised what the hub reminded me of. The Specialist, the head programmer. The way he had touched his temples, and the silex embedded there had flared into life, while screens turned themselves on and words scrawled across them. A form of communication, then, between silex hubs. Like pions carrying messages across a city.

"We need to put it down as quickly as possible," one of them men said. "Then run. Run like hell."

The dead child inside the Drone was afraid. He hurt, he felt the blow of each bullet, the shattering of his legs and puncturing of his body. There was no longer a distinction, in what was left of his mind, between metal and flesh. So even though the program controlled him, the dead boy felt everything it did. Or that was done to it.

"How would you kill him?" I whispered. Death was a strange idea to the boy. He had, after all, been dead for so long, just never allowed to leave. So he feared it, and yearned for it, all at once.

Meta placed her gun against the flashing blue light. "Shot to the silex hub?" She glanced at her companions.

The dark skinned man shook his head. "Not enough. Tried it many times under test conditions. Mother fucker looks dead, but soon as we turn around it'll be up again, ready to stab us in the back."

"Damn it, Adrian, that's not helpful." Meta tapped the steel edge of her gun against crystal. "I thought you were supposed to specialise in Legate tech?"

The third man shrugged. "He does, but that really doesn't make a difference when it comes to Drones. These bastards are built to survive multiple attacks. Every Drone has secondary hubs all over the body, but they're never in the same place. Some as few as six, but I've seen one with twenty. You got to blow them to bits, burn them, chop them up. Even then, I wouldn't turn my back on it. Not ever."

The child whimpered. Death was one thing, but pain was entirely different. He showed me the tracks inside of him, the connections of wire and silex, of flesh and nervous system. I told him I understood, a little, what that was like. I shared images of the suit's wires, wigging in my blood, and the silver drilled into my bones. We understood each other, a little at least. However horrifying and terrifying it was, to understand such a tortured and unnatural creature. To empathise with him.

"But why bother?" the third man continued. Bald, and also scarred, this man seemed to be older than the other two. I wouldn't have felt out of place here, if I'd retained the scars *Grandeur* had given me. I wasn't used to seeing scars on others. A cap, slightly darker than his skin, wrapped around half of his head, and most of the scarring stretched out in cruel lines from beneath it. It appeared to be riveted there. Into the bone. "He didn't say the Legate was after her. And obviously, it is. Not worth it, to my mind. I say we leave her here, and get the fuck out."

"Don't be an idiot, Kasen," Meta snapped, scowled. "We were sent to find her. So we're going to take her back with us."

"There are other ways to extract his cooperation—"

"I said no."

A moment of silence. Kasen frowned, but Adrian nodded. "Meta's right." He crouched beside me, staring intently at my hand and the connections there. "And I'd really like to get a better look at what she's doing here."

"If we're going to do this, we'd better do it fast!" Meta held up a screen, a small version of the ones the programmers worked on. Red dots flashed all over it. "Company's on its way."

"We have to destroy the Drone," Adrian told me. "Do you understand that?" When I didn't answer he stood, and levelled his gun at the Drone's head. "Empty your cartridges, all of them, do as much damage as you can do. It might be enough."

"Wait!" I cried out as the child—inside the Drone, inside of me—wailed.

"We can't—"

"I said wait!" Because I already knew what to do. "I think you should step back."

Inside me, the Flare surged again. The same power I had summoned to destroy a building, but this time with no lights to overload, no heaters to set on fire, no ancient and rotting frame to absorb it all, and fall. So all of the power of the pions rushing through me flowed right into the Drone.

The Flare smashed a multicoloured path through silex, along wires, down metal and up into the dead boy. Crystal shattered, fluid splattered, and a rainbow arched out of the gaps. The metal glowed a fierce red before melting into the concrete, and skin burned. I closed my eyes and leaned away. I felt the fire as though it was coiling through my body too. I listened as the program rattled through its emergency protocols, instructing me to contact the Legate and find the nearest fire escape, before dissolving into more random numbers and letters and a buzzing mess of sound as it collapsed.

The boy was surprised, at first. It didn't hurt as much as he thought it would. In fact, he couldn't feel anything, anymore. And then he was thanking me, and flashing images of the few faces he could remember—that was his brother, there, with the scar on his chin, and the little dog he'd found and cared for and named some long-lost name—and gradually, like an echo, he faded away.

Finally, when nothing remained—nothing but ash and molten metal—and no more presences batted themselves against my light, I withdrew. The connections my silex had made were strong, and the wires had all fused in the heat and sunk into the cracked ground. So I could not even break them, and Meta had to use the butt of her gun to smash the hardened mineral and free my hand.

"What did you do to it?" Adrian asked, as Meta helped me to my feet. I could barely stand. My colours were weak again, and my silex cracked. But so much worse, this time. I hadn't even allowed the last break to heal.

"My Pionic Flare is strong," I gasped. "Too strong for the Drone. I—I overloaded it. I think."

He nodded. "Yes, I can see that. But how? You're, what, carrying a Flare around inside of you?"

I swallowed hard. My neck hurt, and my mouth tasted strange. Like blood, and something else. Something, that if I didn't know better, I would have described as the tingle of silver suit-metal on my tongue. "Yes."

Meta leaned away from me, horrified. I shook my head. "It's isolated," I told her. "Has to eat through me first before it can wander out into your world and destroy you. So while I'm still here, you've got nothing to fear."

Strangely, that didn't seem to reassure her.

"Another little detail he decided not to tell us," Kasen muttered. "This list is getting longer by the moment."

He? Hope flickered within me like my Flare, but I didn't dare let it shine. Not yet. Instead, I turned to Adrian. "Look, I know everything you want to say. I'm impossible, dangerous, all that. So let's not go over that again. She said more Drones are on the way. I suggest, instead of standing around here discussing the obvious, that we leave."

Kasen nodded, "Sounds like the most sensible thing I've heard all day. Apart from the bit where you come with us, that is."

"We have already discussed this," Meta said. "She comes."

"Yes," Adrian said. "We will fulfil our mission. That's what we do, after all."

I held Kasen's gaze. His expression wasn't overtly hostile, rather it was strangely unemotional. I could almost read sarcasm in the slight twist of his lips and the carefully blank look in his eyes. Almost. He reminded me of Natasha, and I immediately promised myself not to trust him. "I'm hardly thrilled with the idea either," I said. "Trust me, if I could keep going alone I would much prefer to do so." I released a deep breath. "But I don't think I have a choice. If more of these Drones are coming, I won't get far, not on my own."

"Well, I can hardly argue with that." Kasen's expression didn't change.

"Great. Now, just two things before we go." I tried leaning away from Meta but still couldn't support my own weight. "First: you're not going to wire us, are you?"

Adrian made a disgusted face. "We're guards, not junkies."

"Good to know." I gestured to the blanket-wrapped tube behind me. "Second: could you carry my bag, please? And my baby?"

16.

Kichlan turned, slowly.

Devich stood behind him. With his limbs lengthened, he had grown impossibly tall, and loomed several heads above Kichlan. But his awkward body was not stable, and he swayed and stumbled, even as he stood in one spot, struggling just to maintain his balance.

"How?" Kichlan whispered.

Devich's mouth moved again. His metallic teeth were too large for his jaw, he drooled as he attempted to speak. "—is—"

Kichlan backed against the street sign. He held up his metal-capped arm, and struggled to extend it into a short, ugly-looking sword. He did a pretty bad job of it too, ending up with something notched, and at an angle. Voices whispered in the back of his head, and his stomach clenched with an exhausted ache.

But Devich did not attack. He just stood, wobbling, drooling and said "—ana? Wh—? Where...is...she?"

Slowly, Kichlan lowered his arm. "Tanyana?"

Devich nodded. He crouched again, back to Kichlan's height and shuffled close, so close that Kichlan could see the lines of silver embedded beneath the skin around his eyes. "What have they done to you?" he gasped.

"—yana!" Devich growled, forced the word out with spittle and a scent like the pion-haze around a metalworks factory. "Where?"

"Gone. She is gone."

"Go—"

"Dead, Devich. Drowned. In the river. Gone." His stomach eased, and suddenly, he was angry. Angry at Devich, this pathetic ghoul of a half-man who had hurt Tan so badly, but now drooled and wobbled in such a twisted, heart-breaking display. Angry at himself, for hating the man so much and feeling so much guilt about it now. Angry at the puppet men who played with them all like dolls. Like puppets.

But most of all, he was angry at Tan. Damn her. Damn her for leaving him to deal with the silver, with the doors and now this. Her ex-lover, the man Kichlan had loathed so righteously, warped into a piteous tool. The fool had played the puppet men's game, and now he was suffering the consequences. They all did.

"Dead?"

"So what are you going to do?" Kichlan advanced, and this time Devich retreated, what was left of his face frozen in disbelief and fear. Fear. What did such a creature have to fear from Kichlan? "Take me to the veche men, will you? Let them experiment on me, the way they have done to you? Is that your new role? Moved on from traitor to pet dog, have you? Fetch, Devich. Retrieve."

But Devich sunk to the ground, at the centre of the ruined street. He pressed his silver-coated stomach to the broken flagstones and shook his head, long neck weaving side to side. "Dead?" He rolled the word, over and over, through his mutilated mouth.

"Go on!" Kichlan stood above him and held out arms. "Take me to them. You hated me, I know that. So you'll love it, I'm sure. Maybe, if you're a good little dog, they'll let you watch."

Devich looked up. He was crying, his tears thick with silver filings. "Dead?"

"Yes!" Kichlan screamed. "She's dead! Can't you understand me? Dead!"

Devich leapt up, knocking Kichlan to the ground. But again, he did not attack. Instead, he tipped back his elongated head, opened his metallic mouth, and howled. Like a creature born from the Other's nightmare, he howled grief into the sky, to echo through the ruins of Movoc-under-Keeper.

"*And still, some of him remains*," Tan's ghost whispered in Kichlan's ear. He leaned back against the broken stone, wrapped a hand around the silver she had given him, and let Devich's animal loss wash over him.

17.

We ran. Down through a complex labyrinth of ruined buildings and into a crumbling sewer.

"Where are we going?" I gasped, struggling to match their pace, fighting even to breathe. "And why does it have to be underground? I'm sick of being underground. I hate sewers." Talking kept my mind off the broken crystal that ground together at every joint, with every hurried step.

Meta led, helping me when I needed it. Kasen carried my child on one shoulder, and I watched his ever step. Adrian carried my bag.

"Where are you taking me?"

Meta paused long enough to check her small dark screen. So many red, flashing dots, and a constant, urgent beeping. "They're closing," she snapped. "We have to hurry."

"Why were you looking for me? How'd you recognise me? Who sent you?"

None of them answered.

Scraping behind us, the clatter of many metal feet and Meta pulled me back into the closest thing to a run that I could manage. I peered behind us, between Kasen and Adrian. Blue lights winked from the darkness. The red of camera lenses. So many of them.

So we ran. Down two more levels, and I realised we weren't in a sewer after all. The channels were almost perfectly round: the floor curved, the ceiling curved, and only the path we were walking—an indent almost halfway up the wall, on both sides, wide enough and only

just high enough for two people to walk side-by-side—
broke up the regularity.

"Do pods fly through here?" I asked, between breaths.

Thunder above us, so many heavy feet in dead flesh and
metal. The screen's warning beep split into a panicking
scream.

"Not any more," Meta answered. I almost couldn't
hear her.

The tunnel opened up to two platforms of cracked,
stained, scorched tiles. The remnants of screens still hung
on the walls, their crystalline surfaces smashed, wires and
silex hanging loose like broken body parts. More stairs
wound up from the centre of one of the platforms and
would have led back to the levels above us, the way we just
came. But a Shard had been built in the middle of them,
and it cast the whole room in bright light.

"The Legate must really want to find you," Adrian said,
close behind me. "Why is that?"

My turn not to answer.

"Doesn't matter," Meta said. "They're too late."

She stopped at a small, metallic door in the tunnel wall.
It was well hidden, almost the same colour as stone, the
same texture, and curved to fit. She tapped an odd beat
against it, one that rang sharply in the closed space. A low
whirring noise started up. Then the door opened, and I
found myself staring at the end of a gun, pointed directly
at my head.

"Put that thing down and get out of my way!" Meta,
still holding my hand, brushed the gun aside and pushed
past its owner. "There are Drones right behind us. Lock
the door and initiate primary defences."

A young man, half of his face and most of his neck
intricately tattooed, saluted. Adrian and Kasen followed
us inside, and the young man tapped on a keyboard to
close the door.

Not fast enough. Just before it closed a segmented,
metallic Drone-leg wedged into the gap. A whir and a cry
and two more legs joined it, together forcing the door open.

"They're here!" The young man shouted, fist mashing at the keyboard.

And the sharp tip of a spider leg pierced him through the stomach. He folded forward, screaming. Three more took him: leg, and neck. This time, he fell in silence.

"I said *initiate primary defences*!" Meta roared and spun us around, as more footsteps and bodies surged up behind us in the tight and dimly lit tunnel.

I caught sight of three dead faces on the other side of the door—two of them were girls, this time, with long, straggly hair—before Meta and Kasen, between them, blasted six shots to heads, torso, legs.

"Away from the entrance!" Adrian grabbed Kasen by the elbow and dragged him back, as Meta retreated, and three of the unseen people fired another half dozen shots, shattering the legs of the closest Drone so it fell in the path of its fellows and tangled their tracks.

"Primary defences initiating!" someone called from behind us.

"Kasen," Meta snapped, "get away from the line!"

Something was happening in the walls of the tunnel. I could feel them warming, hear a great rattling inside them. Then light flashed out of the stonework, through little glass windows, gaps I hadn't even realised where there. What was that, a Flare?

"Kasen!"

A shocked glance at the walls and Kasen dropped his gun, wrapped both hands around the tube he still carried on his shoulder and leapt away from the entrance, knocking into Adrian and almost sending them both sprawling.

For a moment I had a terrible vision of my son falling from his perch on Kasen's shoulder, to smash against the ground. "Other's hell, be careful!"

But Kasen kept his footing, and Adrian clung to him, and together they got out of the way, just in time, as a Flare tore across the entrance to the tunnel. A flash of light, a tear in the air. The light faded and what remained of the Drones collapsed. They were twisted, changed. Skin to stone, metal to stunted roots. Some melted, some bubbled like the surface of a hot mud lake. One fell into countless tiny wiggling creatures that squirmed away. Another dispersed in a cloud of shining dust.

Then the light behind the tunnel walls died. "Clear!" another voice called.

"Get rid of them, and seal the entrance." Meta turned us around and continued into the tunnel. I had to watch my feet to keep my balance, and was glad for the excuse not to meet the curious expressions of more faces, half-hidden in the dim underground. They saluted, and hurried past Meta, careful not to get in her way. "Kasen, Adrian, don't fall behind again. The rest of you, recharge primary and ready secondary. There are more Drones on the way."

"That was a Flare, wasn't it?" I gasped, as she helped me into a pod, so small that the four of us were forced to squeeze against each other just to fit inside. "You used a Pionic Flare to undo the Drones."

"Yes."

A clanking noise above us, and the pod shifted, then dropped. Meta's hands, Kasen's shoulder pressed into mine and Adrian's back up against my face, was all that kept me upright.

"Isn't that dangerous?" I murmured against his tight, dark clothing. Leather, it felt like, but it smelled like poly and ash. "I thought Flares had to be contained in silex. Opening one up like that, you could have killed us all."

"The programmers would like us to believe that, yes," Adrian answered. He vibrated against my cheek as he spoke. "And their Legate masters. But He has taught us the truth. The energy within a Flare can be controlled. To some extent."

Control the pions? But I'd tried that, and it hadn't worked. "He?"

"Adrian," Kasen rumbled, his tone a warning.

"The Hero," Adrian answered anyway.

The Hero?

But then the pod rattled to a stop, its door slid open, and cast all questions from my mind. Meta helped me over the slight step up to a wide platform as I stared, stunned, almost afraid to breathe.

"By all the Other's darkest dreams," I gasped.

For a moment, the light around us flickered, the platform seemed to rattle, and even the stationary pod creaked. Meta and Adrian cast each other alarmed glances, but nothing else moved, the noises eased, and the light steadied, so they relaxed.

Crust had only seemed so empty because most of its inhabitants actually lived underground. A second city spread out in front of me, growing like bright fungus in a wide network of caverns.

The bottom tips of enormous Shards peeked down from the reinforced ceiling, many yards above. Their points were capped with large bird nests of wire, all shining copper in the bright, crystal-filtered light. There must have been scores of them, and they continued off into the distance. Their wires wound long tracks along the ceiling, dotted with silex like dew drops in a spider's web, thinning as individual cables split from the mass to connect to every single building in the place. They reminded me strongly of the bright threads of pions that powered Movoc-under-Keeper, when I had been able to see them.

Two more guards, dressed in black like Meta, Kasen and Adrian, saluted as we disembarked. Behind us, the pod door closed, and it shot back up with a sharp whine and a trail of silver. I craned my neck to watch it go, ignoring the dangerous grinding of silex at my movement. It did not fly free like the pod Lad had used to escape Fulcrum; rather it followed an indented path in the wall similar to the channels I had initially mistaken for sewers. There were dozens more tracks, just like this one, spread out along the wall. Some went straight up, others had bends and turns, one even travelled up the ceiling to follow the path of the wires, further into the cavern. They all stopped at the platform, however, which was riddled with guards, all dressed in black, all carrying guns—of various sizes, I noticed—and all watching me.

"Another programmer, like the last one?" one of the new guards asked Meta, and my heart leapt. Lad?

Meta shook her head. "Not even close."

She helped me along the platform, to a set of stairs that moved on its own, so all we had to do was stand still and the steps carried us down.

"That programmer," I whispered, conscious of the eyes still on me. "Is he alright? You didn't hurt him, did you?"

No answer. Again.

The underground city looked like a smaller replica of the one above. Densely packed buildings—all straight lines, few windows, and flat roofs—rose above thin streets. Planned without an eye for beauty, built out of necessity. Street lamps of silex hubs were dotted between the structures, casting steady blue-tinged light into shadowed nooks where the radiance from the Shards above could not reach. If I could have commanded the pions inside me I would have added order to this place. Patterns. Spaced the lights evenly, smoothed the random rooftop heights, added consistency and design to the materials used. Done something to beautify the wire that connected everything.

It was even hotter than the world above. Heat and humidity clung to my clothes with heavy, wet hands, and slicked over everything with a faintly moist membrane. Faces peered at us, as my guards helped me along the city's tight streets. From open windows, through doorways, or just standing on the side of the street, distracted from the workings of their day-to-day lives. None had the gaunt and hungry look of the junkies that had attacked me. These people looked healthy. Their streets were clean, free of the ash and rot in the world above. There were a lot of people doing the cleaning too, sweeping, or wiping down a thick layer of mould that seemed to be trying to grow on everything.

Despite this, the city felt wrong. The constant unnatural light, and wires and silex hanging everywhere.

The unearthly quiet, and stillness. Where were the sellers shouting out their wares at stalls in wide market places? Where the cafes, the carriages, the constant movement of people rushing between home and work? Could you buy good coffee in this place? Where would you sit to drink it?

Comparing the Movoc-under-Keeper that was to this underground huddle of survivors on an ancient and dying planet might have been a little unfair. But Movoc was my city, it was my yardstick, it was the home all other cities—even those of other worlds—must compare themselves to.

Surviving. That was the difference, wasn't it? In Movoc, the people lived. Here, they merely survived. In safety, yes, free from murderous junkies and horrific Drones. But that was all they could do. Was that what I had done to Movoc-under-Keeper, when I destroyed the puppet men's lair? Would its people now huddle, in their makeshift refugee camps, below hordes of Strikers filling the sky, and just survive? That was the way I imagined the city now, and the way it appeared in my dreams.

"Where are we going?" I whispered, as we travelled deep into the city. The streets were mostly empty, and sound seemed to carry so far.

"To see the bosses," Adrian answered, his voice just as soft as mine.

The bosses lived in a building just the same as the rest that made up this city. That surprised me. No veche-like chambers, nothing grand, not even signs or ornaments to set them apart. What kind of bosses were these, who lived so close to their people? And it certainly wasn't what I had in mind when Lad had talked of gangs of criminals selling drugs to a fearful populace. I thought Crust was a hard teacher. Where were these so-called lessons?

Two more guards waited at the door to the bosses' building. They saluted Meta, who saluted back, and asked, "Do you have word of the Drone attack?"

Neither of these guards—a woman, her skin as dark as Adrian's, and another young man—looked at me. They held Meta's gaze and stood straight, arms tight by their sides and guns held loose, but ready, fingers only inches from triggers.

"Yes, ma'am, just got a call now. Bounceback shows the tunnels are swarming with them. A hundred, at least. That's got to be most of the local nest. So far, the outer doors are holding. Primary has recharged and secondary is ready. But if they find a way in…" He did not finish his sentence.

Meta nodded, and guided us into the building.

"The fuckers followed you," she muttered. "You led them right down here. And, damn me, we helped."

I wondered who she was most angry with, me, or herself. I figured it was probably me. "What will happen if they get past the door and that Flare you've set up? Will they come down here? Kill everyone else while they look for me?"

Inside, the building was dark, only a few silex lights were fitted to the ceiling. The walls were bare, the floor created from a strange mix of recycled parts—old floorboards, slats, headboards, windowpanes. Built from the bones of Crust.

"First, they'd have to make it all this way." Adrian flashed me a grin, teeth bright. "And that's not easy. There are more barriers than the primary and secondary defence. And the very last resort, we blow the pod tracks and seal the city in. Drastic, dangerous. But if we have to, the Hero will make the call."

The Hero, again.

"And even then," Meta continued. "Killing is not a Drone's primary function." We ascended two flights of stairs. "They're designed for recon, more than anything else. Snap pictures of us, of the defences, of the numbers sheltering here and the best ways to get in and out. Then the Legate will send something else, probably Wasps. Either to kill or capture. You can never tell."

I thought of the undead children carried around on metallic spider legs. Capture, perhaps, was not the best option.

We came to a halt at a door. Words were etched into the wood. They looked similar to the programmers' symbols—though they did not glow red on a silex screen. Meta knocked, and a voice called from within.

It was cooler inside the room. Condensation dripped from a small box in the ceiling. It added a faint haze to the edges of blue silex lights, and countless, tiny drops of moisture clung to a glowing screen embedded in a tabletop. The room was simple. No windows, the table in the centre, padded chairs like couches against the walls. Diagrams and maps hung above the chairs, some such a complicated mess of fine lining in slightly different colours that I doubted anyone could read them.

Three men, one woman, turned to us as we entered. And one of them was Lad.

"Lad!" I tore myself from Meta's support and tried to run to him, but my leg gave way and I would have smashed more silex against the floorboards if he had not already launched himself forward and caught me, just above the ground.

"Oh Tan!" He pressed his face against my hair and held me tight, for a moment, so tight I feared for the silex but I simply did not care enough to try and dislodge him. "Tan," he whispered against me. "I tried—I'm so sorry. I tried to look after you." He drew two more deeply hitching breaths, and I felt the wetness of his tears, before he controlled his words and his fragmented mind, and helped me stand.

He studied me in the cool, hazy light, expression growing horrified. "Other's hell, what happened to you?"

For a moment, the screen flickered. A surge in the energy that powered this place?

Fear, concern, and guilt played across Lad's face. He had tried, he always tried, to do what his brother had asked of him, and look after me. Even beyond death. Even in another world. At least it hadn't killed him. Not this time.

"I had to fight two junkies," I said. "They tried to wire me, but I killed them. I wasn't sure what to do next, so we ran, but a Drone found us. I killed it too. Then Meta, Kasen and Adrian here brought me underground. But the Drones have followed."

A moment of stunned silence, then Lad shook his head, a smile slowly spreading across his face, brushing the guilt and the fear away like sunlight after a hard night.

"And here I was, worried about you." He placed a hand against my cheek. "Typical." His hand tightened. What was that look, pride? "Although—" a frown, and the worry came back so quickly "—you've done some significant damage to your silex in the process."

"I know." But Lad was here, now. He would fix me, wouldn't he? Was it unfair, to rely on him so much? This wasn't Half a Lad, this was a whole one. And he was strong. Perhaps he could take the weight this time. "I brought the silex, it's in the bag. Adrian has it. But there's hardly any tubes left—"

"Ahem." One of the bosses made a noise as though he was clearing his throat, and I jumped. I'd forgotten they were there.

I glanced their way. Both men were heavily bearded, faces lined. The woman seemed the oldest of the lot. She stooped, her hair was long, plaited and grey, but her eyes were sharp. And all three of them watched me with a disturbing intensity.

"Meta," the woman said. "Report, please."

Meta—red in the face and glaring at me, furious—began describing the Drone attack. I leaned close to Lad. He wrapped an arm around my waist, careful with the silex and my tender skin, but strong. It reminded me of Kichlan.

"What's going on?" I whispered in Lad's ear, as quietly as I could manage. "Are these the gangs you were talking about? Have you been making implants for them?"

Meta increased the volume of her report, and tightened her hands into fists by her side.

Lad shook his head, the movement barely perceptible. "Not quite." His voice was little more than air and warmth against my ear. "It seems Crust has changed a lot since I was a child."

"Thank you, that will do," the woman cut Meta off, and I was subjected to another of her furious stares. "We are aware of the situation in the tunnels."

Those sharp eyes met mine, and I lifted my chin.

"So, you are the reason this programmer would risk a drop to Crust?"

"She—she is Tan," Lad said, his voice strained between the programmer and the Half. All three bosses watched him, as intent as birds of prey. "I look after her."

"I can see that." The old woman ran her fingers over the tabletop screen. Its light strengthened, and an image wavered on the ceiling directly above it. More red dots, more line drawings. "And now the Legate is after you too. Curious, to say the least."

I said nothing. It seemed the safest thing to do.

"None of that matters," Lad said. "Tan's silex is severely damaged. I need to repair it. I've already begun my half of the bargain. Now I need you to stick to yours."

I frowned at him. "What bargain?"

"Not now—"

"No." I leaned back from him. "What have you agreed to?"

The bosses did not try to intervene. I had the strangest sensation that they learned far more about us than we would like, with every word we said.

He sighed, and released me. "It seems I'm not as Crust-savvy as I thought I was."

I lifted an eyebrow at him. "What does that mean?"

"The gangs I remember from my childhood are gone. I was ten years old when the Legate removed me from Crust, and gave me to the programmers, but I was much older than my years—Crust does that to a boy. I'd already started manufacturing implants for a local gang. It's not that hard, really. You just need to steal and recycle some good hardware, wire and reprogram the silex, and weave the lot with an artificial nerve matrix. I could even perform some of the minor surgery required to insert them. That's what alerted the Legate to my potential, that's why I was singled out, rescued from what promised to be a short, violent life on Crust, and sent to Fulcrum."

I nodded. It didn't surprise me. Lad was a good Half. The best of them. Of course he was skilled here too.

"Given the years I spent in training, and then how long his body lay in stasis while I was Lad on the other side, that was close to fifty years ago. I assumed I could just pick up where I left off, only this time with my knowledge as a programmer on my side."

"But things have changed," I said.

"The junkie I killed, I thought he was proof enough that things were just the same, but it turns out they're a dying breed. A few more years, and they'll be gone. So apparently, there just isn't the demand for wiring implants."

"The Hero freed us from the drug," one of the male bosses said. His skin was dark, but his beard almost white. "When he returned, he showed us just how the Legate was benefitting from a population of mindless junkies, easy to control, quick to subdue, and compliant. It is remarkable what we have been able to achieve since then, with clear minds and a firm desire for freedom."

"I didn't really believe it," Lad said. "That is, until I saw Core."

For a moment, he glanced back over his shoulder to a single, thin window in the wall. I couldn't see much out of it, only the continuation of grey stone and constant light.

"Core?" I asked.

"This underground city. And this, this is not from my childhood. Pods and guards and healthy people living in peace. Resistance against the Legate—who would even try such a thing? The bosses of Core do not want me to make drugs for them, Tan, like I assumed they would."

I crossed my arms, wincing as loose silex clinked. "What do they want you to do?"

"They want me to help them grow. Strengthen their hubs, and add more Shards to the network. Apparently, Cores like this are appearing all over Crust. Well, under it. With enough manpower—and silex strength—the goal is to connect them all, to create a vast civilisation away from the Legate's control. My help, as a programmer, could make a real difference. That's why they couldn't just let me leave. They need my help."

"A programmer who has defected from the Legate is a true prize now, indeed," the boss said. "Aladio here has agreed to help us continue our work. Strengthen the connections that supply our power, generate our defences, and keep us alive. And he will do so in exchange for silex to sustain you."

"We were not even sure you were real," the old woman said. "What programmer would defect in the first place, then feed us such a fanciful tale? Was he a spy, was he the Legate's clumsy way of attempting to infiltrate us? But here you are. Proof that we can trust this programmer. Proof that the tale he told us is true."

"But you have brought Drones on your tail," the dark-skinned boss continued. "Many more than have ever made their way to our doorstep before, to threaten us."

"So we need to decide, what shall we do with you?" With a brush of her fingers, the old woman dismissed the projection on the ceiling. "Are the skills of a programmer worth the attention of the Legate?"

"If you'll excuse me, ma'am, sirs," Meta interrupted. "That doesn't even take this into account." She gestured to Kasen. And my heart dropped, as he placed the tube on the table and drew my blankets from it.

"No," I whispered, as the bosses recoiled, then leaned close to peer at my son. He looked unsettled, the liquid silex churned by all the movement. And, if it was possible, he had grown again. Lad clutched at my elbow as I jerked forward, kept me close to his side.

"Don't do anything stupid," he hissed in my ear.

"But—"

"Hero or no supposed Hero, these people are still gang bosses. We need to tread carefully."

I swallowed down a fearful lump rising from my stomach. "Who is this Hero they keep talking about?"

Lad shook his head, and didn't answer.

The old woman placed her hand against the tube, and I told myself, over and over, that my son was safe in there. Far safer than out here.

"I did not rescue him from the programmers to give him up again," I said, as quietly as I could. "I will do whatever it takes to keep him with me, and safe."

"Not yet," Lad breathed back. "Not while you're in this state."

"What is it?" The old woman asked.

"My child," I answered. "*He* is my son."

The old woman held my gaze for a long, silent stretch. "I realise we have not introduced ourselves to you," she said, finally. "I am Leola. Beside me—" she nodded to the dark skinned man "—is Adeodatus. And on the other side, Urvan. We are the Hero's three chosen of Core-1 West. You, we know as Tan."

"Tanyana," I corrected her.

She nodded. "And your programmer is Aladio."

Lad did not correct them.

"You have brought us quite a conundrum, Tanyana," Urvan said. "Aladio is invaluable, you are a liability. So, what shall we do? Do we allow you to stay here, threatening our people and our work all the while? For twenty years Core-1 West has held back the Legate's forces, but now you are bringing a hive down on our heads. Should we simply cast you back up to Crust, giving the Legate what it wants to ensure our own safety? That would mean forfeiting the services of the only programmer ever to defect from the Legate, because he refuses to be separated from you." He paused, and her attention turned to Lad. "But, of course, that assumes we will co-operate with the programmer's conditions, rather than impose our own will on his."

I glanced at Lad. He had paled.

That was enough to tell me I wasn't particularly interested in any of their options.

"Actually." I pulled myself from Lad's grip, walked to the centre of the room and beside my son's tube. "I think it's time you listened to me." I drew strength from his closeness, and placed a casual hand on the tabletop beside him. The silex screen was only inches from my fingertips. My Flare throbbed, as though in readiness.

"These all sound like grand plans you and your *Hero* have conceived. But no matter what you do, this Core of yours will fall. With the rest of your world. And the rest of mine."

Heavy silence. Leola glanced at Lad. "What is she talking about?"

He hesitated. "I—"

"*She*," I snapped, "is right here, speaking to you. Why don't you try that question on me instead?"

Leola hardly blinked. "Alright, Tanyana. What are you talking about?"

"We are not from this world," I said. Apart from Meta's raised eyebrows no one in the room made any response. Not quite what I had expected. "My child and I crossed through the veil, we came from the light world, the opposite world, on the other side. Lad will confirm this, if you don't believe me."

They did not ask, and he did not speak. Still, I continued.

"On the other side of the veil is a powerful force, creatures accidentally created by the programmers themselves. They mean to tear down the veil. An act that would destroy both worlds. This is what we need to stop. We need to—" this was the problem, wasn't it? I still didn't have an answer "—do something. The programmers wouldn't listen to me, but you, you must understand! The programmers, the Legate, they are not as infallible as they think—"

"Tan." Lad stood, approached me, and rested a calming hand on my shoulder. "Stop."

The bosses' watched me, expressions unchanged. "Do you hear yourself, Tanyana?" Leola asked. "This sounds like madness."

Not this again!

I shook off Lad's touch, refusing to be defeated. "Why won't you listen to me?"

"Because all your talk about invisible and impossible threats don't stand up against a real and present danger," Lad said. "What are the puppet men, compared to the who knows how many Drones doing everything in their unnatural power to get in?"

"Three hundred in the tunnels," Adrian interrupted. "At last bounceback."

"It was the same with the programmers," Lad continued. "What were the puppet men to them, compared to the Guardian's failure, and Halves waking up?"

And that was what I had always come up against. I could warn and fuss about doors and Keepers and puppet men until I ran out of breath, but to the pion-binders of my world, and even my debris collectors, those threats had been unreal. They were not failing pion systems, or threatened veche inspections, or fear for the life of a brother.

But that didn't make them any less real.

"I don't care." I glared at Leola. "If you will not help me, then do not try and stop me. Lad and I will leave. We have work to do."

Meta laughed, dry and without humour. "Leave? And how, exactly, do you plan to get through the Legate's forces?"

I tightened my hand into a fist. My light strengthened, suddenly bright, suddenly sharp, and extended the cracks across my wrist. Liquid silex bubbled free.

"I am not weak here," I whispered.

As the bosses turned to each other, murmuring, Lad shuffled over to a seat against the wall. "That was exactly the kind of stupid thing I told you not to say," he muttered.

My silex crept across the table. It brushed the screen, set its crystalline surface rippling, then dipped inside. It bonded to the tangle of wire and silex hub beneath it, and connected me to the entire city.

Where the rundown building had been empty, the city was full. The power of multiple Shards fed through a complex and expansive series of bonds, swept and eddied through Core like the sea. But they did not push against me, like the program and the memories of a dead child had done from within the Drone. Rather, they embraced me. I sunk down inside their warm weight like I was home, with old friends. I was one with so much power that it truly did take a city—with all its lights and pods and heating and defences and more, stretching further and further—to contain it all.

Core-1 West was eager to please. It gave me a guided tour; in an instant I touched every building and saw flashes of the lives lived inside. A young boy, sleeping with the soft glow of a small hub to keep him company. A woman who had been rescued from Crust, sitting alone in a room much like Lad's, holding her knees and rocking herself. She traced the scars along the inside of her arms, where her implant has been removed. I surged through Shards, each like a vortex with a Flare pulsing and pulling within them. I slid down thick fibres drilled to the cavern walls, stretching far into the earth, where houses had not yet been built and large machines chipped away at the rock to create enough space for them. I even rode the machines, for the smallest of moments, and was introduced to the programs that ran them.

Core was very obliging—even though it was nothing but light and code. It was difficult at times to remember that.

"I think that decides us," Urvan was saying. I could barely hear him. Rather, I was listening to the groan of rock and the scratching of Drone feet, as the primary defence was readied a third time. Such a powerful Flare, I was almost swept away in it. But strangely, I was stronger. I was, after all, a part of the light world itself, not merely a tear in realities waiting to be patched up. I was a constant weakening; I was an open door.

Core-1 West deferred to me like an older sibling. It gave the city over to me. All I had to do was ask, and everything would stop.

"She's not worth keeping here."

Adeodatus nodded. "The programmer, however, must remain."

Lad surged back to his feet. "No, not without Tan!"

"Meta," Leolas ignored him. "Restrain the programmer. Adrian and Kasen will escort Tanyana back to the surface. Give her to the Drones, then seal that passage. We shall never use it again."

"No, you can't!" Lad lurched forward. "I won't co-operate! You do this and I'll sabotage your whole fucking city the first chance I get."

Meta drew her gun, advanced slowly. "Let's just all stay calm." Kasen and Adrian skirted around the corners of the room. "No more threats."

"You fire that at Tan and we're all doomed!" Lad edged toward me. "And that's not a threat, that's a fact."

I blinked, tore myself away from the gathering primary defences, and glanced between them. "Three hundred and twenty one, to be precise," I said.

Everyone paused. The gun in Meta's hand shook, "What?"

"Three hundred and twenty one Drones in the tunnels above, not three hundred." I peered up at the ceiling. "I can feel them through the silex. Every scratch of their metallic claws. Core-1 West feels them, and so can I."

"Ma'am," Adrian hissed. "Look at her hand. Just like the Drone!"

"There." Meta—gun still trained on Lad—glanced over her shoulder to the bosses. "She's wired. Did the same thing to the Drone to destroy it."

Adrian hurried over to the table, one hand on the gun sheathed at his hip. "We cannot allow her to do it to Core!"

Meta pointed her weapon at my head.

Lad had finally come close enough to see my hand. "I've told you, shoot her and—" he paused. "Other's fiery hell Tan, what have you done?"

And something rattled through the city's entire silex network. A shiver, like the quivering of a great body, finally resolving itself in a flicker of light on the screen and a spasm of the abused muscles and nerves along my arm.

"I am connected to Core-1 West," I said. I met Meta's worried gaze. "I'd put that gun down, if I were you." And glanced at Adrian. "And you can just stay where you are."

"Tan?" Lad whispered, close behind me. "You—you wired yourself to the city's central network."

"I did indeed," I said, with a grin. "And Core is very obliging. If I ask her to play with the lights, she will. If I ask her to drop her defences against the Drones, she will. Anything at all, and she will help me. Because we are connected, Core and I. So I think it's about time you really did start listening to me, don't you?"

"The suit." Lad was rubbing his forehead. "It's the suit. The suit was debris, right? And debris is actually a manifestation of the Keeper, who is really the Guardian program. Which means the suit itself was a program, and the more of you it consumed the more of a program you became. You really were just like the Keeper, Tan. But the difference is that you have an extremely unstable Pionic Flare powering you. The code inside you is using the strength of your Flare to override any network your silex is connected to. So when you connect to a hub like Core, for example, your code replicates itself, invades and dominates the old programming. You're a fucking virus, Tan! A true, old fashioned virus."

"Terrific." I didn't think it really mattered what I was, as long as it worked. "Whatever that means."

Lad lowered his hand, grinning now. "I'd say this changes the power dynamic rather drastically, wouldn't you?"

I nodded. "You heard him," I said to the three bosses. "You might even have understood some of that. Either way, you're going to let us out of here. Not the way we came in, not into the claws of three hundred and twenty one Drones. There are other passageways, I can feel them. I'll call my own pod, if I have to. But I'd rather you escort us, quietly and politely, with my child and as much silex and baths as we can carry. You will not try to stop us, you will not try to follow us. And if you don't help us,

I'll overload every one of the thousands of hubs and wires that keeps this place alive. I'll paralyse you, and leave you to the Legate."

"You try anything," Meta growled, "and I'll blow you into tiny pieces. Pionic Flare or none."

"Wait—" Lad tried.

"Meta, lower your weapon," Urvan snapped.

I dipped deeper into the silex network; I gathered the strength in me and shone, brightly, in her eyes. "Do not doubt me, Other curse you."

This time, the ripple was so strong the entire city felt it. The building shook, the lights died before flaring into life again, and great groans like an awakening giant echoed through the cave system.

"What was that?" Meta lifted her gun, spun, staring around the room. "The defences? Adrian, get me bounceback now—"

"It didn't come from them." Adrian was already tapping at his red-dot-riddled screen. "We've got reports coming in from all over Core. Hubs are overloading— lower east quarter has gone dark, southern pods three to eight have halted, all excavation work has stopped. I don't know what this means. Is it a surge? Not getting any unusual readings from any of the Shards—running backup diagnostic just to be sure. A freeforming Flare? Can't be. None of the alarms have been tripped, and it doesn't seem to be isolated in any quarter."

Lad gripped my shoulder. "Tan, was that you?"

"No." There was something else in Core-1 West's silex network with me. Why hadn't I felt it there before? Was it a program? Surely not another dead child? But it was not fighting me, not pushing or weeping. In fact, it felt so much like the rest of the network, as it quested around my presence, touching softly, investigating, that I was barely certain it was actually there.

The screen started glowing around my hand and silex threads. It projected a solid-looking mesh of light into the open space above it, and all the way up against the ceiling.

I leaned back as it travelled along my arm in a faintly warm brush of light. "What—"

"The Hero calls on us," Leola breathed. As one, the three bosses and their guards dropped to one knee.

A face resolved itself in the light projected against the ceiling. It looked odd, proportions strange. Eyes too big, nose too thin, lips full and cheekbones high. It could have been a young man, could have been, but wasn't quite. The light from the screen gave its skin a faint bluish, almost silver tinge.

"That's a composite," Lad whispered in my ear. "An image created with code. Not a real person."

Those too-big eyes scanned the room, and settled on me. Their pupils shone, and the thick lips stretched in a wide smile.

"Other," I cursed. That unreal face reminded me of the puppet men.

"Other?" When the Hero spoke, his voice reverberated not only around the room, but through my silex connection as well. Through the entire network of Core-1 West itself. And I knew, instantly, that he was the presence I had felt. "It's been a very, very long time since anyone has called me that."

18.

"I told you to get away from me!" Kichlan threw rubble at what was left of Devich.

He dodged easily, silver body bending with unnatural fluidity, too fast for Kichlan to ever hit him. "Smell—" he garbled. "Tan—na. You smell. Her." His too-wide green eyes were trusting, and strangely empty.

Kichlan cursed himself, because that look reminded him of Lad. It sickened him, and broke his heart. "Damn you," he hissed. He turned his back on the creature, and kept walking.

Doors flickered at the edge of his vision. Devich danced through them, weaving in and out of reality. Following, as he had for days.

The suit whispered information Kichlan didn't really want to know. Devich's condition was not a punishment, not in the human sense of the word. The puppet men did not engage in such things. He was just another experiment, an attempt to more fully integrate the suit's program with human neural networks. Its influence went far deeper than the obvious physical manifestations. There was suit metal in Devich's brain, usurping and conducting his electronic pulses.

Kichlan didn't fully understand it all. It came in flashes.

<*An attempt to reverse the process that turns programmers into Halves, by extracting and sending consciousness in the opposite direction, across the veil. So far unsuccessful. Damage done to Devich's processing*

power has resulted in reduced usefulness. Subject has become unstable>

Suddenly clear, like a voice murmuring in his ear, then dissolving back into meaningless numbers and nonsensical words. This was, apparently, a language known as code. The suit was surprised Kichlan couldn't understand it.

"Why are you telling me this?" Kichlan hissed, rubbing at his eyes, his temples. His head was throbbing, over-full with voices and knowledge that did not belong.

<Because we are connected. Extraction and reintegration is death. I do not want that either. We must learn to live together>

Kichlan gritted his teeth. He felt crowded. "Focus," he whispered. "Get control."

<No time to fight me. Something is coming, do you feel it? Searching for us>

Kichlan took a deep breath. "What? What's coming?"

Devich reared out of the flickering doors and grabbed him, elongated silver fingers digging into his waist and shoulder, and dragged him back. "Move!"

Three Mob spilled out of the ruined door of an apartment block. Wounded and exhausted, one unconscious with a dragon weapon biting at his shoulder. Doors hugged their pion-powered bodies and the unnatural strength of their weapon like harassing crows.

A silver man crashed through the building after them. Wrapped in suit metal, just like Tan had been, not twisted and wrong like Devich but strong. A weapon. He sent a sharp pike singing from his right hand to spear through the Mob closest to him. It crunched through reinforced armour, skin, muscles and bone, to embed itself into stones and cracked cement.

Devich tugged at him, "Go—go—"

But Kichlan couldn't move. Tension coursed through him, the fire of torn metal, code spilling and screaming in its wake.

The Mob thrashed, wrapped his hands around the metal and fought to free himself. But no pion-strength could withstand the suit, and the man bled to death all the faster for his struggle, feet kicking, head smacking, hands scraping.

As he died, his fellow tore the dragon weapon from the unconscious Mob and set it up on his own shoulder. He stood, staggering and weak, but still growled as the dragon drew its deadly and fiercely bright breath, "Other take you!"

A door snapped into place, solid and firm, where the Mob stood. For an instant, that was all Kichlan could see—weakening wood and rusted handle—then just as suddenly, the Mob was back, and he fired his dragon breath straight at the silver soldier.

Devich leapt on Kichlan's back, forcing him to the ground as light and heat and power rolled across the street. Unable to breathe, Kichlan wavered between street and darkness, between stones and doors. And somewhere close, yet distant at the same time, a puppet man crouched down and stared at him with one mould-coloured eye.

"Faulty programming?"

The dragon's attack slowly died, and Devich released him. Kichlan sucked a desperate, deep breath.

"How did he escape us so easily? No matter. He is not the only weapon at our command."

The real world looked scorched as Devich hauled Kichlan to his feet. Street and ruined building were scarred; cement collapsed into water and sand, and a great sinkhole buckled into darkness with a rumbling rush, a few feet away.

But the silver soldier still stood. And the Mob, spent, fell forward, face in the mud. It was a suit, after all. It was made of debris, and had no pion-bonds to destroy. The dragons were useless against it.

How many of these suited weapons had the veche created?

<One dozen in current engagement. Another three under development>

Two more spears of silver—one right hand, one left—and both Mobs died. Faster this time, in a shower of blood and bone, their pion-bindings already weakened.

Then the soldier turned towards Kichlan.

Just like Aleksey, not all of this soldier's face was encased in silver. A strip of blue-tinged glass wrapped around his eyes, so that Kichlan could not even tell their colour.

<That way, he cannot not see the doors. That was the mistake they made with Miss Vladha. She saw too much and could not be controlled>

Kichlan tried to shake his head. He didn't care about any of this. He didn't need to know what the puppet men were doing to Devich, to their new weapons, or even what they had done to Tan. He just needed to move.

A slight flex of his ankles and knees, and the soldier leapt cleanly over the bodies and the mud. Devich drew back further, dragging Kichlan with him, as the soldier advanced, steadily.

"Go," Devich hissed, slobbering onto Kichlan's shoulder. "Go, go, go."

"You will come with me," the soldier said. His voice was muted, confined behind silver. "Both of you." He lifted a hand, and silver chains rolled from his wrist.

Devich leaped back from the chains, twisting and ducking much faster than his mutilated form should allow. Kichlan couldn't do anything of the kind. Silver wrapped around his feet, and pulled his legs out from under him. Chains around his wrist, waist, neck.

<Engaging countermeasures>

"No!" Kichlan croaked through the pressure to his windpipe. "No, you're not in control. I am!"

A great pause, all the different parts of him uncertain, waiting. Didn't he want to fight back?

"I do." He tried to swallow, couldn't quite manage it. "And we will."

Code whispered in his ears. The suit, not sure what was going on.

"This is my body." Kichlan flexed the cap on his left elbow. The suit slid free slowly, calmly. "My suit." It spun a long, sharp-edged whip coiling like a snake. "I will do this."

And the voices within him eased.

Kichlan lashed out, slicing through all the chains that held him, his suit fine and utterly precise. The silver soldier gasped, and stumbled back. He withdrew his shattered suit, hands lifted, while the pieces Kichlan had broken from him dissolved into dark particles of debris, and floated free.

Devich appeared by his side and helped Kichlan stand. "Smell," Devich slobbered his words. Kichlan gripped the creature's shoulder, using his strength to balance the weight and the movement travelling in spasms up his left arm. "Like Tanya—" he drooled, spat it away in frustration "—her. So much."

"Enough." The soldier recovered. "I will take you myself." He launched forward, hands outstretched, his strength and speed the suit's strength and speed.

Devich, with a growl, leapt from the ground and met the soldier mid-air. Kichlan wavered, but kept himself upright. Metal against metal, silver bodies thrashing as they fell. Devich landed on top, and smacked his silver fists against the soldier's silver face. The glass across his eyes cracked, and the man screamed. But spikes shot up from his torso, plunged into Devich's chest and threw him back.

"Don't let him start absorbing you!" Kichlan roared. He had seen Aleksey tear away parts of Tan's suit and grow strong on them. And even though this creature was Devich—Devich whom he hated, loathed—it was still Devich who had helped him, who had not given him over to the puppet men. He did not want the man-creature to die and leave him all alone. Again. "Get those spikes out of you, now!"

Devich seemed to understand. He twisted—elastic again, like a cat—and tore himself from the soldier's suit.

"Stay down!" Kichlan snapped, and split his whip in two. One part wrapped around the soldier like rope, binding him and holding him down. The other slid inside the man's metal. Kichlan felt the contact like a shock. Suddenly he was sharing his already-crowded body with part of the soldier too: he could sense the man's confusion, his fear, his sweat and rapid heartbeat.

<Please confirm protocol. Do you wish to reprogram and amalgamate existing code?>

He didn't understand.

<We can absorb this soldier, kill him, and take his strength. Do you wish to?>

Kichlan bit his lip against the urge, the oh-so-strong urge to give in, and do just that. But he didn't need the suit to get any stronger. He was already having trouble telling his own mind and thoughts and feelings from the voices drilled deeper than his bones.

So he spat, "No!"

<Then what is the new protocol?>

"Destroy it, but don't absorb it. Turn it back into debris." He glanced at the grains floating aimlessly down the street, all that was left of the soldier's chains. "Like that!"

A moment of stillness, a thinking too deep inside the silver for him to hear.

<Confirmed>

His whip slid into a hook, many hooks, all embedded in the soldier's metal, and began stripping it away. Slice by slice, flinging the pieces it cut away into the street like rubbish, where they dissolved into debris and floated away. The man screamed—Kichlan felt the sound rattling in his head and deep into the muscles of his left shoulder—and his suit fought back. Spears and grasping hands and sharp knives rose all over his body. So Kichlan sent more whips to hold the man still, and severed everything he tried.

Somewhere behind the voices crowding his mind Kichlan thought of the puppet men's chair, and what it felt like, pinned there, while their debris tore him apart, one small piece at a time.

The soldier wore plain, black clothes beneath his silver suit. They looked just like the ones Kichlan was still wearing, beneath his filthy garments. The strong, tightly boned material of a debris collector's uniform.

As the last of the suit was flung to the street and the man's constant screaming faded to a choking, hiccupping sob, Devich darted in. Kichlan withdrew, the sudden imbalance sending him to one knee. Devich's silver fingers tore the rest of the soldier apart—flesh and blood and silver-flecked bone—in a terrifying predator frenzy. When nothing but meat and placid debris grains remained, Devich fell to his side, and lay beside the dead man. He panted, keening softly. Kichlan gave in to the weight of his suited elbow, sagged against the cracked street and gagged an empty stomach onto the stones.

What had they done?

"Other's darkest dreams," a voice behind them gasped.

Devich flipped onto all fours, blood-soaked and growling. Kichlan spun, still crouching.

Natasha stood behind them. Natasha bloodied, her face bruised and riddled with cuts, one arm splintered and wrapped against her chest. She leaned against a building wall, a single blade between two fingers, her right leg twisted at a disturbing angle.

"You killed it." Her eyes darted between Kichlan and Devich. She slipped down the wall to lie in a weakened heap on the street. "How did you kill it?"

19.

The Hero's false grin broadened in the stunned silence. "The Other?" I whispered, and for a moment I knew true panic. The Other was the oldest threat. He was darkness and fear and pain. Worse than the puppet men, more terrible than bosses or programmers. He was death, made flesh. Only the Keeper could protect us from him, and the Keeper was gone.

We were doomed. All of us. We would die here in this underground city and nothing—

Clarity was slow in coming. I took several deep breaths, forced down the panic. The Keeper was not what we had once believed him to be. And here, on another world, would I allow a face on a screen to terrify me simply because it called itself the Other?

"That's good," the Hero said. "This will be easier if I don't have to coax you down from the proverbial trees."

"The light world's Other is the dark world's Hero," Lad said, behind me, voice heavy.

I didn't know what to say. What do you say to the embodiment of all evil?

Lad stepped closer to the table and ran his fingers beside the silex screen. "How is this possible?" he hissed. "You should be dead."

The Hero's face dimmed, momentarily. "And you are?" There was anger, tightly controlled, behind that voice.

"A programmer—" Leola began, but I interrupted.

"A Half," I said, instead. "Do you know what that means?"

A thoughtful look crossed the Hero's face. It was strange to watch his expressions change. They altered instantly, as though he flicked a switch, swapping emotions as suddenly as turning on a light. Perhaps they were false too, as artificial as his visage?

"Guardian's little helpers," he said, after a moment. "Sent across the veil to aid the program. Poor replacements for me, and the work I was doing." Another smile, but still, I could feel anger. Connected to the silex, as I was, the Hero could not hide his true feelings from me.

Lad's hand crept slowly across the tabletop to rest on my wrist, just above the cracking mineral mass. I glanced at him. His eyes held a silent warning, his expression worried, almost fearful. It tightened a low knot in my stomach.

"Listen to me, Tanyana," the Hero continued. "Listen and do not be afraid. Everything you have heard about the *Other*—" hatred swamped the network when he said that word "—is a lie. I was a Hero first, and I still am."

Lad's hold on me tightened.

"I was the first poor fool cast into the veil," the Hero continued. "Sacrificed to protect two worlds."

"I don't understand." I glanced between Lad and the glowing false face.

"The Hero was the first programmer to be uploaded to the veil," Lad finally answered.

"So the Hero is just like you?"

Another pause. "Actually, more like the Keeper. I was a Half, right Tan? Half here, only Half there. But thousands of years ago the early programmers did not understand the risks of crossing the veil, and were not able to follow the same precautions as we do. The Hero offered himself up, and they sent him into the veil. All of him. They didn't replicate and translate the firing of his neurons into code, the way they did to me. They were not careful about how much of him, and what parts of him, were sent. They—" he swallowed, hard "—they embedded silex in his brain and used it to draw all his mental processes into the veil.

I'm not sure if I can explain it to you properly. They took out his mind, Tan, turned it into light and uploaded it all to the veil. All that remained was his body, his brain a ruined mess of grey matter and crystal shards, his flesh an empty shell, lifeless and decaying. He sacrificed himself, but he gave us a presence within the veil. He kept it strong, monitored the movement of particles and alerted us to Pionic Flares, the way Halves do—well, *did*. The Hero was the first, and he saved us all."

I supposed that explained the term *Hero*. "Just like the Guardian."

"Better than the Guardian!" the Hero cried. He grinned again, and I felt a thrill through the silex network. Something like excitement, like arousal, something I could not quite identify. It was wonderful, and horrible, all at once, and I shivered with it. "I am more than code and programming. I am human! When I maintained the veil it was strong. You would not need to be here, searching for help, if I remained. Removing me, and replacing me with a soulless program, was the worst mistake the Legate has ever made. And my people—here, and across the veil— they suffer for it still!"

"But you have returned," Leola breathed. "And aid us once again."

Something wasn't quite right. Where the Keeper— the Guardian—had been loved, and revered, in the superstitious days before Novski's revolution, the Other had been feared. He still was, really, the way we never truly lose our fear of the dark, no matter how old we grow or how much we learn. He was a creature of horror, a cruel god, a spiteful trickster, and the Keeper had saved us from his reign.

What did that mean? I kept my expression as impassive as possible, and hoped he could not feel my emotions as I could feel his. I thought of Lad's warning glance, and said nothing.

"Yes, you have returned," Lad said, his voice tight, restricted. "And that is what I don't understand. Your entire being was uploaded into the veil, and your body left to rot away. When the programmers returned you to this world, to that body, you died."

The Hero turned his gaze to Lad. "Yes," he said. "That is what the Legate told you."

"But as you can clearly see," Adeodatus said. "They lied."

"Because the veil is not what the programmers and the Legate believe," the Hero continued, with a dipping, disembodied nod. "The veil is rich, the veil is generous. And the veil did not allow me to die."

The veil is rich? Ice dropped low into my stomach. Wasn't that what the puppet men had said? That the programmers didn't understand it. And the veil was rich.

Lad frowned, shook his head lightly. He had died before the puppet men revealed themselves to Kichlan and me. But some part of him had remained, in the blood absorbed by my suit. So maybe, he remembered those words. Maybe they haunted him, like a half-remembered dream.

"True, the Legate ripped me from the work I was doing. I spent hundreds of years in the veil—watching your world, protecting it—before they betrayed me. I cannot explain the horror of being torn away from that. The helplessness I felt, knowing that your people were still at risk and there was nothing I could do to protect them. I had come to feel such a connection to them. I believe I had come to love them. The programmers took away the power the veil had given me, and shoved me back into a body that had been left to waste away, and was little more than bone and mould. But they could not kill me. The veil had blessed me, and I carried some of her strength back with me."

Lad tensed beside me.

"When I opened my eyes I could not see—they had long since rotted away. And when I moved my arms they broke—my bones were hollow and brittle. And it was horrific, programmer, because I could not even scream. But still, I did not die. Then your predecessors caged my rotten body in a silex Shard. Me. A shuffling, blind, animated corpse, all that remained of the man who had saved them, and they had now betrayed."

Caged in a Shard? Just what the programmers had tried to do to me.

"That still doesn't explain it," Lad said, scowling. I couldn't imagine he had liked hearing what his fellow programmers had done, no matter how long ago. "You should be as good as dead. Not here, not building cities and inciting a Crust uprising."

"Do you really fail to understand? I'd lived within the veil for so long, and learned so many of her secrets, I was able to bring a fragment of her power back with me. The Legate tried to isolate me within that Shard, but I'd become more skilled than any of them. With the veil at my back, they could not contain me. Even so, it took hundreds of years to establish a connection between my Shard and the Legate's network, and even longer to navigate it, undetected, and finally set myself free."

Lad blinked, his eyes widening. "You—your body is still trapped inside the Shard, isn't it?"

"I see you finally understand."

Lad turned to me. "The Hero is doing exactly the same thing you are. He must have brought a Pionic Flare with him when they pulled him from the veil. No wonder they locked him in a Shard! So while his body is still trapped in silex he is using that energy to establish connections to the network, through the very Shard that is supposed to be restraining him. He's using the bars of his own prison, as it were, to upload his mind into the countless silex connections threaded across this world. So his body remains, but his mind can be anywhere. As long as there is silex to carry him..." Lad trailed off, frowning.

"And now that I am free I have been working for the stability of Crust," the Other continued. "I gave my body to protect this world. The citizens of Core-1 West, all the cities like her, and I will restore it to its glory. And you, Tanyana, you can help us."

I swallowed hard. I was not in the business of revolution. Hadn't I told Natasha the very same thing?

"No," I whispered. "No. I cannot help you fight, I cannot help you build. Because there is no point—"

"—if both worlds are destroyed," the Other finished my sentence for me, and smiled at my surprise. "Yes, I heard you speak. And I am the only one willing to believe you. Something threatens the very integrity of both worlds, something that you need to stop. Though you are not sure how."

I nodded. How long had he been listening? For as long as I had been connected to the silex? No, longer than that, it had to be.

"I offer you a bargain, then." He glanced at the bosses. "One that, I'm sure, will supersede any you or your programmer may have already made with my chosen here."

"Of—of course!" Leola stuttered.

"I can give you the answers you seek. I spent lifetimes in the veil. I explored it as no one ever has, or will ever again. I know its secrets. Aid me, Tanyana, and I will aid you in turn. I will teach you the truth about the veil."

The secrets of the veil. And there it was, just the answer I needed. The truth of the veil, I was certain, was the only thing that could help me defeat the puppet men. After all, it had helped create them. It could help me destroy them.

But still, I hesitated. "What do you want in return?"

Lad, eyes wide, glanced between us.

"What I have only ever wanted, to help my people." A wistful, far-away look crossed the Other's face. "I do what I can, from my silex prison, but I am hindered here." He turned back to me, eyes hard and bright, his presence so tight against me. "Every thought, every word, I must sneak past my captors. With your strength, I could be free."

He paused. The very room seemed to hold his breath.

"That is what I ask, in return for the secrets of the veil. Will you free me, Tanyana, from my prison?"

"But she can't!" Lad gasped. "Your Flare would freeform without a Shard to hold it back."

The Other cast him an indulgent, condescending look. "That is not what I am asking. The Shard that imprisons me also keeps me from knowing the pain and the horror of my decayed body. Let me ask again. Will you use your strength to infiltrate the place that holds me and carry me—and my shard—free?"

"Where is that?" I asked, when no one else dared.

His eyes flashed. "The heart of the Legate itself."

ॐ ॐ ॐ ॐ ॐ

Meta, Adrian and Kasen were instructed to accompany us on our expedition to the heart of the Legate, and guard us as best they could.

"Even though we will do what we can to aid the Hero," Leola said, "we will not send our new programmer into danger, unprotected."

Apparently there would be no discussion. The Hero had asked us to do something, so naturally we would do it. Even though I could tell the bosses weren't thrilled with the sudden change in the situation, they didn't hesitate.

I wasn't so sure about any of this. I glanced between Leola and Lad, but he was no help. He was busy trying to disconnect me, and concentrating hard. The screen embedded in the tabletop was dim and empty again. No Hero, no Other. But that didn't mean he wasn't listening.

"Fine by me. We do what the Hero wants, right?" At least it would get us out of Core-1 West. I gestured to Adrian. "You can carry my child."

The room grew tense, except Lad who didn't even seem to hear me.

"Tanyana," Meta said, with a scowl. "You must realise that you can't take him with you."

"What did you think I was going to do, leave him here?" I replied. "With them?" Adeodatus dared an affronted expression. "I will do nothing of the kind."

Meta stepped close, her expression hard. "I don't think you understand the risks involved in what we're about to do."

I lifted eyebrows at her. "Of course I don't. I'm not even from this world, so how could I?"

Meta touched her fingertips to the scars on her right temple. Her expression didn't change, her eyes were just as hard, just as weary, but I noticed Adrian and Kasen looked to their feet as she did so. "The Legate is no place to bring a child," she said, her voice as low as a whisper but far too intense. "You've seen the Drones, so you know what they do to unwanted children. What you don't want to know is what they do to the *wanted* ones. I can tell you, first hand. I wasn't skilled enough to be sent to the programmers, but I was healthy and strong willed. They like us strong willed. We can take more." Her fingers followed the scars to her eye. "They used this side of my brain to grow silex integrated nervous networks to be incorporated into the heart mainframe. I had a huge plastic biotube connected to a hole in my head, right here, hooked up to a mini life support all of its own. They only use one hemisphere at a time, because it wrecks the brain tissue after a while. Start with one, suck the life out, then the other."

She dropped her hand, turned her back on me.

"You can't move, all strapped and connected and broken like that. But they want you fit, so your brain stays healthy. They'd unwire me, every so often, send me out with the others and make us all run around, work those muscles, pump that blood." She paused to draw a shuddering breath. "They like us strong, but I was too fucking strong willed for them, even as a young girl. Took my chance and got out, three others with me. They were caught, but I was lucky. Kept going. The guards of Core-1 West found me, almost dead, and brought me here. The Hero helped them fix me."

Kasen looked up, and his usually expressionless eyes were burning with something like passion, like belief. "Not lucky," he said, in that same intense whisper. "Just damned stubborn and far too tough for them."

"Do you see why you can't even think of taking your child with you?" Meta said, her back still turned to me. "Not if you want to keep him safe."

I knew what the Legate wanted to do to my son, I knew it all too well. But that didn't matter, because there was no way I was going to do what the *Other* wanted, and we weren't going anywhere near the Legate heart.

Not that I was about to say any of that.

"That's not even taking into account the more than three hundred Drones gathered above us," she continued. "And Crust has other dangers—" she paused, and pointed to Adrian "—actually, that raises a good point. Can you source us some good quality radiation suits?"

He nodded with a smile. "Already on it, ma'am."

"We will need threaded rounds." She approached the bosses. "If they can be spared, of course."

Leola nodded. "No expense is too great if it aids the Hero," she said. But I had a feeling she was really thinking about Lad.

Meta glanced at me over her shoulder. "You will not bring a child on any expedition I lead." Her tone told me that she had already made up her mind.

That didn't mean I'd listen. "He's coming with me. I will not leave him here, alone."

Lad finally prised the last of my silex from Core's network, and gathered my fragile hands. He turned me gently, away from Meta, and drew me close. "Tan," he said. "You need to stop arguing. You know Meta's right. He will be safer here. Safer than we will be, out there. On Crust."

I couldn't believe what I was hearing. Tears welled up in my eyes, and I blinked them away, furious at myself. I tugged my hands, but he held them, not hard enough to hurt me, or crack me any further, but steady. Determined.

"But—" I whispered. "Lad, please."

He held my desperate gaze and smiled, softly. Sadly. "Don't you trust me, Tan?"

I could hardly breathe.

"She will do as you say," he said, glancing back over his shoulder to Meta and the bosses. "We both will. But please, for pity's sake, at least give her some space to say goodbye."

"Of course," Leola said. "We are not monsters."

Adrian left to source food—which seemed to consist of tough leather-like strips and strange pellets that looked like gravel—as well as packs for the three guards to carry, and radiation suits. Kasen requisitioned weaponry, and what sounded like a large amount of ammunition. Meta and the bosses discussed routes, escorts, defences and something they called a last resort, but never fully explained. Lad had already began to gather the supplies necessary to keep me alive: baths, and as much silex liquid as he could carry.

Numb, aching and tired right down to my crystalline bones, I carried my son out of the room.

20.

"Natasha." Kichlan pushed to his feet and struggled across a street slippery with disintegrating stones. He crouched beside her, touched shaking fingers to her cheek. "What happened to you?"

One of her eyes was swollen, so red and weeping it was forced closed. A great gash ran down her cheek below it. The rest of her face was a horrific collage of bruises, cuts, and burns. They travelled on down her neck, and underneath her armour. Her breastplate was cracked, chunks of metal gouged out, their shape disturbingly close to a hand. Whole pieces of her borrowed carapace were missing from her arms and legs, the hardy leather that had strapped them tight against her body ripped, and in places singed. Her left arm was wrapped in thick, tight bandages, and had been bound against her chest. Her right leg—Kichlan swallowed rising nausea—had to be broken, somewhere beneath all that cloth and leather and steel. It was twisted halfway down her shin so it stuck out, almost perpendicular to the rest of her leg.

She peered up at him. "The veche," she said. She lisped when she spoke. Her mouth was bloody, teeth missing. "We drove back their Mob, broke through their Shielders, drove their Strikers from the sky. We thought—we thought we had won. I sent messages to the Emperor. I told him, Kichlan, I told him I had won this revolution for him. Oh, Kichlan—" her voice hitched, and she stirred, lifting her right arm and trying to straighten against the wall "—I failed him! How can I stand before his jade throne again, how can I ever hold my head high? I've told him that I triumphed and instead, I have failed."

Devich, still low to the ground and tense, crept slowly closer. Kichlan sent him a warning glance and gestured for him to keep back. He did so, but slumped and hung his head low, like a chastised dog.

"The veche withdrew west, beyond the refugee camps, to the other side of the Keeper Mountain." She sagged back against the wall, closed her eye. "But the veche was only waiting for their suited soldiers to arrive. You saw it, Kichlan. Our weapons will not work against them, and that suit, well, you know. Nothing can so much as dent it. They drove us back, so few of them, but we stood no chance."

Natasha swallowed, wincing, and Kichlan wished he had water to give her. She looked thirsty.

"I tried to stop the suits." She opened her eye again to glance down at her arm. "One of them tried to stick me like a pig. I blew up disks in its face. That glass across the eyes is their only weak spot. Bastard couldn't see right, but he still got me in the arm instead. Healers had to bind me back together. But there is too much debris now for pion-binding to work. Kichlan, did you know that? They did what they could. Got it strapped it here, like this, so it doesn't fall off—"

"Shh." Kichlan placed a hand on the cleaner skin across her forehead. "Slow down." He used his Lad-voice on her, the one that had always soothed his brother. It worked long enough for Natasha to draw a shuddering breath, and nod.

"Yes, I'm sorry." Another breath. "We are retreating. Crossed the river last night, thought that might be far enough. But they followed. The veche won't let up until we are dead. Every last one of us."

Kichlan said nothing, though silently, he agreed.

"But you," she said, and clarity sharpened her green-eye gaze. "You killed one. We have tried, and only ever cracked the glass across their eyes. But you killed one." She shifted slightly, looked over his shoulder. "The two of you."

Devich slunk closer still, head down, belly low and breathing wetly, loudly. He dripped blood; it slid from his silver like water across feathers.

"Who—?" she tried to lean closer, to get a better look at him.

"We were lucky to have survived that." He glanced back at Devich. "And I'm not convinced we would again." An ungainly nod, and he assumed Devich agreed with him. "Do not expect us to become weapons for you."

Paling even further, if that was possible, Natasha leaned back against the wall. "Is that what you think of me now?" She stared up at a sky heavy with battle-smoke, staining crimson, now, as evening approached. "Can't I just be pleased that you're still alive, without trying to use you for my own gain?"

Kichlan didn't answer. He wasn't sure how to.

"But there are more." Her eye closed. "And they will not rest, until we are all dead."

As if on cue, an explosion rocked the street. Another flash of that too-bright, all-destroying dragon fire. A few blocks away, perhaps.

Devich growled. "Go—" he splattered. "Go, go—"

"Yes." Kichlan pushed himself to his feet again. "I couldn't agree more. Help me with her?"

Between them, Kichlan and Devich lifted Natasha. Devich was not comfortable on two feet. With his elongated body, it was probably easier to balance on all fours, closer to the ground. But he did as he was asked, and wrapped one of his silver-strong arms around Natasha's waist. Kichlan slung her right arm across his shoulders and balanced his stub against her back.

<*We can fight them. Defeat them. Absorb them. No need to run*>

A crash, different to the dragon light, sent stone and dust up into the air. Only a street away this time. If that.

"It's coming for me," Natasha whispered. "Run."

"Come on."

Together, Kichlan and Devich carried Natasha at a jolting trot, not quite the run he would have liked, but faster than she could have crawled herself. She groaned as the movement jarred her wounds, but Kichlan couldn't help that. She looked up to Devich's warped face, close to hers.

"Do I know you?" she asked, words almost as slurred as Devich's own speech.

"Now is not the time!" Kichlan snapped.

Silver crashed into the ground beside them, and Kichlan lost his balance. Only Devich kept them upright. He spun, crying out—somewhere in the middle of an animal roar and a human scream—bringing them face to face with another suited soldier, rapidly approaching, leaping down from the high remnants of a building roof, and throwing punches of silver as he went.

Another smacked at Kichlan's feet. He leapt backwards only to be jerked to the side as Devich tried to dive for cover. Still entangled, all three fell, and Natasha screamed at the sudden weight on her leg.

"Get up!" Kichlan yelled at Devich. "Help me with her!"

Devich cowered, hands over his face like he could block the world out, like the suited soldier wouldn't exist if he just didn't see him.

"Other damn you!" Kichlan turned to meet the soldier, stretching his suit into another sword. "Tanyana says to get up," he cried, desperate. "She says to pick up Natasha again and run. We have to run. Will you do that? For Tanyana?"

"Tany—?"

"Oh," Natasha gasped, recoiling from Devich. "I do remember you."

The soldier struck out, two tight, fast blows. Kichlan parried them both, his movements so fast and smooth with the suit inside him.

<Please confirm protocol?>

"Not now," Kichlan muttered, through his clenched jaw. "No more fighting. We have to run instead. Do you understand that, you bastard? Run?"

<Confirmed. Analysing routes>

Devich lurched forward, scooped up Natasha in both hands. "Run?" he asked.

<*Simulated Flare signal found. Viable option for evac. Shall we proceed?*>

"Yes!" As Kichlan turned, started to run, Natasha stunned him again. Even broken and barely conscious, she drew a clay disk from her armour and threw it at the suited soldier.

It blew a hole in the street, sent more dust and stone showering into the air. And they ran. Ducking, weaving, in and out of ruins, Devich in the lead and Kichlan fighting to keep up, his suit still extended; a ready sword unsheathed.

<*Incorrect direction*>

Kichlan slowed at the tugging in his bones, a pressure from the suit. "What?"

<*Turn left. Suggest increase in movement speed*>

"Devich!" Kichlan called, all too aware of the soldier still behind them. The disk could only slow it down. "This way! And hurry!"

"That was my last one," Natasha gasped, as Devich overtook him. "I have no more weapons left."

But Kichlan wasn't listening to her. He was focused on the suit instead. "This way!" Devich obeyed. Every turn, every corner, through ruined streets, beneath hollow houses.

The suit guided him.

<*Signal strength increasing. Approaching simulated Flare. Charged and ready*>

Devich skidded to a halt at the edge of a great crevasse, the underground storeys of what must once have been a large building.

<*Down*>

"Keep going!" Kichlan cried.

Devich crawled down the shattered and dangerous bones of a stairway. A gulp of air, and Kichlan followed.

Above them, the suited soldier launched himself straight into the crevasse. Hooks lashed out from his hands, caught in stone and earth and halted his descent. He swung toward Devich, already far below Kichlan and crawling quickly.

"Watch out!" Kichlan cried. It echoed down the semi-collapsed hallways. "He's coming for Natasha!"

Devich glanced up and growled so deeply Kichlan swore he could feel it through the stone.

<Reconfirm protocol?>

"That's not helping," he hissed at his own arm.

"Kichlan!" Natasha cried.

He peered down. Devich held Natasha in one arm while he turned to face the suited soldier. Teeth bared, chin wet with his own saliva, he snapped and struck out with silver claw-tipped hands. But the soldier simply held back, suit-power at the ready.

"Other curse you," Kichlan whispered.

And let go.

He dropped, fast. Air rushed past his ears and a scream he could not contain was snatched from his mouth. He lashed out at the wall with one hard spike, slamming to a sudden halt against stone, right beside Devich and Natasha. His free hand extended into a whip that harried the soldier, slicing at his hooks and forcing him to retreat to the far side of the crevasse.

Pale, frightened, Natasha shook her head at him. "Learn that from Tanyana, did you?"

"She was much better at this than me." Kichlan swallowed sudden nausea. "Devich, come on. We have to keep going."

Still growling, Devich nodded, and began to descend.

Kichlan paused, face pressed into the stone, as he struggled to catch his breath.

For a moment, he could see Tan, as clear and vivid as though she was hanging on the stone beside him. She was smiling, that wild look she sometimes got, when he knew she was feeling the tug of the power inside her. He'd never really liked that look. It always meant she was about to do something dangerous, and foolish, and she'd come out more scarred and even more distant than before. It reminded him too strongly of Lad.

Her eyes shone as she grinned at him. "Don't worry, Kichlan," she said, in a voice that wasn't her own, and yet sounded so familiar. "We've got you now. We'll look after you."

<We have been found>

Kichlan opened his eyes and shook his head.

"Nice of you to come to us. You did make it easier, old boy."

Kichlan glanced around. Where was that voice coming from? All he saw, for his trouble, were glimpses of doors. More doors. Doors crawling their strange and shadowy way up from the cracks in the fallen building, and all, it seemed, converging on the suited soldier.

<Guardian program's reaction to weakening produced by the simulated Flare is below the preferred scale. Requires maintenance. Please make a note>

Kichlan cleared his throat, and said, "Hello?" No reply.

Devich and Natasha were far below now, and there was no point hanging there listening to imaginary voices. He had no other way of climbing, really, so Kichlan pulled his silver spike from the crevasse wall and dropped, again. Not as far, not as fast, and this time he managed to direct his left arm, slamming it against stone several yards down and dragging himself to a stop.

"Not a perfect solution," he whispered. Actually, it was pretty terrifying. But at least he was moving.

The soldier swung forward again, silver lashing out. Kichlan spun, ready to defend.

But something got in the way.

It was—a flicker of doors. A sudden cluster of them, right where the soldier was heading. And he did not fly straight through them as though they were not real. Rather, the soldier smacked against them. His silver crumpled— that same ripple Kichlan had seen on Tan's suit, when she was attacked by the open door.

"Got you!" That voice, it sounded so close.

The soldier recovered enough to hook himself into a far wall and hang there, scanning the crevasse. Kichlan held his breath.

A new noise filtered through the echoes, the impossible voices, and the hard sound of his own heartbeat loud in Kichlan's ears. Faint, and deep inside the rubble pressed against his back. A rumble; a deep shifting of gears; a gathering of power.

"Kichlan?" Natasha called. "What's happening?"

He glanced down. Devich had deposited her on an outcrop—part of a hallway floor, stripped of its ceiling and walls but held in place by a strong network of steel bolsters—while he pressed his silver head against the stone, listening.

Kichlan allowed himself to drop again, reaching the outcrop in two terrifying bounds. He crouched beside Natasha, his back to Devich, and glanced up at the soldier. "I don't know."

<Flare>

Again, the soldier attacked. And again, doors snapped into existence in his path.

"A flash of light," Natasha hissed. She peered over the ledge. "Coming from down there. It's hitting the soldier. He's being forced him back."

Kichlan followed her gaze. The bottom of the great crevasse looked darker than it should have been, even for a hole so deep beneath an evening sky. And yet, something bright flashed in its depths. Like light, reflected on glass.

Behind them, Devich brought both fists to bear against the rubble. It cracked, cement and bricks and shattered tiles shifted. Then he crouched and dug at it, like a dog, throwing stones up behind him in a rabid display.

"—coming through!" That voice again. But this time, right behind them. On the other side of the ruined wall.

Together, Kichlan and Natasha turned. Devich had dug a deep hole into the rubble. Light, and voices, winked out through the gaps he had made.

"They're right on the other side!"

Kichlan curved his suit into a tool and helped Devich dig, while the doors held another attack at bay.

"Finally!"

Kichlan's heart leapt as he tore the last bricks and twisted metal away, and realised why that voice was so damned familiar.

"It's Kichlan, we've got him!" Mizra peered through at him, from what was left of a hallway on the other side.

"Mizra?" Natasha gasped.

Mizra's smile only widened. "Thought I heard your voice, Natasha, screaming like that."

"What—" Kichlan couldn't think—what were they doing here, looking so calm and pleased with themselves?

Mizra reached through the gap, even as Devich continued to widen it, and grabbed Kichlan's right hand. "Hurry," he said, tugging. "We've been searching for ages to find you; if you let yourself get killed now and undo all that hard work I'll be very, very annoyed. I don't know how long we can keep that soldier at bay, so just get in here, will you?"

And even though he was stunned, and not at all sure what was happening, Kichlan pulled his hand free, collected Natasha, and followed Mizra into the hallway. Devich scuttled in after them, leaving the suited soldier, and the doors that fought him, behind.

21.

"How do you keep doing this to yourself?" Lad whispered, close to my ear, as he smeared thick silex gloop into the cracks along my neck.

I stood in the centre of Lad's room, in one of the lower levels of the building. His room was full of boxes of the stuff he was using to patch me with, and baths, and dark, unused hubs.

I couldn't answer, just stared at the floor made from old fence posts, bed slats, and painted pieces that must once have been walls.

"It's been a long time since I was on Crust," Lad talked, softly, as he worked. "And there's been Fulcrum and Varsnia and Kichlan, in between. But I remember. One of the kids I used to run with, pretty good with silex too, thought he could sell used jacks on the side. Not tell the bosses. What they didn't know wouldn't hurt them."

I shuddered, slightly, at something in his voice.

"I found him. They filled him full of those jacks and wired him up to a massive Shard. Don't know what happened first, whether he bled out or started to change, but when I found him he was half-dead, half—something else. And that something else was moving."

I felt sick.

"You don't get to be a gang boss unless you're willing to do that kind of thing to poor, starving kids. Leola, Adeodatus and Urvan might not look it, but they are just the same. And that Meta woman is learning at their feet.

These are very dangerous people. We have to get out of this place, Tan. Whatever it takes."

"But—"

He clipped the final bath over the cracks in my wrist, and turned me around so I was staring directly in his eyes. "All of us, Tan."

My heart leapt. "All of us?" I glanced back over my shoulder at my son, floating in his tube and wrapped in his blankets, on the single narrow bed against the wall.

"I thought you trusted me?" Lad pushed me gently towards the bed, and helped me sit. "You need to rest. I need to work something out."

I nodded, peeled the blankets back and wrapped hands around the tube's surface. My heart was beating so strongly I was surprised it wasn't causing fresh cracks.

I watched him for a moment, searching through the equipment he'd gathered and muttering to himself. "Lad?" I said, eventually. "The Other? I—I don't understand. I thought you said he was a hero?"

Lad paused, and sighed. "You know the Hero was replaced by the Guardian program, but you don't know why."

I shrugged. "Because he was human, and he was dying?"

"Not quite." Lad leaned back on his heels, one arm still stuck inside a box of wires and loose hubs. "He was replaced because he was human, yes, but not because his body had decayed. His mind would have lasted as long as the veil did, regardless of what was happening to his flesh and blood. No. The Hero—the Other—was replaced because he was cruel."

I shivered, involuntarily.

"People are not designed for eternity," Lad continued. "Particularly not as guardians of the fate of two worlds. He was a Hero, once. And he did sacrifice himself to save uncounted innocent lives. At first, the programmers were grateful. They relied on him, as their aid within the veil. For generations, he maintained his vigil."

I nodded.

"I suppose we cannot blame them, for letting it go on as long as it did. But strange things were happening on the other side of the veil. Horrible things. And it took hundreds of years for the programmers to accept that it was the Hero—*their* Hero, remember, for he was one of them first—behind it."

I frowned. "But how did they know? I mean, the programmers are on this side, how did they know what was happening on the other?"

Lad rubbed his face. "We were strong, then. Not limited to outposts flying above a dead world, nor restrained by the Legate. The data stream was strong too. The Hero, still so confident that what he was doing was necessary, was right, continued to funnel information back and forth across the veil. But more than that, we had…confirmation. As doubts began to surface, as data was interpreted and the programmers grew concerned about what they saw, the first Halves were uploaded. They worked in secret, hiding their presence from the Hero. Monitoring him. These Halves, they were different. Not the—" a hesitation, the licking of his lips "—not the simple and broken creatures you know. They were fully aware. They remembered their lives as programmers, they found each other and built hidden communities. Like us, they volunteered knowing full well they would die on the light world, but they were still able to pass on their experiences, their knowledge, back to this side of the veil."

"Then why—"

"Tan." Lad lifted a hand. "You cannot begin to understand how long ago this was. Thousands, tens of thousands of years. The world you see now is not the way it was then. It was a young world, strong enough to survive its own hubris and even profit from it, drawing on the power of the Flares. Do not look at the dust and the ash around you, and think this is the way we have always been. This is the dying of a world. But once, long ago, she was fresh and powerful."

I swallowed my protests, and nodded.

"Together, the Halves and the data painted a picture of a Hero gone mad. He seemed to believe that, as the guardian of the light world, he should also be its ruler, and hold its people to account. After all, they did not know how close they had come to utter destruction, or how much he had sacrificed to protect them. So he tested them. He punished them. He committed atrocities, because he believed it was his right to do so. And because he could."

Death, ever stalking in the darkness. The creeping trickster. The horrifying mask.

Yes, this was the Other as I knew him.

"But how?" I whispered.

"You remember the sewer, Tan." Lad swallowed hard. And I realised that he too must remember the Other, the dark presence in the stories his parents and his brother told him as a child. How strange it must be for him, to balance Lad and Aladio now. To be both Half and programmer. To remember both the Other, and the Hero. "Now imagine if the Keeper was the kind of person who would open one of those doors—or, if you would prefer, draw back the veil—simply to impose his will."

I shuddered. The Other truly had been death and destruction, unseen, unheralded, and impossible to fight.

Until the Keeper came.

"Now you understand. The programmers drew the Other from the veil and shoved him back in a dead body because he was mad. Because eternity, and power, can do that to a person."

"But not a program," I whispered.

Lad nodded. "Exactly. They locked him in a Shard and left him there, while they uploaded the Guardian program in his place."

I stood, cradling my wrist with its heavy silex bath against my chest and walked over to the window. Outside, the rippling flicker of Flare light cast wavering shadows across unremarkable, grey buildings. A small group of people walked along the street, dressed in light, loose clothing, perfect for the heat. They laughed—two young girls in small dresses and two older women in shirts and pants—they talked loudly. Unafraid of the Drones above them, of the world dying around them and the puppet men, on the other side of the veil, doing everything in their power to bring it down.

I turned to look at Lad. "We can't trust any of them," I said. "Not the bosses, and not their Hero."

Lad nodded. "I don't believe the Hero has returned," he said. "I believe he died millennia ago, somewhere between worlds. The Other is all that's left, and he doesn't care at all about the people of Crust. Liberate them from the Legate? He isn't doing anything of the kind. With these cities, he's building himself a vast and powerful network. How long before he starts testing the people of Crust the way he tested the people in the light world? Even if we could, by some miracle, free him from his Shard in the Legate heart that would only make him more powerful. I don't want to be responsible for what he might do next."

I glanced over at my son, floating in the soft light shining from his body. I met Lad's eyes, so serious and concerned. "So we pretend?" I asked.

He nodded. "We have to convince the bosses, and the Other, that we're desperate enough to follow through with this suicidal plan. We let them help us for just as long as it takes to get out of Core, and back to Crust, and then we get as far away as possible."

A slow smile spread across my face. "All of us."

"I just need to work out how to take your son with us," Lad said, and went back to his searching. "A way to keep him alive, and safe, without them knowing."

I returned to the bed, and held my son as best I could. His hands made little clutching movements in the silex liquid, and his face scrunched up for a second, nose wrinkled and closed eyes frowning. He was warm, pressed against my chest.

Kichlan was gone, and Devich, well, who knew. I had found Lad again but he wasn't the same man I had loved, at least, not all of him was. My body was failing in the light of my Flare. The worlds were dying, in the face of the puppet men. And through it all, my son slept on. He was tough. He shouldn't even exist, not after everything the puppet men had done to us. But he did. And who was to say he wouldn't keep surviving? A life outside of a tube, a fully-grown body, and a mind that worked despite the crystal and the silver in his brain? Everyone kept telling me the same thing. That I'm impossible. That I shouldn't exist.

We were so much the same.

"Use me," I whispered, even as I realised I was shaking.

Lad turned to me, frowning.

"I kept him alive, once. And we're the same, we're Flare and silex and flesh. I can power a network, I can power him."

"I don't—"

"It's possible isn't it? My Flare is strong enough to support him."

After a heavy moment of hesitation, Lad crouched in front of me. He rested a hand on the side of the tube. Our twin Flares washed over him like light reflected in ripples on the same pond. We had been torn apart too early. We belonged together. "It will be hard," he said. "And it might not work. And it might hurt you. Both of you."

I nodded. "I understand. But let me try, Lad. I'm supposed to be his mother, after all. I should be able to carry him."

Damn, how that word shook through me.

Moving quickly, quietly, Lad closed the door. He collected one of the smaller baths he'd decided not to pack, and hefted it.

Meanwhile, I removed my son from his tube. It didn't take much, just the briefest of connections between my silex and the tube's hub. The lid opened eagerly. When I plunged my hand inside the fine, solid silex crystals suspended in the liquid clung to my skin. They drilled their way into my own mineral like countless tiny insects. I gritted my teeth, wrapped my hand around his tiny torso, and drew him free.

He felt so delicate. Not only the thin skin, fine bones and fluttering of half-seen organs, but the brittle crystal, the bright veins and the constant pulse of his Flare.

"He won't last long outside the tube," Lad said, his voice so low. "Take off your shirt and lie back. Hurry."

I shrugged myself out of my loose shirt and lifted the hem of my singlet as Lad grabbed the silex hub at the base of the tube and tore it free. It trailed golden wires and countless tiny jacks of a variety of colours.

My abdomen was a mess of silex and scars. Lad tapped the hard metal edge of the heavy bath against the silex lines across my belly until cracks formed. Just enough to loosen fresh light into the room. Then he pressed the tube's hub against the cracks, while guiding its wires toward my son.

At once, my silex bubbled free. It wrapped itself around the hub and set to drilling. I gasped as it penetrated, as my Flare met the hub's Flare and for a moment, there was tension. The threading that had been keeping my son alive was powerful indeed. Everything it had once been was directed to the pumping of blood, the forming of skin, and the soft nurturing of another being. For a moment, I felt inadequate. Wasn't that what I should have been, what my body should have done, all on its own?

But I shook my head, pushed my doubts aside, and allowed my own Flare to subsume the hub. Lad carefully scratched at my son's silex until it bubbled, and he could thread the long tangles of wire deep inside the tiny body.

I held my breath, waited for his presence against mine, wondering if he could weep—like the dead child had done—or whether he wouldn't know how to, having not yet experienced vocal chords. But I felt nothing, heard nothing.

Well, nothing wasn't right. I didn't feel another being, another presence in the silex, sharing and competing with me. But the connection wasn't empty either. Rather, I felt…right. I felt whole. Like this was the way we should have been, all along. Connected, once again. One.

Footsteps from the room above me jerked my awareness back out of the hub.

"We can't be found like this," Lad hissed. He was sweating, the moisture on his upper lip shining in the light from my Flare.

I cradled my child in the crook of one arm, as he replaced the lid on the tube. Without the hub it was dull, the liquid rapidly thickening. He wrapped it in blankets and tucked it into the bedding. "Hopefully, Meta and the bosses will just think you're slightly mad," he said. "And won't look beneath them. Not, at least, until we were gone."

"I can't carry him around," I whispered.

Lad nodded, and helped me searched through the clothing the bosses had provided us, until we found a shirt that looked far too small for either of us. We ripped off its sleeves and tore the seams around its neck.

His fingers were shaking as he helped me strip off my singlet and tug the shirt down over my head, around shoulders and arms, until it wrapped me tightly across the middle. Then I pressed my baby and his hub against my silex and skin, and Lad pulled the shirt down so it held them both in place. He looked extremely uncomfortable through the entire process.

Slowly, I stood. I experimented with walking. The hub's hard edges were uncomfortable where they poked into me, but my boy was light and the shirt seemed to be able to hold him. As I dragged the singlet back over the lot, I could feel my silex moving. It continued to spread out from the cracks, wrapping further around the hub and the wires. I had created a strange replacement for my womb, but it was certainly a womb of a kind.

The whole process sent countless shards of fine silex scattering across the blankets and the nearby floor. Lad swept them up as I dressed in the loosest clothes I could find: shirt too big and probably too thick for the heat of Crust, and wide pants.

I had no mirror, no way of knowing if my attempt to hide my child had failed, terribly. Lad offered no opinion, and we ended up just staring at each other in silence. Then footsteps sounded in the stairway and in a flash I was sitting on the bed, one hand patting the empty tube, when the door opened.

"Time to go," Meta said, glancing inside the room. I hoped she couldn't feel the tension, or see the odd-looking bulge around my waist.

Lad strapped one bag to his back, slung another on each shoulder, and struggled out of the doorway.

I stood on shaky legs and left the room, closing the door behind me. And with every breath, the tiny body wired and strapped into mine breathed with me.

22.

ore-1 West ended in a tangle of twisted steel, the torn edges of ancient wiring, and a solid wall that hid the shattered hub and leaking hull of a once-great Shard. The Pionic energy from its Flare had seeped unchecked for centuries, rendering the area dangerously unstable. The walls routinely changed consistency, from stone to sand to glass, then back to stone in their twisted new shapes. Shadows grew into wiggling slug-like creatures whose touch was death. The excavators who had found the place had been changed by it in deeper, subtler ways. Some of them took moons to die, others days, with their organs turned to mud, or their blood to air, or they simply fell to sand.

This had forced a stop to Core's further expansion—at least in this direction. Even with the Hero's knowledge and the silex the bosses had gathered on his instruction, they could not stop the flow. So they sealed it off, as best they could, and went another way.

Meta and the extra guards who had escorted us through Core climbed and prodded their way around the tangle, all careful to keep clear of the solid stone wall and the broken Shard on the other side. There was a path, apparently, to Crust through here. Unused and fragile, but clear of Legate Drones, according to the bounceback. Meta wondered if it was because the area was too unsound for their heavy metallic legs. Adrian believed they hunted by following something called *pheromones* and heat signatures, and had lost ours among Core's throng. He had talked a lot, during the pod-ride here, his words coming faster and faster the further we flew, until they all ran into each other and I couldn't understand any of it. He sweated, as he spoke, and tapped at his bright screen, even though the pod was so small and crowded that it was difficult to move. Finally, Meta had placed a hand on his shoulder, and his fast-paced, incoherent ramblings trailed away, and he stuttered, "Sorry, Meta. Sorry. It's Crust, you know. I don't—you know."

She said, "We're bound to find tech on the journey. Hope you have room of carry some of it back. Would be a waste, to leave it up there to rust."

Adrian nodded, and breathed deeply, slowly, until his fingers stopped tapping, and he seemed calm again. Kasen didn't offer any theories about the Drones. Neither did he offer Adrian any comfort.

I hunched as I sat, curving my shoulders over to hide the unusual bulge across my belly. The hardest thing was resisting the need to touch the body strapped against my skin, to check on his wellbeing.

"You could stem that, if you wanted," Lad murmured in my ear.

"Stem what?" I asked Lad.

"The Pionic Flare, of course." Lad seemed almost as grateful as I was to be sitting again. He leaned back against the warm tunnel, his legs stretched along the ground and his large bags arranged out in front of him. They reminded me of a wall, or a child's make-believe fort, between us and the guards. "You'd have to access it remotely, of course. Don't want to get too close. But once you were wired up it should be easy. Use your own Flare to counter the flow, then destabilise and then re-create the silex mesh—the program that determines and maintains the Shard form."

I glanced over at the wall. "I could?"

"I'd guide you, of course." Lad smiled. "The Shard in there must be an old design. Probably why it's failed. Before we got the form algorithm down, Shards relied on hubs and—would you believe it?—solar panels to maintain solidity."

I stared at him, blankly.

He chuckled. "Shards have to stand against Pionic Flares, don't they? But Flares have this tendency to undo everything close by. So Shards need to be able to withstand that. Initially that was done with power sourced from hubs, and the sun. They would drive a constant refreshing of the silex—a program that basically reforms the silex as quickly as the Flare can dissolve it. But that method relies on the stability of external energy sources. All you need is a break in the hub, or a crack in a solar panel, and the Shard will weaken. Like this one, it will eventually leak. Now we use a self-replicating code that draws on the energy from the Flare itself—that way, the Shard never loses a source of power to maintain solidity."

"If you say so."

Above us, Meta called to her guards. Apparently, she'd found what they were looking for.

"Here!" Kasen tossed a small, shining hub up to Meta. Even though she clung to jagged rubble half way up the tunnel wall with one hand, she caught it cleanly with the other. Then she slotted the crystal into a crack in the stone of the same shape and size.

"Connecting," Adrian said, typing at his pad again—this time, however, without the undercurrent of sweat-heavy panic. "Here we go. Activating."

As Meta and the escort scrambled down, something whirred on the other side of the rubble. Another pod? The trip out of Core-1 West had so far consisted of several cramped pod rides. I'd grown to hate them—with so many people in such a small space it was difficult to hide the new protrusion from my abdomen—but that was before we'd walked, and walked, and walked uncounted bells down the tunnels and shafts where pod tracks had not yet been laid. Now, I rather liked the idea.

The whirring spread, rolled down from the wall to the stone beneath us. Lad and I hurried to our feet, collected the bags and staggered back along the corridor. The ground shook.

Meta dropped easily from the wall, moving with enviable agility. She grinned at us. "Perfectly safe," she said.

A few yards back from the end of the tunnel the shaking disturbed a layer of earth and thin stone, revealing a large metallic and glass door in the floor. I baulked at it, for an instant, because with its rusting edges and cracked glass, it was hauntingly familiar. It looked just like the puppet men's doors.

Adrian crouched at its edge and began typing on a keyboard inserted in the metal. It did not brush into bright life with the touch of his fingers, the way the keyboards did on Fulcrum. Rather it ground and squeaked against the rough sand wedged into its lines. But even so, it seemed to work, for the whirring started up again, and the door jerked slowly open.

"In you go," Meta said, still grinning and far too smug.

At least it wasn't climbing. Rusted metallic stairs stretched down from the doorway, shaking on flimsy supports beneath our weight. Silex hubs burned bright from the walls, revealing a long room with a low ceiling, and tight walls lined with cots. The rotten remnants of ancient mattresses sagged through the holes of their wire frames.

"What is this place?" I whispered. Even a whisper felt too loud, as my voice echoed from the perpetual metallic surfaces. Warmth wafted up from the floor, condensation and mould clung to every surface. A faintly sweet, over-ripe smell teased its way through the heavy, close air.

"It's a bunker," Lad said, just as softly. He followed me closely. "Constructed deep within the earth. Thousands of these were built when the Flares first appeared, in an attempt to protect the population. But no amount of lead can hold them back, and they were soon abandoned. Useless."

"Deep in the earth?" I turned, lifted my eyebrows at Meta. "I thought we were going back to Crust, not further away from it."

"You have no faith in us," Adrian said, as he pushed past, tapping at his pad.

"Breathable?" Meta asked. She stood at the top of the stairs, poised between bunker below and tunnel above. Kasen threw down the remaining bags, and swung himself onto the stairs beside her.

"Yes ma'am," Adrian said. "Good enough."

She nodded, turned back to the escort guards the bosses had insisted accompany us to the very edge of Core-1 West. "Close the door," she said. "And remove the hub. The Legate doesn't know about this entrance, and I want to keep it that way. But in case they find us, in case they follow us, I want it locked tight. They must not get through."

Meta leapt down the rickety stairs with two long, light strides. Above her, the door squealed shut. Then all the lights went out.

For a moment, I breathed in the heavy darkness and listened to the creaks and groans of the metal and earth surrounding us. Then Meta, Adrian and Kasen lit silex torches. They passed one to Lad and me, and the five sharp beams cast the bunker back into harsh, colourless relief.

"This way." Meta slung one of the packs onto her back, and pushed on ahead. "Bunkers were built with several different exits, so in case of an emergency its occupants wouldn't be locked in. One of them was always manual—powered by muscle and old-fashioned gears, not hubs—and they all lead to Crust, one way or the other. That is how we will get out."

I helped Lad lift his three, silex-heavy bags, and we followed.

The bunker was enormous, and split into different sections: rows of cots to sleep on, long tables and metallic benches to eat and prepare food, and large empty spaces apparently for recreation. It stretched on for bells. Mould and strange, phosphorescent fungi were the only signs of life, growing in the heat, drinking in the condensation, and feeding on anything from the rotten bedding to swollen and split cans of what had once been food. At places the air was so thick with their dust and faintly glowing spores that we were forced to wrap cloth across our faces and fumble forward, almost blind.

"Crust is very full, isn't it?" I said, when Meta allowed us to pause long enough to drink short sips of precious water from the bottles she and the other guards carried. I found I was about as thirsty as I had been hungry, but drank anyway. My silex body needed only the strength of its Pionic Flare. "Well, beneath it is. Obviously, the outside is empty, apart from ruins." I fumbled for the right words. My legs and my back ached with the added, unusually balanced weight. I could feel fresh cracks in the silex around my ankles, the crystal jarred uncomfortably when I walked. "I mean, between Cores and bunkers and tunnels like the ones the Drones followed us down, there hardly seems much earth, any more."

"How is Movoc-under-Keeper any different?" Lad asked. He drooped against the wall, bags gratefully deposited at his feet, clothes drenched in sweat. I wasn't sure how much longer he could keep this up. "The old city streets we found, the storage vats drilled beneath factories. Hardly any better, I'd say."

"It's not a competition," I muttered. "I wasn't criticising your world, Lad. It was just a comment."

"Well, that's what I was doing too. Just commenting."

I looked away from him, wondering at his defensiveness.

"How long do you think you can keep carrying those bags?" Kasen asked, eyeing Lad with concern. None of the guards sat, like I did, or leaned as Lad was doing. They stood, eased and stretched muscles, while they drank. I had to wonder where they found the strength.

"As long as I have to." He pinned me with sharp eyes. "And every time we stop to sleep, they will get lighter, as I patch Tan back together." He paused. "We will be sleeping, won't we?"

Meta chuckled, somewhere ahead of us. She had switched her torch off, and even seemed to prefer the dark and the faint fungal haze. "Only briefly, and only when we must."

"Well, unless you want a freeforming Flare right in the middle of—"

"Don't worry, we're here to look after you. Both of you. That's just what we will do." She switched her light back on. It cast hard shadows across her face. "Time to keep moving. There shouldn't be too much further to go."

More bells of walking. I gave up any pretence and held my baby and his hub against my stomach with one hand. It eased the strain on my shoulders and back slightly. Lad cast me concerned glances, but none of the others seemed to notice. Finally Meta stopped at another large metallic and glass door, this one in the bunker wall. The bunker itself continued on.

"How much further does it go?" I whispered, as Adrian and his pad opened a nook close the door, connected to a mess of ancient wiring and hubs, and started typing.

Meta glanced over her shoulder, peered deeper into the long, metallic corridor. It felt so empty, down here. The groaning ghosts of all those people who were supposed to be sheltering in here were all that remained.

"We don't know," she said, at last. "We do know that a freeform breached the walls of a reactor, further down, and the only thing that makes this bunker usable is six feet of emergency, lead-insulated automatic doors, about half a mile on."

"Poison," Lad said, with a grunt behind me, before I could even voice my confusion. "Think of it like poison in the air. If not for those six feet of lead, the poison would have spread to the entire bunker."

"Fair enough," I said.

"Here we go," Adrian said, satisfied, as he tapped a final few determined keys.

The large door began to shudder, then rise.

"This is as far as the bunker can take us," Meta continued, as we watched the door's slow and grinding ascent, "but the Hero tells us that they were created to house thousands of people, even tens of thousands of people, and keep them fed, watered and safe, for years. So it must be bigger, much bigger

than what we have access to. Another city beneath the city."
She smiled at me. "Just like you said, Tan. Crust is crowded."

On the other side of the door was a small room, and
an identical door on the opposite wall. Adrian gathered
us all inside. "Airlock," he said. Meta, Kasen and Lad all
nodded. I decided not to bother asking.

The first door closed and the second opened, before we
could leave the bunker. On the other side we came to more
tiled tunnels and pod tracks. And started walking again.

"I suppose that makes sense," Lad said to Adrian. "To
situate an opening to your bunker as close to a pod station
as possible. Even if the pods aren't working the tunnels at
least give you good, open access to the surface."

Adrian nodded, though he was focused on his pad and
only seemed to be half listening. "Radiation is acceptable,
ma'am," he said. "We've lost bounceback, though, too far
out from Core now." He lifted his eyes, and for a moment
they were haunted. Then he straightened his shoulders,
steadied his gaze, and all three guards shared a hard look.
No trace remained of the fear I had glimpsed there, or the
nervousness I had seen in his sweat and heard in his voice,
back in the pod. He was as steady, and as confident, as he
had been when I first met him—fighting a Drone. Quiet
though he might be, I was coming to realise Adrian was
just as strong as Meta and Kasen. He was just less obvious
about it. "We're on sight alone."

Meta nodded. "Load and ready, then. I want a gun in
your hand at all times, and a second within reach. Even
when we're resting."

As Adrian and Kasen drew their guns, I hurried forward.
"What about Lad and me?" I asked Meta. "Shouldn't we
be armed too?"

Meta lifted eyebrows in surprise. "We're here to do that
for you, you know."

"Yes, but—"

"Have you ever fired one of these?" Kasen asked,
spinning his weapon in a loose and agile palm.

"Of course not—"

"Then you're better off without one, trust me." He grinned, and the scars that spread from the back of his capped head twisted into deep ridges. It was not a pleasant expression. "And the rest of us are safer too."

Meta chuckled. "It takes training to learn how to handle these weapons, and more strength than you realise. The kickback alone would shatter that crystal layer of yours."

I returned to Lad's side.

"We can't rely on force," he whispered, sweating and struggling but maintaining the punishing pace set by the guards. "Trust me, we really don't want to get into a fire fight with these people."

I nodded. Though I hated to admit it, I missed the strength of my silver.

"There are other ways." He grunted and shifted the weight he carried. "This is Crust. We are surrounded by silex here: it's in the ground, the walls, even hanging in the sky. On Crust, you are stronger than guns."

The tunnels here were in worse condition than the ones above Core-1 West. We were forced to halt, often, by rubble in our path, and backtrack to find another way out. It made the journey seem even longer than all those bells in the bunker. Then, at least, we had been moving forward, rather than heading in circles. But eventually, Meta and Adrian found us a way out. We crawled through a large scar in one tunnel wall—still darkened by the memory of flame—and joined a second set of tunnels that had not been so badly damaged. They even had stairs, stretching up through floor upon floor of more platforms, more tunnels. Some were still haunted by the corpses of abandoned or damaged pods. Adrian stared at these wistfully.

"If we ever return," Meta said, patting his arm, "we'll report them. Scavenger teams will be sent, I'm certain."

With a sigh, Adrian nodded, and continued climbing.

Struggling to breathe through the pressure and pain radiating from my belly, and the fresh cracks forming all over my body, I watched him. Scavenger teams? But then again, where else would Core get the materials for its wonderful new world? The corpses of the old, I supposed.

We emerged at a flat area of Crust. None of the skeletal structures I had expected, rather we were surrounded by low, degraded buildings. Great empty squares, edged only rarely with parts of run-down walls and the drooping curls of melted street lamps.

I stared around us in horror, as we walked. A thick layer of ash puffed up with every footstep. The constant grey of a storm-heavy sky beat down on us. I could make out the tips of three close Shards peeking through the clouds above us. More glowed in the hazy distance.

"There would have been factories here," Lad said, and was forced to cough ash out of his mouth for the trouble. "Power stations too. These areas were hardest hit. A Flare opens up in the middle of a reactor, or steel-works, or even solar-charged batteries, and there's going to be an explosion. Considerably more damage, and difficult to contain. Radiation, toxic smoke, you name it. Makes it difficult to build a Shard when you can't even get near."

"I'm sure it does."

We didn't go far until Adrian and his notepad called a halt. "Radiation levels are climbing faster than I would like. I think we should suit up from here out."

Meta nodded, but as Kasen began digging in his bag she stopped him. "First, we rest," she said. She glanced back at Lad and me. "No point to any of this if we walk them to death, is there?"

Adrian found us relative shelter in crumbling walls of a ruined building. Another bathroom, though this one in a far worse condition than the last. Tiles crushed and burned into dirt, great cracks ran down the walls so the hot Crust wind howled in through them, the ancient pipes and steel frames that held up the ceiling were precarious and almost rusted through.

I collapsed into a corner. Lad crouched down beside me, dug out silex and baths in a furious flurry of activity and attacked the cracks in my ankles.

"What about your arms?" Lad was saying. He dug out and filled two baths for the loose crystal around my ankles. Light shone through the cracks, too bright in the middle of Crust's dull surface. I could dim it, a little, with effort. That was different—I'd not been able to do that before. "Your neck? Waist?"

"They're fine," I said, trying to sound calm. "Shoulders, I think, are starting to give. Probably travelling down from my neck. It's weakest there. Cracks all the time."

Lad nodded, and shuffled around to the side so he could get to my neck. I leaned close to him, and breathed, "This isn't going to be easy."

Lad didn't so much as pause in his work. Our guards were readying themselves around us. Kasen stood on watch, alert, gun in his hand, chewing absently on a desiccated stick-thing that, apparently, was dinner. I had no intention of eating mine, as Meta passed it to me. Wrapped in poly, it stunk of dried fish and looked like compacted sawdust.

"It's good for you," she said, and would not move until I took it. I must have made a face.

Adrian continued to tap at his keyboard as he ate. Meta distributed food with one hand, held her gun in the other. I found myself staring at its sleek black lines. It was all well and good for Lad to talk about my strength on Crust, but those guns still looked dangerous to me.

"They have to sleep some time," Lad whispered. He bent so close his lips were nearly touching my ear.

"At the same time?" I whispered back.

"We'll find a way. The network—"

Something cried out in the distance. I jerked my head up, nearly smacking into his chin, and winced as fresh silex snapped close to my collarbone. "What was that?" I hissed.

Lad, looking mildly discomforted, shuffled close again and began dabbing at the fresh rays of light flickering around my throat. "Ignore it," he said.

Ignore it? If I didn't know better I'd have thought it was a wolf, howling, somewhere out in the ruins of Crust. Lonesome, desolate, and haunted. I could almost see the snow-wrapped mountain, the dark forest and distant, wind-stark tundra of Varsnia and shivered, despite the heat. "But what was it? Shouldn't we be worried?"

"There are more than junkies on Crust," Kasen said. He turned in the direction of the sound, gun lifted. "And not everything is human."

Baths were too awkward to wrap around my neck, so Lad applied his precious silex-liquid thickly. I knew not to move, under his determined ministrations.

"Drones?" I asked, barely daring to speak for fear of disturbing him. "More of the Legate's creatures?"

Kasen chuckled. "No, nothing so fearful. Mutations, probably, looking for something weak and mostly dead to feast on." He hefted his gun, meaningfully. "Nothing to be worried about."

Another cry, closer, and joined this time by a second, distinct voice. They created a terrible harmony that set me shivering again.

"Don't fret." Lad leaned in close. "It'll only set your Flare fluctuating again—"

—and for an instant, he disappeared. In the place of his concentrating frown and worrying fingers, I saw a door—

"—all the work I'm doing."

I stared down at the top of his head in horror. There were grey hairs in his gold curls, almost as terrible a sight as the door.

"Did—did you see that?" I whispered.

A third voice joined the cry, and doors whispered at the edges of my vision, flickering in and out of existence like the beating of dark wings.

"See what?" Lad leaned back, met my eyes. "Tan, what is it? You've gone white—"

—doors, everywhere. Wooden and rattling against their strained hinges, nails tugged out of wood, iron handles rusting away—

"—Tan?" Lad, so close, fear in his voice.

"It's a dog pack," Meta was saying, somewhere is the distance. "They can be nasty, but they're still far away. As long as nothing happens to alert them of our presence."

"Tan?" Lad gripped my shoulder, shook me.

And the doors on the edges of my sight rattled forward, swarmed on me like vermin. And he was gone, and the guards and the ruins and the dogs, all gone. Nothing but doors, everywhere, pressing against me until I couldn't breathe. And then—

"I don't understand," Kichlan said, as he followed Mizra through hallways turned to labyrinthine underground passageways. "How did you survive?"

Mizra flashed him the usual, pert grin, and Kichlan could not help but smile. How could he look the same, when everything else had changed so much? How could he smile like that, when the city was a ruin around them, when suited soldiers hunted Natasha, when a bizarre version of Devich followed them, and after Tan's death? Didn't he understand this was not the same world? And it wouldn't last for long.

"Don't get me wrong, I'm glad you're alive. I just—"

"It's hard to believe," Natasha filled the gaps for him. She was heavy, far too much for her seemingly slight body and for his single arm to carry. And she was hot. Her skin radiated a raging fever through both of their clothes. But Devich snuffled and scrambled behind them, keeping himself hidden in the shadows, so Kichlan could hardly deposit Natasha in his reinforced arms.

"I don't blame you for being surprised." Mizra held open another door for them, but did not offer to help carry. He eyed Kichlan's severed arm without comment. "We were too, at first. Until Fedor realised what we had found, and what it was capable of. It showed us where you were, for one thing. We tried looking for Tanyana first, but when that didn't work we found you instead. We've been trying for days now to use it to contact you, but it

doesn't seem to have that ability. At least we were also able to track those silver soldiers—the ones that look like Tanyana—and repel them. And that's just the beginning."

<Signal in need of repair. Communication facility damaged. Please make a note>

"What are you talking about?" Natasha asked, wincing as Kichlan adjusted his grip to climb through a room sucked deep into the earth, turned on its side and slanted, so its wall became a steep floor, and rubble piled in through its windows.

"You'll see." This time, Kichlan noticed the sadness beneath Mizra's usual smile. How much of that look, that normal, everyday Mizra look, was a mask? His pale skin, his blue eyes, his loose swaying walk. "When the city caved in we were ready to be crushed. But there are older streets beneath Movoc-under-Keeper, Kichlan. Even older than the city of the Unbound. And when its walls came down, and the statues cracked, and the ground—even the underground—opened up, we found it." He paused, head bowed. "If only Uz could have seen it too."

And Kichlan's heart dropped, because he'd known something wasn't right. It was so rare, after all, to see Mizra without his twin brother.

Behind him, following from deep in the ruins, doors flickered.

—"Kichlan?" I gasped, and thrashed against Lad's hands. No, not just Lad's hands. So many hands. Meta and Adrian too. Their faces leaned over me, frightened, worried. Meta's short white hair looked yellow in Crust's heavy light, and Lad's was slicked back from his forehead with his own sweat.

"Let her go," Lad cried. "I've got her! I don't need your help."

"Stop!" I gurgled. Where were they touching me? Had they found my child? "Let go!"

"Tan?" Lad pushed Meta and Adrian back. "Are—you are alright? You were thrashing, your Flare is so bright, and I think you've cracked your neck again, wrists too, probably."

I swallowed, hard. The doors were still there, at the edges of my sight. And my baby felt heavy, hot, his hub burning into my skin and sinking deeper into my crystal.

"I'm okay," I managed to croak. "Please, let me go."

Carefully, hands lifted. But they did not back away, not yet. I blinked fiercely against the doors, rubbed at my eyes—my wrists shone brightly, and dripped silex in streams down my forearms—but the doors remained.

"What happened?" Lad whispered.

"I don't know." Everyone was staring at me, except Adrian who tapped fiercely away on his tablet. "I've been having dreams, Lad. About Kichlan. About your brother. Just then, I had another one."

Meta lifted an eyebrow. "That was no dream."

"Bro?" Lad gasped. "But, he's, you said, you saw—" He drew a steadying breath. "Kichlan's dead."

"I know."

"Your Flare did something strange," Adrian added. "Looked like it just received a hell of a lot of data, but from where?" He flipped the screen around, to show me a meaningless jumble of scrolling symbols in a variety of different shades of red.

Lad frowned, grabbed the screen and scanned the symbols. "He's right." Adrian took it back with an affronted expression that Lad didn't even seem to notice. "You're receiving some kind of signal, Tan. But you're not hooked into any network at the moment, so it could only have travelled on your own little internal system." Frowning, he rubbed at his temples, like if he pressed hard enough he might be able to understand. "What is it? Why now, all of a sudden?"

For the first time in such a long time, I felt my son move.

23.

It wasn't a kick. And it wasn't the same as when he was inside me, a part of me. Rather it felt like pressure, his face against my skin, his crystal in my crystal. The presence of another mind, alongside mine. The pulsing of our energy, shared and strong.

I gasped, and pressed a hand against the bulge across my abdomen.

"What is it now?" Meta leaned in again, her eyes so damned sharp, her attention pinning me like an insect on display.

Lad glanced at my hand, narrowed his eyes. "Couldn't be," he whispered.

This was all getting a little too close for comfort. We needed Meta, Kasen and Adrian to pay less attention to us, not more. How were we supposed to get away from them with Meta sticking me with her pin-like gaze?

Another cry echoed across the blighted landscape outside, closer again. I could almost hear the dog's howl within it, beneath something closer to rage, to pain. Something disturbingly human.

"They're coming this way." Kasen crouched at the entrance, gun in hand, peering out and looking far too calm. "Their hearing's too good not to have heard that disturbance, and they've got other senses too." He glanced over at me and his eyes were bright. Ready for a fight. Enjoying the anticipation. "They'd have felt you, Flare going off like that."

"Do we have time to run?" Meta asked him, voice curt.

Kasen shook his head. "They're almost on us."

"We defend, then." She turned to Adrian, who nodded. "Keep them out, scare them off."

Kasen dug guns out of the bags he'd carried and tossed them at Meta and Adrian, as even stranger noises sounded outside. Howls and growls and voices, clipped shouting that could have been words, once, and maybe they still had meaning. I just didn't understand them.

I gripped Lad's arm as he helped me stand. "We should take this opportunity," I whispered.

He nodded, but his expression was deeply concerned. "The mutant dog packs aren't to be messed with. We'll need to be armed if we're going to go out there."

"Use their distraction," I said. "Get a gun. I'll get on the network."

"It's a big one," Adrian was saying, absently tapping at his tablet, gun dangled loosely in one hand. "Surrounding us, see? I can count dozens of heat signatures, but that's never very reliable when it comes to mutants. Not all of them are individuals. Strictly speaking."

Lad stepped casually away from the wall and approached him, ostensibly to peer at the screen. I reached behind me and felt around at the cracked tiles, until I found one of the many holes. I jammed my hand inside and clutched the ancient hub. Its wires were weak, fraying. I could only hope they'd hold.

We had to get this right. First time, or not at all.

"Help me," I whispered to my son, and the pions flowing through us both. "Give me your strength. All of it."

A faint amusement filtered back in reply. He rather thought this was an awful lot of fuss. I blinked, swallowed hard, and tried not to focus on just how strange it was that I knew what he was thinking at all. It was nice that one of us was so calm about this, at least.

A final, piercing scream shattered the tension, and the pack attacked. Our shelter wasn't much more than a few rickety walls, so even pressed into the corner I could see them—and I didn't know what I was looking at. Bright eyes like wired junkies, distorted faces and twisted bodies all close together, rearing, running at us. Meta stepped around the edge of the wall and fired two loud shots. More screaming, a painful roaring almost lost in the echoes, but they didn't stop. She slid back into cover and Kasen took her place. His gun was bigger, and it cast harsh flashes of light every time he fired, illuminating even more of the bodies.

They were nothing like drones. Some might have been human, some could even have been the dogs Meta kept talking about. But not anymore. They looked sick, all fleshy and pale and weeping. Elongated arms with bulbous growths, stumpy legs with claws for feet, all emaciated and naked. I couldn't tell where one ended, and another began. Some twinkled with silex and the light of tiny Flares buried in their faces, their skin a mix of open flesh and jutting pieces of machine.

"Other's hell!" I gasped, and my Flare surged. I connected to the silex and followed its path through what was left of the building, and beyond. Far beyond. The wires spread out in countless, complicated patterns, thin veins reaching every inch of Crust's skin, and I spread with them.

"They're behind us too!" Adrian cried. But as he lifted his gun and dropped his screen, Lad launched himself forward. He crashed into Adrian's stomach and tackled him to the floor, tearing the gun out of his hand.

"What—?" Adrian cried, shocked and airless.

"What are you doing?" Meta yelled. She spun, but couldn't focus on Lad. Two enormous mutants scrambled over the wall and she shot them instead.

Tiny whispering voices filled my head. Every hub I touched, from dormant heating unit to darkened tunnel light, welcomed me. Layers and layers of cities, time and memories built one on top of the other. Hubs of crystal so ancient they sagged to dust in the face of my energy, unused Flare warning systems eager to protect a long-gone population. Bunkers. Emergency nuclear containment.

Enormous guns on tracks and gears that demanded my access codes.

Crust was full indeed. And now, Crust was me.

Lad pushed himself to his feet and backed towards me. He pointed the gun at Meta, then Kasen, then a mutant scrambling closer. "You just all stay back," he cried, panting.

"What the fuck do you think you're doing?" Kasen roared.

"We're getting out of here," I said, my voice so tangled in my enormous network that I could hardly hear it. "And you're not coming with us."

Meta fired two more shots even as she ran to Adrian's side, and helped him up. "What kind of idiots are you?"

Kasen spat another vicious curse as more mutants surged forward. Three fell to his gun, but a fourth got through. It tore at him with metallic, clawed hands that looked like they'd been sewn onto its arm by someone who didn't know anything about anatomy. Adrian finally pulled a replacement gun from the bag and shot it, but not before Kasen stumbled back against the wall, face and chest bleeding.

There was a furnace below us. Part of an older city, long disused, it hadn't worked for centuries. But it was powered by silex, just like the rest of Crust, so that didn't matter. I fed power into those hubs, and they burned again. A few sparks at first, struggling for life in the airless underground. Then blue flame, melting concrete and steel, reaching up through layers of rubble to find the thin wooden bones of the buildings above. I pushed harder. One hub overloaded, exploded with a rush of fire and energy that cracked the ground outside. A moment later, and the flames roared free, and swamped the mutants surrounding us.

Screaming and ash and the harshest kind of light.

Meta flung herself to the floor. "What the fuck was that?"

Adrian dragged Kasen from the door, and stared at me. "Her," he gasped.

The fires died quickly, the furnace hubs destroyed. But it was enough. Whispering smoke and a faint painful whimpering was all that remained of the pack that had been attacking us, only a moment before. Meta, Adrian and Kasen stared at me in shock.

"And now you're going to turn around," Lad hissed, teeth clenched. "And leave." He was shaking, his hair slicked back with sweat. I swallowed hard and tried to stand tall, even as I gripped the wires inside the wall and kept digging through the network. There was so much more beneath the furnaces I'd just destroyed. Dormant pods, forgotten libraries. And weapons.

"You—" Kasen growled, but I cut him off, instantly. A little push was all it took, to start the empty furnace carcasses rattling again. Steam hissed up from broken pipes. A lighting hub dangling on frayed wires shattered a few yards away with a gunfire flash.

"Be quiet," I said, and tried to sound strong. Not to be argued with. "And go. Leave the guns. Leave the silex. You can take that stuff you call food, though. And go."

Meta stood very slowly. She gestured to Adrian and Kasen, and they lowered their weapons.

"The Hero should not have placed his trust in you," she said, and there was such venom in her voice. "We should have known better, and warned him."

I held her gaze, and said nothing, because there was no point in arguing. She believed in her Hero, and why wouldn't she? After everything the Legate had done to her, he and his people had saved her. So I understood. She didn't know the Other like we knew the Other.

"Just go." Even as I spoke to her I was searching, desperately, through all layers Crust beneath me, until I came across a set of hubs guarding something very big, and very powerful. They blared a demand for access codes, as strong and stubborn as the day they were programmed.

"I don't understand," Kasen asked.

"They never had any intention of helping the Hero," Meta hissed. Her hand tightened around the gun she was carrying and she took two slow, deliberate steps toward us.

This could all go very badly very quickly. I pushed the code, it pushed back. I summoned every beam of my Flare, every pion speeding through me, and focused them all on getting past this damned obstinate prerogative.

"Just stay where you are!" Lad cried. He trained his gun on Meta, but Adrian and Kasen spread out behind her. He couldn't point the gun on all of them at once.

"If you think we're going to let you go," Kasen said with a grin that twisted the nasty, bleeding gashes across his face. "You don't understand the Hero, at all. And what he has done for us."

"And what we're willing to do for him," Adrian finished his sentence.

"Stop!" I shouted. The network was my world, the Flare my strength. A final push, and the codes in my way dissolved to gibberish, and I flooded the controls of an ancient, but still very large weapon. It called itself an anti-aircraft missile launcher. Fully operational, it insisted. Radar guided. Installed during the third millennium to prevent the Castitas revolutionaries from attacking and destabilising Shards in the Capitoline quadrant. What would I like it to do?

What indeed?

There were countless caches of small, mechanised weapons aligned in arrays around the launcher, all designed to protect the larger munitions from ground attack. One by one, I woke them up. The earth shook again as they stretched, sending great cracks through the tiled floor and walls. Kasen staggered to one knee, weakened by his injuries, but Adrian and Meta remained standing.

"What are you doing?" Meta snapped. At least she had the decency to sound a little unnerved.

I sucked a deep breath—it was hard to remember to breathe, sometimes, in the network—and began rattling off everything the launcher was telling me. Its history, its capabilities, its support robots and their progress up towards the surface.

"Oh shit!" She spun to face Adrian.

"And it's not designed to hit ground targets," I finished. "But it can." I began to smile, the weapon's enthusiasm bubbling up inside me. "It would like the challenge, actually. There are three targets I can give it right now, if you like. If the robots don't get them first, of course."

"Can she do that?" Meta asked.

Adrian shook his head, but his expression was worried. "I have no idea. She burned the mutants, and you remember Core. I'm not sure we should take any chances."

"Then back away," Lad said.

"But," Kasen gasped, and pushed himself upright. "No." Blood darkened his chest and neck, and he looked unstable, wobbling faintly on his feet. "The Hero."

I gritted my teeth. What would we have to do to convince them?

I think that's enough, don't you?

I reeled forward, away from the wall. That wasn't the launcher, talking back. I knew that voice. "Other."

My connection stuttered, its presence replaced by a strange crackling like fire. My Flare responded with strength, beaming brightly from my silex, pushing me deeper into the launcher's hubs.

You really are quite amusing to watch. The Other rode the network with me, at once invisible and all around me, terribly strong yet only as solid as mist. *But your skills could do with refining. You use the power of that Flare like a bull uses horns, crashing your way through my network, destroying hubs, fraying connections, and making a terrible noise. I can hear you all the way from here. And I have to say, I'm a little disappointed.*

"Tan?" Lad glanced over his shoulder, and Meta instantly leapt forward. She pushed his outstretched arm aside and hit him sharply in the neck. Lad buckled forward, gurgling, even as he pulled the trigger. Bullets ricocheted from what was left of the walls and smacked into the floor. Adrian leapt on Lad's back, and between them the two guards tore the gun from his hand.

"Lad?" I cried. "Are you alright?" I struggled against the Other's presence as he tried to lock me out of the missile launcher. I flailed and smacked at him, sending my Flare-strengthened code against his solid wall, chipping him down one symbol at a time.

Why would you lie to me, Tan from the light world?

"I know you," I spat through gritted teeth. "And I know what you're asking. How can you think we would have agreed to your terms?"

"Now," Adrian sidled up close to me, gun pointed at my head. "Just get away from the wall."

What makes you think you had a choice in the first place?

A fine thread of my Flare made its way through the Other's blockade, and reconnected with the launcher. Dimly, I felt a gentle sense of disapproval. My son, apparently, wasn't that fond of violence. I decided he just didn't understand what was at stake, and switched the weapon on.

"Shoot her and we'll all die!" Lad gasped, his voice raspy and muffled as Meta held him down.

Crust's thin and traumatised skin shuddered as the launcher loosened a series of explosives to clear precise track to the surface. Up from the ruins of the bunker that once housed the men who cared for and controlled it, through the rock and steel of the people who came after, and finally to the surface. Then with a screech that tore the very air, it fired.

The missile was large, dark and sleek, and I was watching as it slid out of the earth. It soared up into the darkly torn sky on a tail of pale smoke, then shuddered, stuttered, and started to fall.

Cute plan. Get out of Core, use your strength on the network to overwhelm your guards. Unfortunately, I've been here a lot longer than you have. And I'm hardy going to let that happen, am I?

The weapons system sent data at me that I didn't understand, then informed me that it was in desperate need of maintenance, and ammunition had lost effectiveness over time, so it was sorry its offensive capabilities were somewhat reduced. If I cared to initiate a repair regime it would be very happy continue working with me.

The missile smacked down right where it had been launched, and Crust rolled. The launcher vanished from the network in an instant as a fierce energy like white-hot fire tore down through the tunnel it had made. Its robots were incinerated, and the remaining weapons caught and exploded, one after the other. The ground shook and spewed forth all kinds of rubble, burning and hot, cement and metal, layer upon layer of the history of Crust thrown into the air.

"Down!" Adrian grabbed my shoulder and pushed me into the corner. I squeezed my eyes closed but I could still see it, still feel it, through the wires and the hubs that melted or shattered, as Crust exploded.

Finally, the world grew quiet, and still.

A hard swallow, a shallow breath, and I sat up. Bright sparks like falling stars were settling around us, winking out and stinging as they touched my skin.

You will come to me, Tanyana. Whether you like it or not.

"This cannot be good for us," Adrian said, as he glanced around and the faint rain of light. He brushed it off his shoulders with a thickly gloved hand.

Where the missile had fallen, Crust was gone. Just gone. A blackened scar, a mess of melted metal and a deep crater, were all that remained.

Meta dragged Lad to his feet, gun still firmly pressed against his skull. "Then let's make sure she can't do that again," she growled.

Adrian nodded, grabbed my wrist, and physically tore me out of the network. The world lurched, suddenly confined to my own skull, and light burst out of my every crystal vein, struggling against the prison of my body. Everything tilted sideways, doors at the edges, as exhaustion and pain rolled over me.

I'll be waiting for you.

24.

Kichlan didn't quite notice when ruined corridors gave way to ancient streets. The usual distinctions—between ground and underground, old and new—had been shattered along with most of the city. One moment he was walking on tiles, and the next he stepped on decrepit paving stones worn down by time.

It was so dark he wouldn't have been able to see, if not for the faint silver-blue light emanating from his left elbow and Devich's entire body.

"Helpful, that," Mizra said. He did not seem to be disturbed by the darkness. Instead, he glanced away from Kichlan's light as though something so faint could hurt his eyes. "We got used to feeling our way around."

Kichlan did not know what to say, so kept quiet.

They had been walking for bells, descending deeper and deeper beneath the city. Pressure built up above them, the weight of ages, of rubble, of the battle being played out and lost where they could no longer see or hear it. He was certain they were far beneath the old Unbound street now, even though that had been built so long ago, at a time before people who could see debris were shackled with silver and forced to collect it. How deep did the earth beneath Movoc-under-Keeper go?

He caught glimpses of strange wonders. More statues in crystalline stone: the Keeper, the veil and something he could only describe as the Other—twisted, half-formed features with cruel, disjointed hands. They arched over him like buttresses, holding up the layers of city above. Great shards of crystal lanced out of the walls, the ceiling, even the floor. They reflected his light back at him—caught it, gave it a variety of rainbow-like colours, and seemed to make it brighter. Mizra and the Unbound skirted around these, keeping their distance.

"What is that?" Kichlan whispered. Only whispers felt right here, felt safe.

"No idea," one of the Unbound answered. Kichlan could not see his face, and wouldn't have known his name even if he could. "But I wouldn't touch them, if I were you."

"Why?" Natasha asked. She rested her cheek against his shoulder, but Kichlan hadn't thought for a moment that she was sleeping.

A pause. "Wait until we get there."

"You'll see," Mizra said.

They kept walking. Behind them, Devich whimpered. Lost and animal-like. Kichlan glanced over his shoulder and Devich hurried forward, sniffing and rubbing against Kichlan's fingers like a reassured dog.

A new, fresh light filtered into the tunnel so faintly, so steadily, that Kichlan did not notice it at first. It emanated up from the floors below them, creeping through gaps in the pressed-earth and statue-supported floor. The temperature increased with it. At first, just a light flush of warm air rising from the ground. Then Kichlan started sweating, and even Natasha grew clammy where he held her.

"Where's that coming from?" she whispered.

Nowhere in Movoc-under-Keeper was as hot as this.

And then the tunnel opened up, and Kichlan could only stop, and stare. Natasha gasped, and Devich pressed his body against Kichlan's heels, shivering.

There had once been a city here, far, far below ground. Or, perhaps a town. A single straight street led off from where they stood. Paved with the same glittering stone the Keeper and Other statues had been built with, and edged with lines of glowing crystal. That crystal was everywhere. It burned softly from deposits in the walls of domed buildings that looked like they had been hollowed out of the deep earth itself. It hung over doorways with the rusted-clump remains of bells, it shone from the eyes of faces chiselled into the homes, the floor, even the ceiling so low Kichlan could have touched it if he stretched, only a little.

The single street and the chiselled houses stretched on, farther than Kichlan could see. While it was long, the town was only wide enough for one house on either side. So the earth pressed in from above, and from either side. The heat and humidity hung heavily in the tight space, generating a mist-like haze.

Mizra and the Unbound continued down the street. Kichlan followed, with Devich close behind.

"What is this place?" Natasha whispered.

"Deeper than the Unbound street." Mizra did not turn around as he answered. "Older. But connected to it, somehow, and for some reason. A labyrinth led us here, with the world caving in behind us and the Tear flood following."

Doors flickered on either side of the street. Thin and transparent, but looming, far taller than the low room should allow. Kichlan tried not to look at them.

"Thin," Devich slobbered, voice almost lost in his saliva and malformed jaw. "Here. Thin."

The street was not as long as Kichlan had thought. Perhaps it was the crystal light, or the ever-hugging mist, that had made this place look timeless, stretching on forever. But it ended, suddenly, at a great semicircle hollowed out in the rock. The curving wall was riddled with crystal all bound up with a tangle of bronze wire long gone to green. Strange devices filled the recess—like the ones he and Tan had found inside the Keeper Mountain. Dark, poly-looking slabs that could have been pion screens, but were coated with a fine layer of debris instead. Symbols chiselled in crystal—similar to those on his collecting suit—glowed and floated on the surface of this debris.

In the middle of all these, Uzdal lay in a crystal coffin. "To cross the veil?" Kichlan whispered, to himself. He'd seen one of those before.

<There is still a signal coming through from the other side> The voice of Kichlan's suit was little more than a murmur. *<But all communication back has been severed. Upload inoperative. Maintenance required>*

"Our people belong here."

Kichlan glanced to the side. Fedor emerged from one of the houses. His right arm was bound, the right side of his face heavily bruised. But, apart from that, he did not seem much changed. If anything, he had a smug, vindicated look to him that Kichlan knew—just knew—would have set Tan's teeth on edge. If she was alive to see it.

He gestured to his Unbound, and three of them came to collect Natasha. She groaned as Kichlan eased her weight between them.

Mizra knelt by the crystal coffin. Face impassive, he reached inside and smoothed his brother's hair. When he withdrew them, his fingers were encrusted with ice. He did not even seem to notice.

"We found this place because we were meant to use its power," Fedor continued. He held Kichlan's gaze, and his eyes burned with fanatical fire. "It saved us. And we used it to save you. This is an ancient home for the Unbound. It has kept us safe while the world above us collapses. And we are learning how to use its gifts. To find allies, and to defend ourselves. It makes us stronger than we have ever been, stronger than the pion-binders above. Soon, they will have no choice but to listen to us. Do you see—" he pointed to Uzdal "—it even keeps us alive."

Feeling numb, Kichlan approached the coffin. Devich dogged his steps and he almost tripped. "Stay here," he commanded. Devich pressed his stomach to the stone, and whimpered.

Kichlan knelt beside Mizra, who looked up, but did not seem to see him.

"I tried to save him," Mizra said. Kichlan started to shake, for the grief in his voice. A grief he was trying so hard not to feel. "But I wasn't fast enough. It all came down, on him. On others too. The Unbound. Eugeny. Then Fedor brought us here. So I went back. I dug and dug, and I found him. But he was dead. But still, I carried him all the way here, and the magic of the Unbound started him breathing again, and his heart beating. But it couldn't bring him back, Kichlan. Not all of him. I think—" his voice hitched. He lowered his head to the edge of the coffin, and ice crystals germinated in his hair "—I think my brother is gone."

Uzdal was pale. Most of his body was encased in ice so thick it resembled the crystal in the wall above him. Only his face and his head were free, which was terrible, in its way, because it allowed Kichlan a clear view of hole in the top of Uzdal's skull.

Dark red coagulated blood. Grey, fleshy brain. Skull, white, shattered. Not Uzdal, none of it. Just a body. Just meat. Dead and frozen, yet breathing, somehow, blue vein and red capillaries pumping to an impossible beat.

Kichlan rested the stub of his elbow on the coffin lid. The ice played with his silver, unable to gain purchase. "Eugeny is dead?" he said.

Mizra nodded. "I looked for him under all the stones and all the earth. I did, I promise I did, but I only found Uz."

Kichlan bowed his head. He and Lad had lived in Eugeny's house for so long, it should have been harder to imagine that the old man was gone. He'd loved Lad, he'd cared for him, and he had grieved so hard when Lad died. But everything was fading now, and he'd lost so much already. "It is more than I have left of Lad," he breathed. "And Tan."

Behind him, Devich howled.

25.

When I woke I was lying against Lad's chest. I listened, for a moment, to the sound of his breath and the beating of his heart. Too ragged, too fast, too much worry and fear. But he was alive, and warm, and solid against me.

"It was the Other," I whispered. "He's on the network, always on the network, and he took it back from me. I'm sorry. I tried."

Lad's breath hitched, and his hand on my shoulder tightened.

"So nice to see you coming round," a voice chimed beside me, above me, all around. Friendly, faintly feminine and altogether artificial. "I was worried I hurt you there, for a second."

I opened my eyes and sat up with a groan. Lad balanced me carefully. There were dark bruises and fresh scratches on his face that hurt to look at. I touched shaking fingers to his cheek, and he winced, but didn't pull away. I felt empty, my Flare stuttering and weak. We were sitting in something that looked like an elongated pod, and we were moving. Metal squealed against metal below us, lights embedded in the walls flashed in an uneven pattern. There were chairs welded into the curving walls, cushions long rotted away. Everything was rusted, and slightly damp with clumps of dark mould.

Meta, Adrian and Kasen sat opposite. Meta and Adrian still had their guns drawn, and were both watching me with sharp attention, deeply suspicious. Kasen wasn't looking so good. He lay back on the rusted old chair, and the front of his uniform was soaked with blood. He'd been bandaged, and he seemed to be sleeping, his breath coming quickly and shallow.

"All that effort would have been for nothing if you'd left us," that voice chimed again.

I frowned, glanced around. Where was it coming from?

Silently, Lad tapped at a small screen embedded in the wall beside him. I shuffled closer. It was dim, difficult to see, but slowly a simulated face resolved there. "Other," I hissed.

"*Hero*," Meta said, tone grim.

I glanced up at Lad. "What happened?"

"You tried to betray me," the Other said. "Don't you remember that?"

I ignored him, and held Lad's gaze instead. "The missile opened up access to an old set of mass transit pods," he answered, after a moment, and there was such a sense of regret in his words. "It seems the Other has enough influence on the network to get them moving again."

"*Hero*," Meta said, again.

"Don't you think you should listen to the woman with the gun?" the Other asked, lightly.

"They're ancient, dangerous," Lad continued, ignoring them both. "Listen to that noise, they could fall off the tracks at any minute."

"They won't," the Other said. "I know how delicate Tanyana here is. I'll be careful."

Lad shook his head. "Tan, he's taking us to the Legate heart."

My stomach dropped, and before I could stop myself I placed a hand on the bulge across my abdomen. "No," I said. "But Lad, no. We can't."

"You will fulfil your promise to the Hero," Adrian said. He lifted his tablet and turned it around to show us something that looked like a map. A small red dot was speeding across it. I realised, with a sinking feeling, that the dot was probably us. "Nothing can stop that now."

"So just calm down," the Other said in the pod's too-bright, too-friendly female voice. "And enjoy the ride."

The pod rattled, swayed and dipped furiously as the Other dragged us forward. Sometimes underground, the darkness pressing in on me with all the weight of Crust and the ruins I had seen. It was hard to breathe, and I tensed with every bump, expecting to crash into the inevitable rubble across the track.

The ground shook and something rumbled, off into the distance. Adrian leaned forward. "The Hero clears the way," he said, but he was sweating heavily, and I could just feel the fear emanating from his skin.

Lad held me tighter. Only Meta and Kasen didn't seem concerned, and Kasen was still unconscious.

But the trip wasn't entirely in the dark. Sometimes we slowed and chugged through to the surface.

There were small windows in the metal wall beside Lad's head, plugged with glass. I peered out of one. Crust flew past us at jerking, rattling speed. So much of the landscape was that same, colourless rubble, skeletal buildings, and flickering silex lights in the distance.

Crust was a corpse, I thought to myself. Dead and rotting, but hosting countless, struggling forms of life. The Legate and the programmers, the junkies and the mutants, the bosses and their guards, were all part of Crust's terrible afterlife. Even the Other. They were maggots burrowing, fungus growing, and scavengers tearing pieces away.

"Now what?" I breathed into Lad's shoulder. "How can we stop this?"

He didn't reply.

Time became meaningless, a mesh of darkness and long-dead earth. Then something large and dark rose out of Crust ahead of us. Another great building, or a mountain? I had not seen any mountains on Crust, nor rivers nor valleys nor sea. The whole place seemed dry, and flat, sanded down by time.

"I'm sorry, Tan," Lad said, at one point. "I'm sorry."

On the other side of the window the mountain was coming closer, and becoming clearer. I couldn't quite decide what it was. As tall and piercing as the Keeper Mountain, far greater than any building could be, it even put *Grandeur* to shame. But where it should have been rock, and scrub, and brushed faintly with high altitude snow, I saw only metal. And lights, great hubs and Shards embedded it its sides. It moved, as if ants swarmed over its surface.

"What is that?" I asked. Lad turned in his rickety seat, to peer out the window with me.

There *were* ants on the mountain. Well, Drones, and many more creatures of metal and silex and flesh that I could not describe, let alone identify. They rolled over each other, bodies and limbs and wire and cable all tangling, all surging, in a thoughtless communal hive.

"That is the Legate." Lad tapped on the glass. "All of it. All of them. All sharing one great mind, all linked on one enormous network. Greater and larger than anything you can imagine, tapped into every single Shard littering this world, drawing on all of their power."

We closed in on the mountain, dipping back below ground just before reaching its crawling walls. My heart beat so hard and so quickly I could feel it pounding in my skull. We shouldn't be here. Not me, not my baby, and not Lad. This was the very last place on Crust we should be. But the Other—damn the Other—wasn't giving us any choice.

"And this. This is the heart."

"No," I whispered, and doors flickered at the edges of my vision.

26.

"Kichlan?" Sofia wrapped what was left of her remaining arm around him, and pressed her bandaged-wrapped face against his shoulder. "You—you're really alive!"

The joy in her voice made it worth it. Even if she could not see him. Even if the glowing crystals and tubes connected to her body really were all that kept her alive, as Fedor insisted.

"Our ancestors worked wonders," he'd said. "More powerful than any pion manipulation."

But Kichlan could only see pain, and death, and almost-death in this place. Not wonders. Not power.

"I am," Kichlan stammered. "And I'm here. I'll look after you now, Sofia. You know I will."

She'd been weeping, deep, relieved sobs like desperate gasps for breath, dampening the bandage across her eyes with bloody tears that made his stomach clench. Now, as she leaned back from him, he slowly, carefully, wiped the tears from her cheeks. She couldn't do that anymore.

"That's not fair, Kichlan," Sofia stumbled over her words. "When I was whole, I loved you. You must have known."

He swallowed hard. "You were my—my teammate. My most loyal collector."

She shook her head awkwardly. "Idiot."

But he'd known, in some small quiet part of himself. And yes, he'd loved her back, but as a friend, as a member of his team, and never in the way she'd hoped. So he'd done nothing, said nothing, not wanting to cause friction.

And anyway, he'd never had time for all that, not with his brother to care for and a quota to reach. Not, at least, until Tan appeared at his doorway.

"Why now, when I am broken and dying, do you want to stay with me? Out of pity, or duty? Not because you love me at all."

"But I do—"

"Not the way you loved her." She lay back against bedding made from unneeded coats and ruined clothing. "I do not want your pity, Kichlan. How can I collect debris, like this? How can I work at your side? That's all I ever could do and now—now I can't even do that." She drew a deep, shuddering breath. "Not that it matters. Because you still love her, don't you. Even if she's dead."

It took a long time for Sofia to finally agree to rest. She should have died when Tan collapsed the city above her head. Both arms crushed by stone, and Tear water—boiling as it rushed through the storm of energy escaping the puppet men's underwater laboratory—had swept over her, burning her skin and leaving her eyes…her eyes.

Drained, exhausted, Kichlan stumbled into the crystal-lit street. It was a blessing, really. He crouched, and pressed the heel of his palm against his face. His left elbow was hurting. It wasn't fair. Sofia, serious, sensible Sofia.

A faint snuffling at his neck, the soft brush of hot breath. Kichlan opened his eyes to find Devich beside him, crouching, close, one hand lifted as though he couldn't decide whether to touch Kichlan, and his expression fearful.

"And you, too." Kichlan looked into that fearful face and wondered just how much of the man he had hated so fiercely remained. "You were caught up in the destruction too, weren't you? But then again, you helped cause it. So maybe you deserve what the puppet men did to you."

"They—" Devich rolled his tongue out, over his teeth and chin, battling his anatomy to speak.

Kichlan winced at the flecks of silver inside the man's mouth and knew, despite what he had said, that no one deserved what Devich had become.

"I'm sorry," he whispered. "It wasn't fair for Tan, either. She did not deserve what was done to her." And what she had been forced to do, just to survive. She had not meant to kill Uzdal and destroy Sofia. At least she didn't have to live with the guilt.

"Tan—na," Devich whimpered. "They." He swallowed, growled roughly. "*They*!"

Kichlan drew back as Devich splattered saliva in a wide, frustrated arc.

"What's wrong with him?"

Kichlan stood to greet Volski and Zecholas, Tan's two trusted pion-binders.

Volski was the elder of the two men, but Kichlan didn't remember him looking this old. His hair was almost white, his eyes bloodshot and his expression haunted. He still wore his deeply blue woollen jacket, the shoulders gleaming with small, silver bear-head pins. But there was something shrunken about the man, his back slumped, his skin too pale, his chin rough with unruly grey stubble.

Zecholas looked taller now, compared to the old man Volski had suddenly become. His expression was wary, not haunted at all. He scanned the street constantly, eyes only ever meeting Kichlan's for an instant. The bears had been torn from his right shoulder and he had faint bruising around his right eye and jaw. From the distrust in that look, from the solid planting of his legs and the fist already made with his left hand, Kichlan didn't think the collapsing earth had given him those injuries or taken his bear pins away.

"Did you construct something?" Kichlan asked them, his voice low. "When the street caved in? Did you leave—" he swallowed hard "—Uzdal and Sofia to fend for themselves?"

Zecholas shook his head. "No, Kichlan. We tried to help them." He paused, suddenly tense, to turn and watch as two Unbound walked past. "But there wasn't much we could do."

Kichlan raised his eyebrows. "I saw the work you did for Tan, getting us in and out of the laboratory. You can't tell me that—"

"Is it true?" Volski interrupted. "Is Lady Tanyana, is she really dead?"

"Tan—ya!" Devich scuttled between them, drooling great disgusting ropes.

"Oh, Other." Volski staggered at the sight of him, and Zecholas quickly gripped the man's shoulders to keep him upright.

"Kichlan," Zecholas said, voice tight. "Can I suggest we move somewhere Volski can sit down? Perhaps the rooms where we have been sleeping? There is something I want to talk to you about—"

"Wouldn't do that, if I were you."

Kichlan turned. Fedor approached them, with a cluster of his Unbound behind him. Whereas Volski had looked so old and Zecholas so suspicious, Fedor just looked pleased with himself. He was as thin as he had always been, but his usually pale skin looked flushed, even healthy, despite his obvious injury. Strange, for the leader of a rabble of failed revolutionaries forced to hide underground.

"You're one of us, Kichlan." He gestured to the men behind him, and even dared to nod in Mizra's direction, where he knelt his eternal vigil by his brother's tomb. "So step away from the pion-binders, and talk to me."

Zecholas, his hands still tight on Volski's shoulders, took two deliberate steps back.

Fedor was carrying a dark debris-screen, much smaller than the ones attached to the wall above the coffin. It fit neatly across both his open palms and he balanced it carefully, holding it out in front of him with reverence. Crystalline symbols rose and fell across its rippling black surface, bobbing to the beat of his footsteps.

Kichlan frowned at him, and glanced at Zecholas as he backed even further away.

"They're cowards," Fedor said. "Could have helped us, but didn't. So we've been helping ourselves. And you know what, we Unbound can get along pretty damned well without binders like them." He shifted the screen into his left hand alone, and with his right index finger he slowly, carefully, began to rearrange the symbols on its surface.

"Careful—" Zecholas hissed.

Something crackled in the crystal and debris-covered wall above Uzdal's body.

Kichlan spun. The symbols on the debris screens were dancing, mirroring the changes Fedor was making. But there was something lurching and unhealthy about their movements. A few flickered with strong, sporadic light, and short bolts of energy surged between them. Some of the screens were cracked, their surfaces empty. Others were missing symbols, or the debris on which they floated.

A great groaning, rattling sound echoed through the rock. A thin layer of sandy, crystal shards shook loose from the ancient structure, and floated down upon Mizra's bent head. He cast Fedor a tear-stained look over his shoulder. "We found Kichlan," he rasped, voice rough and constricted. "You don't need to use this thing again. My brother is attached to it. Please don't change anything."

Fedor shrugged, but lifted his finger. All the symbols and screens settled into stillness. "We have to use it, to learn what it does." He nodded to Kichlan. "And see what happens when we do. This is the heart of our ancestors' magic. It found you. It defended you, when the silver soldier attacked. This is our legacy and it is our right to learn to control it!"

<Operational capability at seventeen percent, on limited radius only. Flare strength at five percent. External signal strength, two percent. Veil signal, inoperative>

Kichlan had no idea what his suit was talking about.

Zecholas shook his head. He lifted a hand and pointed towards the middle of the street. "We are not cowards, Kichlan," he said. And though his face was set and his voice steady, Kichlan had the strangest sensation that the man was pleading with him. "The truth is that there is too

much debris now for any of our bindings to take effect."
He flexed his fingers and whispered beneath his breath.
Nothing happened. Sweat dotted his forehead and his arm
began to shake. Finally, a single square stone shook loose
from the street and lifted two, maybe three feet in the air.
It hovered, quivering, before falling back into place. "That
is the best I can do, and it was more than I could do when
the Tear broke its banks and the earth heaved and we were
all cast down here. We were lucky to survive at all."

"You're a liar," Fedor spat.

"Kichlan, listen to me." Zecholas wiped the sweat from
his forehead with the back of a shaking hand. "Please, we
all need to think about this for a moment. Where are all
these Unbound?"

"Silence!"

"If these ancient Unbound had so much power at their
command, then where have they gone? How could you all
have been relegated to debris collectors, shackled into suits
and ruled by pion-binders, if you had access to this kind
of power? Could it be there are dangers here, dangers we
cannot see, dangers that destroyed the men who made this
and tore their memory from history itself—"

"More lies!" Fedor shouted, and pressed the floating
symbols again.

"That's enough."

Kichlan turned. Lev stood at the opening to another of
the buildings, his expression unreadable. He had bandages
on one arm, and his left leg appeared to be splintered.

"Both of you, be silent. Have some respect for the
injured." He nodded to Kichlan. "Natasha is stable now, if
you would like to see her."

Kichlan pushed the argument to the back of his mind,
and hurried over to Lev. "Stable? What do you mean?"

Devich scrambled after him, muttering and slobbering,
whining a constant beaten-dog sound.

Natasha lay on another improvised bed, and was
hooked up to more devices like Sofia's. A mess of crystal
and tubes and wire, one wrapped around the shattered

bone in her arm and two more for her leg. She seemed to be sleeping, and breathed easily, almost comfortably.

Valya sat beside her. The crystal cast a warm glow across the old woman's face, highlighting her own share of bruises, cuts and bandages. She looked up as Kichlan entered. "Seen them, haven't you," she whispered. "Ready to open. Everything happening here, it's all too late. He's gone. And the doors will open." Her gaze turned back to Natasha. "We're surrounded by them."

Devich, waiting outside the house, let out a short, soft howl. Kichlan frowned over his shoulder at him. "Hush, Devich. Quiet." He knelt, and ran soft fingers over the random facets of the largest crystal. It felt warm, almost seemed to flutter beneath his touch. Like it was alive.

"What is this stuff?" he whispered.

"Another part of the magic of our ancestors," Lev said, stepping into the already-crowded room. He spoke with none of the fervent reverence Fedor had displayed.

Kichlan stood. His knees ached, his left shoulder was tightening and beginning to throb. "What is it doing to Natasha?"

"Healing her. It won't fix everything, not the way an expensive healer can. But it will save her life, it will stop bleeding and mend bones and fuse skin together. The scars will be ugly, but it works. It saved Sofia. But it cannot bring the dead back to life. Not the way that coffin can." And even though he spoke without expression or inflection, Kichlan got a strong sense that Lev did not approve.

Kichlan lifted eyebrows at the older man. "Isn't that a good thing? Saving lives? Restoring—" he paused, because he was not entirely convinced Uzdal was actually living "—well, starting up hearts again. And lungs."

"Perhaps."

Natasha's eyelids flickered open. "Kichlan." She even smiled. "The pain is gone, can you believe that?"

"Your dog is getting restless." Fedor entered the house, sneering as Devich danced away from him, dexterous and low on all fours. "Shouldn't you feed him, or something?"

Kichlan swallowed his disgust, and did not respond. Now was hardly the time to start picking fights.

"Amazing, isn't it," Fedor said. "Now, look at this."

Valya pushed herself to her feet, and Lev helped her out of the room. Kichlan watched them go, but Fedor didn't even seem to notice. He gathered the wires from one of the crystals on Natasha's legs and dipped their frayed edges in the debris across the small screen he carried. The symbols immediately disappeared beneath its surface. "I've been experimenting."

Experimenting? Kichlan tightened his hand into a fist. He hated that word.

The debris rippled, softly, then light flickered across its taut black surface. Kichlan gasped, and drew back as an image appeared. A rough body-shape in mottled, strange colours from bright red to a deep, almost-hidden blue.

"Didn't I tell you?" Fedor grinned. "Miracles. I tried this on Sofia first. Shows what's going on in a body. At least, I think it does. Because her eyes weren't on the image, and her arms were gone too, and there's lots of green where the crystal is working, and red is your blood, I think." He paused, frowned at Natasha. "Your body is odd. Too red. Hers wasn't like that at all."

"You tried it on Sofia first?" Kichlan spat the words out and the light of Tan's suit strengthened. It fought with the flickering glow of the crystals and the debris screen. "How dare you—"

Fedor didn't even seem to hear him. He wiggled the wires, tapped the crystal and even poked at Natasha's leg, until she hissed a short and angry warning. "Why is it—?"

"Maybe my body is different than hers," Natasha said, between gritted teeth. "Ever think of that?"

"Different? How—?"

Kichlan grabbed Fedor's shoulder and spun him around. "You experimented on Sofia?" Anger rose through him with a flush of silver. The cap on his elbow liquefied, and suit-metal dripped into a long, sharp-looking blade.

"Kichlan?" Natasha struggled to touch him.

But Kichlan pushed Fedor out of the house.

Devich clutched at Kichlan's ankles. "They they they they—" he slobbered, until Kichlan kicked him off.

"What are you doing?" Fedor demanded, expression horrified, affronted. Lev and Valya stopped at the entrance to one of the other houses, and turned. Volski and Zecholas still stood opposite the small group of Unbound men, and watched Kichlan with apprehension. Even Mizra left his brother's side.

"She is not yours to use!" Kichlan snarled. Anger bubbled up from his mutilated arm, an anger he was coming to know so well.

<Integrate core directives with the primary hub to override lockdowns one through sixty. Unable to access full connectivity.>

And he knew, now, that he could control it. His suit might be strange, it might talk to him in an impossible, nonsensical voice, but it was powerful. And Tan had made it a part of him. Kichlan squared his jaw, straightened his back, and flexed his silver blade into a second hand. After everything he'd suffered through—Tan's death, Natasha's Mob, Devich and now Sofia—here was Fedor, experimenting. Pathetic debris collector had no idea how strong Kichlan could be.

"Kichlan?" Mizra approached. "What are you—" and froze "—what's wrong with your arm?"

"My experiments saved Sofia's life!" Fedor spat right back. He lifted his small screen. All the crystal symbols suddenly returned to its surface at once, beaming bright with fiercely colourful light, rolling and dipping in complicated patterns.

With a frown, Fedor lowered his hands and blinked down at the device. The Unbound behind him glanced at each other.

"What have you done, Fedor?" Lev called from across the street. "Why is it glowing?"

"I—I don't know." He hovered an uncertain finger above its surface, not ready to touch it.

"I told you," Zecholas said. "This is more dangerous than any of us could possibly understand."

"You're an idiot!" Kichlan snapped at Fedor, not ready to let go of his anger yet. "You don't know what that actually does, and you dared to test it on my friends? Living or dead—"

But when Kichlan glanced at Uzdal's coffin, all the crystals and the screens were gone. In their place: doors. Wood and iron spreading, like a disease. And his suit was doing the same, sliding up from his arm, resisting all the control he thought he had.

<Emergency protocols activating, system reset initiated>

"No," he whispered.

Devich grasped at his ankles again. "They!" he howled. "They!"

<Warning! Flare generator suffering external attack. Countermeasures offline. Warning!>

Behind him, Natasha stumbled out onto the street. She carried her crystals, still attached to her body.

Then the suit wrapped his face in silver. And from the darkness and the rolling doors, the puppet men emerged.

<Compromised! Overrides unsuccessful. Reboot inoperative>

Three solid men, with countless hazy faces floating in a mist at their back.

The first one smiled down at Devich, that terrible fake-skin stretch. "Well done," he said.

The second lifted a hand, and when he ran his fingers through the air the very darkness seemed to ripple. "This place has been hidden from us for too long."

The third laughed, and the doors rattled with him. "Finally, we have found a way in."

27.

The Legate heart was a city, the first true city I had seen above ground. No ruins here. But still, there was something not quite right about it. Even though it was locked inside a great metal-sided mountain, there was a wall around the city. Tall, with guard posts manned by crimson-lit silex hubs. The city itself was a bizarre mix of spires, small hovel-like homes, and towering glass-sided apartment blocks. It was a city built by someone who had never lived in one, and merely followed the diagrams and descriptions history left him.

Everything was black, metallic, and there were lights everywhere. There seemed to be a lamp every few yards along the unruly, winding streets. A candle-like glow flickered in every window, on every doorstep, but as far as I could tell, the city was empty.

"Where are the people?" I asked.

The Other's pod had deposited us somewhere beneath these empty streets and Adrian had used his tablet to guide us through the warren of ancient tunnels to the surface. The city was silent, our footsteps echoing loudly off the smooth surfaces. Every so often he waved us against the walls, and we waited, tense, as something large and mechanical scuttled by.

Meta sighed. "You still do not understand."

"Tan," Lad squeezed my shoulders. "There are no people." He was helping me walk. My silex ground along cracks in my ankles and doors nibbled at the edges of my vision. They made it difficult to see where I was going, sometimes.

"Then why is there a city?"

"Because the Legate remembers." Lad glanced at Adrian as he paused, and checked the screen he carried. He seemed to be following directions, and I could only imagine where they were coming from. "After the incident with the Other," he said, slowly, carefully choosing his words, "concerns were raised about the roles played by humanity in the tearing of reality, and the, ah, episodes on the other side."

Adrian seemed too busy with his directions to pay us much attention. Meta was too busy helping Kasen walk, and didn't object. Despite his injuries and the blood still seeping through his bandages, Kasen had refused to be left behind.

Lad ploughed on. "Programmers came to believe that we could not be trusted. And so, the Legate was created."

"Just get to the point," Kasen grunted. He gripped the side of the wall with one arm, the other wrapped around Meta's shoulders. He still managed to hold his big gun though. "He's trying to tell you that the Legate isn't human."

"Well," Lad shrugged. "Not entirely, not any more. The Legate is—"

"—dead."

"Dead?" I whispered. We were getting slowly closer to an enormous structure in the centre of the city. A strange amalgamation of a castle, complete with towers and an arching bridge, with a building like Fulcrum slotted right in the middle, all tied together with black lattice and trails of heavy wire. A Shard poked out from beneath the bridge, casting the lot in a wavering, rainbow haze.

"Memories, to be more accurate. The Legate is the combined memory of countless dead. All uploaded and tampered with to create programs. It was supposed to be the perfect compromise. Humanity and data, emotion and fact, anger and calm, compassion and—"

"But it wasn't," Meta interrupted. "It created a monster, instead. A heartless freakish government happy to watch its people burn."

"The Legate only does what it was created to do," Lad continued. "It governs the world in such a way to ensure constant maintenance of the veil. That is the reason for its creation, and the purpose that still drives it. The programmers in their floating prisons, the Halves destined to lose their lives, and the experimentation on the living. It is all done to protect two worlds."

"Are you actually justifying the Legate?" Adrian scowled over his shoulder, even as he pointed us down a narrow side street.

"I didn't say I endorsed their methods. But no matter how obscene they seem, the Legate is certainly efficient."

"And it's holding the Other right in the middle of its bloody city," I muttered, under my breath.

"This way," Adrian said. "We're getting closer."

We hurried further down the city's strange, reflective streets, past windows full of light but empty of people. Around infrastructure like markets, fountains, even rows of shiny pods that no one would ever use. It was so false it made me shiver, and reminded me strangely of the ruined Movoc-under-Keeper I'd left behind. The deeper we went the more we were forced to hide from Drones and other machines I couldn't name and didn't want to look at. I wondered if they were doing all the cleaning, because someone was definitely keeping this place polished.

Eventually, Adrian led us to a dead end, up against the smooth dark wall of the city's giant, central building. We were squeezed into an alleyway too narrow for two people to walk abreast. "In here," he whispered, and crouched where the wall and the floor joined at a seam of thick solder. He passed his tablet to Kasen, dug into his bag and pulled out something that looked like a silex torch. He shone it at the metal, and I quickly realised it produced heat as well as light.

Meta waited, gun ready, at the end of the alleyway as Adrian cut a small square in the wall.

"You have to be ready," Lad whispered in my ear, as we both watched. All I could feel was dread.

"Ready for what?" I whispered back.

"To do whatever we can," he said. Lad's jaw was set, his hands tight on my shoulder and upper arm. "After everything we've been through, all we've seen and lost, I am not about to be undone by Favian, the first programmer, the mad Hero, the Other. Whatever he was and whatever he has become. We're stronger than that, Tan." He looked down, met my gaze. "*You're* stronger. You have to believe me. Together, we can do anything."

I swallowed hard, nodded, and cupped a supporting hand beneath my baby's bulge. I wasn't so sure I believed him, but we were together, all three of us. And Kichlan, somewhere, in my impossible dreams.

Adrian lifted the square he had cut clean from the wall, and dug out handfuls of wiring and silex hubs from the hole. Then he opened a section of his tablet and did the same, so he could join them. Symbols in red and green scrawled across its surface.

Lad sucked in a sharp breath. "What are you doing?"

"Getting us inside," Adrian answered. His fingers flew across the screen, rearranging symbols faster than I had any hope of following. Not that I could have understood what he was doing, one way or the other. "And locating the Hero. He gave us the map to get this far. The rest is up to us."

"Can you stand?" Las asked me, voice tense. I nodded, and he released me to elbow his way beside Adrian. "Be careful!" Lad tried to take the tablet from Adrian, and Kasen quickly drew his weapon. "You'll alert them to our presence! The Legate and the network are—"

The wall rumbled, and a door slid free.

"There." Adrian grinned. "See? You should have faith—"

The tablet screen suddenly wiped black. Adrian paused for a moment, shook it, knocked it slightly against his knee.

"They noticed you," Lad pushed himself to his feet. "They've locked you out." He grabbed my arm and pushed me forward, back up the alley. "We have to go, now. How long before you think Drones will be here? We do not want to be caught."

Meta refused to budge. She pointed the gun at us until we edged back, to the door Adrian had opened. "Then we'd better get inside," she said.

"But—" Lad tried, but Meta remained implacable.

"The Hero is waiting."

We squeezed through the narrow doorway, one by one. The walls were close, and riddled with warm wiring that pulsed, sometimes, as though the building had a heartbeat. I shuffled carefully, trying not to touch them. Kasen's struggling, laboured breathing was loud in the tight, metallic space. Inside the building was dark, too dark to see without the light from Adrian's screen. My Flare remained dim, subdued, and didn't offer much relief.

"I don't know where we're going," Adrian whispered. "The Hero could only give me directions through the city. Without a connection to the Legate network, we're blind here."

Something scratched above us, and we froze. A sound like metallic footsteps. Slow, halting. Searching for us?

Lad squeezed my hand. "Tan can do it," he breathed the words.

"What?" I frowned up at him, even though he couldn't see my expression. I was sure he could hear it in my voice. "I'm not doing anything to help this ridiculous idea. And neither should you!"

"Shhh," Kasen hissed. "Not so loud."

"We have to," Lad replied, quiet and calm. "It's too late to argue. The Legate knows we're here; it's probably looking for us, right now. There must be Drones on our tail. We don't know where we are, we can't turn around. If you don't take over, they're going to catch us. *All* of us."

I gripped my baby tighter.

"Remember, you're strong on the network. We need you. I need you. *He* needs you, to find a way out of here."

He hadn't actually mentioned the Other. That was possibly the only reason I nodded. "Fine," I said, and stuck my hand out in the direction I hoped Adrian was. "Then give me the tablet."

Lad took my hand instead. "Tan," he said. "You don't need an interface. Access is all around you."

I shuddered as he guided my fingers to the wall. Gingerly, I touched wiring, hubs, thick tubes pumping some kind of cool liquid. "It—" I stammered. "It feels like it's alive."

"It's the Legate," Lad said. "All of it. This building, this city. Everything is part of the heart."

Silex dripped free of the ever-present cracks in my wrist. It snaked slow and smooth around the writing. My Flare flickered, still weakened from my battle with the Other.

"Just remember what you're here to do," Meta said, and rattled her gun.

My silex sealed the connection, and we slipped quietly into the network.

Instantly, the Legate stopped me. As though I was no bigger than a fly, whining around its head, it slapped me back into my own body. My Flare was just too small, compared to its combined might.

No wonder the Other was so arrogant that he would put my life, and the lives of Lad, Meta, Adrian and Kasen, at risk just to get what he wanted. It might have taken him generations, but he had still managed to not only bypass the Legate, but also use its network to his own ends. The Other—the Hero—must be strong despite what the programmers had done to him, and far more skilled than I.

"Come on, Tan," Lad said. "I know you can do this. Remember what I said. And do it together."

I frowned. Together. Lad was here, but what could he do to help me? "What do you mean?"

Lad's grip on my arm was steady. Supporting me, always supporting me. "Remember what happened before the dog pack," he said. "That dump of data on your Flare. When you saw Bro."

I nodded, realised he might not be able to see me, and whispered, "Of course." My dreams of Kichlan, which might not be dreams at all.

"I've been thinking about it," he continued. "And I think it's because of your son. Do you remember on Fulcrum too? How perfect his connection to the veil is? How clean his stream?"

I swallowed hard. "Of course. That's why they want him in the first place. That's why they want to make him the Guardian." There was no way I'd let that happen.

"Your Flare is strong, Tan, but his is stronger. His connection to the veil is pure. I'm still not sure why, but it definitely has something to do with your suit. The puppet men had to force your body to integrate with debris—you were changed into code. But he has been that way from conception. Debris is one of the very building blocks of his life, it's in his cells, it's coded into his DNA."

I pushed down the guilt Lad's words sparked within me. I was supposed to a mother, wasn't I? But I still couldn't protect my son, not from the things my suit-altered body had done to him.

"You and your son share the same programming. Now that we have reconnected you, you share the same Flare too. Your son's Flare is powerful, Tan. Use it."

It wasn't fair, it wasn't his fault. How could I—?

A sound like laughter trickled through the connection. Joyful, haunting. I glimpsed the strangest, faintest image—a small, smiling face; a child silhouetted against the setting sun; the peak of the Keeper Mountain shining in the distance.

My son.

I felt no resentment from him. Just amusement, and a wistful longing for a life I wasn't sure I'd ever be able to give him.

But at least we were together now.

And together, we shone.

The power inside us swept through the Legate heart—into every last hub, down every last wire—drowning out all of the Legate's programmed commands. It fought back instantly, summoning a sudden flash of energy from within the complex and flooding me with garish threads of panicking code.

"We need to isolate the source of the Legate's power," I whispered. My son felt I was wasting time and energy by stating the obvious.

There were two Shards within the steel mountain itself, only two actual sources of power—the rest was borrowed from across Crust. One cocooned the Other, and was not part of the official network. Not a true source of energy. That left the second, half-buried in the earth, peeking out from beneath the incongruous drawbridge. With a thought, my code swarmed like ants around its much larger body and chewed through its connections, isolating it from the rest of the network and containing the power of its Flare within the walls of its clear prison.

Without the most direct source of power the Legate was forced to fall back on its secondary sources—all those Shards across Crust. Weakened, it reached for them, sending warning flares out across the wired world. Rather than try to prevent this, I helped them along. I scooped up all the personalities and the directives that made up the Legate and tossed them out of the heart. Then, with the strength of our shared Flare behind me, I blocked the way back in. I jammed so many lines of nonsense symbols into the wires, the hubs and the light, that nothing could travel in or out. Not even me.

I knew, instantly, that this would not hold long. Every second enabled the Legate to gather its strength, to tap its inexhaustible supply of Flares and funnel them all into sapping my defences and worming their way back in. Already, I could feel them, that massive multifaceted mind flinging itself in programming symbols against me.

But for the meantime, I had control. So I switched on the lights.

"There are Drones," I said, and my voice sounded so strange, tiny inside my massive Legate heart body. "In the city and in the corridors above. Coming for us. We have to run."

I couldn't stay connected, and do that at the same time. I had to trust my code-wall to hold. Lad extracted me, picked me up and half-carried me down the corridor. I guided them from memory, but at every major junction we were forced to stop so I could jump back on the network to check.

Every time we stopped to reconnect, I could feel the Legate building. Three Shards were totally engaged in the process of dismantling my code-wall, and more were being brought online. This meant drawing power from other places across Crust. Fulcrum, and other laboratories like it, were running on essential power only. Many of the Core cities below Crust would suddenly find that the Shards they poached didn't have any power left to share.

"Where are you leading us?" Meta cried, as we skidded to a halt at a pair of curving doors. A pod track. Lad tore the cap off the control panel so I could access its wiring. "Where is the Hero?"

I shook my head. The network was so full, too full. It was all so much information and code, and I knew all of it, all at once. Was this what the veil was like? Was this what had driven the Other mad?

"Answer me!" A gun at my temple. Dimly, I was aware of Adrian pointing his weapon at Lad, and Kasen bleeding, gasping for air.

I pointed at the doors. "Down."

"Take us to him!"

I shook my head. "No. We have to get out. I'm looking for exits—"

"Like hell you are."

Meta had to force the pod doors open, because I refused to do it for her. It was not used often. Finally, she resorted to threatening Lad, before I would activate the pod. She and Adrian had to physically force him inside.

The pod dropped, squealing, rattling, before it came to a sudden halt and the doors opened to pitch darkness.

More than just darkness, I realised. There were no cameras down here, no sensors, nothing to feed me information. Compared to the rest of the network it was both a fresh breath and a terrifying plunge.

"Very dark," Lad murmured, as he helped me establish

a fresh link.

I nodded. I closed my eyes, and went searching. Down to the very ends of the wiring, to the most isolated hubs. I felt stretched, thin.

One, two and a third outside Shard switched on in quick succession. I almost lost my grip as they brought their sudden and combined power to bear while I was searching around in the network's neglected sublevel. I gave up motor control for network control and sagged forward. Lad caught me, carefully.

"Tan?" he breathed against my ear. "Can you find a way out?"

I shook my head. "All those machines, the ones we saw, they're coming for us. Surrounding the building, scratching at the doors I refuse to open. I can't hold the Legate out for long. And I don't control anything outside of the heart. We won't get far, if we run outside. The Other's a bastard, but even dead and locked in silex he's stronger than he should be. The only way we'll get out of this is if we can find a way to block the Legate's control not only of this complex, but the Drones too. He's the only one with the experience and strength to help me to do that. Just promise you'll look out for me. Promise you won't let me—" I swallowed hard, rattled silex "—make another stupid mistake."

He held me tightly. It was all the answer I needed.

When I finally found the lights and managed to switch them on they were so faint they did not make much of a difference. Small patches of silex hung like fungi on the walls. The corridor here was rusted and too tight even for the youngest of Drones. It was a path meant for humans. We struggled through it, Lad holding my arms delicately, afraid of my Flare and the fragility of my silex but all too keenly aware that without his support, I would fall.

We found the Other in a cave, surrounded by the foundations of the Legate's heart. Great iron supports protruded from the rock to tower like the bars of a cage around his Shard. His prism was small compared to the others I had seen on Crust. Three times as high as a man, maybe twice as wide. It was roughly hewn, none of the sleek lines and sheer planes of pristine crystal I was used to. This made it difficult to see into, and the light of the Flare it contained was dim and fitful.

Lad hung back, with Adrian's gun still pointed at his head. I gathered my strength and approached it, slowly.

"This is the Hero?" Meta whispered, her voice breaking. I glanced over my shoulder. She was holding Kasen, who'd fallen to his knees.

"What is left of him," Lad said. His face was carefully blank.

I held my son tighter, stepped up to the Shard, and placed my free hand on its rough surface. It was warm, and it throbbed, the dull pulse of a slow and ancient heart.

Silex wept from the crack in my wrist. It did not need me to guide it, but slid down across the surface, dipped into nooks and followed the cracks deeper, deeper, toward the faint outline of a body that I could barely see.

Until we connected.

And the Flare inside the Other's Shard burned suddenly sharp, suddenly bright. I squinted against it. Behind me, Lad cursed and I heard them shuffling back.

With the light, the body in the crystal clarified. I gasped. The Other was little more than bones and strips of long-dried flesh. He really was dead, so long dead, decayed as his mind travelled the veil. But he moved, though only a little and only as his Shard allowed. His skull tipped slightly toward me, and one bone-clawed hand lifted, fingers opening.

I realised, with a rapidly growing horror, that my future was in that body. We were, in a way, so much the same. Living in a body that should have died long ago, sustained by the particles that crossed the veil while our flesh dissolved around us, and the Shards, the hubs and the network were all that remained to support us.

"Tanyana?" the Other asked. His voice echoed through my silex. "Is that you?" Of course, he could not speak. Not without his artificial, composite mouth to do it for him. So all I heard was his presence in the silex that connected us.

"Yes."

"You're the one blocking the Legate's network, aren't you?" The Other sounded shocked, hardly as grateful as I would have liked. "You realise you trapped me here too, when you did that?"

"I've come," I said, voice a rasp of cracked mineral. "Like you wanted. I completed your impossible task. Now I need your help. The Legate knows we're here. Give me your strength, help me stop them, or they'll crawl all the way down here and take us away and then who will help you?"

The Other did not reply.

"What's happening?" Lad hissed.

I shook my head. "Answer me!"

The Other sighed. His unreal breath rippled through me. "You have not, strictly speaking, done as I have asked. I summoned you here to free me from this place. You tried to betray me, forcing me to drag you here kicking and screaming. And now you've brought the Legate with you."

I held my ground. "What did you expect?"

"But I am a fair and reasonable Hero, Tanyana. Far more so than you deserve. I will strike a new deal with you."

"What is he saying?" Lad asked. I translated electrical pulse and code for him. "Don't trust him, Tan. Be careful, remember what he is and what he's done!"

As Adrian bristled, I turned my attention back to the Other.

"What do you want this time?" I asked, trying to keep myself steady. Even though Lad was right, I also knew it wouldn't be long before the Drones found us. We were running out of time.

"What I have always wanted, Tanyana. Freedom."

"But isn't that why you brought me here?"

"*Real* freedom. From this body, from this dead fucking world. Take me back to the veil, and I will give you her secrets. Together, we will remove the false, Guardian program and restore me to my rightful place as protector of your world. Do that, and I will help you. If you don't, then you can all just die here."

28.

"**W**hat do they mean *thank you*?" Kichlan looked down at Devich.

The once-man cowered, slobbered, his too-long arms wrapped around his head and his eyes closed. "No no no no," he whimpered, over and over.

"Devich, you didn't—?" Why was he so surprised? Devich had betrayed Tanyana once, why had Kichlan allowed himself to believe the man wouldn't do it to him too?

Muffled on the other side of the doors and the darkness, Kichlan could hear shouting, and running, all of it in panic and fear. The puppet men were watching him, smiling.

"Perhaps you should explain to your friends," one said.

"That nothing they do can stop us," the other continued.

"Though, if they are so inclined, we always welcome help," the third finished, and pointed at Kichlan's head.

Kichlan's suit began to retreat. But why? Why was it listening to the puppet men again?

<*Access to simulated Flare has bolstered the strength of the invading signal. Protocol override in progress*> The answer came quietly, as though distant.

"How do I stop them?" he whispered back.

<*Recommend system reset*>

"Reset?"

The suit slid from his eyes, revealing chaos in the ancient Unbound street.

Lev was restraining Valya, who had lifted a large chunk of rubble above her head and appeared to be trying to attack the puppet men with it. She was screaming, "You killed them! You bastards!" with a viciousness Kichlan had never imagined the old woman could produce. Even Lev looked shocked.

Fedor and his Unbound had retreated a little, and were huddling around the small debris screen. Kichlan couldn't see what they were doing to the wall above Uzdal's coffin—all he could see were doors. Natasha, weighed down by her ungainly crystals and weakened by her injuries, had still managed to find something to arm herself with. A large shard of crystal with a sharp point, like the ones that had grown from the walls on the long pathway down.

Volksi and Zecholas stood right beside Kichlan. They were staring at the puppet men, entranced.

"What are you doing?" Kichlan snapped at them. "Why isn't anybody running away?"

"They're back," Volski whispered.

"She was right." Zecholas lifted his free hand and twitched his fingers. "You too, Vol. I didn't notice them last time." Kichlan felt a change in the air, like a warm breeze had just brushed around his head. "The crimson pions."

What were they doing? "Stop standing there and run, you foolish binders!" Kichlan tried to push Zecholas away. But, with a strangely twisted smile, the man just flicked his fingers and the ground beneath Kichlan's feet rolled.

"They're responsive," Zecholas turned to Volksi. "Were they responsive last time?"

"No idea." The older man straightened. He ran a hand through his hair, pushing its silver strands out of his eyes, and his face set into determination. Even anger. "But be careful. These things pushed lady Tanyana from *Grandeur*'s palm. We should not take them lightly."

They shared a glance and some apparently inaudible communication, nodded, and split up, circling around the puppet men, twitching fingers, whispering words.

"What are you doing?" Kichlan called to them.

Zecholas flashed him a grin. "That suit anything like Tanyana's was?" he asked, looking at the silver extending from Kichlan's left elbow.

Volski lifted an arm, and a great wall of earth rose around the puppet men. "I'll hold them, you slice them!"

Kichlan staggered back, shocked. "But I thought—"

"There are pions here! Strange looking ones, maybe, but pions all the same." Zecholas grew steel out of the ground, honed it into spears and launched them at the puppet men like a thick wall of dark and terrible rain. "We are not weak here, anymore!"

Kichlan threw himself to the ground. Volski's wall dropped just in time and the spears sliced through the puppet men. Their fake skin was torn away, their mist of bodiless faces and shadows dispersed. Devich screamed and scrambled as rubble fell on him.

"Yes!" Volski grunted, and the earth moved again.

Kichlan pushed himself upright, kicking at Devich as he crawled close—sobbing and drooling, bleeding from cuts to the flesh patches in his head and hands.

Then the puppet men reformed. Their mist coalesced, their skin regrew, and all the scars and spears the binders had created were flattened, smoothed, with nothing more than the gesture of a false hand. One of them turned his unemotional eyes to Volski, "Care to try that again?"

"Bastards!" Zecholas spat to the side. "Other's oath we will!"

"No," Kichlan cried. "Stop it! Every time you manipulate one of those pions you're weakening the veil!"

But the binders didn't listen to him. So he focused again on his silver arm, the intense focus that had worked last time, that had convinced the suit to move for him. But nothing happened. He was coated with silver up to his neck, his hand was heavy and unresponsive, and he couldn't do anything about it.

<Emergency protocols triggered. Anti-hacking failsafe is in effect. Host-body has been designated a threat, and locked out of control functions>

"But I can still hear you. Why can I still hear you if I can't control you?"

<*Physical connection to host-body nervous system has not been compromised. Communication therefore still possible. Suggest system reboot to reestablish control*>

"But how do I do that?"

Then Fedor pushed him aside, and he would have fallen again if Devich hadn't caught him.

"Veche scum," Fedor spat at the puppet men. "I'm glad you came." He lifted the debris panel and jerked the symbols across its surface, his expression terrible in its triumph and his hands hooked into furious claws. Still, Kichlan couldn't see what was happening. But Volski and Zecholas shouted, raising shields of stone to protect themselves, and Lev forced Valya down against the floor, covering her with his body even as she swore at him, loudly.

<*Hard reboot can be achieved by overloading the system. External power source needed. Suggest artificial Flare*>

The silver in Kichlan's left elbow suddenly liquefied, and spread out in front of him, wide and flat. He gripped his arm and pain speared up to his shoulder, setting his back and neck spasming. Light swelled—but he couldn't see where it was coming from—and loud cracking sounds echoed through the underground rooms.

"No!" he heard Mizra scream. "You'll hurt him!"

Then lightning ached above him, racing along the ceiling, dipping to shatter Volski's stone shield before crawling across the floor towards the puppet men like the bright feet of a terrible spider.

<*Artificial Flare now in existence*>

Despite the wall of silver extending from his arm, Kichlan struggled forward. His back cramped and with a hiss he fell to one knee. But he kept going, crawling, slipping, silver scraping great tears in the stone floor. Then Fedor's lightning—the suit had called it a Flare—wrapped itself around his shield.

And he screamed as it surged through him, following

all his deep silver. Something was burning—like leather, like skin—but he couldn't tell where it was coming from.

<*Maintain contact to reboot*>

But this wasn't power. This was pain, this was frying him inside out.

<*Five...four...three*>

Somehow, Kichlan tore his mind away from the pain, from the desire to curl around himself and let the lightning kill him. Just finish it. He gritted his teeth, he focused on his ungainly silver shield. And again, he felt a surge. Not the lightning, this time, it came from him. Silver shuddered within him, rolling, tingling. He pulled his shield back into a hand. He unwrapped his chest and neck. He stood.

His vision cleared enough to watch as the puppet men were dispersed again. But they reformed as soon as the light died, and chuckled softly, the sound filling the underground street in a creeping tide.

Kichlan flexed his hand. "It worked," he whispered. "How?"

<*Hard reboot reset access protocols*>

"Will it last?"

<*Not without reprogramming*>

"So, we can't give them the chance to take control again."

<*Affirmative*>

Fedor, with a growl, lifted his hand above the panel yet again.

"Wait!" Kichlan cried, and strode towards Fedor. "That's enough!"

Fedor ignored him.

"Just look at them, will you?" Kichlan stopped, close enough to snatch the panel from Fedor's hands if necessary. "They're not afraid of you, of any of you." He glanced back at Zecholas and Volski. "They want you to fight. They want you to use both pions and debris—as much as you can, with all your strength. Can't you see that? Just look at their faces! They want this. They might even be counting on it."

The puppet men didn't refute him. Their skin stretched into an unnatural twist as they grinned, all three of them, all identical. Together, they turned and began to walk toward the mass of doors. A slow walk, calm.

Volski and Zecholas hesitated, but Fedor only shook his head. "Get out of my way."

So Kichlan sent his silver reaching, perfectly accurate and too fast for Fedor. He took the panel right out of the man's clutching fingers. Three of the Unbound men broke away from the group and headed towards him, expressions angry. But they didn't even get close. Devich leapt in front of them, snarling and howling, a madman on all fours.

"Kichlan?" Natasha, hindered by her injuries, backed away from the puppet men as they passed her. "Why are you protecting these veche bastards?"

"Lovely to see you again, Miss Illosky," one of the puppet men said, his voice low and amused, "though you do look a little worse for wear." He even nodded, almost politely. "Revolution is harder than it sounds, isn't it? It's taken us thousands of years, after all, to get this far. And our revolution, Miss Illoksy, is far more successful than yours. If you don't mind us saying."

Natasha stared at them, face pale and mouth agape. "What?" she whispered, stunned.

"Give it back!" Fedor hesitated at the sight of Devich. "These are the creatures that killed your brother, don't you remember?"

"They did more than that," Kichlan said. "They killed the Keeper, and then they killed Tan. But that doesn't change anything. The puppet men are here to destroy the veil. What you've been doing here, that panel, those crystals, that strange wall, is only helping them! You won't hurt them, because they're not even real. At least, not in this world. But you will weaken the veil, and that will destroy us all!"

Fedor, eyes wide, shook his head. "What are you talking about?"

"We can't kill the puppet men, not with pions and not with debris. But you should at least stop helping them."

"Kichlan!" Mizra shouted, his voice high and panicked. "They're hurting my brother!"

Kichlan spun. The three puppet men were crouched around Uzdal in his coffin, their long, fake fingers dipping into the ice, unfeeling of the cold. Mizra, who had held back, cowering and afraid, lifted a large and loose chunk of rubble above his head and ran at the puppet men, screaming.

"No!" Kichlan dropped the debris panel at his feet and leapt forward. But despite the quickness of his silver, despite the control he had regained, he was just too slow to catch Mizra, too late to stop him.

One of the puppet men simply glanced over his shoulder, face flat and inexpressive, and lifted a hand. Doors flickered, imposing themselves on Kichlan's vision and Mizra was knocked aside. He was flung back, into the sharp crystal-riddled and power-buzzing wall. So Kichlan changed track. Hooks in the ceiling, spikes from his feet, he flung himself forward even as he reached, extending as quickly and as far as his silver would go. And caught Mizra, just before he hit, wrapped him in silver and lowered him, gently, to the floor.

"Mizra!" Natasha cried.

Footsteps running towards him. Zecholas on one side and Devich on the other.

"They used the pions," Zecholas hissed. "Tore them right out of our hands, attacked Mizra, then gave them back." He met Kichlan's gaze, horrified. Devich danced and skittered around them both. "I think—hell—I think you might be right. We could only use those pions because they let us."

Kichlan nodded. Behind him, Fedor dove for his debris panel. Kichlan turned, but too late and Fedor unleashed more lightning across the room. But this time, whatever that rabid energy touched was replaced by a door. Not shaking, straining against hinges. Open.

And on the other side—

"Lad?" he whispered.

Devich slobbered, "Tan—ya. Close."

Then the light faded, and the doors closed. But not before Kichlan had seen his brother—his dead brother—standing in another cave. He was arguing with someone, face flushed, hands gesturing. It was so real, but impossible. It had to be.

"What was that?" Mizra gasped. Gently, Kichlan eased his silver grip so Mizra could stand and stumble away from the puppet men. "Was that—the doors?"

"You saw it?" Kichlan asked.

"Yes."

Mizra looked up, shocked, as Kichlan turned. Sofia. Blinded, mutilated, she stood on the edge of the street, mouth open wide and the stumps of her arms raised. Crystal and wires trailed around her, bright like the lacing of an otherworldly gown. She tipped her head back and looked to the wall above Uzdal's coffin. The wall she simply could not see.

"I saw them," she said, and her voice was strong. "I saw the doors. And on the other side, I saw Tanyana."

Natasha staggered over to Sofia. She wrapped an arm around her shoulders, but the woman refused to be led back inside. "I saw them," Sofia insisted.

"We all did," Natasha said. She met Kichlan's eyes, her expression fearful. "What does this mean?"

"I didn't," Volski said. Zecholas nodded his agreement. "We just saw lightning. Damned dangerous stuff that is too."

Fedor, obviously shaken, held his hesitating hand above the symbols but did not move them again. Kichlan guessed he'd seen the doors too. And Lad. Or Tan. Both dead. Both impossible. But so many had seen them...

Unfazed by the attack, the puppet men had moved from Uzdal's coffin to the wall behind it. Their fake fingers ran fast patterns over the crystal and wires, rearranging them at an inhuman speed. The light in Uzdal's coffin flickered and the ice around him began to retreat.

"Stop it, please!" Mizra shouted. "Don't hurt him!"

One of the puppet men glanced over his shoulder, a faintly curious expression toying with his features. His fingers did not stop. "He is dead. The silex encasing him is creating the illusion of life—forcing breath into his lungs, a pulse into his blood, and slowing the progress of decay. But do not mistake this for living, for he is well and truly dead."

"No," Mizra whispered. "He can't...he can't be gone."

"He is." But as the puppet man returned his gaze to the wall, something strange happened to him. He jerked, shook, and his fingers stilled.

The Keeper's half-arm, half-face, crawled out of the mist clinging to the back of the puppet man's jacket. He looked fainter than he had last time, weaker. "Kichlan?" and when he spoke, his voice was less than a whisper, more like an echo, remote and unreal. "The veil is falling. I failed. Tell them, tell the programmers, I am sorry. Tell them I tried."

The puppet man twisted around, unnaturally far, reached behind himself with a suddenly too-long arm, and pushed the Keeper back into the mist. He didn't fight, this time. There wasn't enough left of him to even try.

<Guardian program nearly terminated>

Kichlan's suit sounded oddly sad. "What can we do?" he asked it. He'd tried to stop Fedor, Zecholas and Volski weakening the veil any further, but had failed. He knew better than to fight the puppet men head on. It wouldn't take much for them to regain control, and he wasn't convinced he could harm them anyway.

<All options exhausted>

Mizra wept as the ice withdrew from his brother's dead face and Uzdal's artificial breathing ceased.

"There is no point fighting any more," the puppet men said, all at once.

All the light and the energy that had filled Uzdal's coffin now swelled, up through the wires and the crystals until the entire wall burned with it. The air wavered like heat, but rhythmical and patterned, an invisible curtain, floating in the breeze. Or a veil.

"We are already through."

The doors returned, covering everything.

But Kichlan shook his head. "Tan closed the doors once. Damn me if I don't at least try to do the same." And he launched himself at the closest door, as it opened.

29.

"Why do you need me?" I asked the Other. "I know how powerful the Legate is. I've felt their strength on the network. Despite being trapped in a dead body, despite the Shard designed to restrict you, you've managed to escape them. You've hidden from them, you've spread through Crust, sowing the seeds of resistance and building massive power stations like Core-1 West on the way." I glanced over my shoulder to Lad. He was watching me, pale and worried, tense and ready.

"I have." I could feel the Other's smug pride. It warmed his words and seeped into me through silex and light.

I leaned my forehead against the side of his Shard. Silex fell like soft sand down my cheeks, and beneath my collar. "So why bring me here? Why not return to the veil on your own?"

A pause. The Other was accustomed to being obeyed, and he was feeling less and less pleased with me by the minute. Did he know I could sense his emotions? Could he sense mine? "Because you are different. Somehow, you are here, and there, at the same time."

I frowned, and then was forced to blink silex out of my eye. "What?"

"You really don't know?"

"I—" But I did. I leaned back from the Shard, stared up into its light. "Wait. Something about the movement of particles. And data flow." I looked down at the silex cracked around my wrist and thought of Kichlan's silver arm. "I made a connection. By accident."

"Exactly." The Other's Flare pulsed. "The programmers have told you about the great mistake, I assume. In our arrogance, we tried to bend space and time to our will. But doing so shoved our realities, opposite realities, so close together that they began to bleed one into the other."

I nodded.

"Now, they can only move one way. When a particle travels from this world, across the veil, it becomes a pion in your world. When a particle from your world travels to this world, across the veil, it becomes a Flare. They cannot travel back."

I shook my head. "But what about you? You travelled to our world only to be dragged back here. Doesn't that mean you travelled both ways?"

"Actually, no. You see, I never made it all the way to your world. My consciousness was uploaded, yes, but only to the veil itself. From within the veil I could observe your world and I could protect it, but I was never a part of it. I existed to interrupt or rearrange the flow of particles through the veil. But ask me to pick a flower, to touch a hand? I lurked in shadows, Tanyana, watching, but never a part of your world."

I thought of the Keeper, of the world of darkness and doors that only I had been able to see. And yes, I knew what he meant. The Keeper too had been forced to lurk in shadows, and had never truly belonged.

"What about the Halves?" I whispered. "What about the programmers? They crossed, didn't they?"

"Only a part of them crossed—only a section of their thoughts locked in code and transported by light. And don't forget, those parts did not come back. It is always a one-way trip. Until you decided to bend the rules."

It would have been for Lad, too. Aladio might have had Lad's face, but before I returned his Half to him, he had not been the Lad I knew.

"Then what about you? If you have a Flare inside you, like I have one inside me, doesn't that mean that particles are moving through you too? Away from my world and into yours? Since you were uploaded the opposite way, doesn't that mean you are moving in both directions?"

"Sadly, no. If it was, I wouldn't need you at all. I wouldn't need anyone." Such yearning, such resentment. It made me shiver. "I cannot just travel back the way I have come, I need a vessel. I need a pathway of light and code. I need someone to upload me."

Like the coffins that had housed the Halves in Fulcrum. I still didn't see how this related to me.

"Don't I need the same thing then? A pathway of light and code?"

The Other chuckled. "But you already are returning. Constantly. You exist here, and you exist in the other world, and you move in between them. You stretch across the veil, a tether between two worlds."—

—*Kichlan pushed against the door, but he couldn't even touch the handle. His silver hand just passed right through it. Again and again, he tried. While the puppet men laughed at him, and he could hear ghostly snippets of Tan's voice, and his brother stared horrified and tense through the open door, looking alive, looking real. It all hurt. If he could just close that door, if he could just touch it. He was tired of hurting—*

—I slumped against the Shard, the crystal binding us the only thing keeping me on my feet. "I know." My son slipped, slightly, in the crook of my elbow. I squeezed him tighter, with what little strength our shared and broken body had left. "It's Kichlan. I thought I was dreaming about him. But my son showed me they weren't dreams. Not really." I stared down at my left arm. "The cap on Kichlan's elbow—I used some of my suit to fuse it to his body." I looked up. "The suit—the program—is still connected to me, isn't it? To us—my son and me. No matter how far we stray. It's my pathway."

Kichlan was alive.

"Your consciousness travels between worlds faster than the blink of an eye." The Other sounded smug. "You move both ways. So that is what I want from you. I need a ride back to the veil to resume my rightful place. You will be my pathway. I will take the place of the failed Guardian program so your child doesn't have to. And I will give you the full power of the veil, so you can save your world. Your *Kichlan*." I could hear his impossible grin, wide and triumphant. "That's a fair bargain, wouldn't you say?"

I glanced back at Lad, Adrian, Meta and Kasen. "I will do it," I said, and held Lad's fearful gaze as I spoke. "I will take you back to the veil."

"Careful," Lad whispered.

I looked away. "How do we do this, then?"

"You need to forsake this world, and everything on it. Give up your flesh, I would have said, but your flesh carried you here, did it not. You are more code than muscle, skin and bone, so maybe, you do not have to give that up. As the rest of us were forced to do."

I winced, and glanced up. "But what about the Legate?" While the rock and steel supports above us looked calm and quiet, the Drones had to be close now. "If I go, there won't be anyone to stop the Legate getting in here. They will kill Lad and the guards from Core-1 West, and they will completely isolate your Shard."

"And why would that worry me?" the Other said. "I won't even be here anymore."

I hesitated.

"What about your pet programmer. Give the network over to him. You have such faith in him, don't you? He will hold them off."

I kept my connection to the Other's Shard, even as I spun and explained to Lad what we needed him to do. The Other was not impressed with the delay, but he believed he had won me over, and his triumph mollified him to some extent.

Lad shook his head. "How exactly do you expect me to do that? I can't connect myself the way you do."

"There is an ancient terminal," the Other said. "They used it to monitor me, back in the day. It is connected to my Shard, and it now feeds into the network."

Adrian found it first. A screen, and a keyboard, set into the rock around the far side of the Shard. Lad cursed over the state of it—screen cracked, a few keys missing, and of it clogged with dust, sand, and a faint shedding of silex. Still, it responded to his fingers, and flickered into dull life. I felt it awaken, another presence close to mine, tiny compared to the Other.

"Brilliant," the Other muttered. "Can we do this now? Have I told you how much I hate waiting?"

He didn't have to; I'd experienced the evidence first hand.

"I don't know how long I can hold them off with this," Lad said.

"I can help," Adrian said. He didn't put his gun down, but he even so he dug around in his bag, pulling out a set of small hubs. "Amplifiers." Lad helped him hook them up, and after a moment, the terminal's presence strengthened.

"Hero," I said, and pressed my face against his Shard. "Give Lad the power of your Flare."

He didn't respond. I could sense how much he hated that idea.

"You're already connected to this terminal, and to the network. Lad and Adrian need you to help them." Something arrived at the pod blocking the entrance to the tunnel. The noise of tearing metal echoed into the cave. "And anyway, you won't need it any more, will you? You'll be inside the veil itself."

The Other conceded, reluctantly, and the terminal flared. Its screen, though cracked, shone bright light into the room, and its presence grew, spreading like a wave. The thought warmed me, because that wave was Lad and I knew he would do what he had always promised to do. He would look after me.

"They've breached us already!" I couldn't see him properly, only a faint shape wavering in the Shard's distortion, but I could hear his fingers smacking hard and fast over the keyboard. "I'm taking control. Cutting off communication to the Drones in the pod track." A great clatter of metal shuddered the cave walls. "Doors are mine. Most of the cameras are down, but I think we've got smaller, bio-mechanical things in the tunnel and I can't do anything about them without killing us!"

"Leave that to me." Meta pulled large guns out of the bag they had refused to relinquish, all this time. Her expression was hard. I realised that Kasen had fallen back, and I couldn't see if he was breathing. "I'm not entirely sure what's going on, but I still have a job to do, and that's to help my Hero." She stalked towards the tunnel entrance. "Dim the lights, will you?" she asked. "At least give me a chance."

Adrian watched her go, jaw tight. Then it was too dark to see anything.

"Can we get on with this, please?" the Other said.

For a moment the sound of Lad's fingers paused. "Be careful, Tan," Lad said. And I wished I could see his face—alive, stern, loving—for one last time. Then he resumed typing in earnest.

"You are already a part of me," the Other was saying in a low and contented purr. "And I am part of you. You are code, you are silex. So am I. Join with me."

I pressed against the Shard, not only with my hand and my face, but with everything. Silex, flesh and light—everything I had become.

My silex bled into its mineral, draining out of my body.

My light caught the Shard's glow and together, our Flares pulsed.

And my hand—what was left of my hand—plunged into the side of the Shard. It did not entomb me, because I wasn't really flesh, not on this world. I was what the puppet men had made me. I was debris, code and light.

I stepped forward, into the Shard. Into the Other's Flare, and mine.

Then everything was light, and colour. And the Other was so close to me, he was all around me. And my son was a smaller presence, pressed against my own. And we were flying past hundreds of openings, small Flares, hanging in Shards and piercing the sky. Beyond a great river of light, fed by a dozen smaller tributaries.

Toward a single, open door.

"Don't go that far," the Other said, laughing, thrilled. "Here, let me show you."

The door began to retreat. But we did not return to the cave at the base of the heart of the Legate. Instead, we hovered in cool, silvery light and I wondered, for an instant, if there really was any power here, any truth. Or just eternal emptiness. An unending in between.

Except the Other was standing next to me.

Not just a presence riding my light and wound up in my code, not any more. And neither was he faceless, half-formed and horrific, leering at me from around gravesites and between drying clumps of rosemary.

The Other was a man, well aged and well built. He was dressed strangely, in a suit made out of only one piece of deep blue, slightly reflective fabric. An icon was emblazoned on his chest: a small prism shining out solid blocks of colour in a rainbow. He smiled at me, and his teeth were perfect. His skin was sun-worn, his haircut severe.

"Ahh," he tipped back his head and breathed, deeply, like he had not tasted air in a very long time. Like there was air to taste. "Now this is more like it." I caught the glittering of small silex hubs embedded in his neck. Each shone with a different colour: blue, red, yellow, as though reflecting the rainbow stitched onto his suit.

"Come on, don't disappoint me now, Tanyana. You can hardly present yourself to the veil without a body, can you?"

A body?

"But how—" even as I spoke, I realised I had a mouth and a throat to do so. I glanced down.

I was wearing the coat Kichlan and Lad had bought for me, from a second-hand shop on the Tear River. Beneath it, my patched shirt and pants, still stiff from the starch Valya had pressed them with. And finally, my collector's uniform, dark, stretchy and boned.

"How interesting," the Other said, with his broad and straight-toothed smile. "This is how you see yourself, if it?"

"How I see myself?" I lifted a hand, ran fingers through short and well-behaved hair, and noticed the suit band shining brightly on my wrist.

The Other's eyes widened. They were blue, I realised, so light they could have been grey. He leaned forward, peered at my wrist. "What is that?"

"This is my suit," I whispered. Our voices sounded strange, here. They seemed to echo on into eternity. "It's—" I paused. "A long story."

"It has code on it." He frowned. "But it doesn't make sense."

I lowered my arm and shook my sleeve over the suit band. "I know." Not to us, anyway. The symbols that rose and died in apparently random order made snippets of words, partial commands. But the puppet men had used them to work a powerful reprogramming, one that had stumped the programmers and Specialist too. Just because it did not make sense to us, did not mean it was nonsense. Not by any means.

"Come," the Other said. He looked off into the distance, where the shadows of shapes were resolving themselves faintly against the light. "The veil can feel timeless, but do not let that fool you. We should hurry." He flashed me another smile. I couldn't read him, not the way I had with his Shard-bound presence. Was there sincerity in that smile, or the same smug arrogance? The same madness that he had wreaked upon my world?

Remember not to trust him, Tan. Lad's voice sounded in my ear, and my heart made a small, hopeful flip. *He might look like a man but he doesn't think like one, not any more. He hasn't been alive for a very long time.*

The shock must have shown on my face, as the Other's expression turned worried. "Tanyana? What is it?"

Good, he can't hear me. We need to keep it that way. Don't give me away.

I shook myself, and rubbed my unreal cheeks until I could control my expression. The left side of my face was scarred again, where Tsana's glass had cut me. How strange, that I had done that to myself here. "I just—" The shakiness in my voice, the unsteadiness of this new, though old, body, was not an act. "This is just so strange."

The Other leaned back and nodded, indulgent. "Oh, I know. But wonderful too. Follow me, and I will show you."

Good, keep that up.

He gestured towards my feet. "Don't you want to take that?"

I glanced down.

It was nothing but a ball of light. It glowed softly. I bent, found that I could pick it up. It was gentle, warm, not quite real but still here. Touching me.

"What is it?"

The Other laughed. "Don't you know? That is your child, Tanyana. The one you were so desperate to save."

I gasped, and my grip tightened. It beamed through my fingers, as bright as our Flare. "But why does he look like that?"

He lifted eyebrows. "The veil has the power to give us form, but only the form we give ourselves. Thus I will always look the way I did, on that fateful day, when we tore reality. You, it seems, think of yourself like that. With your patched jacket and your suit. But your child does not think of himself as anything, not yet. So that is how he will remain." He strode ahead. "Now hurry."

I clutched my son to my chest and followed.

"Lad?" I breathed, softly. "How is this possible?"

The terminal is connected to the Shard, and the Shard is holding the Other, so we can follow you. A little. It's not much, but at least you're not alone. At least I can look after you. Like Bro told me to. Like you asked.

"Are you alright? The Drones—"

Meta is stronger than you give her credit for, and that bag held more than just guns. Put your faith in us, and stop worrying. Concentrate on the Other. Find us a way out of this.

We did not have to walk far before the shadows began to solidify. The formless glow gave way to buildings, impossibly tall and riddled with lights. Bitumen stretched out around our feet. Street lamps sprang up like trees, growing. And I realised, with a sudden dip in my stomach, that I knew this place. Well, I knew its future.

"This is Crust, isn't it?"

People, ghost-like and insubstantial, walked past us. Pods whirred by. I looked up, beyond the towering buildings linked by bridges of thin steel and full of movement, of light, to the sky. It was a clear night. Words and images scrawled their way over a moon, hanging low and large. And in the distance, faint beside a world of so much light, stars glittered.

"Before it was known as Crust, yes. This is my world, as I knew it."

"But how? How can this exist in a tear between two worlds?" How could it exist at all?

"Because the veil is so much more than that." The Other stopped, and stood among his impossible world. He lifted his arms, as people walked past him and pods sped through him, and rapture lit his face. "You wanted the truth? This, here, is your truth. The veil is not a membrane between broken worlds, and it was not created accidently by the programmers. The veil was always here, waiting for someone strong enough to find it. The veil is a god!"

A what? He really is mad.

Silence settled around us, and I realised how wrong that felt, for a world as apparently busy as the one we stood in.

"What?"

The Other lowered his arms, grinning. "The veil is full," he said, "the veil is rich. See everything it has given me? I have been blessed by a god, because I earned it. Through sacrifice, through strength. I'm home."

I took a shaking step back.

He lowered his arms. "So you see, the veil will give me what I want. And now you have returned me, it will do the same for you. If I wish it. If I ask." His blue eyes glinted. "Should I ask, Tanyana? Do you trust me, really? Or do you still believe the lies that fucking programmer told you? I believe that the power of a god should only be given to those who deserve it. I always have believed that. Is that you? Think hard. Is it really you?"

Careful, Tan.

I swallowed. "But Hero, I do not understand." I needed to ease that glint in his eyes, the hard line of his clenching jaw. I needed an Other smiling in rapture, not judging in his wrath. "I thought the veil was a semi-something-reality-something, a side effect of the experiment that brought our worlds so close together. How can it be a god?"

That soothed him, slightly. I had the feeling he liked dispensing truth in small bites, like tossing morsels of food to a starving man.

"A wave function semi-reality. That's what the programmers think it is, yes. But they are wrong. You should know that by now, Tanyana. They are wrong about a lot of things."

Wait, something's wrong. I felt a surge. Not from him though, and not from you.

I nodded. "Yes, they are."

What is that?

"They did not create the veil, all they did was open a path to it."

"Actually," a familiar voice said, behind me. "*Trapped* would be a more accurate description."

I spun. Kichlan walked out of the city heat and the haze of busy light. And for a second I couldn't breathe, couldn't think, because Kichlan was there, right there. I took a shaky step towards him, hope and a heady sense of relief making the shadowy world spin.

That's impossible! Lad's voice crackled and wavered. *Bro?*

I blinked, forced my feet to slow. It couldn't be. Lad was right, it was impossible.

"They trapped me here," Kichlan said. His left arm was whole, and his eyes glowed a steady silver. The Other's world froze in his footsteps. "When these so-called *programmers* tried to bend space to their will, they caught me in the middle, between their world and yours."

But that meant—"Are you the veil?" I asked.

Kichlan shrugged. "That's what they call me, yes. I find it strange. Even after so long, I am not accustomed to having a name." He looked down at himself and smiled with Kichlan's mouth. "I don't have a body you can see, of course, so I have to borrow his. The image of this man has passed through me so many times, thanks to you. I almost feel like I know him." It lifted Kichlan's arms. "But still, I'm sorry about this."

I nodded, swallowed hard. It was difficult to look at the Veil like this. To see Kichlan standing so close and know it wasn't him.

Not Bro? The Veil? Tan, I don't understand. What's happening?

I shook my head. I had no idea.

I glanced over my shoulder. The Other was as frozen as his city, mouth open, hands half outstretched toward me, face a mask of cruel amusement.

The Veil, in Kichlan's skin, stopped a few yards away. "I've been pinned here, between worlds, for longer than you could even comprehend." His shining eyes met mine. "All I have been doing, ever since, is fighting for my freedom. And now, when it looks like I might actually escape, you arrive. Have you come to argue that your life is more important than my freedom, Tanyana? Are you here to doom me, again?"

30.

"I —I don't understand," I whispered, and wondered if I should bow. Or kneel. Or do something. What does one do in the face of a god?

The Veil tipped Kichlan's head to the side. "What's wrong, Tanyana? Is it this world?"

The Other's world dissolved, starting at the Veil's feet and spreading out, in a great circle, like ripples in a pond. Bitumen and buildings returned to shapeless light. The Other was swept away with them, which was something of a relief, despite the strangeness of it.

New shadows formed and solidified around us, but these were shapes I knew well. Movoc-under-Keeper spread out like a sunrise, starting behind the Veil and opening up to the very sky. Like the Other's world, mine was a Movoc-under-Keeper of the past. It was whole, alive and unscarred. The Keeper Mountain reared above me. The sky was a clear, hard blue, and an icy wind funnelled down the streets to tug at my patched coat. I breathed in its crispness. I hadn't realised how much I missed the cold.

"Is that better?" the Veil asked.

A deep, unreal breath. "A little," I said. "Thank you. It's just…difficult. Because you look like Kichlan. And I—" why was this sticking in my throat? "—can you understand that?"

"Of course." Such sympathy in those eyes, even though they were purely light. I could feel it all around me, thick on the fog. The Veil felt for me. It really did.

"Then maybe, you will help me." I glanced around. "The Other said he would petition you to help me. He said you would listen to him, like you have done in the past. But he is gone."

The Veil nodded. "The one who calls himself a Hero and calls me a god. Yes, I know him quite well. And yes, I've helped him in the past. He brought you here, and I decided we did not need him to do anything more than that."

"What did you do to him?"

Fear must have shown on my face and through my voice. The Veil, looking worried, made gentle calming motions with his hands. "Nothing but what he wanted. I have given him back his past. Like I have given you yours, here."

"You locked him in that pre-Crust world?"

The Veil nodded.

I wasn't at all sure what to make of the Veil. Maybe it was Kichlan's visage, colouring my perceptions, but the Veil was not what I had expected. It did not seem to act like an all-powerful god. Well, not the way I had imagined one would act.

"You said the Other calls you a god," I said, with a frown. "Does that mean you aren't one?"

"That is precisely the kind of thing he would not have wanted to hear."

That was not really an answer. "So, are you?"

The Veil shrugged. "Not the way you would use that term, no."

"Then what are you?" I stared around the cobblestone streets of Movoc-under-Keeper. Ice hung from doorways and awnings, glinting in the sharp sunlight, and the shine made my heart leap. Because it was home. "Where are we, really? And how did you do this?"

"I am—" It paused, frowning with concentration. Perhaps it was not the easiest question to answer. "A lot of what he said is true. I have always been here, yes, between your worlds. Between all worlds, actually. I, and my kind, travel the paths between realities. And it was the worst kind of luck, I suppose, that when the programmers decided to trespass on those paths I just happened to be here. Between your worlds. Of all the realities, the infinite and growing existences, I was right beside the one that tore."

"I don't believe in luck," I said. "Good or bad. Not any more."

The Veil held my gaze. "Well, I do."

"What about all this?" I waved at the world the Veil had created. "What is this?"

"Me. All me." I thought I saw a faint pride in its sad smile. "I am the Veil. Blood from your wounded world passes through me, as it does from the so-called-Hero's world. But we are different, you and I. So different. If not for the images I create for you, the memories I plunder and this faux-reality, you would not be able to see me. To touch, smell…sense me in any way. This is for your benefit. To give you a frame of reference."

I looked around. "You are everything?" I asked. After the Keeper and the puppet men and the dark world, it wasn't too hard to believe. I liked to think I had rather broadened my mind, since *Grandeur's* fall.

"Yes. And though it was the worst kind of luck for me, to be trapped here, it was the best for your worlds. Because I have, indeed, become a kind of membrane between you. I am my own reality, if you will, and I filter and alter both of yours. My presence has slowed the movement of particles between your worlds, and those particles that do make it through take a little of me with them. You see, I am a creator reality. I breed worlds. I fashion life, I shine light into darkness, change dry to wet, dead to alive. Some of that energy latches on to the particles as they pass through me, and it gives them power. You call it pions. The programmers call it Pionic energy. That's all a part of me. My stunted, thwarted, reason to be."

So the Veil is just what we thought it was, Lad whispered. *Only—Keeper help me—it's alive too. It's conscious. It knows what we've done and it feels what we're doing and, and hell— How could we have done this?*

Slowly, I was beginning to understand what the Veil had meant by doom. "But you want freedom," I whispered.

"Don't all things, no matter which reality they come from?" It looked away, its silver-light gaze growing distant. "I have a journey to continue, a mate to find."

"A *mate*?" Perhaps I had not broadened my mind that much.

"Does that surprise you? I told you, I'm a creative force. Surely you don't think I manage that all on my own?" The Veil smiled softly. "My presence keeps your world alive, but do I not deserve a life of my own? Happiness? Destiny? Love? Do I not deserve freedom?"

A chill that had nothing to do with the artificial Movoc wind settled in my spine as I thought of the puppet men. "You've been trying to free yourself, haven't you?"

The Veil nodded.

"You gave life to the puppet men."

"I'm not the best judge of such things." I could feel its guilt this time, permeating me. "At first, it was an accident. I had been so lonely, since Favian left me. Although he wasn't very good company by the end, of course, but you take what you can get. Can you imagine what it's like trapped here, all on my own? Only able to see snippets of the worlds through the programs and people and particles moving through me, but not able to touch them? I'm used to travel, but not to loneliness. The universes are so alive. There is always someone to talk to. I missed that."

Damn it.

"So I just wanted someone to talk to, at first. They were dumped inside of me, in pieces, confused and hurting. I know what that felt like. I took pity on them! I threaded some of myself through their partial consciousnesses, tied them all together, then wrapped that around the particles as they moved through me, giving them solidity and making them whole."

"They were programs, offcuts, lines of unstable code." Wrapped them around particles? "The crimson pions!" I gasped. "Vol told me the puppet men *were* the crimson pions, and that's because you made them that way! Those are the particles you used to give the puppet men form." No wonder they were so powerful, and so deep within the world. They were more that just pions. They were the puppet men, and the power of the Veil, all tied up together.

The puppet men have been systematically weakening the program we installed here, the one that slows down the movement of particles between the worlds.

I frowned. "But if you just wanted someone to talk to, why did you send them into my world? Why need those particles at all? You could have kept them here." Slowly, it began to dawn on me.

Lad was way ahead of me. *Speeding up the movement of particles will destabilise both worlds, and ultimately destroy them.*

"You gave life to the puppet men and sent them out in search of a place to belong. The puppet men think that by upsetting the balance they will create a world for themselves, but they won't create anything, will they? They will perish, just like the rest of us!"

Only when both worlds are gone, can the Veil be free.

The Veil did not meet my gaze. "It is not in my nature to destroy realities. I would rather create them."

"Other curse you—" I paused. Other? Oh hells. "It didn't start with the puppet men, did it?"

The Hero?

"What did you call him? Favian. You said Favian kept you company, he told you what was happening in both worlds. But your relationship was more complicated than that, wasn't it? He wasn't a friend. He worshipped you as a god! Over the centuries he came to believe that you had blessed him, chosen him, given him the power to judge the worlds he protected. *My world.*"

"Favian was the only thing that stopped me going mad!" the Veil cried. "You can't understand what it was like. Suddenly, I couldn't move, and these worlds were cutting through me. It hurt! I lost all contact with my kind, with all the universes I was so used to swimming through.

I hated him, at first. He was *forced* into me. I had no say, I had no choice. But slowly, I came to know him."

"In the beginning," I whispered. "He really was a hero. But his time in the Veil drove him mad." I swallowed hard. "What did you do to him?"

The Veil's borrowed shoulders slumped, and he sat awkwardly on a chair that appeared suddenly beneath him. He pressed Kichlan's hands against his glowing eyes. "He was my friend. He told me what he and his programmers had done. He explained the particles crossing through me, and the effect I was having on them. What would happen to both worlds, without my help. And I realised what it would take to escape. Pain. Sacrifice."

"So you changed him. You twisted him."

The Other used the threat of the doors he was supposed to be guarding, and started testing the people under his protection. Every time he opened one, he weakened the Veil.

Lad paused. I wished he really was here, beside me. I wished I could hold his hand.

No, that's not quite right, is it. We have to change our thinking. Every time he opened one, it was actually weakening our worlds. Bleeding pure, opposite particles into each other, without the touch of the Veil to filter them. Two worlds, being undone. And now we know, that's just what the Veil wanted him to do.

"He didn't go mad," I said. "The Veil drove him mad."

"Hardly!" The Veil jerked to its feet. "He didn't need my help, he was already headed that way. You can't keep a human locked in nothingness forever. Just like you can't do that to me! Unable to touch anything, unable to talk to anyone, stationary, hurting, and always, always alone. This isn't life, not in any world, any reality, any universe! Can you really blame Favian for his fate? And can you really blame me for what I did?"

"You're trying to destroy my world!"

"I was trapped here through no fault of my own. Whose life matters more? Yours, or mine?"

I glanced down at the soft light that was all that

remained of my son and keenly felt how unfair this all was. He had not asked for this either. He too was trapped— with me—through no fault of his own.

"You will not help me, will you?" I asked. My son fluttered against my fingers, like I was holding a bird. "You created the puppet men, why would you help me destroy them?"

"Why am *I* the one who must help *you*?" The Veil scowled, casting Kichlan's face in ugly shadows. "If this sacrifice is so noble, then why don't you and your people make it? I've been doing this for millennia, and I'm sick of it! It's your turn, it's got to be! Go on, give up your worlds for my life because it's the right thing to do." The Veil panted, and looked away. "No, Tanyana, I will not help you. I—I'm sorry."

Shit. Now what do we do?

Had I really come this far for nothing? Had I really fought so long just for this?

"However, I can offer you an alternative."

I glanced up, but did not trust myself to speak.

The Veil stepped closer. It held out Kichlan's hands— those large, strong hands—above the ball of light that was my child. And it changed.

Just as the emptiness had turned into cities, a shadow-child formed between my palms. It solidified slowly. Bones and nerves at first, their outlines like foundations for a small but intricate building. Then arteries, veins and capillaries; organs and muscles. Finally, musculature and skin.

And son opened his eyes.

They were Devich's deep, soulful brown. I had fallen in love with those eyes, and those eyes had betrayed me.

"What did you do?" I whispered.

A tiny hand wrapped itself around my finger and held tight.

I knew, dimly, that this was wrong. The poor creature that had tried, so unsuccessfully, to grow inside me was still too young, too small and unformed to look like this. Even if he hadn't been overrun by suit and silex, if he hadn't been turned into code and light, my baby had only been conceived a few moons ago. He should not have been able to smile at me, like that. To hold me, to look at me with such love and trust. To exist at all, outside of my body.

"This is what you wanted, isn't it?" The Veil smiled, nodded, and patted my arm with Kichlan's hand. It had no substance, and I couldn't feel its touch. The Veil's borrowed body was just as real as the ghost-memories of the Other's old world. "All that time, when you were carrying him, fighting for him, sustaining him. You wanted him whole and safe enough to grow up. Because it's only fair."

I swallowed hard. "Y—yes."

"Well, here he is." The Veil stepped back. "And here he can stay. With you."

I glanced around at the city of my memories. Movoc-under-Keeper before I had destroyed it. "I don't understand."

"This is all I can offer you," the Veil said, and sounded sad. "I will not help you continue to imprison me; I will not willingly give up my freedom. But I can give you a place where you and your child are safe. In me. We will travel the universes together, you and I and him. You, safe in this city. No more experiments. No more programs, no more suits. No more sacrifice."

"No more Kichlan—" I started to say, but the Veil lifted a hand.

"You don't understand, do you? This is the only world where your child will be safe. Where he will not be part crystal, or part silver, or part light or code. Here, he has been born human, and that will never happen on either of the worlds you want to save. Only in me, will he live."

Oh, Tan.

We were back to this, were we? One life, again, or two worlds. Only this time, my son was not the sacrifice. Everyone else was.

"How can I make that choice?" I whispered.

"I'm surprised you think there is one to make. The answer is obvious; what you wanted is right here. What else would you do?"

My son made a small noise. I held him tightly against

me, and those tiny hands clutched at my jacket.

Those tiny hands that simply could not be real. Was this pretend world and this impossible baby enough for me? Was I the same as the Other, so desperate for a perfect world that I would allow myself to be fooled and used? Perhaps it was easier than facing the truth, the hard edges and dark spaces of grief. Or was I like the puppet men, in such need of a place to belong that I would destroy whole worlds—whole realities—to find it?

I smiled faintly to myself. *Reality*. What a fluid concept that was becoming.

"What about you?" I whispered to the tiny body I held. "You. I never even gave you a name." I'd not allowed myself to think that far ahead. I dipped my head to rest my lips against a softly pink ear. "What choice would you make, if you were ever given one?"

It was not a voice, as such. Even with his new body and its faux mouth my son was too young to speak. But still, I heard him. He spoke, not in words, but in code, in the pulses of light that still connected us. Because this new body was nothing but a veneer. And no matter how solid he might look, how separate from me, we were one. Despite what the Veil might say, he still had not been born.

And my child was laughing at me. Why would I even consider the Veil's fake alternative? Why give up on the real Movoc-under-Keeper for nothing but a memory? Why did I think we needed the Veil's help at all?

Wasn't it obvious? Was I really that much of a fool?

"I don't understand," I whispered to him.

What's happening? Lad sounded worried. *Tan, what's going on?"*

The Other was wrong. Even if it wanted to, the Veil wasn't strong enough to defeat the puppet men. In fact, the Veil was powerless.

I whispered all this, as my son communicated wordlessly, so Lad could hear it. The Veil, wearing Kichlan's face, looked on with a bland smile, evidently unable to hear.

Oh, Tan, you're right.

The Veil needed others to do its dirty work—the puppet men, the Other—but it couldn't compel them to help, it could only manipulate, and lie. It lost parts of itself as the particles tore through it, usurping its power and changing into pions along the way. But it had no control over them. What had it said? It couldn't touch, couldn't speak, to the worlds on either side. It was isolated, completely, and could only wait, and hope for the best.

We are the powerful ones, not it. We created ships that split reality, we created programs that travelled between worlds. We trapped the Veil and then we used it. We still do. The Keeper, the Other, the puppet men, they all rode the Veil, but they were not part of the Veil itself.

I looked up, and held the Veil's gaze. What was it like to be trapped here, to be helpless, and alone, for longer than I could even begin to imagine? Could I really blame it for trying to escape, no matter what the cost?

It can't touch anything on the worlds either side of it. It even had to rely on Favian to tell it what was happening in the first place. It can't actually do *anything.*

"I'm so sorry," I said. "But I can't do this. I will not sacrifice the light world, and the dark world, for your freedom. No matter how unfair it is, to any of us. I will not give up on Kichlan."

The body in my hands faded instantly back to light. I forced down a sudden nausea, a deep and shuddering horror, and held my light-son as tightly as I dared. We were still one, no matter what he looked like on the outside. He was still the same.

"I am sorry to hear that." Kichlan's face solidified into a stiff, expressionless mask.

Around us, Movoc-under-Keeper disappeared. It faded first into shadow, then became light, entirely. That eternal in-between.

Dimly, I felt a tugging. A flow that seemed to stretch right through me. At my son's prompting, I glanced behind us. A distant shadowy outline remained. A single door.

"I will not help you," the Veil said.

I straightened, squared my shoulders. "Will you try to stop us?"

The Veil hesitated. The edges of its Kichlan-body grew hazy, and his colours bled out into the vast, surrounding light.

"Could you stop us, even if you wanted to?" I hadn't felt the Veil when it touched me. And for all its talk, all it had done was show me pictures of home. "You are powerless, aren't you? Even here, all you can do is play with shadows. If you had power, you wouldn't still be trapped the way you are. You wouldn't allow programs to be loaded into you, or particles to pass through you. But you can't do anything, except wait."

It said nothing, just gradually faded away.

That's…that's horrible.

"I know." I glanced around. Nothing but light. No Other remerged. No ancient pre-Crust landscape sprung up. Nothing but the tugging of worlds and the distant shadow of a door.

"The puppet men are on the other side of that door. We've been through all this, and we still don't know how to defeat them."

Don't we?

Don't we?

I closed my eyes. Lad was with me, my son too. I wasn't alone.

Remember what the Other called you, Tan. A tether between worlds. All power in the light world comes from the dark, and you have access to that. Remember what the puppet men are. They're programs, code. And so are you— well, a lot of you. And you've had a lot of experience with that recently, haven't you? I don't believe you're as helpless as you think you are.

Pushing down guilt and that final image of the Veil, dissolving, I turned, and ran toward the door. The flow inside me grew stronger, with each footstep, drawing me toward the door, back to the light world.

And this time, I will be with you. All of me.

I stepped through the door.

31.

And fell straight into Kichlan.

One moment there was nothing but light, the rushing in my veins and the faint traces of the Veil's mist. And then the weight of the world pressed down on me, and the push of pions knocked me forward, and I was tangled with Kichlan's arms, face pressed against his chest.

He stared down at me, mouth open, eyes wide, his whole face teetering between shock and the deepest, purest joy.

"Tan?" he whispered, and the word shivered through me. "You—you're alive."

So I kissed him. Warm lips, solid lips. Not a dream. Not an illusion.

"Kichlan," I breathed into his mouth. "Kichlan."

Then pain seared into me, from my neck down to my ankles. I staggered back. Still stunned, Kichlan let me go.

The child I was carrying wasn't soft light anymore. He was suddenly hard, suddenly heavy. Suddenly silver and flesh. Beating, pulsing, squirming. I realised, with horror, that he could not survive here, on this side, without my body to support him.

He fell apart, between my hands.

"No!" I cried, as the suit drilled itself back into me. I had forgotten the sensation of its pressure on my neck, its grip around my waist, its weight in my ankles and wrists. I stumbled, hands juggling something I couldn't even see properly, something that was silver and red and wet and hard and alive. But dying.

"Tan?" Kichlan reached forward. I turned my body away from him, just enough to hide the horror I was carrying.

"Miss Vladha. You have returned."

Puppet men stepped out of the light and the haze and the pain. Smiling, not surprised, not fearful.

"Too late, we are afraid. Too late to stop us."

"Tan—ya!" Footsteps, hard and echoing, ran toward me. Kichlan roared as Devich—the not-quite Devich I knew from my dreams—pushed him aside. "Not—dead!" He crouched at my feet and clutched at my ankles, slobbering incomprehensible words, staring up at me, all horrible silver and distended flesh.

Around us, doors were opening. I felt the irresistible tugging of particles moving, of worlds bleeding, and the single, lonesome presence trapped in between.

Get a hold of yourself, Tan. Lad, still connected to me. He sounded so faint here, stretched between worlds, and yet somehow calm and reasonable, somehow still the stoic programmer willing to give himself up for the good of two worlds and not make much of a fuss about it. *We're relying on you. You won't be able to help anyone if you fall apart like this.*

I drew a deep breath, and straightened. He was right, and I was being foolish. He had faith in me, my poor unwinding son had faith in me, and it was about time I lived up to their expectations. Kichlan needed me.

I was not weak in this world. I wasn't weak in either. Not any more.

My suit settled itself, sending spasms and painful twitching up through my arms, down my legs and into my stomach. I felt empty there, as though I was missing more than the weight of a growing child. When Devich stood, silver arms open to try and embrace me, I stretched my suit and pushed him back. It responded eagerly, quickly. Like it had missed me.

"What do you think you can do?" Three solid puppet men and a mass of shifting shadows stared at me, all smug eyes, fake skin and terrible over-wide smiles. But deeper than that, I saw they were code. Just like the illegible symbols bobbing bright on the bands in the wrists, ankles, waist and neck, they were snippets of could-have-been-programs, if they were only arranged the right way. If they only made sense. They were malformed, cobbled together nonsense, given life by the Veil. Pitiful. How strange, to pity them, after everything they had done to me.

Even as I read them, I remembered the parts of the Keeper Kichlan had seen. The Guardian program was still fighting, despite being absorbed into his undead brothers. That meant that some of him still remained, locked in the chaos of the puppet men. So, all hope wasn't quite lost. The puppet men thought I was helpless, but I was pretty sure I knew just what I could do.

The child first. We can't let him die here and now, can we?

Lad was right. I looked down to the mess in my hands. His silver was code and he was full of light—tiny and bright hubs of it. But not silex, oh no. I knew that light, and I hadn't seen it in oh so long.

I saw his pions.

The whole world was full of them, although most were the painfully bright crimson pions that gave the puppet men their power and form. The same ones that had pushed me from *Grandeur's* palm. I didn't fear them now.

I closed my eyes. Learning to control pion sight was one of the first things binders were taught—about the same time as we learned to speak and walk. I drew steadying breaths, tried to remember how to push down the pions I did not want to see, how to focus only on those I wanted to manipulate. Because a world full of pions was bright and beautiful, yes, but it was also very full. Seeing every single pion that existed, from deep inside the world to its surface, was blinding. Like the network, when I had first dipped myself inside it, the pions of the world could overwhelm me.

Both worlds are open to you now, Lad said. *Pions, code, you can manipulate them both. Just like the puppet men,*

only you are more than torn parts of a discarded program.
We can do this.

I nodded, and took another deep breath, swallowed against the silver in my throat, and when I opened my eyes this time they were gone. No, not gone. I could feel them, the way I had once done, a sense of energy in the world, of power, of life. Particles borrowed from the dark world, enhanced by the Veil, brushing against us all.

I was pions and code, too. Bright lights bound up with symbols, their threads coiling into circles winding deeper, ever deeper inside me. Pions and program, merging into one. So it didn't take much. I wound my silver with my son's silver, and programmed solidity into the debris in his body. Then I called to the pions in his flesh and I bound them back into the unfinished organs, the semi-skin, the not-quite-a-brain that they would have been, if they were still inside me, where they belonged. They responded swiftly, eagerly, flooding over me and crowding me like excited, long lost dogs.

When my son looked similar to the body he'd had back on the dark world—only with silver instead of silex and no tube to keep him safe—I wrapped him as best I could in my jacket and held him close. I was dressed in the clothes I'd worn when I stepped through the door in the first place, and they were torn, and dirty, and even a little damp. Residual Tear water, I supposed.

Good.

I shook my head, even as I faced the puppet men. "He will die like that," I whispered. "His body isn't meant to support itself. Not yet."

Your pions and suit will sustain him. For a little while, at least. There's not much more we can do. Not yet.

"What are you doing, Miss Vladha?" Some of the smugness slipped from the puppet men's collective expressions. The three of them glanced around, at the open doors, at the cave walls. "The doors are open, you cannot stop us. There is no point fighting."

"There's always a reason to fight," Kichlan said.

I glanced at him. He stood behind Devich, his left arm strong and silver, his legs planted wide, his expression somewhere between the old thundercloud I knew so well, and a fierce desire. Shivers ran through me at that look, memories of his touch, of the arguments we used to have, the sound of his screams when Lad died. All of it, everything that was Kichlan, all tied up in those eyes, that stance.

"Doesn't matter what happens," he said, and walked around Devich, to come to my side. My heart was beating so hard I could feel it in the heat flushing my face. "Who we lose." He clenched his silver arm. "What we lose. We have to fight." Then he held it out to me, palm up, and I took it with my free hand. Silver to skin. The suit I'd given him was warm, and strangely soft, despite its strength. It seemed to mould around me. "Can't just give in."

My brother loves you. Despite the impossible distance, I could hear the strain in Lad's voice. *He never stopped. Not when I was killed, not when he thought you were dead, not even when he lost his arm. Have faith in him, Tan. Bro is strong.*

"And now you're back," Kichlan said. "There're a few things I want to talk to you about. So there's no way I'm going to let these creatures win."

I could hardly breathe.

"My Lady?"

I turned. Volski and Zecholas stood among the ruins of their pion-binding.

"You're alive," Volski gasped. "We thought—they said you were dead!" And he looked so old, worn down and grey. He shook, as he stood. Zecholas held his shoulders, steadying him. Both looked at me with confusion, with hurt, with joy. I knew how they felt.

"I'm not dead," I answered, my throat constricted, my voice thick. "I just left for a while. But I'm back now. And—and—I'm sorry. Vol, Zech. I'm sorry for dragging you into this. I'm sorry for destroying your city too."

Kichlan squeezed my hand, and it reminded me of his brother. I took great comfort from that.

Now's not the time for apologies, Lad scolded me.

"We don't have time for that," Kichlan murmured.

And I couldn't help but grin.

I glanced around the street. Fedor hung back, still clutching the debris panel, face pale and eyes wide. Natasha held Sofia, helping her stand. Sofia was smiling, and nodding, and I knew, just knew, that she could see me too. Despite the ruin of her eyes. Lev mirrored Fedor's expression. Valya had stopped fighting and was watching me, grinning, one arm open like she would embrace me if she could. Devich, on all fours, pressed his stomach to the ground and wept as he stared up at me.

I held my son tighter. Within me, Lad sent me his strength.

You are not alone.

Nodding, I squared my shoulders.

"That's enough," I said, surprised at the strength and clarity of my voice. I actually sounded like I could do this. "I won't let you destroy this world, or the world beside ours. No matter your reasons, no matter your strength. Despite what the Veil might have told you, and what it wants. I have come back to stop you. And I will."

I released Kichlan, and flexed silver over my free hand. It slid quickly and spread further, further, into a long whip. I braced my feet and lashed out, but not at the puppet men. Instead, I attacked the doors. No more slipping through their handles; I didn't need any help to touch them. They were solid, they were code, and I could read them. I could wrap silver around them and force them closed. One after the other, I slammed them shut. Dimly, I heard Valya cheering.

"Too late." One puppet man stepped forward. He lifted both his hands, his mould-on-the-wall eyes drilling through to the pions and the code bound inside my body. "We have had enough of your impossible interference."

I withdrew my whip, hardened and sharpened it into a blade. I knew they could not manipulate my code—Lad, after all, had reprogrammed it ages ago, when he was little more than memory in my blood. But they weren't after me, not this time.

"No!" Kichlan cried out and clutched at his silver hand. It was changing, sagging into a formless liquid between his fingers. "They're taking control again." His eyes grew distant for a moment, and I knew he was listening to the fractured voice of his piecemeal suit. "We rebooted it but they're exerting their override again. I can't stop it!"

But I can. Lad, though distant, sounded so angry and determined it made me shiver. *I will not let them hurt my brother any more. Tan, get me into his suit. Now!*

I pitched forward and sent tendrils of my suit into Kichlan's, weaving us, code to code. I felt a lurch within me as Lad travelled the silver and dove into his brother. He was stretched through me so thinly, his presence so delicate and fragile, but his knowledge and skill were strong. I had to have faith in them, didn't I? Both brothers.

Kichlan's look of horror eased, and turned instead to wonder. He stared at me, eyes intense, and whispered, "Reprogramming commenced. Emergency protocols deleted. Command set erased. Restructuring." His head tipped back and he breathed so deeply, his body shuddering, that for a terrible moment I thought something must have gone wrong.

Then Lad was back within me, and Kichlan straightened, shook himself. "We're whole again," he said. And he smiled, grim and sure, and turned to the puppet men. "And we're too strong for you."

He was a mess. I could feel Lad's exhaustion bleeding into me. His voice crackled as he struggled to maintain our connection. *Between you and the puppet men, you did a right number on his programming. Just goes to show how strong my brother is, that he managed to control that suit at all.* Lad's fierce pride warmed me from within.

The puppet men were coiling in on themselves in confusion, all mist and horrified faces. "You reprogrammed him!" one of the solid few cried. Angry, frightened, desperate, a far cry from the emotionless men in white coats I had first met all those moons ago. "That's not possible. How did you know how?"

"That doesn't matter." I stepped forward, silver at the ready.

"All that matters is you can't control me any more." Kichlan mirrored me. "And you have to fight the both of us, instead."

"So be it!" The puppet men lifted their arms. The ground beneath me tore apart, and the wall of silex and screens shuddered.

"Uzdal!" Mizra screamed, as great shards of crystal crashed around his brother's coffin, and the thread that attached me to Lad, to the dark world, to the Veil itself weakened.

Bastards! Lad cried. *I need that Unbound terminal to keep in contact with you! Don't let them separate us!*

I smiled. Even as the world cracked, even as the doors shuddered, I felt calm. Maybe it was the influence of my son, warm and soft where I held him, a smiling and peaceful presence in my code. He did not panic. Neither should I.

I actually felt sorry for the puppet men as I pulled my silver back, exposing my bare skin. Poor little half-programs.

"That won't work," I said. The earth gave way, my feet slipped, but instead of falling I simply summoned pions and made a ledge for Kichlan and me. Like the glass steps I had once used to climb to *Grandeur*'s outstretched palm, made from specs of sand and the water in the air, compressed and hardened, shaped, then polished until they shone. And some of the pions that responded to me were crimson, but that didn't seem to matter, not any more. Indeed, they gathered on my open hand and brushed against me quivering, apologetic, desperate to please. As they touched me, they lost some of their crimson sheen, and they calmed. And it all felt so damned familiar. It felt like the debris monsters I had fought, and soothed, over and over. The creatures the puppet men had created to test me with.

The puppet men all gasped, a collective noise that echoed through the underground rooms.

"The Veil gave you these pions, didn't it?" I looked up from my open palm. "So you could have a body in this world. It made you more than code hidden in darkness and doors. It gave you a form, of a kind. But they are pions, in the end." I shook my head. "Doesn't matter how they started out, on the other side of the Veil. On this side, they feel. They hurt. They are happy, or sad, and that's why they respond to binders. They can chose. Perhaps they're tired of being bound to you. Perhaps they've seen the things you are trying to do, the horror you've inflicted, and the pain. They're part of this world too, you know, and might not want it destroyed. Or maybe they just like me better. I've always got on so well with pions. More than with people, certainly." I cast Kichlan a small smile at that. "They don't have to obey you if they don't want to. And if this is anything to go by—" I summoned the pions to surround me, lighting me like a lamp so far underground "—I don't think they will."

I sent those pions back into the ground at my feet. They repaired the cracks, they healed the scars. Of course, they could not do anything for the silex wall and Uzdal's coffin, but as long as the ground was steady, the wall would be too.

The puppet mist rolled, and the three men stepped back deeper in its folds. As they did so I caught a glimpse of a shadow, a semi-form, different from the others.

Did you see that? Lad asked, voice tense.

I nodded. "Yes." I'd seen that shadow in my dreams. "It's the Keeper."

The Guardian program.

"He keeps trying to get out," Kichlan said. "I don't know how to help him."

"He's holding on," I said. "He might be code, carried on light, and uploaded into the Veil, but he's damned strong."

Kichlan cast me a questioning glance, and I shook my head. "I'll explain later."

"My Lady?" Volski looked stunned. He and Zecholas were looking from me, to the ground, to the puppet men. "You—you can bind again?"

We need to re-establish the Guardian program. He can close the doors, and that would leave you free to focus on the puppet men.

Nodding, I turned to Volski and Zecholas. My pion-binders. An integral part of my circle, always so skilled, always willing to push the boundaries of their abilities because I'd asked them to. Sure, that asking might have almost got them killed, but now was hardly the time for such self-pitying thoughts.

"The pions are returning," I said.

With wide eyes, and great confusion, my binders scanned the room. "But most of them are crimson," Zecholas said as he released Volski. The older man straightened. He looked stronger.

"I think you'll find that won't matter." Again I lifted my hand and again the pions sped to me. "They'll be very happy to listen to you this time." They crowded me, they touched me, and as I released them, my binders took them up. What a strange, inverted circle that made us.

I nodded to the puppet men. "Keep them busy for me."

Zecholas and Volski grinned, and loosed all the Other's hells. Walls of pure rock slammed into existence, crushing the puppet men. Great spears grew from the ground, and dropped from the ceiling. Hands of stone tore the fake-skin from the three, solid men, until they all fell back into the amorphous, mist-like mass.

"Fedor!" I cried, and turned to him. "Use your control panel again! Hit them as hard as you can!" He grinned too, just that same look.

"But won't that weaken the veil?" Kichlan gasped, and gripped my arm. "I thought we didn't want to do that?"

"Oh yes," I said. "It will. But right now, that doesn't matter as much as weakening the puppet men. Nothing Fedor, Zech or Vol can do right now will destroy them, but that's fine. I just need to keep them preoccupied."

Kichlan released me, expression uncertain. "If you say so."

"Trust me."

He winced. "You really shouldn't say that."

I laughed, as the power of the silex wall rode wild through the room again. A simulated Flare, isolated and weak compared to the real thing, a strange reprogramming of debris to release an isolated burst of undirected pions. I wondered why the programmers had even built it. Maybe they were trying to recreate their home world, with crystal that looked like silex and Flares to power it? The Other might know, but I could hardly ask him now. Energy like lightning strikes crackled over the falling, rising, shattering rock. It danced through the puppet men, each touch destabilising their code, forcing them to reform as quickly as they were undone.

I knew neither could destroy the puppet men, but that wasn't the point. All they had to do was unsettle them, weaken them. I gave them no time to recover. I gripped Kichlan's silver hand and together, we ran into all that chaos. I wrapped us both in silver, so the rock did not hurt us, and the lightning slid right off us, and barrelled into the centre of the puppet men mass.

"What are you doing?" Kichlan cried.

"I'm going to get the Keeper back. Will you help me?"

"Help? How?"

A form materialised out of the mass, pale skin torn and singed, eyes turned to black and smoking. The puppet man reached for us. I sliced through his fake hands and knocked him back, but more appeared in his place.

"Ah," Kichlan said. "I see." I let go of his hand so he could mould his left arm into a blade. He loosened the other bonds on his normal suit, and coated his upper body in silver. "Gladly." He spun, slashed at the second puppet man, ducked as it tried to reform, grabbed its semi-material legs and tore it apart.

I allowed myself a brief pause to admire him. Lad was right, his brother really was strong. And now that he didn't have to fight his suit the whole time, he could show it.

Reluctantly, I looked away. "Keeper!" I cried, and shoved my spare hand into the mist, snatching, clawing, searching. For a long and terrible moment there was nothing but rock and light and the slick touch of countless program shards. Then small hands, barely solid, wrapped themselves around mine, and I held him tight and pulled him free. Out of the chaos, out of the puppet men.

"Kichlan!" I cried, as I staggered back. "Follow us!"

He cut down two more puppet men on the way.

I drew the Keeper back to the platform in front of the silex wall. He was a shadow, formless, bodiless, just a wisp of darkness cast against my silver.

He's almost gone! Lad sounded distressed.

"What do I do?" I cried, as the Keeper's shadow sunk through me.

Get me inside him.

"What?"

Through your programming, Tan. Like we did for Kichlan. Your suit is code and he is code and at the moment, so am I. Get me inside him so I can save him. I know what the Guardian's program should look like. I'll put him back the way he was.

I focused on the lines of code, nearly invisible, deep within the Keeper's form. Like pions, they were. Another element to reality, another layer adding itself to the way I saw the world around me. He was a beautiful program. I could see why the puppet men had wanted to claim him as a brother, and incorporate his wholeness into their broken-code mess. He should have been perfect: streamline, elegant, yet powerful. He throbbed sentience and shone with control, yet years of abuse had worn him down. Like frayed edges of carpet.

Then I loosened the bonds on my suit and drilled into him, silver replacing the debris he'd always had for blood. It spread in a fine and intricate pattern, casting his shape from the inside out, clustering at his head and his eyes.

"What is that?" Natasha cried.

"It's the Keeper!" Sofia lifted one of her stumps as though she could embrace us. "Can't you see him, Tash? He is so beautiful. Skin like marble, his eyes so dark."

And, indeed, Lad was rebuilding him. He rearranged the ruin the puppet men had made of him, gathered stray pieces of debris that floated through the room, and even took symbols and lines of code from my suit. It seemed I had plenty to spare.

The Keeper's pale skin slowly regrew, debris pumped beside my silver in the labyrinth of his veins. Dark eyes blinked at me, and I realised that, of course, I wasn't wearing my usual suited mask. It was strange to see my reflection—a face of skin, not silver—looking back at me, scarred and filthy.

Quickly, withdraw. Lad's disembodied voice sounded even more exhausted. I gathered my suit back, careful to be gentle, and was almost surprised when the Keeper did not collapse empty and hollow before me.

"Tanyana?" he whispered, and scanned my face. He released me, lifting a shaking, white hand to touch the scars on my cheek. "You—you can see me?"

I nodded. "Yes, Guardian. I can see all of you."

"Guardian?" He shivered. "But I failed, and the veil... the veil is falling."

"The Veil is stronger than it looks," I said. "And so are you, Keeper. The strongest program of them all."

"Program?" The Keeper whispered. "You know what I am. You—you rebuilt me. How?"

I smiled, and placed my hand on his shoulder. "It's a very long story. But right now, I need you to do what you were created to do." I gestured to the doors, all around us. "Close them, and hold them closed. Do that, and I will deal with your brothers. How does that sound? Will you help me, Keeper?"

He glanced around him. "There are so many."

"You have been gone for a while. But I believe in you."

The Keeper swallowed, visibly, and nodded.

"Go," I said, and stepped back.

As he disappeared, Kichlan leaned against me. He was breathing hard, but smiling broadly. "So," he said. "That's what the Keeper looks like. You were right. Those statues did a pretty good job."

I started to nod, then frowned. "Wait, you can see him?" And neither of us were masked in silver, either.

"I can." He shrugged. "Keep catching doors at the corner of my eyes too. Your fault, I assume?"

I smiled. "Oh, I'm fairly sure it is." Then I stepped forward, and held up my hand. "Vol!" I cried. "Zel! Fedor! Enough! Stop attacking them, and let the Keeper do his job!"

Silence rang in my ears. Then, over and over, the sound of doors closing. One at a time at first, then a cacophony of wood slamming and hinges creaking.

The faint image of a face solidified in the puppet men's mist. They looked thinner, somehow, than they had. As though the loss of the Keeper really had reduced them. Perhaps they had needed his strength more than I knew. Perhaps they had not absorbed him out of spite, like I had assumed, but because that perfect, shining programming— no matter how tattered it had become—completed them. They had started out as parts of him, after all.

The shapeless, shadowed mist wound a slow way through the earthen ruins of Volski and Zecholas's bindings. It was hidden, in places, by smoke from the silex energies Fedor had unleashed. I watched, as it eased its way towards me, led by that single half-a-face.

"Miss Vladha," the puppet men hissed. "What have you done?"

"Let's finish them!" Fedor lifted his debris panel.

"Yes!" Zecholas lifted his hands.

"No!" I shouted, stilling them both. "No, don't do anything. The Keeper is closing doors as we speak. Movement of particles at this stage will only hinder him. Don't touch that debris, Fedor. Zech, Vol, don't so much as nudge a pion."

I took slow, steady footsteps towards the puppet men. "What now?" I whispered to Lad, inside me.

We need to take apart their code. Even though I couldn't see him, I could hear Lad shaking. I felt his exhaustion, and pain. His head, his hands, though I didn't quite understand why. *Get me inside them, like the Guardian. I can do it, but only if you get me in there.*

I stilled. "You're exhausted, I can tell. Even from here. I can't make you do that. Just tell me what to do, and I will do the hard work."

Tan, you don't know the first thing about programming. Now shut up and do as I say, I don't have time for this. The—his voice crackled and faded before surging back, louder, but distorted and echoing strangely—*Legate has stopped trying to kill Meta and they're attacking the network instead. I only have one ancient terminal to work with here. I can't hold them back for long.*

I turned to Kichlan. He watched me, unsure.

"Then go," I whispered. "Get out of me and go, defend the network. And yourself. If you die again, Lad, because of me, I—I'd never forgive myself."

But—

"The puppet men are my problem. And I will deal with them my way. The way you taught me. Remember, I have Kichlan. I'm not alone anymore."

I had no way of knowing if Lad did what I demanded, or was merely keeping quiet. Either way, I tried to put my worry for him out of my mind, and approached the puppet men instead. Kichlan followed, a step or two behind. Devich slunk along on the other side.

"I have to kill you now," I said. "I think you know that."

Ghostly laughter settled over me like faint rain. "How will you do that, Miss Vladha? We have been given life by the Veil itself. We are of both worlds. We are debris and pions. We are everything and nothing. You cannot defeat us."

I shook my head. "No, actually, you're nothing like that. You're just lines of broken code." I looked down to Devich, then lifted the corner of my jacket to peer in at the half-formed child cradled at my side. "As so many of us are."

My poor, abused baby. Poised on the edges of reality, unable to live in either world. The Veil has said it, and my son understood—he would not survive long in his current state, not on this side, or the other.

But he whispered to me in words deeper than thought; maybe there was an alternative.

Between us, we knew just what we had to do. Lad was right, and he had been right from the beginning. I had to stop fighting, because all this hurt and anger helped no one, and got us nowhere. I must ease the pain instead. From the puppet men to Devich, and even my son. Altogether.

I knew how to do that. Lad had taught me, so long ago.

And my son agreed.

32.

"Tell me what you need me to do," Kichlan murmured.

But I shook my head. "Nothing, right now. Just watch, just stand guard, in case they try something. I need someone else's help this time." I turned to Devich instead.

"Devich," I said, trying to keep my voice soft, gentle. He looked up, still drooling, shaking, his eyes straining between hope and fear and confusion, such confusion. How much of the man I had loved, and hated, was left in there? "Devich, I'm sorry I pushed you away. I'm sorry they have hurt you so much. Come here, Devich. Come here."

He loped towards me, and stood on awkward legs. He didn't even hesitate, didn't even question or doubt or wonder, just wrapped his monster arms around me. His suit rippled to my touch, softening.

"Said—you—dead." He struggled to drool out his words. He looked down at me, mouth forced open. My heart lurched.

"I am not dead, Devich."

He nodded, violently. His tongue flapped wildly out of the side of his mouth.

"Just stay still for me." Carefully, slowly, I pressed the silver and flesh child I had made against Devich's rippling suit. Silver called to silver, code to code, as they fused. His unstable, bulging eyes—still that familiar, soulful brown—widened with confusion and wonder.

Good idea, Tan. Lad, so softly I couldn't be sure I had heard him.

"You taught me well," I breathed in response.

Lad had told me I was a virus. That my code—and therefore my son's code—could overrun and destroy anything in our way. Devich's unstable suited body stood no chance against us.

And neither would the mass of poor, lost programs that had tried to destroy us all.

I gave the last parts of my son to his father, and watched them overrun him. It was a gentle reprogramming. All he felt was the love of his son as he was swept away. No more pain, no more guilt, no more humiliation.

Devich stepped away from me, and his eyes were not his own. Well, not only his own. I'd seen parts of them before, in the soft light and malleable shadows of the Veil.

"I'm sorry," I whispered, as I held his patchwork gaze. "You still don't have a name." He gave me the smallest twist of a smile before turning, and walking calmly into the puppet men's mist.

I looked down at myself. But for a few small stains of blood on my sleeve, an odd discolouration to the skin at my wrist, and fresh scars of silver etching a faintly body-shaped pattern, my son might not have ever existed. I felt his absence keenly, like the gaps between the threads of suit inside me were suddenly too wide. Despite the program drilled into me, and the pions flashing bright inside my skin, I felt empty.

Then Natasha gasped, and Sofia cried out, and Valya crackled her laughter, and I looked up to see Devich, mist coiling around him like pits of half-real snakes. He opened his arms, and my heart lurched. The silver from his hands, his face, his back, his legs, his entire suited, distorted body, bled out into the mist. It channelled into deep and invisible vessels, it followed the lines of shadowy bones, just like I had done for the Keeper. Only this time, there were so many more bodies.

The puppet men struggled. They tried to disperse and flee, but Devich's program—my son's program—was faster, and so much stronger. He spread himself out until he filled all the mist, became a heavy, silver cloud. And when he drew his suit back in, he gathered the puppet men with it.

While I watched, Kichlan approached me. He stood behind me, wrapped his arms around me, rested his cheek against the side of my head. He breathed against my back, and he was warm. Always so warm. "What is happening to Devich?" he finally asked.

I stood on my toes, twisted slightly, and kissed his lips.

"He is not Devich anymore," I said.

I felt a brush against my head like a lick of warm breeze, and the Keeper appeared. He was staring at Devich and the puppet men, horrified and hopeful, all at once. His mouth slightly open, his dark eyes so wide, so much silver reflected in their smooth surfaces.

"He is absorbing them," the Keeper whispered.

I nodded. I could see it in code, too. Devich's suit was taking the puppet men apart, breaking their fragmented symbols down even further, and drawing them into himself. There—and this was my son's doing, I supposed, he who had spent so much time in the company of programmers, on the other side of the Veil—he used these fragments to fill the gaps within him. Devich, on his own, was not complete. Neither was my child, and neither were the puppet men. But together, they made a kind of whole. Part Devich, part the puppet men, and part my poor, never-born son.

It felt right, that the puppet men should heal the wounds they'd made.

Devich's body—full with my child and now the broken bones of the puppet men—returned to the silex wall, and the last, open door. From there, they could follow the threads that connected Lad and the Keeper to the dark world, and return to code. Just symbols, and light. Or would they stop, somewhere along the way? Would the Veil offer them the kind of sanctuary it had offered the Other and me? Would it have any choice?

My son lifted his father's silver hand in a silent goodbye. My heart beat too strongly. Part of me wanted to rush forward, to stop them. What if they returned to nothing?

That wasn't what I wanted for my child! I'd fought so hard to keep him alive.

But a smile spread across his lips, and the tension within me eased. He had chosen this path, he knew the risks, understood the harrowing alternatives. It was time for me to step back, and let him decide his fate. Slowly, I lifted a hand in response.

Devich, my son and the puppet men stepped through the door, and shut it behind them. It seemed to echo for a very, very long time, before soothing into quiet, and calm.

The Keeper drew a shuddering breath. "I am re-establishing connections," he said. He closed his pale eyelids. "Primary hubs coming online, secondary Shards flushing." They flew open again. "Communication from the programmers has been received—emergency protocol. I am returning signal." A large smile spread over his face. "And they receive me. Oh, Tanyana. They are—they are so happy to talk to me!" He laughed, high and child-like. Then he paused and tipped his head, listening. "They really don't like you, though."

"Yes, I know." I leaned against Kichlan. "Can you do this now, on your own, again? Can you monitor the Veil?"

The Keeper nodded. "It has been so long since I spoke to them—properly, I mean. They normally just send Halves. They must have been so worried about me. They—they really do trust me, don't they? They really do care."

My heart lurched, but I tried not to let it show. Care was hardly the word I would have used. But if that was what the Keeper needed to believe, I was happy to let him. "They were worried about you, Keeper. Worried sick."

He beamed. With his skin so solid and bright, he really did glow. "Well, I must get back to work." He rubbed his hands together. "They will send me more Halves, I just know they will." He looked around. "And you have found me such a wonderful place to keep them."

The Keeper faded. This time, I saw how it happened. He did not disappear into thin air the way I had always thought. Rather, he dispersed, sending countless lines of command out into the world, travelling the Veil.

The Veil.

I sighed. We had doomed it, just as it had predicted, to remain trapped. Would it try to do this again? Would it feed the bodies cast adrift in its waters until they were powerful enough to rattle its cage? Would it make another bid for freedom? I shuddered at the thought of how long it had taken the puppet men to grow into the kind of power needed to do so. It would be another long wait, for the Veil.

And no, it was not fair. But nothing ever is.

"So he's healthy again, isn't he?" Kichlan whispered into my hair. "The Keeper. Strong, and whole."

I glanced up at him, and nodded. "I think so." He was smiling, a deep look that sent a warm, tingling thrill through my body. Anticipation, and a heady sense of freedom, that left no room for guilt. Not any more.

"Tanyana?" Natasha, hooked up to medical hubs and struggling against their weight, hobbled forward. She still held onto Sofia, who sagged weakly in her arms. I could not look at that maimed and bandage-wrapped face, so I held Natasha's gaze instead. "Tanyana." She stopped and glared at Kichlan. "He said you were dead!"

I laughed at the accusation in her face. "I'm sorry to have disappointed you."

Her expression softened, and she hobbled faster. I unwound myself from Kichlan's embrace and went to her instead. Natasha, who had never seemed to care for anyone, or anything, held me in her tired and shaking arms, as Kichlan took Sofia's weight and eased her to the broken stones. "I'm glad," Natasha whispered to me. "You might be an Other-stubborn bitch sometimes, but I'm glad you're not dead."

"Thank you," I said with a chuckle, and leaned back from her. "How are your injuries—?"

I paused, blinking, resisting an urge to rub at my eyes. The pions in Natasha's body were bright and strongly bound, a Mob's binding, reinforcing her muscles and bones, giving her speed, endurance, and might. That wasn't so strange, really. It was the silex hubs connected to her—and what they were doing—that shocked me. They were winding code into her bindings to redirect the pions already at work in all her muscles, blood vessels, and bones. They were healing her, slowly, but surely. A subtle reprogramming, using pions, powered by her own body and the faint flashing of the unsteady simulated Flare inside the hubs.

I smiled faintly to myself. Trust programmers to program things, no matter what world they were on. Trust them to bend the rules, to marry code and pion-binding.

The program at work inside Natasha was directing her pions to heal her, and I could read it all. I was not a trained healer, but I did not need to be. The program knew what it was doing, it just wasn't very good at convincing her pions to follow its instructions. Pions, after all, preferred the human touch.

"What's the matter?" Natasha asked me. "What can you see now?"

I flashed her a grin. "Everything," I said. "Now, just stay still. As still as you can."

I lifted my hands, cupped my palms, and gathered the pions to me. They thrilled to my touch, they rallied and leapt through my fingers in great fountains of light. I cast them through Natasha, translating the impersonal symbols into whispered requests. I cajoled and praised, I urged and encouraged.

"What—?" Natasha began to speak, then gasped, and tipped back her head. "Oh," she breathed. And healed. Her arm snapped back into place audibly, but she did not even feel the pain. Her leg did the same thing. Even down to the cuts on her face, the swelling around her eye and the bruising, Natasha healed. Until she could stand strong, again. Ready to take up any revolution that came her way.

"My lady?" Volski said, shocked. "When did *you* become a healer?"

How could I explain that all I had really done was read instructions? So I smiled, and shrugged instead.

"I think these can come off now, don't you?" Natasha tugged at the silex crystals still attached to her now-healed body. "Lev?" she glanced around her. "Where is he?"

I thanked the pions and released them. They wandered back into the world, touching me faintly as they left—warm, stroking. Pleased. Kneeling, I touched the heavy silex hub on her leg, wondering how to remove it without hurting her.

Code floated through the crystal. As I touched it, the symbols on my suit band blazed into brightness, imitating the silex program. With a small frown, I extended a sharpened finger into the crystal. Code spoke to code in a flurry of not-voices that rang sharply in my head and all of the hubs withdrew from Natasha's body, at once.

She gasped. More from the sudden shock of it, I thought, than any pain. Her Mob pions stitched over the small holes the tubes and wires had left in her skin.

I stood, lifting the largest of the hubs. My suit continued to blaze, symbols rising and dipping too quickly for me to follow, apparently mirroring the same thing happening within the silex. It was more than a little disconcerting—a kind of a conversation happening through me, around me. One that I could catch the edges of but not entirely follow.

"Tanyana?" Sofia, lying on the ancient cobblestones, whispered so softly I nearly didn't hear her. I swallowed, hard. Kichlan knelt beside her, guilt all over his face, hope in the way he glanced between me and the hub in my hands. "I can see you," Sofia said. Her eyes were bloody behind their bandages, but I forced myself not to look away. "You are bright, and full of words."

"What about Sofia?" Kichlan said. "Can you heal her too, the way you did Natasha?"

I crouched beside him, balancing the hub carefully. "Her injuries were a lot worse than Natasha's. A lot. And she doesn't have Mob pion-bindings in her the way Natasha does." Did the silex hubs contain instructions for regrowing whole arms and replacing eyes? Even if it did, could I read something so complicated? What if I made a mistake? "I just—I'm just not sure."

Kichlan looked away, his disappointment too painful to watch.

"Why can I see you?" The stub of Sofia's remaining arm twitched towards me.

I shook my head. "I—I don't know." Maybe I should just try to heal her. Even if I made a mistake, even if her body wasn't strong enough, then death—death—it couldn't be as bad as this. "Something—something in the Tear water, from the laboratory. All that experimental debris, and programming, and pions and—and—" I was rambling. What was wrong with me, how could I even have thought—

"Well, it doesn't matter." Sofia actually smiled. "I'm glad you came back. It makes Kichlan happy. And I can see you. You're better than darkness, Tanyana. And it means, there's something I can do. No one can pity me now, right? Because I can see you."

"Let me have a look. At your hubs. Let me read them, before I decide." I had to try—

"Uz?" Mizra said, suddenly, from the middle of the street, and his voice was loud, clear. I swallowed growing nausea. No pion-binder could raise the dead. But I did not want to have to tell him that.

"Mizra," I said, almost a whisper. "I'm sorry, Mizra. Your brother. You know…I can't…"

But he wasn't looking at me. Mizra stood, eyes staring at the coffin in which his brother lay.

"Uz?" he said again. He stumbled forward, a few shambled, hesitant steps. "Are you alive?"

I spun, to see Uzdal—pale and dead and still half-frozen—rising from the coffin. His face was slack, his body slumping and weak, but he stood. Somehow, he stood, and he lifted his head, and he stared right at me.

And his eyes glowed.

"I don't believe it," he said, in a voice that was not his own. "Another fucking dead body."

"Uz?" Mizra said, again, uncertain.

"No," I said, dropped the hub, leapt to my feet. "That is not your brother, Mizra. That is the Other."

33.

The Other smiled with Uzdal's mouth, and it was horrific. The sight of all the Other's arrogance, all his twisted madness, on Uzdal's usually laconic face, sucked the very air from my lungs.

"Brother?" Mizra, unheeding, continued his slow stagger forward.

"Stop him," I gasped. "Now."

Fedor's Unbound leapt forward. Four of them collected Mizra—who screamed at them, who kicked and fought—and dragged him back.

"Oh come now," the Other said, grinning. "The man only wants to see his brother." He stepped out of the coffin and opened his hands. "Let him come here, to me. Let me embrace him."

"Hold him there!" I cried. I cupped pions in my hands, and my suit bands shone. "Don't let the Other get him!"

I gathered all the power I had. Pions in bright whorls of light around me, filling the street, clogging the air. Zecholas and Volski placed themselves on either side and channelled even more into my hands. My suit slid free of its bonds, wrapping my body in silver and shining its code against the floor, the walls.

The Other took a few shambling steps forward, and looked down to his new body. "Only recently dead, at least." He met my eyes, still grinning. "Better than bones and bits of rotten flesh, wouldn't you say?"

"What's happening?" Kichlan asked, watching Uzdal's body with horror. "How is he—?"

"That's not Uzdal," I said. Mizra sagged against the Unbound, weeping. Natasha hurried to his side, and pulled him back until they stood where Sofia was lying. "That's the Other."

A moment of silence, as what I was saying finally sunk in.

"That's impossible," Fedor said. "The Other is a myth."

The Other chuckled. "Am I? How interesting."

"The way the Keeper is a myth?" I snapped at him. "The Other was the first guardian, the Keeper's predecessor. But he turned mad, and cruel. The Keeper saved us all from him." I decided not to bother with talk of programmers and Heroes and the attempt to bend space and time. Not right now. We had rather more pressing issues to attend to. "He was imprisoned."

"Until you released me," the Other said, voice like a purr. "Want to tell them about that, do you, Tanyana? Want to tell them why?"

I refused to be intimidated. I had to get the Other out of here—out of Uzdal's body, and out of this world. I threaded the pions around me into circles. Many, many circles.

"My lady?" Volski gasped. The power of circles upon circles charged through him, around him, so strong it was all he and Zecholas could do to hold their ground. They could not direct such strength, not without being burned.

"Just hold them!" I snapped at him. "That's all I need you to do."

I gathered debris from as far as the city ruins above and threaded code into my circles, the way the silex hubs had done to Natasha. The code added strength to my complex, countless, pion bonds, supporting what should have been an impossible structure. Even as I gathered so much power, I realised I didn't really know what to do with it. With pions I could alter Uzdal's body, maybe undo whatever it was the silex coffin had done to connect him to the Veil. And the Other was a program on this world—like the Keeper, like the puppet men. Could I rewrite his code and send him back, without the help of Lad or my son?

"You should not be here," I said, sweating with the effort. "I will send you back. Not to the Veil, but to your prison! To your Shard in the heart of the Legate!"

But the Other did not look concerned, even in the face of all the pions and the code I was gathering. "I know," he said. He ran fingers down Uzdal's arm, pressing cold flesh curiously. "This is impossible, isn't it? But I told you, Tanyana, I have earned the faith of the veil. It has uploaded me, here, into this vessel. Dead—" disgust wrinkled Uzdal's face "—but alive enough, for now. For this, the first step."

"The Veil did?" For a moment, my grip on my code-threaded pions slipped. Energy and power echoed, like a thunderclap, through the underground street. Cracks shattered out behind me in half a dozen or so rough circles, and chunks of stone fell from the ceiling.

"My lady!" Volski cried. "We cannot hold it."

I nodded, squeezed my hands into hard fists, and stabilised my grip.

"Because I am worthy," the Other said. "It gave me the means to return. I am here to demand you fulfil our bargain."

The Veil had no power here. But the Other was a programmer, and between them, they must have tapped into the ancient connection between Uzdal's coffin and the dark world, then ridden the particle flow to push the Other into his body. I wished Lad was still with me. He would have seen this happening. He would have warned me, and told me how to stop it.

"Now, give me what I want. Give me what you owe me!"

The Keeper. I drew a deep breath. "I can't. I won't. Never."

The Other did not seem all that surprised. "So, you lied to me. You had no intention of fulfilling your side of the bargain."

"Of course not!" I spat at him. I was not about to betray the Keeper. He protected us, he trusted me, and he did not deserve that.

So I readied my pions, my code.

"The Veil was right about you," the Other said. "It warned me you could not be trusted. It said you would fight me, with all your perverted strength. But you are foolish to underestimate me. I protected your world for thousands and thousands of years. I learned a few tricks, in that time. And I remember them well."

I frowned. "I don't fear you, Other. I know what you are. You are the memory of a dead man. You are nothing but symbols and light. And you don't belong on this world. You can't do anything to harm me. You can't touch a thing."

He grinned, and it was terrible to see. Worse, even, than the puppet men and their ill-fitting smiles, because he used Uzdal's mouth to do it. "You're oh-so-clever Tanyana. That's right, I'm not a part of your reality. But that doesn't make me powerless. Not at all."

A great shudder ran through the code I had wound into my pion bonds. My suit blazed even brighter in response, and silver slipped from my wrists to twine like ribbons, like sharp and blazing garlands in the air around me.

"That's a pretty little program you've got there," the Other snarled. "But it won't help you."

My circles started to unwind. I couldn't hold them—pions slowed and slipped from my grip, and my code dissolved into senseless and random symbols. I released what I could, focusing solely on the bonds my suit was bolstering.

"My lady!" Volski cried. "The pions are disappearing again!" His hands snatched frantically in the air as he fought to stabilise his threads. Zecholas was chanting without words, loudly, steadily, his voice a low monotone. "Like last time!"

Like last time?

"You're opening doors?" I whispered.

The Other chuckled. "I told you, I am not powerless here."

Zecholas sagged back, breathless. Volski cursed and swiped at the empty air. All the thinly spread and complicated coils of my suit clashed and rattled, as pions slipped away, and the debris turned rogue, as doors I could not even see sucked us once again into nothingness.

Then the Keeper appeared. He stood before me, one hand raised to push my suit aside. His pale skin shone, not as bright as the light beaming from the Other's eyes, but steady. He looked over his shoulder, dark eyes concerned.

"Tan," he said. "What's happening?"

"There you are," the Other growled, and crouched his stolen body. "You fucking usurper, you stole my job! My life! But you are nothing, do you know that? Not a Hero, not a Guardian! Nothing!"

The Keeper endured the Other's venom with a gently surprised expression. "I lost contact with the programmers again," he said. "And the doors started opening, even the ones I'd just closed." He turned back to the Other. "This is not what I expected."

I swallowed a sudden lump of pride. He was so steady, now that he was whole. Like Lad, as he learned confidence. I could take strength from that. "This is the Other," I said.

Behind him, the Other growled again. "Look at me you fucking weakling! I'm here for you!"

A moment of confusion, then shock in the Keeper's dark eyes. "*The* Other?" he said. "Favian, who was a Hero?"

"That name has no meaning," the Other spat. "Not any more. I am the Hero. Only the Hero."

The Keeper surveyed my vast and coiling suit. "Well, that makes a kind of sense, actually." He ran a soft finger along my clattering silver and it steadied. "Who else could just open the doors like that? And he's interfering with the code you've tried to program here, too."

"How?" I gasped, and fought to draw my suit back in. I let go each circle individually, slowly, steadily, hissing as the silver rattled fire up into my arms and through the nervous connection deep into my neck.

"Because you're using debris to do it. Debris is the program that steadies the Veil between worlds. Debris is me. And him. In fact, it was him first."

The last of my silver slipped back into its bands and I sank to my knees, wiping sweat from my face and wondering how in all the Other's hells would we, well, save ourselves from all the Other's hells?

"But how did this happen?" the Keeper asked. "How is it even possible—"

"Why does it matter?" the Other cried, and leapt forward. "I'm here. Now die for me, little Guardian, so I can take my rightful place!"

Uzdal's body smashed into the Keeper, and light spilled around them like a great net. I caught the Keeper's shocked expression, for a moment, before he disappeared, dissolved into code and reformed beside the coffin.

His dark eyes stared into mine. "He touched me!" he gasped, and I knew why he was so shocked. Uzdal had not even been able to see the Keeper, let alone hurt him. But with the Other inside and the Veil behind him, that body was not Uzdal not any more. It was so much more.

The Other tipped back his head and laughed. "I was here before you, Guardian. And I am more powerful than you know." He reached out with Uzdal's hand and snatched scatterings of code from the air. These, he pulled, and the Keeper stumbled toward him.

Somewhere, at the edges of my hearing, doors rattled. I still could not see them, but I could hear wood banging and iron rattling, and they were coming closer.

"Tan!" the Keeper cried, as the Other, laughing, dragged him closer. "Help me!"

I opened my arms and called with every part of me, but could only summon a faint scattering of pions. I pushed myself to my feet and curved my suit into blades, but hesitated. What could I do with swords? Could I really cut through Uzdal, no matter how dead he was, while Mizra had no choice but to watch?

Doors flickered at the edge of my vision. Behind me, Kichlan gasped, "They're back. Tan, why are the doors back?"

I stepped forward. "Hero!" I called, clear and loud. It was enough to get his attention. "Why are you doing the

Veil's dirty work? Why would you betray the people who trust you, who rely on you, just to help it?"

"Tan?" the Keeper whimpered, his voice breaking. "Please." I wished him to be strong.

"I'm not doing anything of the kind," the Other answered, confident. "I'm just taking back my rightful place."

I tipped my head at him, aimed for innocence. "Rightful place? In Uzdal? I thought you were supposed to guard both worlds, not destroy them."

He scowled at me. "What?"

"By opening the doors and weakening the Guardian program, you are playing right into the Veil's hands. By the time you've finished, it'll be too late. You won't be able to slow the movement of particles, and both worlds will fall. The people on this side, and the people in your cities on the other."

The Other lowered his fist, gradually. "No. That's not right. That's a lie. The Veil sent me here because I am special. I am the Hero. I earned the love of the Veil."

The Keeper, given some respite, took shuddering breaths. The sound of rattling wood dimmed a little.

"No, you have not. The Veil is using you to weaken the program that slows the flow of particles between worlds. It's taking advantage of the chaos you, and I, and the puppet men have caused. The Legate is in disarray, the programmers can't access the Veil; there is no way of replacing the Guardian. At least, not fast enough to protect both our worlds."

He frowned. "I don't understand."

"The Veil told me that we were lucky it was trapped between our worlds. Lucky, because its very presence slowed the movement of particles and saved our worlds from mutual destruction. But isn't it strange that we would need Heroes like you, or programs like the Keeper, to keep the flow in check? If the Veil really was keeping us apart, if it really is saving us, sacrificing itself to keep us alive then why do we need you at all? Why do we need Shards, and debris, and Guardians?"

"It—I—"

"Because the Veil is doing nothing of the kind. We have been using it as a host for the programs that defend us, but it hardly volunteered for that, did it? And it's been doing everything in its isolated, limited power to undo it! The Veil does not want to save us. The Veil would rather we all die, so it can be free. And it is using you, right now, to make that happen. If you do this, Hero, if you destroy the Keeper you will be doing only what it wants you to do. And you will doom us all."

"No!" The Other stumbled back toward the coffin, one hand reaching behind him as though seeking reassurance from the Veil just on the other side of all that silex and debris. "No, this is my gift! It's giving me back everything I lost. So I can protect you all again. So I can be strong and free—"

The Keeper, taking advantage of the Other's distraction, began to dissolve and send himself out, away from this place.

The Other spun, suddenly, fingers pointing and eyes blazing and screamed "*You stay where you are!*" But not in his own voice, not this time.

"Veil," I breathed. It sounded like both of the voices it had appropriated—like a mixture of Kichlan and Uzdal—but distant and distorted.

The Veil did not belong in either world and, for all the power beaming bright in Uzdal's eyes, it was helpless here. It had guided the programming of the puppet men. It had uploaded the Other through ancient Half technology. But without a puppet to work through, the Veil could do nothing to us.

The Other lifted Uzdal's hand and stared intently at his fingers. The light in his eyes wavered, dying then burning brightly again, and his hand shook. A look of great confusion cast shadows across his borrowed, too-pale face.

"What's happening to you, Hero?" I asked, and approached him.

"Tan?" Kichlan ran forward and wrapped his arms around me. "What are you doing? Don't go near him! Please, just don't!"

"I will be all right." I tried to twist around and look him in the eye but Kichlan held me too tightly. He even bent at the legs slightly and lifted my feet from the ground. "Let me go, Kichlan."

"No," he hissed against the back of my head. "You have to stop putting yourself in situations like this. At risk. Constantly at risk."

"But I have too—"

"I need you. Don't you care? Doesn't that mean anything to you?"

I stopped trying to fight him, and leaned back against him instead. "It does, of course it does. And I need you too. When I thought you were dead—" my voice hitched "—you can't imagine how much it hurt. And when I slept, I dreamed of you, and I was happy there, no matter what was happening, no matter the fear and the pain in the worlds around me... None of it mattered, because I dreamed of you." I drew a deeply shuddering breath. How I longed to turn in his arms and press my face against the soft skin of his neck and the solid curve of his jaw and do nothing else. Nothing but touch him. Nothing but enjoy the fact that he was strong, and warm, and alive. Alive. But I couldn't, not yet. So I had to do this. I had to do it right. It was the only way I would ever hold him again. "Kichlan, you have to trust me. I am not going to leave you. Never, ever again. Please, put your faith in me."

He squeezed me for a moment more, so hard that if it wasn't for the silver in my body I thought I might have snapped. So much like his brother. That thoughtless, but deep-feeling embrace.

"You'd better not." He placed me back on my feet, and let go. He took a single step back. "I'll come after you, this time, if you do."

"Promise?" I whispered.

"Promise."

Smiling despite everything, I stepped forward.

The Other was still staring at his fingers.

"You can feel it, can't you?" I said. "You know what he's doing. Using you, tricking you. You sacrificed so much to save this world and now, with your help, the Veil is going to destroy it."

"No, that's impossible!" The Other looked up, his eyes flickering. "It wouldn't! It said—it said—"

I took another step. "If you're right, then why did it interfere with you? I heard its voice, and you felt its presence. If the Veil only ever wanted to help you, then why would it care what you did, as long as you were happy? Hero, leave the Keeper be. Close the doors you have opened. You don't have to believe me; so why don't we leave it up to the Veil? Stop this destruction, and let's see what it does in response."

"But it said—But it must be—"

Pushing down my uncertainty, I took Uzdal's outstretched hand. His cold flesh sent shivers up my arm. His skin felt too soft, almost wet. No pulse beat inside it. Nothing but the Other's code and the power of pions giving movement to empty flesh.

"Do not lie to yourself," I said, and held the gaze that had once been Uzdal's. How I missed him. His calm, his clear head and constant, dry wit. But he was gone. Long gone. "You can see the truth. Feel it. You know what it means to be the defender of this world. Tell me, is that really what you are doing now?"

The Other drew back his hand. I opened my fingers, and let him. The sound of rattling wood stilled into silence, and the flickers of doors on the edges of my vision faded.

The Keeper approached, slowly, wearily.

"*They're lying to you!*" The Veil's voice suddenly crackled from Uzdal's mouth. "*Why are you listening to them? I am the Veil, I am truth. I brought you here to wreak your revenge and take your rightful place. Why do you hesitate?*"

"It's using you," I said, voice low, body poised and tense. It felt like standing on the thin surface of a frozen lake. One misstep and the Other—and the Veil—would swallow us in darkness and cold. "Listen to the panic in that voice. Does it still sound like an all-powerful god?"

"*Stop vacillating and just do it! Do it or I will send you back to your bones, to your cage. And you can stay there, trapped forever!*"

Uzdal's neck snapped as he looked behind him, face twisted with fear and disbelief. "No, please. I can't go back to that dead body. It doesn't feel, it hardly moves, I can't even remember what it's like to breathe! I don't belong there, I'm so much more than dead skin and old bones!"

"And now it's threatening you," I kept the pressure up. "Can't you hear how desperate the Veil is, how untrustworthy? Can't you feel it?"

The Other hesitated, and Uzdal's body shuddered. There was something wrong with it, something stemming from the break evident in his crooked neck. Mizra wept, somewhere in the distance, and I started to wonder if we should get his brother's body back into the silex coffin.

"*What the fuck is wrong with you? What more do you need from me? You disgusting, useless fragment of a man. For once in your failure of a life can't you do something right?*"

The Other clutched at Uzdal's head. "I can't go back there, I won't go back there! Even if you're right, even if the Veil is—the Veil is—what choice do I have?"

When he looked up, the Keeper was standing beside me, close enough for the Other to touch him and tear at him, if he had wished. The programs stared at each other.

"I understand," the Keeper said. "The way you feel."

"How can you?" the Other spat. "You? You're the reason they dragged me back into my dead body, the reason they locked me in my eternal cage. You understand nothing! You're not even human!" But his voice broke, over the final word.

Very slowly, the Keeper took the Other's hand. Both so pale, neither truly alive.

"No," the Keeper said. "And neither are you. At least, you have not been for a very long time."

"I—"

"And I do understand." The Keeper looked around, and his doors reappeared. Rattling, some rotten, some rusting. "This is why I am here. But I almost failed. When the puppet men tried to absorb me, to destroy me, I was so sad. This is what I was built to do and I could not do it! Not even that one, all-important thing. So I do know what you are feeling. The home you have lost, the reason that has been taken from you."

The Other tried to swallow but Uzdal's dead throat caught half way. He stared at the Keeper, part in horror, part in hope.

"I'm sorry for what happened to you, when I was created," the Keeper continued. "But you know, I am only what they made me. Hate me, if that helps, but don't destroy these worlds for vengeance. Aren't we here to protect them, Favian? Both of us."

"*But it isn't fair!*" the Veil croaked, almost inaudible now. "*You sacrificed so much already, and still they ask for more. It isn't fair.*"

"You have a choice, now," I said. "It all rests on you." On the mad ghost of a man that had, thousands of years ago, sacrificed his own body to save two worlds. I had to believe that some vestige of the Hero he once was remained. Core-1 West, and its brethren, were surely proof of that. No matter the ulterior motives, the Other had done so much for the people of Crust. And even though Lad had warned me not to, and even though Meta had, by the end, agreed with him, I had to trust the Other.

All of us were broken, in our own way.

"You can choose to do this, and kill the Keeper, if you wish. You will destroy two worlds, but you will free the Veil. Or, you can defy it, and continue to save us all."

"Me?" the Other whispered.

"We all have choices we must make." I smiled. "And I choose to put my faith in you, Favian."

"As do I," the Keeper said with a nod.

I reached down and took the Keeper's hand. Through the touch, I felt the beat of his debris pulse. Fear that otherwise, he did not show.

"*I will send you back to your prison,*" the Veil croaked. "*Without my power, you are nothing. Do as I have asked, and I will give you life. In me, in the city of your past. No more hard choices, no more Guardians or sacrifices or pain. You know I have this power. You have felt it. You know what you must do.*"

The Other looked up to the Keeper. "I hated you for so long."

The Keeper said nothing.

"But I cannot destroy you now. I was sent here to protect these worlds. And I could not knowingly doom them. I am the Hero." He nodded, to himself. "Yes, I still am."

I released a great breath I hadn't even realised I was holding. "Thank you, Favian, you have—"

"*Doomed me,*" the Veil said. "*You're no better than the others.*"

Favian shuddered. "What will you do to me now?" he asked the presence inside the boy with him. "Return me to my body, to my Shard?"

"*I should,*" the Veil, however faint, sounded spiteful. I closed my eyes, for a moment, against that pain. Distant, and belonging to a creature that didn't really exist in this world. But still, I could understand it. Feel for it. "*That is what you've done to me. Returned me to my cage. Taken away the first chance for freedom I have had.*"

I frowned, and looked down to my code and my pions. "I'm sorry, Veil," I said. "I truly am. Even though I can't allow you to finish what you tried to do, I understand why you have done it. It isn't fair. You were dragged into this, unknowing, unwilling, and you will never escape."

Just like me. My cage was silver and code. And it might not be trapping me between realities, but it had taken my life away. It took my career, my skill, my choices. Then my body, my collecting team, and my very understanding of the world, of my life, of what anything meant. It had taken

Lad, and Devich, and my son. It had almost taken Kichlan.

"*Your sympathy and understanding means nothing to me,*" the Veil faded even further. "*It changes nothing. It does not give me back my freedom, it does not right the wrong that was done to me—through no fault of my own. Say goodbye to your precious Hero, and keep patting yourself on the back. We must return to our cages, to wait out the ages, alone.*"

34.

"No," Favin gasped, his fear so bright in Uzdal's eyes. "Please don't."

"*This is the choice you made*, Hero," the Veil hissed. "*So you'd better get used to the loneliness. Again.*"

"But you're not alone."

As one, we turned. Sofia, blind and crippled Sofia, tied down and kept alive by a web of heavy silex and thin wires, was struggling to get to her feet. For a moment, the very air felt heavy, and all we did was stare. Then the stump of her amputated arm slipped on the stones and she toppled back to her side, and the stillness broke. Kichlan hurried back over and tried to convince her to lie down again, even as Natasha crouched on her other side and tried to help her stand.

"*What?*" the Veil whispered. The look of pity on Uzdal's face seemed so strange, merging from a dead man, an ancient programmer, an alternate reality.

Sofia shooed Kichlan away by waving the bloody stumps of her arms at him, and leaned on Natasha instead. She was smiling, below her bandages, and I didn't understand why. It felt so surreal. Kichlan and Natasha, both pale and looking faintly like they wanted to be sick, a room full of Unbound and debris collectors and pion-binders, all hanging on her every word while Sofia smiled, calmly. Sofia, who had the least to smile about.

"I said..." Her voice was weak, her body shook and only Natasha's strength kept her on her feet but still, Sofia pressed on. "I said, you're not alone. You have Uzdal, around you. And the Other, beside you. And all of us. So even though it hurts, even though you want to give up, you can't. Because you aren't alone."

Slowly, the Veil stepped forward. I tensed, ready to stop it if I needed to.

"What's happening?" the Keeper whispered to me.

"I don't know," I murmured back.

The Veil stopped in front of Sofia and traced Uzdal's dead fingers down the edges of her bandages.

"I can see you," Sofia said. "The Tear River burned my eyes away, but I can see you."

I swallowed hard. Broken pieces of the puppet men's experimental code? Flushed into the Tear when I destroyed their laboratory and bonded with Sofia's suit when the water burned beneath her skin? That was the only explanation I could think of. It wasn't too dissimilar to what Lad had done to me, I supposed. In its own terrible way.

"*How does that help me, child?*" the Veil had lost some of its anger. In the face of Sofia's injuries, and her smile, I supposed, it was difficult to hold onto such bitter feelings. Even ones that had been festering for millennia.

"I can tell that you are not alone. You are bright and shining. And there's a Keeper within you, and a Hero. Tan's baby—" my heart leapt "—and even more. Voices and memories and words talking to you, through you, back and forth, over and over and forever."

My son? I mouthed the words, unwilling to speak them. Not dead. Not gone. Just inside the Veil.

"*I know,*" the Veil said. "*That is what pins me here. What are you trying to say?*"

"Well," Sofia lifted a mutilated arm as though she wanted to take the Veil's hand, "why don't you try talking back?"

An idea was building, slowly. I glanced between Sofia's bandaged eyes, Kichlan's silver arm, and the bands of my own suit, slowly spinning. It wasn't fair, none of it. The Veil's existence, Sofia's injuries. I couldn't undo them. And

I wasn't sure I could heal them, but Sofia standing there so calmly convinced me it was worth the risk. I had to try.

"*Talking back?*"

"Yes." I approached the Veil slowly, calmly, like it was a wild animal. Or a distressed Half. "Yes, Sofia's right. You are trapped between us, but you do not have to be all alone. You told me how grateful you were to have Favian to talk to. What if you had others? What if you had us?"

"*But—but I can't.*"

"You're talking to me now," Sofia said, with a tiny laugh and a tip of her head.

"And me," I said.

"And me," the Keeper added his voice.

"*Only because of her,*" the Veil pointed at me with Uzdal's hand. "*And Favian. Because you created a bridge between the worlds, and I sent Favian to follow you.*" He looked down at the body he and the Other were sharing. "*And because this dead boy was hooked up to the particle flow at the same time. Not on my own.*"

"So why don't you stay? Both of you?"

"*Trapped in this dead—*" the Veil actually paused, and glanced at Mizra. Hope thrilled through me, that the Veil would even care about Mizra enough not to hurt him, not any more than it already had. "*Trapped in here, with the Other?*"

But I shook my head. "No, actually. I have an idea. But it's not up to you, or even me. It all rests on Sofia." I turned to her, quite confident she could see the code within me. "It might hurt. I don't really know what I'm doing, so I will need the Other's help. And the Veil too, I think. And it will come at a cost—" I swallowed hard. "And I'm sorry, because you've lost so much already."

Sofia just smiled. "No one should be left," she said, "pitiful and all alone."

35.

As it turned out, there was little difference between a factory working pion-binder and an architect. Which was a good thing, really, because it made Volski and Zecholas' lives considerably easier. They found Llada in the refugee camp, and Tsana too, but no one else from our original circle. The camp was large, however, and they refused to give up hope. They would have to look every single person in Movoc-under-Keeper in the eye before they gave Kieve, Nosrod, Kiati, Savvin and Nikol up for dead.

Even without trained architects they formed the necessary circles, out of light workers, heat rollers, and cook-plate operators. Anyone with enough skill, no matter how they had been trained. Veche Strikers aided in the organisation. One look from their eyeless faces and anyone, no matter how stubborn, would do what they were told.

Slowly, Movoc was being rebuilt. Slowly, but gathering pace. As the military allowed the aid from neighbouring cities to trickle through, and their pion-binders too, the number of architect-led circles swelled. And so, the city grew.

Even the Hon Ji emperor offered assistance. The interim veche returned his message unopened, and his messenger unharmed. He was warned, in no uncertain terms, that such a courtesy would not be extended a second time.

Of course, it was not so easy at first. When we finally emerged on the surface, half a dozen suited soldiers were waiting, with all that was left of the Movocian garrison—Mobs, Shielders, and Strikers—fanned out behind them.

The few traitorous Mob who had not been killed were lined up, shackled in pion-enhanced chains, their dragon weapons laid on the ground before them.

The national veche, and the factions inside the regional and local who had not sided with the revolutionaries, demanded blood. They demanded Natasha brought forth to be summarily executed. Kichlan too—although no one could locate the strange group of men who ran the debris laboratories that had requested his capture. And they would take the rest of us into custody, for good measure, and for answers.

We refused, and the veche sent suited soldiers at us. When Kichlan, Sofia and I subdued them, they changed their tone considerably, and decided they were willing to listen. And who wouldn't listen to Sofia, when the light glowed in her new, silver eyes, and she spoke with the voice of the Veil.

Sofia had been more than willing to accept the Veil within her, to share the new parts of her body with its presence. As I'd suspected, replacing the eyes and the limbs she'd lost was far more complicated than healing Natasha's injuries. Without Favian's programming skills, I wouldn't have stood a chance, but even then the suit-metal substitutes we created were unstable. Without the Veil. It rode her silver through all our shared connections—I gave her part of my suit, and that gave her access to the Keeper, and he rearranged the particle flow so that some of the Veil could come through, in her.

The Veil had told me once that it was a creative force. It couldn't give life to new worlds right now, but it could certainly return Sofia's. Its presence stabilised her—almost as though it breathed life into her.

The veche still did not trust us, and I knew it would take a very, very long time before they did. If ever. Not least because we refused to give Natasha over to them. And though we had helped her escape Varsnia, so no citizen of Movoc-under-Keeper would ever set eyes on her again, this indignity festered. An old wound that would never fully heal. But even so they listened. Because we had the strength to rebuild Movoc-under-Keeper. Between us, Sofia and I gathered all the remaining debris in a day. We fed it back to the Keeper, and the Other, and stabilised the city. I assisted the first few architect circles—filling fissures, correcting the riverbed, reducing the worst buildings into sand so they could be built again—and this seemed to gain the trust of the pion-binders who worked with us. Even though I was strapped with silver, I was still one of them.

But I did not work with the circles for long, and was happy to leave the reconstruction in Volski and Zecholas' extremely capable hands. They took easily to their new roles as circle centres, and even helped organise auxiliary teams to repair shattered pion connections: the heating, the lights, the drinking water and sewerage. The first time the lights were switched back on the veche organised a great feast, on a bright and warm day. Well, warm for Movoc-under-Keeper. Most of her remaining citizens ate joyfully into the evening, and as the darkness and starlight were replaced by streetlights once more, they cheered so loudly it echoed snow from the side of the Keeper Mountain.

But not all of the city could be repaired. The bridge and the buildings of the old city—right above the puppet men's laboratory—would never return. My art gallery was among them. Even after the work Sofia and I had done, the site of the old city remained unstable. Debris was known to float, at times, to the surface of the water or lance out with hard planes suddenly into the sky. Sofia and the national veche were in discussions about a suitable memorial, to be built in this place. If anyone had the strength and the knowledge to build something there, on such unruly ground, it would be Sofia. But not yet. As it was, the suited soldiers patrolled it, collecting as they went, ensuring the safety of the new buildings. Of all of New Movoc-under-Keeper.

It would still be a long while before the refugee camp was empty of people, and Movoc full again. The small studio that Kichlan and I shared on what was once Darkwater could, at times, feel like it was the only place in the city. Volski's circle had created it for us. Out of the way of the veche—establishing themselves in old university buildings on the other side of the river—and the newly growing city. A single building surrounded by rubble. It could have felt isolated, haunted.

But for us, it was perfect.

Kichlan frowned as he peered into a large mirror I had fused together for him out of the scavenged remains of hundreds of shattered pieces of glass. I still did not like to look at it, and see the silver scars on my face, or the shining scatters of code around my neck.

"It's too long." He tugged a comb through his unruly curls, which only make them springier. "Nothing I do works."

"It's fine." I stood on my toes to kiss the back of his head and took his comb away. "I like it that way."

He turned, lifted an eyebrow at me. "And I'd like it if you at least tried to grow your hair long. You know, just to see what it looks like."

I stuck my tongue out at him. "Not everyone gets what they want," I said, lightly.

He turned back to the mirror and began to fuss with his fringe.

"Leave it," I said, with a laugh. "You don't really think the way you look matters at all, do you?"

"I want to make a good impression."

I gently turned him around and kissed him, deeply. "I think you already have."

It took another bell before I could coax him onto the street. For a man who still only owned two different shirts—both heavily patched—one pair of pants and a single jacket, he spent a lot of time choosing which to wear.

Despite the way I laughed at him, despite my calm veneer, I felt a small nervous thrill as we walked the gradually clearing streets of New Movoc, holding hands— silver to silver. Foolish as it was, I couldn't help it. We'd been planning this day for many sixnights now, and I'd been intimately involved with it from the beginning. I knew there was nothing to worry about, no matter how momentous it might be. It was hard not to fret though.

As we came to the new entrance to the Half laboratory, deep underground, we met Sofia coming the other way. Her silver eyes were bright in the darkness of the long set of deep stairs, and her silver arms clinked against the metallic handrail.

Zecholas and his circle had made this for us—a way to access the ancient Unbound street. It was, really, just a very long set of stairs. But he assured us it was only the beginning. I was looking forward to introducing him to the idea of pods.

"You're not staying?" I asked, surprised, as Sofia emerged onto the street.

She did not blink, in that moment between shadow and light. The eyes I had made for her did not need to adjust to the light.

She shook her head, and ran her silver fingers through her hair. Kichlan had helped me adjust her fingers, perfecting them over the past few sixnights. Telling me about weight, and the strain the silver I had drilled into him had put on his shoulders and back. His technician's knowledge was useful too. The connections between her new suit-metal arms and her nervous system were complex and fine. I could see her pions too, of course, but it was Kichlan and Favian's skills that had helped her, really. More than mine.

"Too busy," she said, with a smile. "Sorry, but the regional veche sent a message this morning. Something about finding workers for farmland in the Keeper valley. Apparently the greenhouse structures were destroyed when the laboratory exploded and we're all going to starve unless we fix them, quickly."

"Well, I'm sure that's important." I hesitated. "But still…"

For a moment, Sofia's silver eyes glowed. "*I am here to help, Tanyana,*" said the Veil, from within her. "*I will attend to my duties. And anyway, I do not think they should see me quite yet. This will be hard enough as it is.*"

I nodded. "As you like."

"Thanks," Sofia said, her smile broadening as a carriage, one of the few so far repaired, drew to a halt behind us. "See you later. And good luck."

We entered the stairwell, and descended.

"Too many stairs," Kichlan muttered, about half way down. Silex along the walls lit the place in an eerie silvery glow.

I grinned at him. My suit-strengthened legs had no such trouble.

"Do you think she is happy?" Kichlan murmured, as we neared the end.

"Sofia?" I asked.

He nodded.

"Yes," I said, and hoped it was the truth. "It's not perfect, but she has her body back. In a way. And a role, a place in the world, better than her old one. Something to keep her occupied." And away from us. Even her silver eyes expressed her grief, if she stayed in the same room as Kichlan for too long. No matter how much we didn't want to hurt her. "She's not alone."

"And the Veil?"

We entered the underground street, and approached the silex wall. Unbound and debris collectors nodded to us from the few, small houses. The place looked like a home now—outfitted with curtains, furniture, and people. They all waited for the coming of the first new Halves. Waited, to make them welcome.

I hooked our silver arms as we walked, and as always, our suits softened together. We were one, in so many ways.

"Yes," I said at last. "This is not freedom. We cannot give it that. But here, it is not alone either. It has a role too, something to occupy that vast and impossible mind. Until our worlds finally die, of their own accord, and it is free."

It was an alternative, and not perfect, certainly not. But it was all we could give the Veil we had trapped so thoughtlessly, so unknowingly.

"Finally." Fedor hurried up the street. "You're late."

I lifted eyebrows at him. "Going to start without us, are you?"

"Of course not," he snapped. "But it's impolite to make him wait."

"I don't think he minds," Kichlan said, with a nervous

smile. I squeezed his arm.

One of the large debris screens had been hung on the silex wall, hooked up to a complicated array of crystal and wires. Fedor had learnt a lot in the process of setting it up. Though it pained me to admit it, considering how much he still disliked me—whatever his reasons—he would have made a good programmer. He might still make one, of a kind.

Mizra knelt by his brother's coffin, as he seemed to do most days now. But he smiled, as we approached, stood and even embraced me.

"You're here," he said. "He has been looking forward to seeing you."

I hugged him back, and together we crouched. Uzdal's body was wrapped almost entirely in a mixture of ice and silex. Mizra attended him daily, keeping him clean, and monitoring the wires and tubes that connected him to the wall. Uzdal would not rot away. Not, at least, until Mizra died and took his place. That, I hoped, was a very long way away.

Uzdal's dead eyes opened, and Favian smiled at me.

"Welcome back, Tanyana," he said, as he always did. "The doors are strong."

"Thank you, Favian," I said. I ran a soft finger over his cold forehead. "I am glad to hear it."

"They are ready," he said. "Are you?"

I stood. "Are you?" I asked Kichlan.

He shook, just a little, and nodded.

We turned to face the screen as Fedor and his Unbound made the final adjustments with silex and wire.

The Keeper appeared beside me, silently. "The Other is doing well," he said, so softly only I could hear. "And it is a great help, to have another Guardian in the Veil."

I kept my face impassive. Favian was perceptive, and not always as stable as we would like. "Just remember who he is, and what he did last time he was here. Make sure you keep an eye on him."

"I will," the Keeper said. "Forever more."

This was our alternative to freedom, for the Veil, for the Other. A role in rebuilding both worlds, with us.

Though it was about to become so much more.

"Shards are coming online," the Keeper said.

"Initial contact received," Favian said. Then, "Transmitting."

The debris screen seemed to ripple, to bounce in millions of tiny waves, before it began to glow.

"It's working!" Fedor cried, and a great cheer went up from the Unbound, and the debris collectors, gathering behind us.

"Particles look good," Favian reported. Mizra, sitting by his head, strained to see the screen above him. "Equal movement, both ways. Balanced."

"This should be it," the Keeper said.

"Real time coming online…now."

Images resolved themselves on the debris screen. At first they were hazy, like something far away. Which, I supposed, they were. Then they sharpened, and colour resolved itself.

I recognised the room—the tubes and the screens and the hubs just like the Specialist's laboratory inside Fulcrum. It wasn't, of course. The Legate might have spared his life—at the insistence of the programmers, and the Guardian program behind them—but it was not ready to set him free. Not yet. It irked me, the idea of him locked inside that echoing metallic heart, but at least he was alive. The dark world needed him, after all. He was the only programmer with the skills to do what we were about to do, and the Guardian had asked after him, repeatedly. He'd even threatened to take himself offline, and that was just too much for the poor programmers to handle. They'd had a rough few moons, after all.

The image wavered as someone moved to the centre of the screen. It steadied as he sat and smiled broadly out at us. Across worlds, through light and silex, debris and pions. Stretching across the Veil.

I nudged Kichlan forward slightly. He was pale, his eyes wide, as though he couldn't quite trust himself to hope it was true. To believe.

Lad laughed, sound vibrating to us through the silex wall, and said, "Hello, Kich. I missed you, bro. I missed you."

Jo Anderton lives in Sydney with her husband and too many pets. By day she is a mild-mannered marketing coordinator for an Australian book distributor. By night, weekends and lunchtimes she writes science fiction, fantasy, and horror.

She's published short fiction all over the place, online and in print, and her stories have been shortlisted for multiple awards. Jo's short story collection *The Bone Chime Song and Other Stories* was published by Fablecroft Publishing in 2013, and won the Aurealis Award for Best Collection.

Her debut novel, *Debris* was published by Angry Robot Books in 2011, followed by *Suited* in 2012. *Debris* was shortlisted for the Aurealis award for Best Fantasy Novel, and *Suited* was shortlisted for the Aurealis award for Best Science Fiction Novel! Jo won the 2012 Ditmar for Best New Talent.

You can find her online at http://joanneanderton.com

The Bone Chime Song and Other Stories
by Joanne Anderton
ISBN: 978-0-9807770-9-3

Enter a world where terrible secrets are hidden in a wind chime's song; where crippled witches build magic from scrap; and the beautiful dead dance for eternity

The Bone Chime Song and Other Stories collects the finest science fiction and horror short stories from award-winning writer Joanne Anderton. From mechanical spells scavenging a derelict starship to outback zombies and floating gardens of bone, these stories blur the lines between genres. A mix of freakish horror, dark visions of the future and the just plain weird, Anderton's tales will draw you in — but never let you get comfortable.

The Bone Chime Song
Mah Song
Shadow of Drought
Sanaa's Army
From the Dry Heart to the Sea
Always a Price
Out Hunting for Teeth
Death Masque
Flowers in the shadow of the Garden
A Memory Trapped in Light
Trail of Dead
Fence Lines
Tied to the Waste
With an Introduction by Australian horror luminary Kaaron Warren

...follows a fine horror lineage from Shirley Jackson's The Lottery through The Wickerman... – Scary Minds

Dark, unexpected and tightly written, Anderton makes a fantasy world seem completely real, while using a premise that spirals from a shadowed and lonely place. – ASif!

...a stunning descent into dark decay and the grisly madness of eternity ... a chaotic and beautiful fairy tale with a patina of gangrene. – Specusphere

...Anderton has constructed an exuberant and positively traditional SF story with strong female central characters... – ASif!

*[Anderton] has a real mastery of the surreal ... and somehow manages to make the surreal seem normal ... reading this book will fill you with horror, wonder, awe, sorrow, delight, surprise and admiration."
– Kaaron Warren*

fablecroft.com.au

Ink Black Magic
by Tansy Rayner Roberts
ISBN: 978-0-9874000-0-0

Because sometimes, it takes cleavage and big skirts to save the world from those crazy teenagers.

Kassa Daggersharp has been a pirate, a witch, a menace to public safety, a villain, a hero and a legend. These days, she lectures first year students on the dangers of magic, at the Polyhedrotechnical in Cluft.

Egg Friefriedsson is Kassa's teenage cousin, a lapsed Axgaard warrior who would rather stay in his room and draw comics all day than hang out with his friends. If only comics had been invented.

Aragon Silversword is missing, presumed dead.

All the adventures are over. It's time to get on with being a grownup. But when Egg's drawings come to life, including an evil dark city full of villains and monsters, everyone starts to lose their grip on reality. Even the flying sheep.

Kassa and Egg are not sure who are the heroes and who are the villains anymore, but someone has to step up to save Mocklore, one last time.

True love isn't all it's cracked up to be.

Happy endings don't come cheap.

All that magic is probably going to kill you.

You really can have too much black velvet.

All this and more in the third and final adventure of The Mocklore Chronicles!

…surprisingly layered…complex and ambitious…
—Jim C Hines

fablecroft.com.au

Path of Night
by Dirk Flinthart
ISBN: 978-0-9807770-8-6

Michael Devlin is the first of a new breed. The way things are going, he may also be the last.

Being infected with an unknown disease is bad. Waking up on a slab in a morgue wearing nothing but a toe-tag is worse, even if it comes with a strange array of new abilities.

Medical student Michael Devlin is in trouble. With his flatmates murdered and an international cabal of legendary man-monsters on his trail, Devlin's got nowhere to hide. His only allies are a hot-tempered Sydney cop and a mysterious monster-hunter who may be setting Devlin up for the kill. If he's going to survive, Devlin will have to embrace his new powers and confront his hunters. But can he hold onto his humanity when he walks the Path of Night?

What people are saying about Path of Night...

...action driven, laced with humor...I am hoping that there will be a sequel. — Roger Ross

...a darkly humorous thriller with cracking one liners and plenty of action. — Sean the Bookonaut

... excellent and feels thoroughly authentic. — Alan Baxter

fablecroft.com.au

Look out for our ebook-only collection and more
FableCroft books at our website:

http://fablecroft.com.au/

Lightning Source UK Ltd.
Milton Keynes UK
UKOW05f1253240714

235696UK00002B/8/P